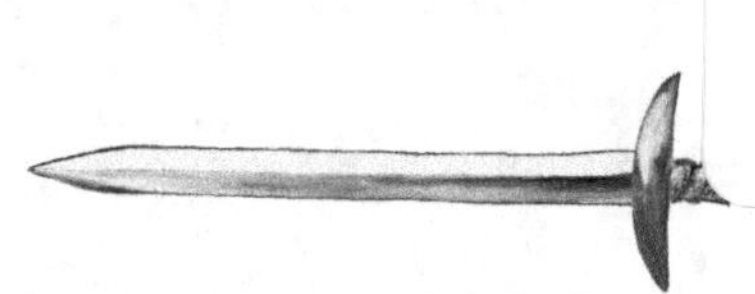

Their horses hadn't made it more than a handful of strides off of the bridge over the Sapphire when Adam made an unhappy noise and reined in tightly.

"Adam?" Damien inquired with some concern. "What's wrong?"

The tall knight looked almost greenish. "Something I ate must *really* not have agreed with me."

Damien reached his Healer's sense out to deal with the problem. Indigestion – or even food poisoning – shouldn't take more than a moment to fix. Though they'd all been eating the same things, and Adam's iron stomach really shouldn't have been the first to react if there were an issue with improper preparation.

To the King's surprise, he could detect Adam's nausea, but no *cause* for it.

No, *more* than just *nausea...*

The tall knight practically slithered out of his saddle, collapsing to his knees practically *underneath* his horse in the least graceful dismount Damien had ever seen *anyone* accomplish, let alone his skilled Champion. The King hurriedly hopped off his own tall, roan palfrey to take Adam's abandoned reins and move his Champion's warhorse aside before it accidentally stepped on its rider.

Which should be unlikely, but... Adam collapsing to the ground was also <u>unlikely</u>.

A
Lovely Mess

Book Six of the
Chronicles of Ilseador

(The Heart of Ilseador Saga)

Mangala McNamara

Also available in eBook and hardcover editions.
McNamara, Mangala
A Lovely Mess/ by Mangala McNamara Indiana: Rising Dragon Books, 2025
 pages, 2 maps
(McNamara, Mangala. Chronicles of Ilseador; bk. 6)
Summary: King Damien needs to reclaim the last Lost Province — after checking on the well-being of the one he took back from the evil sorceress and the one he is Bound to as Duke-Consort. Not to mention sorting out the unusual relationship he has with his Heir, Jason, and with his Champion, Adam Loveress.

ISBN 978-1-960160-68-3 (pbk)
1. Kings and rulers - Fiction. 2. Wizards and Magic - Fiction
ISBN 978-1-960160-69-0 (hc); ISBN 978-1-960160-67-6 (eBook)

ISBN: 978-1-960160-69-0
First Print Edition: February 2025
10 9 8 7 6 5 4 3 2 1

A note to sensitive souls:

Damien had to face true evil when he was kidnapped by Azella the Unpitying. His control - and understanding - of his magickal Power also grew tremendously. But in order to achieve that growth and learn what he needed to protect Ilseador (and the people he loves) he had to do - and be - things that don't fit with his view of what kind of a person he is... or should be.

Now he needs to figure out how to move forwards from that - and somehow let himself believe that he is not going to follow in his grandfather's footsteps.

And there's only one person who can help him do that... if Damien will only listen... But Adam has his own 'ghosts' to deal with...

Proceed with caution...

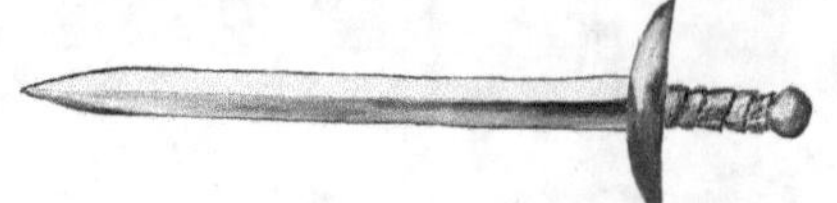

CONTENTS

And for your delectation...
An excerpt from the first
book in the Chronicles of Ilseador:

The Rebel Duchess

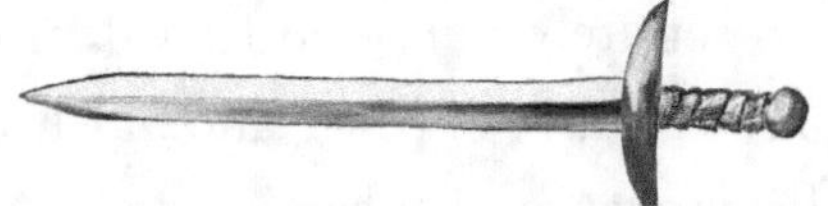

PROLOGUE

a visit to Farivera

THE UNNATURAL BLUFF STOOD OUT starkly against a sky that seemed at war with itself.

Damien stood silently on the ramparts of Count Felix Marsham's castle, looking south as roiling dark clouds seemed to keep trying to envelop the ridge... and losing to cheerful gusts of wind that pushed them back in favor of cheeky little puffs of white that seemed almost egregiously innocent against an incredibly bright blue sky.

"The weather's been quite odd over there, since just before... um..." Count Felix broke off his somewhat inane comment as Damien turned to give him a very dry look.

"We're all quite grateful, Your Majesty," the Count tried again – for the hundredth time. "I can't tell you the number of times we all wanted to send to the capitol for help."

"Hmmn." Damien turned his attention back to watching the part of the weather that it seemed only he could see – the sylphs determinedly pushing back against the gloom that Azella was trying to spin around her Keep. Exactly *how* he could see the sylphs at this distance, he wasn't sure, but it was entirely obvious to him what they were doing.

Damien sent a little extra energy from the Realm to aid in their efforts as, behind him, Adam chased off the obsequious Count.

It probably wasn't entirely *politic* to let Adam do that, but the King just wanted a few minutes of peace and quiet. Count Marsham would be General Direlien's problem come morning anyways. Damien and the miniature Court he had brought with him – the knights of his Royal Guards and the ladies-in-waiting and gentlemen-of-the-chamber who served him more properly as the Secret Cadre of his Royal Guards – would be departing with sunrise.

General Direlien and his five thousand soldiers should be enough to keep Farivera under control while its people – including the feckless Count Marsham – got used to the idea of once again being subjects of the Ilseadoran Crown. After several decades under the thumb of the Evil Keep to the south, it was... likely to be quite an adjustment.

Not that the good General could do a great deal if Azella the Unpitying herself decided to do something about having lost her influence here... but the spells of warding that Damien had woven over Farivera a month ago should alert him in that case. And he could *Vanish* himself back here in no time at all to – again – face the Evil Sorceress.

Damien leaned his elbows, pensively, on top of a crenelation in the battlements.

He had thought that – *finally* – he could see himself as the Sorcerer-King that his people did. The man who had defeated Lord Prydeen in a mage-battle in the very Throneroom, then glowed a bright silver light and Healed everyone who had been damaged during Harald of Siovale's coup, including the father of his soul-bonded bride, who had nearly bled out.

The accolades *(and, be honest, the **fear**)* that had accrued to him after that had made Damien deeply uncomfortable. The magick that he'd used had been Gifted to him by the Realm, as far as he could tell, with the Monarch's Sword being the tool which allowed him to 'ride the dragon,' rather than be the one ridden.

It had been a very near thing. The Realm had been severely damaged during the reign of his grandfather, King Reginald *(now being called 'the Ruthless'),* and It so desperately needed Healing that It tried to devour Damien whole every time he sat upon his Throne. The Sword and his soul-bond to Genevieve, his Queen *(and the former Rebel Duchess),* were all that kept him from succumbing to that seductive, desperate *need.*

Damien was, in many senses, the most educated man in the Realm. He'd spent nearly ten years living in the Royal Library *(after his grandfather had executed his parents before his eyes when he was ten)* and had occupied himself by reading his way through a great deal of its contents. Nowhere near *all* of it, no matter what his wife seemed to think, but his reading had been wide-ranging and he'd found everything interesting, so... a great deal of it indeed. And with his prodigious memory, he was able to call disparate facts to mind quickly and cross-correlate them to make it seem that he knew even more than he really did.

His memory and his years in the Royal Library had allowed him to fake his way through the first few years of being king. His wife and father-in-law had helped him learn the administrative aspects that his grandfather had held so tightly... but their experience was with a remote, largely isolated mountain province. What they could teach him had only a tenuous connection to governing the entire Realm – or even the gigantic city of Emeralsee itself. Not to mention that 'Duke' Aldred was weak after years of captivity and Genevieve's skills were better used on the battlefield.

Still, faking his way through ruling had seemed far less dangerous than faking his way through the use of *magick.*

After all, it was *magick* that had turned his grandfather from a somewhat arrogant and ambitious prince into an Evil Wizard Tyrant who had ruled for eighty-three years – and long past his natural lifespan. Likely he'd still be ruling today if his own Apprentice, Lord Prydeen, hadn't grown tired of living in the shadows and sought his own chance to take all the Power.

Damien had embarked on a desperate mission of trying to acquire all the available *(legitimate)* knowledge about magick in the world. His own innate Power might not be that impressive, but given how the Realm supplemented him, he had a great deal of 'weight' to throw around. It would be all too easy for him to smoosh things – or people – entirely unintentionally if he wasn't careful.

(Although Adam – the Captain of his Royal Guards, his friend and mentor and forever-Champion even before he bore that title instead, and the only person who tried to keep up with him in this mad quest for magickal knowledge – kept trying to insist that Damien's abilities owed as much to his personal gifts as to what he borrowed from the Realm.)

And while he was trying to fake his way through ruling and magick, and Genevieve was going about recovering the Lost Provinces that had defected to pledge to other Realms under King Reginald's aggressive disinterest, there had been the other problems.

The soul-bond demanding that they produce an Heir to the Realm despite every attempt ending in a tragic early miscarriage… and the slow but inevitable destruction of Genevieve's health.

The Realm demanding that Damien and his Queen 'feed' it on their own intimate joys – and thereby adding to the pressure of the soul-bond and making it further impossible for Genevieve to ever fully recuperate from the most recent miscarriage.

And, of course, the prophecy which the foul Lord Prydeen had told – or cursed them with – upon his dying breath: that Genevieve would never bear Damien's firstborn until she'd born a child sired by his Champion… their dear friend Jason Solway. Who was completely devoted to his own longtime-lover, Adam Loveress.

Or so they had all thought until Damien, in desperation to save Genevieve's life *(and his own, since the soul-bond would drag him down after her… and then the Realm after them both in civil war without a Named Heir)*, had finally told the two men about the prophecy. And they'd agreed to allow Jason to secretly sire the royal couple's first child…

…and that had come with all sorts of *extra* complications that still made Damien blush to consider closely…

...and then Jason and Genevieve had discovered an unheard-of *second* soul-bond between the two of *them,* just the day after Adam and Jason's wedding and Jason's crowning and Naming as Crown Prince...

...and all of it on the very eve of an invasion of pirates and the Evil Sorceress, Azella the Unpitying, who had stolen Damien away and given him access to study materials regarding magick that surely existed nowhere else in the world...

The same beautiful, Powerful young woman who resided up there in that Keep that Damien was now staring at so fixedly.

Damn her.

A light, but determined step behind him, bootheels ringing softly on the worn old granite of the battlement gallery. Not that Damien needed that sort of auditory signal to tell him someone was there. Or who it was.

"I told Marsham that General Direlien wanted to go over some of the deployments you and he have discussed," Adam said, that usual sardonic lilt to his voice laced with exasperation. Or was it irritation. "Doubtless he's going to want to argue about them over dinner, but at least it got rid of him for now."

"Thank you," Damien said without turning around.

Adam... was another whole piece of his problems. And that was frustrating in and of itself, because Adam had been a source of *solutions* since the King was fourteen years old.

"So. How long are you going to stare at the White Witch's Keep?" Adam asked, leaning up against the same crenelation, but facing the opposite direction so that he could look at his King. Damien didn't have to turn his head to know that the tall blonde knight's arms were folded, his ankles crossed, his position comfortably settled enough that he could outwait Time and the Gods Themselves.

"I don't know. She knows I'm watching, you know." He didn't bother correcting Adam's terminology. A true witch was a sort of low-Powered mage, usually one with an affinity for the magickal Element of Earth. Adam's reference was to spare the presumably tender ears of his sovereign the rhyming word that was certainly the one he was *thinking.*

Though how he could imagine Damien was *innocent* in any sense of the word, the slightly younger man didn't understand. Adam was the one person to whom he'd given most *(though still not quite all…)* of the details of his tenure in Azella's Keep. No one who had survived that place could be considered an 'innocent.'

Adam snorted. "That's a bit of a vanity, and you know it. Even if she *is* looking out this way – which I'd imagine she does fairly often, if only to grind her teeth – there's no possible way she can see you, here. There's no way she can know you're watching. *We* can barely see her damned Keep from here."

Damien shrugged. He *knew* Azella was watching him – or at least the distant outline of this castle – just as *he* was watching *her* Keep. There was still a connection between them. Not one he could explain – not a bond of magick or soul. But it was there just the same.

Perhaps he would never be free of her.

Adam sighed and turned, unfolding his arms and wrapping one around Damien's shoulders. "It's over."

Damien resisted the urge to lay his head – to rest all the weight of his worries – upon Adam. As he used to do. That… was entirely fraught now, and *another* one of his worries.

"I don't think it will ever *really* be over between us," he said softly.

How could it, after all? Azella was an Evil Wizard, Heir to her master who had built the Keep and raised up that unnatural promontory a thousand years ago… and whom she had killed. She would also live as close to forever as made no difference to anyone who wasn't willing to steal the life-magick of others to sustain themselves. She would be there for all his lifetime, and likely trouble the Ilseador he passed on to his children and grandchildren.

Damien had explored the question of how to evict her from the margin of his Realm – or even to… extinguish her. His conclusion was that he didn't have the Power…

Well, his conclusion that he couldn't be sure wasn't tainted by his unwilling empathy for her. Azella might be Unpitying and unmerciful in the extreme… but she was also a young girl trapped *(choosing to be trapped, though the original choice had been her master's)* in an unaging body, with a mind clever enough to learn knowledge but never able to mature to true wisdom. A princess reft of her royal origins, by what tragedy of fate or design, Damien had not *(yet)* managed to determine.

He had fallen a little in love with her during his enforced stay in her Keep. Had allowed himself to do it, knowing that her intent was to turn him aside from his own principles and responsibilities – and loves – and make him into her fit mate. His own goal had been to soften her... to offer her his love in all honesty – and no matter the personal cost – in order to divert her from the path of Evil.

He had failed, of course.

But the attempt – and the things she had done to him, and to others to manipulate him – had left him in a tangle.

A... *broken* tangle.

Not that he had the leisure to be broken. Not with Azella upon his southern border, Queen Estelle of Deltheran – still in possession of the province of Elendria – to the west, a rather uneasy truce with King Haveeer of Mercasia and another with the Jeweled Queen of Vindalia to the north. Not to mention his own hordes of untrustworthy nobles.

And knowing what he now did about the entire *society* of Evil Wizards – complete with cruel and terrible infrastructure to serve their needs – lying somewhere to the west and south...

Azella might be the most Powerful, but she would hardly be the only one to try his borders... hardly the only one he needed to fear would try to take away his loved ones...

"No, I suppose not..." Adam's arm tightened around him as he sighed. "Still. You're safe now. If – *when* – you face each other again, it won't because she has you in her power."

"I hope not." Because that would mean Damien had already lost everything.

Surely it wasn't too... *unmanly* for him to take comfort in Adam's nearness. Everyone in the Realm knew that Adam had been one of the ones who found him in the Royal Library and trained him up to be a king, didn't they? A man could always benefit from the advice of his mentor of long years.

"I am your sword and shield, my sweet prince. Against Azella or any other. As I have always been. And will always be."

Supremely comforting…

…except for the endearment.

And except for Adam angling in for a kiss…

Damien wriggled himself a little away – Adam's arms fell instantly, not confining him.

Gods, but he'd been dodging Adam's kisses for weeks. A problem made all the harder by the fact that Adam was now his Champion and *de facto* bodyguard and it was his duty to sleep across the inner threshold of his king's door. Or… somewhere in the rooms or tent that the king occupied.

It didn't help that he wasn't entirely sure he *wanted* to be dodging those kisses.

But this… this *infernal mess* that the four of them had created… no, that *Damien* had created *(not that he could still see any other thing he might have done to save Genevieve's life)*… it had to be ended. It *had* to.

Faraway Dawil might indulge in these ideas of 'triad-marriages' – though even they went only so far as allowing it for the commoners, not the Lord of Wave himself. Lord Tedros' Amberdeen princess – the mother of his older children – was not acknowledged as his wife despite ten thousand years of the Sacred Marriage between the Elemandros line and the Sea-Queen being supplemented with a human spouse. *(It should have been Lord Tedros' princess that was accepted, rather than the Wavian noblewoman he'd married so much later… but political realities were what they were, and no one wanted to see a half-blooded Amberdeen prince or princess on the Turquoise Throne.)*

Damien had pushed that envelope as far as it could go – sanctioning Jason and Adam's wedding and seeing it sanctified as part of Jason's Confirmation as Crown Prince. And he'd explicitly accepted Duchess Laura's marriage to Duchess-Consort Carmencita as part of the treaty that restored Alpinsward to Ilseador. There was already unrest among the people regarding the change and the City Guard in Emeralsee had needed to provide protection for more than a handful of bold couples who followed their example. Out in the countryside... reports didn't always have all the details, and countryfolk were often slow to change their ways anyhow.

Besides, it wasn't, it *shouldn't* be *wrong* for a man to cleave to his soul-bonded wife, should it?

(And never mind the mess of Geneveive's second soul-bond to Jason...)

"Adam... Farivera's only just come back into contact with the rest of the Realm," Damien offered the same, rather lame excuse he'd been using for days. "People here don't know that you practically raised me. They'll... read more into things than...."

Adam's lip curled wryly as he refolded his arms and settled against the crenellation again. "Than you want them to see?"

"Than a man receiving advice from his mentor," Damien answered as he folded his own arms and settled into a stable, swordsman's stance.

It was a bit *prim,* and he knew that. But what else could he say? Or do?

His Champion snorted. "If that's how you want it, Damien."

It was on the tip of his tongue to say it wasn't what he *wanted,* but then Adam likely *would* kiss him, and then...

...and then he'd be lost.

Damien Alsterling had never wanted to be king of Ilseador. It had merely been the only option if he didn't want to *die.*

And kings... couldn't please themselves. At least not if they didn't want to walk the paths his grandfather had done.

Something in his face apparently spoke to Adam, because the tall man's golden-hazel gaze softened. Adam could read him better than anyone else, even despite the trim little beard Damien had begun sporting a couple of years ago – likely because of that *empathy* he'd admitted to so recently.

"Nevermind, love. We'll get it sorted out eventually." Adam chuckled. "Though not before Count Marsham and General Direlien make you resolve their disagreements about deployments, it seems. Given that they seem to be hunting you down."

Damien glanced over his shoulder to see the burly military man and the almost elderly Count making their way across the gallery. Each was carefully avoiding contact with even a brush of the other's cloak. Neither one would likely appreciate that they had identical glints of determination and ire in their eyes.

He turned back to close his eyes for a moment, summoning the soothing sense of his Library around him. No, he'd never wanted to be king. But it was his nonetheless.

Adam's hand on his shoulder spun him around to face the oncoming nobles – the General was the scion of a family from the Emeralsee northern coastline, not far from where Adam had grown up.

As Damien opened his eyes and fixed an appropriate expression on his face, Adam's voice whispered almost in his ear, "Not *too* much longer though, my sweet prince. Not *too* much longer."

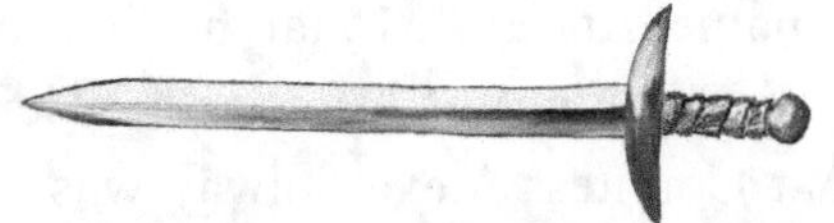

Chapter ONE

Responsibilities

"We've never come to Elaarwen this way before," King Damien Alsterling mused. "It looks... different."

The Siovale plains were behind them now; they were deep into the foothills of the Elaarwen mountains. The bridge over the Topaz River lay just ahead.

Sir Adam Loveress, King's Champion – among other things – snorted. "Of course it's *different*. We're used to coming up alongside the Emerald and passing through Cedarwen." He shuddered. "And bypassing Brindlewell."

Damien gave him a sympathetic glance. "Alexa can't last forever."

The Countess of Brindlewell had caused no one anything but pain before Damien had banished her to her estates. She was not Adam's mother-in-law... thanks to Damien's discovery, the previous Autumn, that Adam's then-husband-to-be, Jason, was actually Alexa's *grandson* and *not* her son, as they had all thought for thirty-five years.

And more importantly, that Jason was actually a cousin of the king himself and the only other living person who could legitimately carry the Alsterling name. And the Monarch's Sword had spoken for him, validating Damien's choice of Jason as his Heir and making it completely clear that Countess Alexa Solway was *not* Jason's liege-lady and had no right to control him.

The Champion's expression was dour. "I'm sure she'll try. And I wouldn't put it past her to try to haunt the place even after she finally does die." He gazed off into the distance... though distinctly *not* in the direction of distant Brindlewell. "Not that I can imagine Jason will want to have anything to do with the place. But his brother, or one of his sisters, will still have to rule there... He hasn't said anything about whether he'll want to go back someday. To... visit."

Damien glanced around them for possible listeners, mostly out of habit. His magickal connection with Ilseador ensured that he was always aware of his surroundings. But Adam – and Jason – had trained him to be alert since he was seventeen and long before his magick had manifested. And what he said next might walk well walk the line of things they dared not speak in public.

The rest of their party – knights and ladies of the Royal Guard, both official and Secret – were spread out well away from the pair of them. A half-dozen were ahead, acting like frivolous nobles on an outing. Another group trotted along behind. Others ranged out to the sides.

No one was within hearing distance.

"I'll still deed you a place of your own, you know," Damien offered a little hesitantly.

He'd been looking for a chance to have this conversation with Adam, to make this offer. Not that he wanted his dear friends – his *Champion* and his *Heir* – gone from Castle Alsterling, but everyone needed a certain amount of space, right? And if Adam and Jason were feeling at all trapped by the roles they had taken up in Emeralsee...

"Whenever... whenever you *want* it," he added. "And, um, *wherever.*"

Wherever there were Crown lands that he could deed away, anyways.

His best friend and Champion blinked as if to dismiss whatever he'd been thinking of and turned his usual glower on his king. "Don't be an idiot. You need us with you and Genevieve. And *we* need to be near the baby. The *children.*"

The *children.* Of course.

All of them as yet unborn, but Adam's *visions* had assured him there would be at least four, despite Genevieve's rather advanced age for embarking on having so many.

The first had been sired by Jason, to meet the terms of evil old Lord Prydeen's prophecy and save Genevieve's life after ten miscarriages in five years. Her life, and by extension Damien's, since he was soul-bonded to his Queen. In Adam's vision it was a little girl with reddish hair more golden than her mother's – and hopefully everyone would believe that she resembled Damien's long-dead father rather than her true sire. It was possible, after all. She would be born in a few more months and they would get to see.

The second was to be a boy with coal-black hair – Damien's, undoubtedly.

The last – Adam had managed to share his *vision* with Damien across their *empathic* bond – were twins. A girl with that same black hair and a towheaded boy. Damien's again, presumably.

And they didn't dare even hint that the eldest had been sired by her 'Uncle' Jason. Not even to *her,* because how could a toddler keep a secret? Perhaps when she was older...

Damien already loved little Giendra Marlerite fiercely. She was *his,* no matter who had sired her, born of his soul-bonded wife and Queen...

Of course, Adam loved the baby just as much – sired by his own true-love and wedded husband... who was *also* – if secretly – soul-bonded to Genevieve.

None of it had anything to do with *Damien,* and he should be resigned to that idea. He knew how much Adam adored children, after all. How long his Champion had been importuning Jason for the pair of them to adopt.

That had been to his own benefit as well, when Adam had insisted on half-adopting a certain orphaned young prince who had been hiding out in the Royal Library for four years. He – and Jason – had been the parents Damien had needed.

A lovely mess indeed.

Damien nodded briefly, and hopefully not *curtly*, and turned his gaze back to the bridge their horses' canter was rapidly approaching. "Of course. I just don't want you to feel stuck. I know I ask a lot of you–"

He felt the warmth of Adam's horse brush his leg as his Champion brought them almost too close to ride safely, and looked up to meet that always-understanding if usually-sardonic golden-hazel gaze.

"Fool king." Adam's tone belied his words... though Damien had come to realize that this was an endearment from the man who'd looked after him since he was fourteen. From the first person who had *loved* him since his own parents had been so brutally murdered.

Adam's voice went quiet. "My sweet prince. Even if it were possible to separate Jason and Genevieve, *I* won't be parted from *you*. Baby or not."

Damien gave him a tentative smile. "As I suppose this trip has proven. I just wish..."

He flushed, and looked fixedly down at his horse's ears.

Dammit. He hadn't wanted to *say*, to *suggest*...

They *had* to get the four of them sorted out into something *sustainable*.

Something that didn't involve censoring every word... given that Adam was his closest advisor besides – and sometimes even *beyond* – Genevieve. And Jason was Crown Prince and Heir to the Throne until the damned Monarch's Blade spoke for one of the children. Until the children were *old* enough to try them on it, though the prophecy claimed that it wouldn't be their precious soon-to-be-born first daughter that the Sword would speak for.

Something that wouldn't risk *civil war* if their secrets were ever outed.

Something... *separate*.

Except Damien had firsthand experience of why *separate* didn't *work* for a soul-bonded pair. He and Genevieve had both nearly *died*... Though the demands of the bond had been muted so long as she was pregnant.

He couldn't do that to her *again* by separating her from Jason.

Nor harm Jason that way either. Even if it weren't just *wrong*, Jason was... well, the *second* person to care about him after Adam.

Another... lovely *mess*.

But Damien hadn't been able to resign himself to the impossibility of the situation. He kept poking at it, trying to make all the puzzle-pieces fall into a recognizable – a *familiar* – pattern that anyone could look at and that didn't need layer upon layer of secrets.

The only way it even halfway began to make sense was if they could somehow put everything back as close to the way it had been last Fall as they could. Or rather last Summer. Or earlier. Except with *children* and *without* Genevieve nearly dying of her pregnancies.

The other... *things* needed to go away. To stop. To... be as close as possible to *never happened*.

It was... necessary.

For the survival of the Realm – and of Damien and his small, strangely-shaped family.

Because even a whisper of... what had happened before... could light a fire under his far-too-restive population.

They needed things to settle.

They needed people to go back to their own concerns and for any salacious rumors to have a chance to die away.

They needed to be two *separate* pairs. Jason and Adam. Damien and Genevieve.

And *that* was what he needed to convince *Adam* to resign himself to, as well.

Adam gave the King a wry look that was far too... interested, likely responding to the sentiment that Damien hadn't intended to express... ever again.

What he – what either of them – *wished*... would just have to go hang.

"Me, too. But it's about as wise in Elaarwen as it was in Siovale," Adam replied. "Or with this small troop of Guards with us every moment. There's not much justification for me to sleep in your tent out here in the wilds. It's safer out here than when we had a whole army with us and were in potentially unfriendly territory."

Safer... because the loyalty of this handful of Guards was without question, but the army might contain any number of disaffected men or women. Not to mention that they'd been traveling through Siovale, whose dukes had rebelled three times in the last two decades, and then Farivera, which had been ruled by Azella the Unpitying – and her Evil Wizard master before her.

Having Adam sleep in Damien's tent – and that tent again surrounded by their loyal Guards – had a measure of paranoia to it. But not *unwarranted* paranoia.

Not that Damien had let it go farther than *sleeping*. Despite Adam's... *inviting* comments about just how well the King had warded his tent.

Temptation... was to be resisted.

The Champion – the *new Prince-Consort to the new Crown Prince* – had an entirely different perspective on the whole situation.

He'd spent the entire trip looking for opportunities to get Damien into bed with him. Not that he'd pressed the matter when the King had made up excuse after patently fake excuse. Which had become increasingly challenging with his Champion sleeping across his threshold as a proper bodyguard. Warded tent or no.

"At least no one has actually turned out to be unfriendly," Damien felt he had to point out – again. It might even make a good distraction from what Adam had *really* meant. "The nobles in Farivera seemed grateful to return to being a part of the Realm at last. It wasn't *their* idea for the county to have been yielded up to Azella's mentor by the Duke of Siovale."

That would be not the young and newly-confirmed Duke Mark, nor his father, Tomas, the duke who had tried to usurp Damien's throne two months ago, either, but Tomas' long-dead *grandfather.* Nor was it clear how many generations before *that* had been the first contact between the Elseviers and Azella's deathless master.

The sorceress had suggested that the man had lived a thousand years – and that timing dovetailed with the Fall of the Turquoise Empire and the chaos that had swept the Empire's former vassals, which included both Ilseador and, on the other side of the Tree-of-Life River, Sindala. It would have been the perfect time for a rather private-minded Evil Wizard to nibble away at the margins between two countries with Bound and Crowned Monarchs and establish his own vile Keep.

By the time the chaos settled and the Monarchs of the time were able to focus on their own lands again, the Keep and its master would have been harder to detect. In his return visit to Farivera, Damien had found it difficult to detect *now*, despite knowing full well that it was there. Like a pearl in an oyster or a boll within a treetrunk, the Realm had layered protective walls around the canker.

Decades it would be, to heal all the wounds inflicted by the Dukes of Siovale... though hopefully the new one would break the trend.

"I'm still not sure how far we can trust Count Marsham," Adam commented, but waved off Damien's inevitable disagreement and reminder that he'd taken the Count of Farivera's oath and it had held through the magickal Binding. "Time will tell. And it won't hurt that General Direlien is staying in Farivera with that Division of the Army for now. If anyone can handle things, *he* can. Including reopening contact with what's left of Sindala."

"Yes..." That, at least, was something they agreed on.

But...

"A Division in Farivera, another two in Elendria..." Damien muttered. "A third in Alpinsward. A fourth supporting Tariana in Embervest... I still think we should pull that one back since the Jeweled Queen gave us back Everfields."

"In the wake of the news of your demon-battle," Adam pointed out – again. "*Genevieve* doesn't think we should pull back, and between Everfields and Minglemere and her home county in the foothills, Her Grace of Embervest has more bandits to deal with than anywhere else in the Realm. You've said yourself that you understood why we lost Everfields and Minglemere when your grandfather pulled back the troops supporting Embervest. Besides, we still have a full five thousand-man Home Guard in Emeralsee."

"We won't though," the King fretted. "Not if Genevieve wants to keep a full Division in Siovale. The Home Guard will go back to being the 'hospital Division,' with all the men and women who need to recuperate and no one really able to *fight*."

Adam raised an eyebrow. *"She's* the master strategist, as you keep telling everyone who'll listen. And the only reason we'd need a full, fighting-capable Division right outside Emeralsee, is if Siovale decided to invade again. Which shouldn't be a problem if we already have a Division occupying the province."

"Nor with Mark as Duke and marrying your sister," Damien relaxed marginally, smiling at the memory of the young duke kneeling at *Adam's* feet and begging permission to officially court Marianna. The young lady-in-waiting had come along to Siovale to guard her King as a member of the Secret Cadre...

Adam, however, winced. "Hunh. I'm just as happy that Mama will hear about *that* while we're still in Elaarwen. Actually... the letter I sent her should be getting to Lynncrag about now."

"It's a wonderful match," Damien suggested. "She'll be married to the Duke of Siovale."

"To the son of the man who just tried to usurp your throne," Adam said dryly. "Who's *also* the *nephew* of the one who tried to usurp you *six* years ago."

"To the young man Marianna clearly loves and who just as obviously adores *her,"* Damien corrected.

His Champion sighed. "Well, *I* agree, but you know how stubborn Mama – *and* Papa – can be if *they* don't."

He hadn't spoken to his parents for over ten years when they refused to accept Jason as the love of his life.

"I... think they've grown a little since then," Damien replied.

Adam snorted. "I *hope* so. For Mari's sake. Though he'll have to talk to Mama and Papa himself eventually." He winced. "I shouldn't really even have given them an interim permission. Mama is going to use that as another reason why I'm not meant to give up Lynncrag."

And so, they'd circled back around.

"Lynncrag... *would* be close enough to Emeralsee for you and Jason to go back and forth," Damien said quietly. "You could see the children as much as you like. And then – if Prydeen was right about this baby – Jason could ask me to cede her to him as his own Heir, once the Sword speaks for one of the others."

They wouldn't even have to explain it. People adopted younger cousins as Heirs all the time. *(Though it **would** be unusual for a baronet to adopt a princess...)*

Adam gave him a quizzical look. "And just how is that supposed to work while I'm your Champion and Jason is Duke of Emeralsee and Crown Prince? And with Genevieve needing an Heir to Elaarwen? Not to mention that, even if we bring the children down to Lynncrag regularly, she won't *know* the place like..."

He sighed. "Like *I* don't. I haven't lived there since I was eleven. Mama should designate Desirée as her Heir. So far, she's the only one of us with children and she's lived there all her life."

It wasn't really any of Damien's business, who one of his quaternary vassals chose as an Heir. Except that this was *Adam's* home.

"I just think you should have a place that's yours, and yours alone," he said, trying to sound reasonable.

Adam raised an eyebrow. "It sounds more like you're trying to get rid of us."

"*Never.*"

It came out rather too vehemently, and Damien carefully kept his eyes focused on the road ahead.

A chuckle, and Adam's horse brushed his leg again.

"If we were alone on this road, my sweet prince, I'd pull you over onto my saddle and make sure we both believed you meant that."

Well, and wasn't that an... *odd* thing to say.

And he had to sternly suppress the shiver of... wishful anticipation that was surely as much a reaction to the *feelings* that Adam was unintentionally *projecting* at him.

Almost certainly unintentionally.

Or at least he could pretend that he thought it was unintentional.

But Damien couldn't really pretend he didn't understand what his Champion meant.

"Adam..."

"It's all right, Damien. We've only been trying to figure ourselves out for fifteen years now. We'll surely get it right one of these days."

His shoulder was buffeted with a friendly – but not *overly* friendly – clap, and then Adam eased off a bit, letting their horses drift apart into a more normal spacing.

The King had to fight not to hunch his shoulders in – misery? Guilt?

At least Adam hadn't used his 'disappointed swordmaster' voice that still made the slightly-younger man jump. Though that touch of amusement laden with understanding was almost worse somehow.

Damien dared a glance at his oldest... friend.

Golden-hazel eyes met his own silver-grey ones, and one corner of Adam's mouth tipped upwards in wry acknowledgment of all the things they couldn't say out here on the open road, surrounded by their guards.

Damien couldn't help returning the look – *and* the smile.

It occurred to the King, as Lady Alanna dropped back from the vanguard to have a word with her former captain and Adam gave her his full attention, that *resignation* had had no part in that last interaction. Neither Adam's nor, he had to admit, his own.

Gods, but this only kept getting harder.

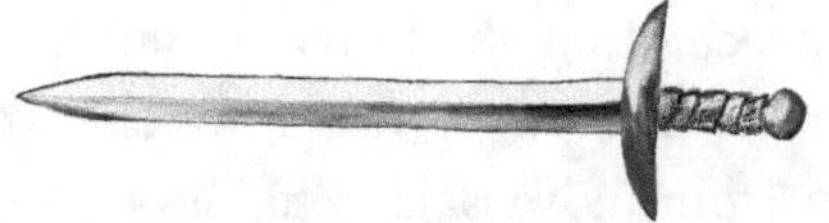

Chapter TWO

Necessities

THEY REACHED THE BRIDGE OVER the Topaz and crossed without incident. The span was well-maintained and of solid construction – there was a great deal of commerce between Siovale and Elaarwen, after all.

There always had been, but it had increased significantly after Genevieve had married Duke Tomas' younger brother and Siovale had joined the Rebellion.

The alliance had brought Siovale's impressive mounted warriors and vast herds of well-trained horses onto the side of Duke Aldred's Rebels. It had given the starving mountain people access to Siovale's vast grainfields and the other products of the rich and prosperous lowlands.

What it had given Siovale was more questionable, though simply finding a way to start fighting free of Damien's grandfather's tyranny might have been sufficient at the time. Tomas Elsevier had claimed once that he and his nobles hadn't dared rebel until they knew that

Elaarwen – with the natural fortress provided by the mountains – would welcome them if the Royal Armies stood likely to roll over Siovale. More likely it had been that Genevieve and her father carried royal blood and any children she bore to Harald would have had that same claim to the Throne; it was now clear to everyone that Farivera's defection from its vassalage to the Dukes of Siovale had been more of a ruse than a reality.

The alliance of Siovale and Elaarwen had not, however, eased the bottleneck of other resources that the Rebellion needed. Ilseador had only the one terribly good harbor at Emeralsee and a handful of halfway decent sites where it was worth bringing shallow-keeled boats in along the shore north of the city... all of which were still located in the royal province. The roads to countries like Deltheran, Mercasia, and Vindalia routed through provinces that had stayed loyal to the Crown. And the one tiny port at the far southern tip of Farivera was only marginally useful, inconveniently faraway... and no longer under the control of the Dukes of Siovale.

Additionally, neither impoverished Elaarwen, nor prosperous Siovale were much noted for their weaponsmiths, nor did they have connections abroad that might have been used to tighten an economic noose around King Reginald's reign.

Luckily, they'd had other, secret allies to do that and to smuggle them weapons to replace what was inevitably lost over the years-long struggle.

All of which was very old news, since the Rebellion had been formally ended shortly after Damien's coronation nearly six years ago... or more properly after *Genevieve's* coronation as his Queen. The Rebel Duchess ruling Ilseador was deemed by most everyone to be a satisfactory outcome, not least by Damien himself.

Nonetheless, the strengthened economic connections between fiercely independent Elaarwen and Siovale had continued. Thus, the healthy state of the road and bridges and the number of trade caravans that they had passed going in both directions.

Grain and other vegetables went into the uplands. Furs and gemstones came back down to the plains. The Siovalese had developed a taste for wearing the thick, cold-weather pelts of the fur-bearing animals found in the mountains. There was a bit of mining in both provinces – tunnels in the mountains and open pits in the flatlands – but most of what was removed from the Elaarwen mountains were precious and semi-precious gemstones and small quantities of rare ores that were used to improve steel. Elaarwen's fiercely independent hunters and farmers prised those valuable substances out in their spare time and had little interest in developing larger and more lucrative operations.

Large amounts of iron, coal, and various salts were mined more effectively – and enthusiastically – in the Alpinsward range to the north of the broad flood-plains that stretched west from the ocean.

For some reason, the *feel* of this part of Elaarwen was subtly different than what Damien was used to from his other trips. Somehow more... *aware?*

He was Bound to all of Ilseador as King, of course, but he was Bound additionally to Elaarwen through Genevieve as her Duke-Consort. As a result, he'd always had a finer sense of the place than anywhere besides the royal province of Emeralsee where he'd been born and from which he ruled.

It was possible that the difference was simply one of perception. Damien's own Power as an Earth-mage was now under much better control after his harrowing Winter as a prisoner – and student – in the Keep of the Evil Sorceress at the southern tip of Farivera.

It was also possible it was simply that the area between the Topaz and Sapphire Rivers had a different set of flora and fauna, given the greater availability of water in the region. It wasn't exactly marshy – most of it, anyways – but it was a milder climate than in the mountains and yet protected, by the rivers and the sharp peaks to the south, from the vast, peripatetic herds of the eastern grasslands. It was only the biannual Spring and Fall floods that overwhelmed this bit of riverland that kept humans from making permanent homes here, but the animal life seemed more resilient.

Or it was even possible that the area felt different because this was the lowest points in all of Elaarwen. Only Cedarwen itself – at the confluence of the Emerald and Sapphire rivers and which was also regularly flooded – was at a lower altitude. The grade of this road coming up from Siovale was a great deal less steep than the main one that followed the Sapphire up from Cedarwen – but it was a great deal longer.

None of this probably mattered any great deal, but Damien was rather distracted with sorting all of it out and barely noticed that Adam was uncharacteristically quiet as they rode along together.

They'd crossed the Topaz shortly before noon. It was only a short ride on the good road across the somewhat marshy meadowlands between the two rivers to reach the second bridge, which was also in excellent repair. The Spring floods were long-enough gone to have left the intervening area verdant and burgeoning with wildflowers. Damien was glad that they were riding straight across rather than camping here – he could tell that those oh-so-green meadows would be a little too squishy for sleeping comfort, but the road itself was largely dry to the hoof.

The whole troupe had to close up a bit to get across the Sapphire, taking the usual care to avoid setting up vibrations in the bridge decking. Horses fell into step somewhat less easily than humans, but it was still wise to be cautious. Damien noted that Lady Alanna was taking care of the matter – and had delegated a handful of Royal Guards to be sure the packhorses didn't create any problems.

He set aside the logistical considerations and simply let the Land welcome him home. It was always on the west bank of the Sapphire that he really *felt* like he was in Elaarwen.

Though it was… interesting that Elaarwen didn't really notice him as much in the meadowlands between the rivers. Perhaps it was because the very high mountains that separated the two streams a little farther to the south were all but impassable.

Cloudcroft was off in that direction, Damien knew, and between the rivers as well, if the Land – and his maps – described it properly. It was his father-in-law's personal holding now and some important family history had taken place there. Damien had been up to the high-altitude cottage-holding a couple of times with his wife. But the peaks surrounding Cloudcroft were particularly sharp and forbidding – the only safe approach was from the direction of Castle Stellarine and the small town that was generously termed Elaarwen's capitol 'city.'

Their horses hadn't made it more than a handful of paces off of the bridge over the Sapphire when Adam made an unhappy noise and reined in tightly.

"Adam?" Damien inquired with some concern. "What's wrong?"

The tall knight looked almost greenish. "Something I ate must *really* not have agreed with me."

Damien reached his Healer's sense out to deal with the problem. Indigestion – or even food poisoning – shouldn't take more than a moment to fix. Though they'd all been eating the same things, and Adam's iron stomach really shouldn't have been the first to react if there were an issue with improper preparation.

To the King's surprise, he could detect Adam's nausea, but no *cause* for it.

No, *more* than just *nausea...*

The tall knight practically slithered out of his saddle, collapsing to his knees practically *underneath* his horse in the least graceful dismount Damien had ever seen *anyone* accomplish, let alone his skilled Champion. The King hurriedly hopped off his own tall, roan palfrey to take Adam's abandoned reins and move his Champion's warhorse aside before it accidentally stepped on its rider.

Which should be unlikely, but... Adam collapsing to the ground was also *unlikely*.

Lady Alanna was at his side almost as soon as Damien had gotten the horses a step or two away, and accepted the reins that the King thrust at her.

"What's wrong?" the commander of this detached unit of his Royal Guards – Secret and otherwise – asked with concern as Damien turned to Adam.

The tall, blonde knight was kneeling, hunched around his stomach and with a hand pressed tight over his mouth as if trying to restrain himself from vomiting by sheer willpower alone.

And... apparently that was *exactly* what was going on, because Adam lost his internal battle before Damien even had a chance to try to help. At the same exact moment, he lost control of his projective *empathy* and Damien had to fight to keep *himself* from vomiting as well, as he absorbed Adam's idiopathic dizziness.

"I don't know, Alanna," the King said distractedly. Though a part of him couldn't help noticing that Alanna wasn't affected by Adam's suddenly erratic projective *empathy*. "He thought it might be something he ate – but I'm not detecting anything like that in his gut."

He knelt on one knee a little behind Adam, putting a hand on his Champion's forehead and another on his back. The swirling dizziness seemed to recede a little as he did so – Damien's own at least.

Damien *thought* it was his own anyways. He was having difficulty distinguishing his own reactions from Adam's right now.

This... was an unpleasant side-effect of the emotional entanglement of a pair of receptive/projective *empaths* that he hadn't anticipated. Sorting through all of this right now, to be able to help Adam, promised to be... *another* lovely mess.

And was surely yet *another* argument for why Damien needed to find some *other* solution for the four of them. How could he possibly take care of Adam and Jason and Genevieve if they were so tangled up together that he couldn't even tell which of them was feeling what? It had made sense when Damien had felt his soul-bonded wife's morning sickness, but... he *wasn't* soul-bonded to *Adam*...

"Is anyone else feeling poorly?" Damien looked up at the young woman who was still hovering.

He shouldn't have to *ask* that, dammit. He should be able to send his Healer's sense out to the rest of their troop to see for himself.

But that swirling dizziness of Adam's was swamping out all of the King's finer senses.

Or maybe it was his sympathy for this man he loved more than he wanted to, and not magickal *empathy,* that was distorting Damien's perceptions. He should be able to *tell* which of those it was, dammit.

Alanna shook her head. Her eyes were scanning around at the various knights and ladies and gentlemen who were now converging on the three who were on the ground, though most of them were staying back and keeping a proper perimeter guard.

"Not as far as I can tell, Your Majesty."

Sir Angelos Eldridge, Damien's cousin on his mother's side and Alanna's second-in-command, reined up as he also came in close enough to converse. His concerned gaze checked over Damien and Adam before going, quite properly, to Alanna for instructions.

Alanna gave him a small shake of her head, eyes still on Damien. "Your Majesty?"

The King sighed and began to rise...

...and Adam moaned and began retching again as soon as Damien's hand left his brow.

Well... *that* made no particular sense. The King wasn't using any of his Healing magick. Nor should it make a difference whether he was touching his patient if he had been.

"*Damien...*" Adam managed to eke out in a painful whisper, "*don't leave me... please...*"

The fact that he used the King's name in public was as much of a testament to the situation as the actual words, unexpected as those were. Whether *Adam Loveress Alsterling* had ever pled for *anything* in his life before this moment might have been questionable.

Well, other than his mother and father's understanding. When he was seventeen, Damien had sat uncomfortably in the hallway outside of the baronetta's suite at Lynncrag, while Adam spent *hours* trying to reconcile his parents to his relationship with Jason. The young prince had been out of earshot – and Adam's brothers and sisters and Ciriis Celavell had all tried to pry him away – but he hadn't been able to make himself go even a few steps farther. It wasn't as though Adam had been aware of his own awkward attempt to be supportive – the frustrated young knight hadn't even noticed 'his prince' huddled there in the corridor when he had finally stormed out, swearing never to set foot in his childhood home again.

Damien had scrambled to catch up to him, and thank goodness Ciriis had already packed for all three of them and Adam's brothers had readied their horses. Damien would have followed Adam back to Emeralsee on foot and without so much as a crust of bread otherwise.

"Of course not," Damien agreed, quickly replacing his hand on Adam's forehead. Leaving anyone in such a state when he could do something about it – not that he was really sure what he was doing in this case – wasn't in his nature. Let alone *Adam*.

It must be a placebo; Adam *believed* that having Damien touching him could help, so it worked for him. And having Damien move away had the opposite effect. It was clearly all in his head.

Not that Adam was prone to fantasies, but Damien knew that his friend was a creative and imaginative man and a quick learner *(and no, he didn't mean that as a **double entendre**)*. It was why Adam had become the King's closest advisor, after all. He *noticed* everything and *thought* about everything and he made broader connections between all those things quite nearly as well as Damien did himself.

Though... the King had *felt* for himself Adam's renewed nausea and the increase in the swirling dizziness when he removed his hand. Not that he could *explain* it.

"We'll camp here, Alanna," he told the commander of his Guards as he tried to find a more comfortable position to kneel in without letting his hand leave Adam's forehead. Almost absently, he *Vanished* away Adam's vomit, leaving the grass and soil clean and dry. "We won't risk upsetting Adam's stomach further by trying to pick him up. Just get my tent set up and I'll *Vanish* the two of us into it."

Kneeling on one knee with his hands on Adam... was not something Damien was going to be able to continue during the amount of time it would take to set up the camp; his legs would go numb before the tent was ready if he couldn't find a better position. Not to mention that he had no idea what to do *after* he got the two of them into his tent, though at least he'd be able to fumble around without an audience.

Nausea and dizziness had *causes,* dammit. Causes that should yield to his Healing, just as they always had before.

The problem must be this new *openness* that he had with respect to Adam. His *empathy* was too deeply engaged; he was *feeling* everything Adam was and that was keeping Damien from being able to focus his mind properly on the problem. And without being able to focus his *mind,* he certainly couldn't focus his *magick.*

Clearly, *that* was the problem.

Just as it was with everything *else* in his life.

"*Water... please...*" Adam whispered. He wasn't quite as nauseous and dizzy now that Damien's hands were on his head again, but he was all-too-obviously *not well*.

"I don't think you can keep anything down right now, Adam," Damien said dubiously.

A very slight shake of the tall man's head was instantly regretted by both of them.

"*Just... want to rinse my mouth...*"

"All right." Damien looked over at the scramble of knights, ladies, and gentlemen assembling his tent in a clearing to the north, some hundred feet off the road, and starting on a few others. A thin stream of smoke from behind the group suggested that someone was working on dinner.

"Angelos!" the King called out to one of the nearer men who seemed to have been left on guard-duty, and the young man hurried over.

"Your Majesty?" Sir Angelos Eldridge asked.

He was shorter than most of the rest of the King's knights, black-haired and dark-eyed with a nose and cheekbones that matched Damien's own. As made sense, since he was the King's cousin on his mother's side. He was also as excellent a swordsman – a *fighter* – as his appointment to the Royal Guard implied, and good with people – as his assignment as second-in-command of this troop implied.

Second-in-command to Lady Alanna, but he was introduced as the 'official' commander to everyone from General Direlien to Count Marsham, since Alanna had never had the chance to earn her shield.

It was Angelos' unhesitating deference to the woman that had earned him this assignment.

Unlike many of Damien's knights, Angelos accepted that the Secret Cadre of ladies-in-waiting –which now also included a handful of gentlemen-of-the-chamber – were his equals, or even superiors, in terms of being able to defend the Ilseadoran royals. In Alanna's case *(and that of a diminishing few others)* most particularly, since she was a veteran of the Rebellion and if she hadn't earned her *shield,* she had still taken down more than one knight who *had* while facing the Royal Army on the battlefield.

Assuming Damien's expedition around the Realm went well, Angelos would be confirmed as official Second to Captain Tim Ancellius on their return to Emeralsee. Alanna was already Commander of the Secret Cadre... and Tim's *real* Second. Sir Marcus, the knight who currently served as Tim's official Second, had been chafing under this structure and refusing to take the more discreet Guards seriously, even after being repeatedly trounced in the practice ring by one or another of them.

"Water for His Highness, if you please," Damien asked his younger cousin politely. "From the river, if you would." Because the leathery-tasting water residing in various waterskins would likely not help Adam's situation, and Damien's magick could at least purify drinking water for his sick friend.

"Right away, Sire," Angelos said, and headed off.

Damien frowned. His cousin seemed unsteady on his feet for some reason. But he put aside the thought when Adam moaned softly again, and went back to rubbing soothing circles on the tall man's back, his other hand steady on Adam's forehead.

Adam seemed a little better after rinsing his mouth out several times and pouring the rest of the contents of the metal cup that Angelos brought back over his sweating head.

Damien hadn't really agreed with that last idea, given both that Adam seemed to be in a *cold* sweat and that he had to keep his *own* hands on Adam while the tall knight drenched himself. Late Spring air was damned chilly in the Elaarwen foothills, and wet skin – and cuffs – didn't help with that at all.

Well, at least he could help *himself* with his magick by driving off the chill. And dry their clothes and Adam's hair. Even if the *only* thing that the frustrated King could do for Adam's mysterious ailment was keep his hands on the other man.

On his *skin,* specifically.

It wasn't touching Adam's head that was helping, it was touching his *skin* – which they discovered accidentally when Damien moved the hand that was on Adam's back to sweep the dripping hair out of Adam's face and one finger contacted the tall knight's ear... and Adam's dizziness ratcheted down another notch.

A little more experimentation made it clear that the skin was critical – even holding Adam's hand helped – but touching his face or his neck still made more of a difference.

Which wasn't really *useful.* Damien was hardly going to subject both of them to more of this nausea and dizziness than he had to, just to spare their dignity, but... having to put his hands on Adam's face was... damned *awkward* as well as looking a bit... odd. Not that holding hands with his Champion was all that much more dignified than kneeling at his side like this.

The Healer-King (as Adam had called him once) settled himself crosslegged in front of his friend, taking care to keep at least one hand on Adam's face the whole time. He put the other on the other side of Adam's face as soon as he was set, which seemed to be the most he could do about the situation.

They met each other's eyes... and Adam tried for a measure of his usual cynical expression.

"A bit indiscreet, this," the Champion said softly. His throat was still raspy with the irritation of having vomited, though at least this time the words weren't forced past a rising gorge.

Damien snorted just as softly. "Why? Because it looks like I'm about to kiss you, holding your face in my hands like this? Or because I'm going to have to *Vanish* us into the tent together and *still* in this position?"

It might be a good thing that his hands were mostly covering Adam's cheeks. Though the tall blonde knight's flush was fairly obvious even past Damien's concealing fingers.

He *thought* he'd managed to use his magick to keep his *own* flush from showing.

The King half-expected Adam to suggest that he could cope on his own and tell Damien to take his hands away after his comment.

He readied himself to make the counter-arguments. That even if it wasn't *Adam,* who was one of his best friends and who had looked after *him* through all manners of travails, he was a *Healer* and would never leave someone in pain that he could do anything to ameliorate. Useless though this seemed in any practical sense right now.

But Adam said nothing of the kind, though he did gingerly extract one of his own hands from its position on his abdomen and gently touch the back of Damien's where it cupped his face. He also made a brief, abortive gesture towards *Damien's* face, his warm, golden-hazel eyes searching the King's, then sighed and put the hand back on his stomach.

Despite how he *knew* Adam was feeling right now, Damien couldn't help but think of how the hard, flat muscles of that stomach felt to the touch. And the soft, soft skin of his lov– his *friend's* – abdomen. Skin that still bore the marks of scars from his years on the battlefield fighting against Genevieve and her Rebels.

Years spent fighting to preserve the Realm that Genevieve now *ruled*.

Years... that Adam had *also* spent helping one frightened young prince grow confidence and strength and claim the throne. And that he'd apparently *also* spent trying not to think about how attracted he was to that young prince...

Who had also been oh-so-tentatively in love with h*im*.

Not the direction Damien should be thinking in right at this moment.

Though what else was he supposed to do, with his hands on Adam's face as if holding him in place for a kiss that he knew they both wanted... Though not out in public here, where their Guards could see them...

Their Guards, yes, because Adam wasn't just Sir Loveress anymore. He was *Prince Consort* Adam *Alsterling* – and he bore the surname because of his *husband, Jason*. Damien's other mentor. And cousin. And Named and Confirmed Heir to the Throne.

And Damien's beloved soul-bonded wife's other soul-bonded love...

Who was likely making love to her *right now*...

Or possibly not *right* now, given that it was only late afternoon.

But Jason likely *would* be, tonight. As he had on the previous nights they'd been gone on this expedition to Siovale and Farivera and Elaarwen. Damien's soul-bond to Genevieve still wasn't fully recovered from the damage done to it by Azella the Unpitying, but truly strong emotions – such as sex – easily made it across.

After all, Genevieve belonged to Jason *almost* as much as she did to Damien. A soul-bond washed away all other oaths... And while there were legends of the very occasional *triple* soul-bonds, there was no real precedence for a *second* soul-bond that manifested years after the first... and without the first diminishing in any measurable way.

Only at the farthest points of their travel had Damien been unable to tell with tantalizing detail exactly *what* his wife and his... *friend* were doing with each other. And the fact that he was *feeling* what *Genevieve* was feeling... didn't help ameliorate his reactions a great deal, given that he knew what it was like to feel Jason's touch rather more directly.

And then there had been Adam sleeping just feet away and inside his wards... a temptation that he'd resisted only by telling himself that he *had* to. For the good of the Realm. For his future children. For his own sanity. And for his love and respect for the two men who had given up so very much to care for him and see him to his throne and now to help defeat that damned prophecy.

After all, even with that second soul-bond in place, it wasn't Damien's marriage to Genevieve that was at risk. It was Adam's marriage to Jason.

Though *they* had a bond that Damien could detect as well. It seemed to have been forged by the actual marriage-ceremony in token of how very much they loved each other. A soul-bond-by-choice, as it were.

No, *Adam and Jason* were clearly meant to be together.

"Your lashes are full of tears, my sweet prince."

Damien hadn't even noticed he'd closed his eyes. But they were blurry when he opened them to see Adam's again.

Blurry enough that he could pretend that he wasn't seeing that expression in his... his *sworn knight's* face that he'd only ever seen when the two of them were all alone...

Or think about how Adam mostly used that nickname when they were making love...

The which they had done to prevent Damien from reacting instinctively and badly to Jason and Genevieve meeting the demands of Lord Prydeen's prophecy and their own soul-bond... And then again, later, after Damien had won free of Azella the Unpitying because Damien had been so... broken... from his experiences with the Evil Sorceress and because Jason and Genevieve had both been taken hostage by Tomas Elsevier in his bid for the throne.

The *White Witch of Farivera,* as Adam had called her. He hadn't come up with anything more poetic than *'traitor'* to describe Tomas.

It had merely been... a matter of *needing Healing.* The same was true for Damien's boyhood... *fascination* with both Adam and Jason when they had lured him out of his safe refuge in the Royal Library when he was fifteen.

And Damien was a man grown now. His wife – his *soul-bonded and pregnant wife and Queen* – was safe and home in Emeralsee and ruling the country for him while Damien toured Siovale and Farivera to take the oaths of his most ructious vassals. And now Elaarwen, because he'd promised their people that he'd visit there as soon as he could. *(Doubtless the rest of the Realm would soon be demanding he spend such tender attentions on It as well... though hopefully not until after his baby daughter was born.)*

He was a man grown now, and he was *Healed,* dammit, from all the guilt of not being here when Genevieve had needed him. Of having to bend his own principles near – or past – the breaking point in what Adam had insisted on calling his 'undercover operation' in Azella's Keep. Of having put his people at risk of another civil way for having not Bound Tomas tightly enough despite the perfidy of Tomas' younger, bastard brother. Of having *trusted* the man with the safety of his wife and unborn child and Realm.

It had been over a month since they left Emeralsee.

Since Damien had been in Genevieve's arms – since *Adam* had seen *Jason.*

That was *all* this was.

"Your Majesty? The tent is ready."

Damien looked up to see Lady Alanna standing... some ten feet away for some reason. Her eyes were still supervising her subordinates as they prepared the campsite, rather than meeting his own, though the King didn't think any of them needed that kind of attention. Setting up camp was nearly automatic after a month on the road, after all, though they'd rarely done so this early in the day.

On the other hand, an attentive eye to detail was what kept them all safe, and while young Mark Elsevier's Oath to Damien had held – and actually *glistened* with the young man's grief and earnestness – it was wise to remember that Tomas hadn't Rebelled twice in twenty years all on his lonesome. Nor even solely with the help of Azella and her foul *compulsion* spells.

The plains of Siovale and the valleys and mountains of Elaarwen were rife with people who remembered all too clearly that the *royal* banner wasn't always the one they followed. Though hopefully Alanna's alertness would never need to be tested again.

"I had your bedrolls placed side-by-side," the commander of his Guard detachment was continuing, still not looking at them. "Given that we don't know how long it will take you to Heal Prince Adam. I'll send Angelos in to help with your boots and things once you've moved. And we'll keep the usual covered plate with the enameled green bird on the lid by the fire with your meals in it."

Alanna – and Angelos – had taken Damien's ability to *Vanish* himself and others and other *things* from place to place without a great deal of fuss. So had Adam's sister Marianna, and Jason's sister Elaina, though Jason himself hadn't been so sanguine. The rest of the Guards... had had varying reactions from Lord Aaron's sardonic comment that such a skill would have been handy in his days as an assassin to Marcus's still-bug-eyed expression every time the King used his skills.

And Adam had accepted it as part and parcel of Damien without a fuss.

"The red-cased pillow is on your bedroll, Sire," Alanna finished.

The red-cased pillow and the covered dish with his meal were... *targets* that Damien could shoot for without having to know precisely where they were. He trusted the Realm to prevent him from trying to make two objects – including himself – occupy the same physical space, and if he knew a place well, he could *reach* in to take things from it or place them therein. Or move people about the same way. But he'd recently discovered that he could target a particular object as well, without having to be familiar with the space it was in, and that had led to a certain broader flexibility.

"Thank you, Lady Alanna," Damien replied. "Ready, Adam?"

The question of whether or not the tall knight was ready was obviated because Damien smoothly transferred the pair of them into his tent before Adam could answer.

The interior of the royal tent was spacious and high – it was meant to serve as Genevieve's command tent as well as sleeping quarters, after all. Normally there would be an entire set of wagons carrying the Queen's map-table and even furniture and tea-services for greeting visiting nobles and royals.

It had served the same function for the King on this trip, but just now the tent held only a small, folding table with a lantern on it, his and Adam's saddlebags, and the paired bed-rolls. He'd left behind the majority of the tent's accoutrements when they began the trip up to Elaarwen, and would have left the tent – and the wagon it traveled on – if not for the enchantments he'd rather laboriously attached to its weave. And because Lady Alanna had rather pointedly noted that they would rather have the inconvenience of a wagon than potentially lose their king *again*.

"Hunh," Adam commented. "I'm almost getting used to that."

Damien managed a chuckle. "I wouldn't think I'd *Vanished* you from place to place often enough to warrant that."

Adam's eyes sparkled almost like normal and his hand came up to mirror Damien's and cup the King's cheek. "Well, there *have* been a few rather *memorable* times."

Indubitably. Beginning with Adam 'catching a ride' when Damien had transferred himself and Megan Solway down to face Azella the Unpitying and the Pirate-King... and then Azella had sent the Champion back up to the ramparts alone.

But by the look in his eye, Adam was remembering a couple of times when Damien had gotten the two of them moved to allow Jason and Genevieve a measure of privacy in the weeks between the defeat of Azella and Tomas Elsevier and their departure on this perambulation of the Realm. A measure of privacy that had torn at both of their hearts, and – as their loves' emotions had overflowed the soul- and marriage-bonds – had helped them make some... *memorable* memories themselves.

Adam began to lean forwards, the gentle look in his golden-hazel eyes giving away his intention although his lips weren't yet pursed... Damien couldn't dodge him just *now,* after all...

...and the bell attached to the rope dangling outside the tent's entrance jangled, sparing Damien from having to hurt his friend's feelings by pulling away or turning his head.

Or... no.

Of course he would have turned aside.

Of course.

Genevieve had laughed and called it an extravagance, when Damien had had the royal tent outfitted with a doorbell. He hadn't known such things weren't *done* and had assumed the designer had simply forgotten to include one when someone had shown him a diagram of the tent that he'd been commissioning to replace the one his wife had worn practically to shreds during her 'negotiations' over Alpinsward. Jason said that Genevieve had been entirely bemused when the new tent had been setup for her at the start of the Elendrian campaign.

But she'd made a few appreciative comments about the doorbell since then.

"Your Majesty?" It was Angelos' voice. "May I assist you or Sir Adam with anything?"

"Just a moment..." Damien glanced over at the tent entrance, then back at Adam. Whose hand had fallen away from his own face at the first tinkle of the bell. Discreet, as ever.

Damien raised an eyebrow and Adam shrugged slightly.

Worth a shot.

Carefully, the King removed one hand from Adam's face, finger by finger.

The Champion gritted his teeth and swallowed hard as the last finger lifted. Damien could feel the nausea in his tall knight.

But this was ridiculous. He wasn't *doing* anything. He wasn't *stopping* doing anything.

The King pulled his palm from Adam's other cheek, leaving his fingertips in place...

...Adam quickly squeezed his eyes shut – Damien could almost see for himself the sudden surge of swirling, unnatural colors that the knight was trying to avoid...

Adam's eyes popped open again just as quickly.

"It's worse with my eyes *closed*," he grated, sounding both ill and irritated.

Damien sighed and put both hands back. Both of them heaved a sigh as... erm, *heaves* again became unnecessary.

"Yes, please come in, Sir Angelos," Damien called out. "It appears that nothing has changed."

"Your Majesty?" Angelos inquired politely as he knelt at Damien's side. "How may I assist?"

"Can you help remove our jackets and boots, please, Sir Angelos? And, um, our weapons?" Damien asked, taking care to avert his gaze from Adam's.

Which was certain to be extremely sardonic.

It was a spouse's place to assist one with arming or disarming, after all.

A spouse's, or a body-servant or personal squire.

Or, in the King's case, a gentleman-of-the-chamber.

It wasn't the job of one of His Majesty's knights – especially not the commander of his current set. And he'd never let Adam do this for him in all these years.

But it was Sir Angelos that Alanna had sent to them, rather than Master Derrick or Lord Lewis.

Still, proprieties.

"Or maybe, um, you could ask Derrick or Lew to give us a hand...?" Damien added a little belatedly as his younger cousin knelt down beside them.

Sir Angelos looked up from where he'd begun dealing with the buckle of Damien's sword-belt. He had to duck under Damien's arms and lean over his lap to do so. "If you prefer it, of course. But I'm happy to help. Alanna thought... perhaps you might prefer aid from a cousin. Not that Derrick and Lew can't be discreet, of course..."

Was the young man *blushing?*

"There's nothing to be *discreet* about," Adam said dryly. "It's not like everyone out there didn't *already* see that I can't sit up straight without His Majesty's Healing touch right now. Illness isn't anything to be embarrassed about. It happens to everyone eventually."

Though he sounded a bit overly firm about it. Likely Adam *was* embarrassed over inconveniencing everyone.

Certainly, there wasn't anything *else* to be embarrassed about.

Not that anyone should have noticed anyways.

Angelos prised Damien's sword-belt off and stood to remove belt and scabbard and Monarch's Blade over near where their saddlebags were set.

"Of course, Captain," he said again, then made a sound that was clearly a forced chuckle. "I don't think we're any of us letting you anywhere near the cooking again, sir."

"I didn't burn the bacon *that* badly this morning," Adam groused, but with a note of relief in his voice. He didn't even bother to remind Angelos that he wasn't his *Captain* anymore.

"No, sir," Angelos replied. "But it's the general opinion amongst the rest of the Guards that it's the size of the lumps in the porridge that are giving you your current troubles. Seeing as how you seem to have been the only one of us who actually managed to *eat* any of them."

Adam snorted – he was definitely feeling better, though he wasn't trying to test it again.

But Damien had caught something else.

"'Amongst the *rest of* the Guards,'" he repeated. "Not you, cousin?"

Angelos had returned for Damien's dagger-belt. He didn't look up.

"No, Your Majesty. Not me. And... not Alanna."

The King met his... *Champion's* wry look over the young man's head.

Well. Perhaps it had been too much to hope that *all* of their observant, careful people would have managed to miss how Adam was looking at him. And... how he was looking back at his... Champion.

Not really a liege-lord-to-knight look, though Queen Marian's ghost did claim that she'd stocked the position of Queen's Champion with her lovers when she'd lived and ruled...

"And just what do you think *is* the cause of my 'current troubles,' Sir Eldridge?" Adam asked crisply.

Oh. Oh, yes. That.

Damien's second belt came free, and the young man extracted himself from under the King's arms to look at them. He looked... rather pale and ill himself, Damien noted.

"I think – *we* think – it's something to do with magick," Angelos answered. He gave Damien an uncomfortable look. "Not that we know enough to be making any such pronouncements, Your Majesty. But it's why Alanna sent me in to talk to you. You see... *I'm* feeling poorly as well. Though not as bad as the Captain – I mean Prince Adam."

Adam had been Captain of the Royal Guard until late last Fall. He had trained Angelos, along with the other young knights – up from squires or even pages, the training of the Realm's knights being part of his purview when he held the title. The slip-up was habit, though the younger man looked embarrassed.

"*Just* you?" Damien asked, frowning.

"Yes, Sire," Angelos nodded, then gave them a small smile. "And *I* didn't eat any of Prince Adam's cooking any more than anyone else."

Adam snorted. "That doesn't explain anything, lad."

But Damien was frowning as he rapidly ran over things in his head. "You were with your father the day of the ice-storm, weren't you, Angelos?"

The young man nodded. "You kept him back a moment after the Council meeting and I guided him to Prince Jason's suite." He looked down. "Captain Tim was... unhappy that I didn't make it back in time to help guard you and the Queen and Prince Adam in the Throneroom. Your Majesty."

Damien's brow unfurrowed. This might be the clue he needed to help... well... both of them? "You got caught up in the spell, didn't you."

It wasn't really a question.

"Yes, Sire." Angelos sounded nervous.

"You can call me by name," Damien told him absently as he tried to fit all the pieces together. "In private anyways. We're fairly close cousins, after all."

"We... weren't sure how you felt about that... Damien," Angelos said hesitantly. "Father said that I shouldn't press you on it. That you had all the reason in the world not to trust our family after what Uncle David and Aunt Alexa did..."

Damien's mother's parents *(who had arguably been the young prince's pensioners, given that the cottage and the farms for its support that King Reginald had settled upon his second-youngest son and his wife should have come to their son upon their demise)* had replied to the desperate letter he had sent them at age seventeen begging them to let him come home by telling him never to contact them again. That hadn't all been their own idea. Adam and Ciriis Celavell, who had been helping Adam and Jason raise him, had asked them to tell Damien he couldn't come back, though Damien hadn't known that until last Fall.

And he'd eventually visited his grandparents – after he'd been crowned – and they'd made what amends they could. Then.

But at seventeen, Damien had been utterly devastated. Ravenscroft was where he'd been born and where he'd lived the first eight years of his life. Grandpa Dave had given him 'pony-rides' on his knee, and Grandma 'Lexa had made him warm drinks and cuddled him in her arms over bruises. His cousins had been his playmates and friends until his other grandfather, King Reginald, had summoned Prince Eric to bring his small family back to Emeralsee's city and Castle Alsterling.

It had been too much to expect that a failed squire with too many children to support could dare to thwart his king by sheltering their mutual grandson... after his daughter and son-in-law had been executed at that same king's command in the very throneroom itself.

Damien... understood that. Now.

At seventeen... well, he had then, too, honestly. He'd just hoped so desperately that seven years after his parents' demise was long enough to make it safe to go home at last.

Angelos' father, Eugenio, was the Baron of Elderwyld now. It had been Eugenio's mother, Baroness Dara Eldridge, who had been Grandpa Dave's much older sister.

None of what had passed should redound to that branch of the family, though Damien couldn't deny that he'd hesitated on approving this young knight's application to the Royal Guard last year – and not because of anything to do with the young man himself. Despite his slightly short stature, Angelos had been considered at the top of his training class.

No, to his shame, Damien's hesitation had centered solely on the young man's surname.

Speaking of things the King still needed to Heal from.

Though, he'd quickly developed a fondness for his young cousin – and Angelos' kind and subtle sense of humor – shortly thereafter.

Damien winced. "I meant to talk to Eugenio about... that."

He had, really. Had even set up an appointment to do so, following Jason and Adam's wedding.

Twice.

But between the sudden advent of the ice-storm and then being taken hostage *(or whatever)* by Azella... it hadn't happened.

And now, knowing that the Pirate-King – Jason's father – was Baron Eldridge's younger brother....

And the Elderwyld barony was a fairly minor part of even the province of Emeralsee – he simply hadn't had *time* in the month he'd been home to try to visit. Or to have the baron come visit. Or...

Not that any of that explained his reticence in talking to Eugenio Eldridge during the *previous* five years since he'd been crowned.

And no, he hadn't been relieved *in the slightest* that all those horrific things had happened in the nick of time to spare him from keeping those appointments last Fall.

"It wasn't their fault," Adam put into the awkward silence. "Ciriis Celavell and I asked Lord David and Lady Alexa to tell Damien he wasn't welcome in their home. And we explained why. Damien needed to be at Court so that King Reginald would Name him Heir when the opportunity arose, not hiding out in Ravenscroft – or even Elderwyld."

Angelos shrugged. "Father says they should have offered to have him visit anyways. Even just for a short while. And even if it upset the Old King. Because His Maj– *Damien* is family. Father didn't know what had happened until years later. When Uncle David was on his deathbed, actually. And now there's the whole mess with Uncle Evan..."

He shook his head and gave King and Prince a wry look. "It's beginning to look like we'll *never* have a chance to sort this out. And... Father really would like to. He was very close friends with Aunt Miria."

Damien's hands started to sag away from Adam's face – in shock. "My... my mother?"

He replaced his hands as Adam moaned slightly and started to curl up against the returning nausea.

Angelos nodded. "Father wasn't of age to inherit when Grandmother died, and Uncle David – *Great*-Uncle David, I suppose, since he was Grandmother's brother – served as his Regent. The whole family was living at Elderwyld then anyways, after all. They didn't have Ravenscroft until..."

"Until my parents were wedded and Grandfather awarded it to them," Damien finished a little numbly.

He should have known this. As Genevieve always teased him, he'd practically memorized the Royal Archives... which included regencies for underage Heirs. Not to mention that there really wouldn't have been anywhere else for his grandfather's family to have lived other than under his sister's roof. Of course, Mother would have grown up close to her cousins.

Angelos nodded. "Father says that *your* father started to show up at Elderwyld when Uncle Evan was six or seven years old. He says he was sure for the entire first year that Prince Eric was making up the whole thing about Prince Robert having been Uncle Evan's father as an excuse to court Aunt Miria. And that it wasn't until he actually took Uncle Evan to Court – several years after they were married – that he really believed it."

Damien had read some of his mother's correspondence with her cousin in Elderwyld regarding Evan Eldridge Alsterling... Intellectually, he'd known it was Baron Eugenio she'd been writing to, though she'd used a nickname... Which should also have suggested they were close...

"Damien, are you alright?" Adam asked, having recovered himself from the nausea again.

The King swallowed hard. Nodded.

It was just that he hadn't thought to be talking about his long-dead and much-missed parents today.

"Father... says he used to go up to Ravenscroft pretty regularly," Angelos continued hesitantly. "When your family lived there with Uncle David and Aunt Alexa. He said he used to carry Princess Kandra around when she was little and tease Aunt Miria about how *she* had a child and *he* wasn't even married yet."

Damien blinked hard. Mother, Father, his grandparents whom he'd visited before they died but never really managed to forgive for pushing him away... and now the sister he'd idolized? How much more could he take of these... gentle, painful stories?

He'd begun to be able to talk about them – his parents and sister anyways – recently without the pain becoming too much to bear. Or... he was trying, at least. He wanted to be able to tell his children about the aunt and grandparents they would never know without crying. He wanted his children to love their memories the way he did – not think of Mother and Father and Kandy as people who made their own father cry.

So... he'd been trying to talk about them now. To get used to doing so. Marli – little golden-haired Giendra Marlerite, but Damien had given her the nickname in his thoughts – would be born soon. And if she had anywhere near as good a memory as he did, it was important that he take the right tone with her from the very beginning. No telling what her infant mind might keep and hold precious...

Not that it was easy to find opportunities to mention his parents or Kandy in casual conversations. Years of him avoiding doing so had trained everyone around him to do the same... and there really wasn't much reason for the names of the former Crown Prince and his wife and daughter to come up.

But... Angelos was family. *Close* family, for all that he'd have been a baby when Damien's family had moved to Emeralsee. Of course he'd have stories. He and his father and... others at Elderwyld. They were probably even stories Damien wanted to hear...

Adam was looking worried. He had better say something...

"He..." Damien had to pause and clear his throat. "Baron Eugenio must have done the same with me, I suppose. Though surely, he must have been married by then...?"

Angelos looked a little relieved. "Yes. My oldest sister is a little older than you."

He flushed again. "Tonia didn't make it to the wedding and coronation. She was laid up with having my third nephew. And the others had stayed home to take care of her. So, I was the only one there with Father. I *know* it was only supposed to be your sworn vassals who took part in the... the *spell.*" He winced. "Though I don't think hardly any of them even realized that was what it was. They seemed to think Sir Jas– I mean the Crown Prince – was using *his* magick to do something, not... not... having *us* use *ours.* After all, we'd all seen the Sword Choose him by then. Twice."

"But *you* knew?" Adam sounded skeptical, but Damien was aware that his Champion's fine mind was quickly turning over everything the younger knight was telling them despite how ill he felt. It was undoubtedly vital to know that the Emeralsee nobility – at minimum – didn't realize that Damien had allowed the Land to wake their magick.

Not that that state of affairs was likely to *last*. Magick once freed was likely to start slipping out everywhere.

Angelos had that hangdog look again. "Father did. And, um, so did I. We Eldridges have... a certain history..." He looked uncertainly at Adam. "Magick pops up in the family every now and then and we... train for it. To make sure we know how to handle it when it does."

When, not *if.*

That sounded like it was rather more frequent than 'every now and then.' Especially if *all* the Eldridge children were 'trained' to handle it.

Well. *That* was something that hadn't made its way into the Royal Archives.

Though perhaps not all that unexpected, either.

Power, Damien had been discovering was very attractive to someone else who had it. And with both his father and his Uncle Robert choosing brides from the Eldridge clan there was clearly a great deal of Power in that bloodline.

And his grandfather, actually; King Reginald's last wife, Queen Eliza, had been an Eldridge... though of a slightly more far-flung branch.

Perhaps it had been the Eldridges' magickal lineage had been the draw for all of those men.

And Lady Alanna... She wasn't an Eldridge by *name,* being the daughter of a baronet in Cedarwen, which historically pledged to Elaarwen by way of Brindlewell, though both that county and barony had been Crown vassals since the start of the Rebellion. Her family had fled to Siovale when Damien's horrible uncle, Prince Oskar, had expressed his unwholesome interest in Alanna's older sister.

Damien's knowledge of the families of his fifth-degree vassals – who weren't legally required to register their marriages and offspring with the Royal Archives and didn't always choose to do so – was much spottier than with regards to the higher nobility, but he thought he recalled that Alanna's grandmother had been an Eldridge. Or maybe her great-grandmother. It had been someone connected to Queen Eliza, he recalled, so rather distant kin to the Eldridges of Elderwyld.

Abruptly, all of the pieces fell into place.

"That's what you and Alanna noticed, then," Damien stated. "None of the others come from families with a particularly *magickal* background. Just you and..."

He looked sideways at Adam. The Loveress clan's *empathy* wasn't common knowledge. Not that the Eldridge affinity for magick was either...

"*I* don't have *magick,*" Adam said a little stubbornly. "No one in the Loveress fami– ah. Hmmmn."

It was a bit hard to make that claim *now,* when most everyone knew that his youngest sister, Marianna, had been able to break the King's own wards. And his youngest brother, Martin, was studying to be a Healer. Another sister had briefly been a novice priestess and Damien still hadn't heard the story of why Fontaine had left her vocation.

And then there were those oh-so-helpful-for-parenting *ForeSeeing visions* that Adam and his mother and his *other* sister, Desirée, all seemed to have. Not that anyone outside the family should be aware of those.

Angelos gave them a small smile. "I'm sorry, Captain. I didn't want to have to out the Loveress family to His Majesty like this. But if he *knows*... maybe he can help *both* of us."

Adam glared past Damien's hands at the younger knight. "And how do you *know* anything about my family?"

Damien's cousin frowned. "Surely you know that my sister, Juliettta, was your brother's first wife?"

Adam's mouth dropped.

"That would be Lorrie?" Damien asked for him. "Lorenzo, I mean?"

Angelos nodded uncertainly, his eyes flickering between the two older men. "Yes."

Damien watched Adam's face, wishing he could give his belo– his *friend* some greater comfort, but not daring to move his hands. Surely Adam needed not to be dizzy and nauseous from whatever-this-was even more than he needed to not be... dizzy and nauseous at the reminder of how much of his family's life he had missed in his determination not to give in to his parents' small-mindedness over his relationship with Jason.

The Loveress clan had been – and was again, now that the Baronetta and Lord George had come around and sought their oldest son's forgiveness – extremely close. The weeks Damien had spent with them when he was seventeen had been the closest thing he had experienced to his childhood in Ravenscroft with the Eldridges since his other grandfather, King Reginald, had required his parents to return to the capitol. If Adam hadn't fallen out so badly with his parents – and Ciriis hadn't seduced Damien into being her starry-eyed shadow – the young prince had been wondering if he dared ask Baronetta Linda if she would let him stay *there*.

Not that Adam and Ciriis would have let *that* happen either, as he now knew. Nor would the motherly Baronetta have been wise to have allowed him to do so.

He harbored no resentment for Adam over any of it. How could he? Adam had suffered as much as he, but had never flagged in his care and consideration for his young prince.

His feelings about Ciriis... were a different matter. For a variety of reasons.

"You must be aware, Angelos, that Adam didn't have any contact with his family for... a long time," the King said gently.

The younger man's chin dropped. "Oh. Yes. I'm sorry to... Juli and Lorrie didn't want to make a big deal about it all, given that, well, King Reginald..."

He winced, alert to how he was treading on *other* potential hazards. "They didn't even really have a *wedding*. They met when he came out to visit some of our neighbors and then she went home with him after some correspondence between your parents and ours. And... she came home again a couple years later, shortly before I went up to be a page in the capitol. She said it wasn't anything about Lynncrag or the Loveresses or Lorrie. It was just that she missed home."

That seemed... odd to Damien, and clearly to Adam as well.

Angelos flushed before either of them could say something. "I *was* only ten, Sire – sirs. I'm sure there's more to the story that I didn't get to hear. But she only had good things to say about everyone there when I was around. Father said once that it might have been an attraction based on Power... and that those don't always last. And that's what led to the discussion I remember about how the Loveress family has magick. Like we do. Sire. Damien. Um... *cousin*."

Adam looked disgruntled...

"So how do *you* feel, Angelos?" Damien decided to put things back on a track that would get them somewhere... less trying.

The young man sighed. "Rather awful, though not so bad as the Captain, obviously. I don't have a great *deal* of magick for myself, but Father said the business with the ice-storm woke up what I do have a bit more. I've... felt like the Land has been *watching* me ever since we crossed the Topaz. It... got a great deal *stronger* after we crossed the Sapphire."

Angelos shrugged. "I can handle it. It doesn't seem to particularly *like* having me here, but it also doesn't seem to think I'm much of a threat."

Damien did the little mental thing that let him access his ability to *see* magick.

And, yes, Angelos had a soft glow about him. A rather soothing aura, actually. Apparently that peaceful and gently humorous outlook he presented to the world was him all the way through.

"I'm not sure if I can manage the whole trip to Elaarwen, though," Angelos admitted. "I don't want to abandon my post... and I'm not quite at the point where I need to beg for your permission to go back. But... if it gets much stronger, I'll be more of a liability than a Guard."

The young knight looked... deeply disappointed in himself. He knew, after all, that this was a trial for the position of Captain Tim's official Second.

Not that this was any of his fault.

What was it about *Elaarwen* that was making this so difficult?

They'd all been up to Elaarwen before... Angelos and Adam included.

And it couldn't just be *magick,* or Damien himself would be in terrible straits.

The boy – the young knight, his *cousin* – was looking at Damien hopefully...

"You've given me some ideas," the King answered that look slightly mendaciously. "But even if you have to go back, I won't hold this against you. I'd rather Tim have a Second who's responsible and alert enough to know when he needs to step aside."

"Thank you, Your Majesty." Angelos lowered his eyes. That was... something, though it opened up the opportunity for one of his peers to demonstrate *their* capacity to fill that place as well. "Shall I help with the rest of your weapons and things?"

"Please do," Damien nodded.

Adam had two free hands, so he removed his own belts, though Angelos carried them out of the way. And removing his jacket – he still wore the uniform of a Royal Guard, though without insignia – was fairly easy. Since the nausea and dizziness was solidly under control, even extracting his boots wasn't too bad, though Angelos' help was definitely... helpful.

Removing *Damien's* coat and boots was a bit more challenging.

It turned out that Adam touching *him* was the equivalent of Damien having his hands on Adam's face, so they were able to take it turn and turnabout to get his arms out of the coat sleeves. The boots were almost easier.

"Shall I send food in?" Angelos asked as he prepared to exit the tent, all of those items neatly laid out on the far side of the huge tent. He looked more than a little green himself at the thought of eating and Damien guessed that the younger man intended to go to bed hungry. Which was not a particularly sustainable solution either, though not particularly dire for today if Damien could find a solution shortly. Young men might always be hungry, but they didn't *actually* die of starvation overnight.

Adam shook his head. "Alanna said she'd leave that covered dish with the bird on it where Damien could *Vanish* it in here when... when it will work. I... don't think I could handle being around food right now."

The King sighed softly. *He* could use some food. But he couldn't very well leave Adam to his own devices... even if he weren't going to be stuck *feeling* every bit of misery alongside his... *friend.*

He wouldn't starve overnight either, after all. Or so he could tell himself.

Angelos gave them both a sympathetic look. "I understand."

He put a hand to the tent opening, then paused before drawing it back and looked at Adam. "We haven't ever thanked you, I don't think, sir. We Eldridges. For taking care of... of *Damien* for us."

Adam looked down. "Hmmn."

"Uncle David's choice was *his,* sir," the younger knight said earnestly. "*You* were doing the best that you could. And all you did was *ask*. He... could have been braver. And you took care of my cousin even though it meant *you* had to deal with King Reginald yourself. We all know you're Baronetta Linda's Heir. You could have resigned your commission and gone home at any time."

He smiled a little wryly. "Juli says that was why your parents were so upset about... about you and Sir Jason. Because *he* wasn't willing to come to Lynncrag with you and leave Prince Damien. And they wanted home where you'd be safer. *Both* of you, she says."

Adam's eyes had gone wide...

Enough revelations for one day.

"Thank you, cousin," Damien said. "I'll see if I can figure out some solution for you and Adam both by morning."

Angelos nodded, confidence in Damien shining out of his dark eyes. "I'm sure you'll find it, sir."

And he ducked out of the tent.

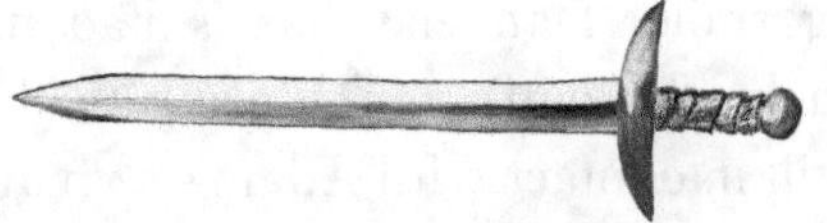

Chapter THREE

Instructions

DAMIEN SIGHED AS HE TURNED back to regard Adam. They had returned to the positions that they had begun in after Angelos' helpful ministrations were done: Adam kneeling and Damien crosslegged in front of him with his hands on Adam's cheeks.

"That was a lot to tak–"

It turned out that *lips* were even more effective at meeting that requirement of skin contact than hands on cheeks. Some distant part of Damien noted that Adam felt... pretty damn good, actually.

The kiss was... *almost* chaste.

And *entirely* fiery.

"Adam..." Damien wasn't entirely sure what he wanted to say. 'No' seemed entirely wrong... though that might simply be because it had been nearly a *month* since he'd seen Genevieve...

He kept telling himself that, but it didn't seem to get any *truer* with repetition.

"Did you set the wards, my sweet prince?" Adam asked with a rather... *glowing* smile. Damien's hands had migrated entirely naturally to the back of Adam's neck during that lovely interlude. Where they *were* still in contact with Adam's skin after all...

Though somewhat less so. And Adam seemed *less* nauseous and dizzy than when Damien's hands had been on his cheeks.

Odd. Not that *any* of this made sense.

"Damien? The wards?" Adam asked again.

"I... did..."

As soon as Angelos left, actually. Mostly by habit after several weeks of living out of this tent. But it meant that they couldn't be discerned by eye, ear, or magick by anyone outside.

"Good." Adam's smile was far more than *suggestive* as he bore his king down to lie flat on the bedrolls for another kiss that was... far less chaste. And far more *thorough*.

It all felt so *good*.

How could this be so *wrong* when everything about it felt so *right?*

So *right*... until Adam paused in his explorations of Damien's neck with his lips and propped himself slightly out of reach of kisses.

"Damien, my love..." He sounded as reluctant as the younger man felt to have any *pause* in this...delight. "Do you want this?"

"What do you think?" Damien said a bit impatiently as he tugged Adam closer for another kiss.

The tall knight's smile was there, but he wasn't yielding. "I don't want this to be... only for *me*. Even if it seems to be doing an excellent job at curing whatever ails me–"

"*Elaarwen watching,*" Damien muttered, and removing a hand from around Adam's neck to run it down the soft, fabric-covered line of Adam's back and then *up* his front...

The tall man chuckled, catching those errant fingers and pressing them close to his chest... his *heart*.

"Maybe so. But it still isn't *right* if it's something you don't want, love. I need to hear you say it. In words. Tell me to stop – or tell me not to."

"Don't stop." The words were out of Damien's mouth instantly, instinctually.

Stopping seemed utterly beyond comprehension at this point. He didn't want Adam to *stop* kissing him. And *touching* him. He wanted *more* of it. He could *feel* the lovely things his own actions – and reactions – were doing to his lover and he wanted more of *that,* too. Making Adam feel wonderful – not just not-sick – was just as important as how Adam was making *him* feel, after all.

And... it suddenly seemed that Adam should *know* that.

Not that he just wasn't *unwilling...*

Adam had relaxed and was bending in for another kiss at his words,,, but Damien pressed him away with the hand that was still trapped against the tall – the *handsome, sexy* – knight's heart.

That quizzical, unsure look was back in Adam's golden-hazel eyes as he instantly yielded to the slight pressure and backed off.

"Damien–?"

"I want you to make love to me, Adam," Damien told him – firmly, if shyly. "I... want *you.*"

If this was *wrong,* he decided, he would just accept the consequences as he was trying to accept how *awkward* it was to say these things aloud.

His beloved knight's eyes softened, and his gentle smile seemed worth all the *awkwardness* in the world. And possibly worth all the *wrongness* that might be laid at Damien's feet for this as well.

"I love you, my sweet prince," Adam was murmuring between kisses as his hands divested them both of their remaining layers of clothing and Damien did his level best to make sure he didn't ever lose enough direct skin-to-skin contact to let Adam feel sick again.

Whether it made Healing sense or not. And... that was his only reason. Of course.

"I love you, too," Damien whispered back, deciding to set all the other things aside for right now. Making Adam well should surely take precedence just now... right?

And... *this* seemed to be, ah, *working* extremely *well.*

Adam seemed completely recovered from his mysterious illness – *the Land watching him,* Angelos had said. Not there wasn't copious amounts of skin-to-skin contact between them as Adam peeled layers away, and that was what had appeared to make the difference in how Adam felt.

What exactly the Land was *watching* now was enough to make the King blush.

Extremely copious amounts of skin contact, and Damien could barely *breathe* for the joy of it all. Why had he been so adamantly opposed to making love with Adam again? It all seemed distant and unimportant as his Champion – the man who had *championed* him from the moment the lonely and terrified fourteen-year-old Damien's *empathy* had reached out for love and found a safe harbor in the nearly-knighted squire's heart – as *Adam* showed him all over again that while they might not have a soul-bond... they had something very special together anyways.

There was, after all, nothing *quite* like the feedback loop between a pair who were both Powerful *empaths.* 'Joy shared was joy doubled' indeed... though the downside had been clear earlier when Damien had all but vomited himself with Adam's dizziness.

"That... that *hurt* more than I expected..." Damien said softly when they were done and resting quietly together.

Adam chuckled and kissed him behind the ear. "You didn't seem like you wanted me to *stop,* though."

"No..."

He definitely hadn't. Though he'd been a little surprised at Adam's willingness to continue.

Jason liked to 'play a little rough' and Damien had discovered he enjoyed that as well on occasion... but his impression had been that *Adam* didn't. He knew for a fact that Jason never showed that side of himself to *Genevieve,* for all that she was aware – since she shared a soul-bond with her husband and the Crown Prince each – of what they did without her. Though, of course, Genevieve was the survivor of her horribly abusive first marriage.

Damien's soft admission earned him another – very gentle – kiss.

"I didn't think *you* liked it... rough," Damien commented a little shyly. "I... actually thought you felt pretty strongly about that."

"I've let Jason show me a thing or two," Adam told him, his tone casual. Carefully casual? Hard to tell... "I'm trying to be openminded, since you both feel differently."

Openminded... and more willing to discuss this than Damien really was himself. Though... the dark-haired man felt he needed clarification on this point. He'd caused Adam enough tribulations – he didn't want to be the cause of breaking his Champion's sense of self any further. But...

"You... seemed a bit more than *openminded* about it, Adam."

And that got him another very relaxed-sounding chuckle... so apparently that casual tone was real. And this time Damien couldn't help but notice how he could feel the delightful shiver of Adam's humor all the way down his own body.

"*Jason* isn't nearly so tender with his language, my sweet prince. You're asking why I was okay with making love to you when I could *feel* what you were feeling. Part of it is just how very much I *wanted* you, of course... and with so long since the last time I actually got you into bed, this was more or less inevitable–"

Damien twisted around to look up into Adam's eyes with a frown. "What are you talking about?"

Adam gave him a wry look. "It's always a little *rough* when it's been a while, Damien. Jase and I have been apart enough that I'm rather overly familiar with the problem."

...which was another thing to lay at the King's feet, since it was he who had asked Jason to guard Genevieve on her negotiations while Adam stayed home in Emeralsee to look after *him* as the Captain of the Royal Guard should...

But...

"I... There wasn't any, um, *problem* like that when I came back from..." Damien's voice trailed off as he realized...

The *wry* look from those beautiful golden-hazel eyes became so *compassionate* that it was hard to meet Adam's gaze. That or... there might be another reason Damien's gaze was skittering away.

"No," Damien's forever-Champion said softly. "There wasn't. And since that was somewhat at odds with what you *told* me went on at the White Witch's Keep... Well, let's just say that there was more than one reason why I made sure that *that boy* wasn't so available to trouble you."

That boy being Jeremy. Azella's 'Power-slave' whom Damien had taught to play chess and to use a sword, and then freed to follow him to Ilseador. And who had not been able to stay on the eight-fold path of righteousness that Damien had left for him... he'd ended up recaptured by the Evil Sorceress. Azella had allowed – no, say it straight, *had given Jeremy over to* – a demon to *possess* him. Damien had then had to fight the demon to save his Realm and exorcise it from Jeremy's body... and prevent it from slaying Adam, who had been struck unconscious by a blow from Azella's magick just moments before the battle began.

By the time Damien had recovered from his battle with the demon and cleaned up the mess from Tomas Elsevier's treason and attempted coup – including breaking the compulsion spells on Genevieve and sleeping for two days straight – Jeremy had found a place at the side of the wounded Lord Aaron. The too-beautiful former Power-slave – who had told Damien he had been bred for his sexual allure – had lost his huge natural capacity to hold onto magick as a result of the demon's *possession,* and was quite as soul-wounded as Aaron, who had lost half of his abilities as a spy and assassin and member of Damien's Secret Cadre of Royal Guards when a Siovalese soldier had chopped off his left hand.

The two of them had seemed to be making a pair of it when Damien's expedition had left Emeralsee.

"You... said you made sure he had a distraction... before he became one," the dark-haired man said faintly. "I... thought you meant... um..."

He wasn't sure how to say it. Or if he wanted to.

After all, at least half of Jeremy's allure had been that huge well of Power, and that was thoroughly gone. Power called to Power, after all.

Adam's Power, however, for all that he denied it vehemently, blazed brighter than the sun when Damien accidentally glanced at him using his ability to *see* magick. And it did so for no reason that the King had been able to determine, given that Adam might be his mother's Heir, but he wasn't Bound to the land.

Nor had *he* participated in Damien's abrupt and impromptu awakening of the Power of most of the Realm's nobility, that Angelos had unintentionally gotten caught up in. Adam hadn't been at his mother's side or even his newly wedded husband's. No, he'd been at Damien's side, separated from Jason *again* by his King's needs...

Perhaps thinking about poor Jeremy was actually preferable to...

"You don't have to tell me anything you don't want to, Damien," Adam said gently. But apparently what Damien wasn't saying was... *vivid* enough emotionally to send Adam's eyebrows up as he absorbed it.

And then to laugh.

"Oh, ho! You thought I was suggesting you'd want to keep him on as a *lover?* When you had *Genevieve* back? And *Jason?* And... *me?*" Adam snuggled him closer as Damien felt his face burning with embarrassment. "My sweet prince, *that boy* never had a chance. No matter how pretty he is."

"No, he didn't," Damien mumbled into Adam's chest, but it didn't cool his face at all to admit that.

Because that made it entirely obvious that Adam had made sure Jeremy was, ah, *occupied* such that he wouldn't be a *distraction* for Damien because he *knew*... Though he'd said he *did,* just from his own observations...

"You never have to say anything you don't want to," Adam said again. "But surely you can't be embarrassed about this with *me.* Or with Jason," he added thoughtfully. "Though I imagine *Jase* might want *details* if you were willing to talk."

And that was a whole other reason not to bring any of it up.

Damien had had a little time to mend, emotionally – mostly due to Adam – before Jason and Genevieve had been rescued from their captivity in Siovale. The King hadn't let either of them see more than a hint of what his time with Azella had been like.

And Jason had his own set of memories of having an Evil Wizard as a lover and doing their bidding. Though he had been in love with Prince Oskar and had left him – the first time – with a broken heart, but not a broken soul. And a certain appreciation for possible *future* lovers...

Damien didn't voice any of those thoughts either, but the Champion rolled his eyes. "I wasn't worried about *him,* either. Jason is the very definition of loyalty." He snorted. "Though there was a kind of look in his eyes when he finally got a chance to really see the boy – that suggested he kind of *wished* he would consider giving me something to worry about."

And that was a little alarming in and of itself, though Adam seemed entirely at ease and amused by the whole notion. Presumably because if Jason had chosen him – eventually – over Prince Oskar, with whom Jason had actually been in love, there really was no reason to worry about anyone *else.*

"I'm not embarrassed..." Damien decided not to go into what was surely an even more dangerous topic. How deep Adam's confidence in Jason went... was a question he did *not* want to find out the answer to.

"Not... exactly anyways," he self-corrected. Better to bare his own soul than make another naked unwilling after all. And it wasn't as if his burning cheeks didn't give him away anyways. "It's just... I've told you about all those *compulsion* spells Azella used on me."

Adam nodded. "And your concern that it would make you more vulnerable to more of the same in the future. Though we don't have much in the way of evidence for any of that." He paused. "And... I already guessed that you didn't tell me about *everything* she cast on you."

Damien looked away. A mere movement of his eyes, since Adam had them cuddled too close for him to turn his head. Safe...

"This... was really just more of that. I suppose. She... I guess she liked to *watch*. It would be after I was asleep and when I was... refusing her. She'd keep me in a doze and then..." He made a little gesture. "Honestly, I was never actually certain it wasn't all just a dream. A... recurring dream." He winced. "A... rather *good* recurring dream. I wasn't *there* in the dream. It wasn't... wasn't *them.*"

Adam raised his eyebrows. "You couldn't tell what had happened when you woke up?"

Damien shrugged, knowing he was blushing.

"I mean, I could tell that..." He sighed. "Look, Adam, in my *dream* it wasn't *Jeremy* at all. It was *you*. I didn't particularly *want* to think about what parts of it might have been *real*. Since you weren't actually... actually..."

His voice broke and he tried not to sob...

Adam cuddled him close. "Since I wasn't actually there."

Damien nodded. It was just over two months ago. Still far too close to *now*. Still too *real*.

A piece of him had been expecting – *dreading* – Azella coming down to confront him the entire time they had been in Farivera. Unlikely though that would have been now that she knew that Damien was stronger than she was. That he could even defeat one of her demons.

Damien didn't *fear* her – never really *had,* which might be an unfortunate statement about his intelligence, though it really spoke more to his naïvete. His *former* naïvete.

But... Azella could make some trouble for him if she chose, spreading rumors about just what all she had made him do while in her keeping. Merely the truth would be damaging enough, though she could embroider the bare facts as much as she liked, there being no one to call her out, and no way to defeat rumors anyways, even with truth spreadeagled naked in the bright sun.

Though likely Azella would think of such efforts as beneath her, which was another clue to her own royal heritage. If she could not win him with her own allure, nor force him through her most puissant magick... then she would behave as the princess she'd been born and pretend she simply had better uses for her time and efforts. The spreading of damaging rumors was a tactic used by *lesser* nobles.

Damien knew he could probably figure out what royal family Azella had been born to. He certainly had enough details to allow Aryllis to do so – without even delving into the ones too uncomfortable to share with the cool, quiet woman who was his friend and former lover and Spymistress.

Right now, though... he wasn't sure he wanted to know more about Azella's origins. He was already too sympathetic to her, despite all she had done to him. And all she had attempted to do.

Somehow, he couldn't help seeing the lonely, hurting girl she was. The one who had been trapped in that on-the-cusp-of-maturity body – and was now choosing for herself to keep it. She would never grow up...

"You learned you didn't *need* me to be there," Adam said gently. "And that is worth... a great deal. For all of us, but especially for you. But I still wish I could have been."

"Hmmn." Damien didn't really feel he could disagree. "How are you feeling now, Adam?"

Not that he couldn't tell the other man's physical state for himself... usually. But since this 'ailment' didn't respond to his Healing, who knew what else it might have confused?

The tall knight took a moment to do an internal survey.

"Better," he pronounced. "Entirely fine actually, though there's... sort of a sense that it may not last."

He paused thoughtfully. "I... can feel what Angelos was talking about now. That the Land – and I imagine that would be *Elaarwen* and not *Ilseador,* though what the difference is I do *not* understand. But Elaarwen is *watching* me. And not feeling terribly charitable about me."

Damien frowned. "This makes no sense. The Realm told me when I reconnected with It, just before coming home, that It appreciated *you* particularly. Because you took it more seriously, I think."

Adam raised an eyebrow. "More seriously than *Genevieve?*"

Genevieve was Bound to the Realm as Queen. Though she had been Bound first to Elaarwen.

Ilseador's Bound King shrugged. "That's what It told me. They. The Realm is definitely plural."

"So, what's different about Elaarwen?" Adam asked reasonably. "And... how is Elaarwen even a separate entity than Ilseador? Are the other provinces distinct as well?"

"To some extent," Damien replied, hunting within his own sense of the Realm for an explanation that would work for someone who *wasn't* so Bound. "They sort of have to be, or I couldn't Bind the different parts to different people. But *this*... seems unusual."

"I certainly *hope* it's unusual," Adam muttered. "It'll be a bloody hell of a mess if we suddenly can't have any of the nobility traveling around the *rest* of the Realm."

"Or Elaarwen either." The tall man winced slightly, perhaps realizing he'd implied that the Queen's province wasn't all that important.

Which it wasn't, in the grand scheme of Ilseador's economy or agriculture. Or, well, *anything,* really, beyond its connection to Genevieve. The province bred bandits – that preyed on the adjacent provinces – and regularly needed help sent from the more prosperous parts of the Realm to allow the people to recover from horrendous Winter storms; violent Spring floods that knocked out bridges and unwary travelers as the snowpack melted in its odd, abrupt way; unexpected late Summer rains that ruined the meager harvest from the steep slopes *(every two to three years, so they shouldn't really be that unexpected, but Elaarwen never generated a surplus)*; early Autumn snowfalls that killed off livestock; avalanches; failed crops; mine collapses *(though most mining was done to the north in the Alpinsward range)*; and so on.

It had only been Duke Aldred's pact with Duke Tomas of Siovale that had allowed his feisty, impoverished mountain people to survive during the years when Genevieve's father had set the province in Rebellion against the Crown. And it was only Aldred's – and Genevieve's – excellent claim to said Crown that had persuaded Tomas to support them.

Well, that and Genevieve's willingness to stay married to his duplicitous, abusive, half-brother, Harald.

Damien gave his own small snort of amusement. "There aren't a great many people who go to Elaarwen for the lovely weather, I'll admit. And almost never nobles from other provinces."

Excepting during the Rebellion, of course. But that was over.

"Do you feel up to eating now, Adam?" the King asked.

They'd regenerated a certain amount of his magick in the way such things were done best, but his body needed actual food to sustain itself as well. Most of the *magick* had drained off into the Realm – into *Elaarwen* – anyways. Though it served as a great reservoir there that the King could access at need.

Adam winced again.

"Not... not really. Though I think I could tolerate being near the food while *you* eat." He gave Damien a wry smile. "I wouldn't dream of coming between you and an actual meal."

It was another running joke between the two of them – and Jason to some extent. Lady Theresa had been very... *forgetful* about making sure her young charge had enough to eat on anything resembling a regular schedule. The only 'regular' meals the young prince had eaten had been the very occasional ones taken in the stomach-churning presence of his grandfather and the always-diminishing number of his cousins and aunts and uncles.

Damien had gotten used to eating odd things at odd times and, by the time Jason and Adam had discovered him, he had found it challenging to sit through an entire meal. Training him to do that had been one of their many hurdles... but like the rest, there had been no choice. A future king needed to be able to sit still through state banquets, after all.

They'd done it largely by letting him snack on treats as much he liked the rest of the time. Essentially, they had bribed him to tame his essential and eternal restlessness by restricting access to the higher-value foods his starving body craved, but that his boyish palate had deemed less appetizing.

"It's probably a miracle that I didn't get fat with all the sweets you gave me those first few years," Damien told Adam wryly as he sat up in preparation for *reaching* for the covered dish Alanna had promised them would be waiting.

He was careful not to let the skin-contact between them lapse. Adam was feeling better, but *Elaarwen was watching*.

"As much as *you* move around?" Adam laughed. "Not likely. And once we had you riding and learning the sword, you needed all those extra sweets just to keep up with all the work we were giving you."

The tall Champion didn't bother to sit up himself, merely tucking his hands behind his head as he watched his... 'sweet prince' find a comfortable seated position on the bedrolls. The dark-haired younger man tried to hide his flush as he thought those words.

Adam's relaxed, narrow-lidded smile suggested that he'd caught either the thought or the blush. Or both. The tall man looked... rather like the cat that had gotten into the cream.

Damien let his hand rest lightly on the soft, scarred skin that covered Adam's well-muscled stomach. Merely to maintain that necessary contact. Of course.

Trying to hide his discomfiture, Damien rolled his eyes as he *Vanished* the covered dish away from the fireside to appear under his other hand. "I don't move around *that* much."

Dinner was a savory stew, just as he'd expected, with the meat and vegetables cut up fairly finely for quicker cooking time. Someone had made the little bit of extra effort to brown the meat before adding it in order to bring out the deeper flavors. A plate that made a separate compartment above the stew and had to be removed to access it had kept a pair of flatbreads warm... if slightly soggy with condensation.

It had been stew almost every night they were on the road. And porridge with dried fruit and nuts – but no sweet, salted butter, alas – alongside rather overly blackened bacon for breakfast. And hard sausage with cold, flatbread gone leathery from the previous night's cooking and hard, sharp cheeses.

Count Marsham and his Fariveran vassals had set tables nearly as poor, which perhaps was no great surprise after so many years without contact with the outer world. Farivera had fertile lands, but apparently various plant diseases had wiped out most of their varieties of domesticated plants and the livestock had followed thereafter. They'd turned to hunting for meat, but had eaten out the deer long since, relying solely on rabbits the last five years. And the rabbits had become harder to find.

The Fariverans had been almost pathetically grateful for Damien's offers to provide seeds and bulbs and livestock. Apparently, the Evil Wizards to whom the Dukes of Siovale had yielded up the province had been utterly uninterested in managing their human stock by replenishing such basic necessities. *(Exactly what use Azella and her predecessor had made of Farivera, Damien had yet to determine.)*

The peasants had looked even more poorly off than the nobles in their age-worn finery... which spoke poorly to Damien's sense of things. In his opinion, the nobility existed to provide the safe and prosperous structure that the Realm's people deserved and the fine lives of physical ease that nobles enjoyed should only ever be compensation for the hard work they did in other ways – ensuring the free flow of trade, providing security for citizens and travelers, building and maintaining physical infrastructure and so on. Or, in his case, managing the underlying magickal fabric of the Realm and averting things like all those natural disasters that so plagued Elaarwen when he could do so without causing more difficulties.

Clearly Felix Marsham and his people hadn't felt such a burden – as, indeed, neither did a number of Damien's nobles in less ravaged parts of the Realm. If their Oaths of Vassalage held, however, meaning that they were blessed by Ilseador Itself through the magickal connection that the Oath built, the King had no real excuse to remove such men and women from the rule of their lands. He had to trust that the Realm knew what was needed, for all that it abused Damien's own sensibilities of the rightful relationship between lord and liegeman.

And... it was entirely possible that Marsham and the men and women whose oaths *he* held had simply been putting as good a face on it as they could for their new King. No one wanted to look shabbier than necessary in such a situation. And they *had* told Damien – and Adam, and his Royal Guards of both ilks had heard more quiet words – just how bad things *had* gotten. They might have been trying to put a good face on things out of respect for the King's significance, but they weren't constructing 'Potemkin villages' to hide the dire straits of nobles *or* peasants.

Count Marsham had given Damien a list of all their needs – and been dismayed that the King merely nodded, not even taking the long scroll *(on parchment, not paper, and clearly a one that had been scraped clean for re-use)* nor writing it down. The Count had actually taken *Lady Alanna* to task for not doing so – or seeing it done, since the young woman was currently serving as King's hostess for his traveling mini-Court.

At which point, Adam's eyes had sparkled with that mischievous and sardonic glint that said Damien had better do something or *Words* would be *Exchanged*. And he'd yet to see anyone best his Champion verbally any more than at swordplay. At least Adam had seemed more amused than irritated on behalf of his protegée *(all of the Royal Guards, but particularly the Secret ones being quite close to their former Captain).*

Damien had given his lo– Adam a quelling glance, then turned back to the Count and rattled off the entire list. With additions that he'd already noted as needs, even so early in their visit as this confrontation had occurred.

Food, first and foremost, immediately.

Seeds, bulbs, and cuttings. Sheep, goats, and cattle. Chickens, ducks, and geese. Deer and rabbits for the forests *(and squirrels, beavers, raccoons, songbirds, and other wild creatures… which had likely become game to peasants with slings; though he didn't list those, instead planning to encourage wild creatures to migrate into the emptied spaces later on… after the traditional livestock were re-established).*

Lumber, since the province hadn't had access to Alpinsward coal or Zialest charcoal and had denuded its own forests. Iron – first to be brought in as finished supplies of nails, saws, awls, and needles, thence to be followed by loads of ingots. Likewise, copper, tin, and other less common metals.

And humans. The Fariverans hadn't had much to use for the training of smiths and tanners and weavers and many of them had died off these last score of years without passing on their skills. Herbalists had stripped their gardens and had apprentices who couldn't tell mints from nightshades – King Reginald's rule had driven

Healers away and the ancient presence of Azella's master suggested that Farivera had possessed few to begin with. Foresters hadn't had forests to manage since the trees were cut down and the larger game eaten.

And the birthrate had fallen off drastically as women hadn't been healthy enough to conceive, let alone bear and nurture babes. Alanna had been told that entire communities would go to half of their poor rations to try to adequately feed bearing women and women with babes at the breast. Which spoke well for the people... But midwives would be needed to be brought in and then trained as the population recovered.

Perhaps they'd simply been lucky that they hadn't ended up using stone knives. As it was, it was clear that Farivera was on the verge of a major population crash merely through mismanagement and neglect and lack of opportunity. Damien's zigzagging run through the province two months before had brought a lusher fertility in his footsteps than had been seen in decades, and those who had walked along even a portion of his path had quickly been noticed to be healthier.

Such a vaguely directed spell of well-being hadn't been *enough*, of course. Damien had spent rather more of his time in Count Marsham's castle – *connected* as it was to the province, even as Castle Alsterling was to the Realm – meditating than the Count had really appreciated. And then *eating* more than the impoverished provincial could agree with, for all that the royal party's supplies had been brought in with the Army's own and were no drain on Farivera. And *sleeping* a great deal of the rest of the time.

Damien was aware that Adam had explained to the irate old man that the King was using his Great and Puissant Magick to Heal even the people in the province's most distant fiefs of various illnesses. It hadn't mollified Marsham until word started pouring in from his local population. Whether he believed that Damien's reach went so far as the most distant fiefs... hadn't been possible to tell.

Count Marsham's eyes had looked... hopeful.

Though he still wouldn't discuss his former evil overlords to the south except in the most general terms. It was clear that he didn't *really* believe that they were truly free. Felix Marsham had been – by his own accounts – a wild young fellow when they'd been cutoff from the Realm. He'd spent much of his time at King Reginald's Court and had known both Genevieve's father and Damien's own, being their age-contemporary.

He'd had stories about *them,* too. Though not such homey ones as Sir Angelos had just given. That Ducal-Prince Aldred had been a wild young man didn't terribly surprise Damien – Genevieve must have gotten that from somewhere, after all.

But the pained look on Count Marsham's face in describing his own father had been unexpected. No one had ever had a bad word to say about Prince Eric that Damien had ever heard. Felix Marsham had... *implied* that Damien's father had been uptight and snobbish, a stickler for rules and entirely caught up in his own importance as a Prince of the Realm. Marsham had sort of admitted that he hadn't met Lady Miria, and that perhaps marriage and fatherhood had mitigated some of that when Damien's baffled look made it clear that that wasn't the father *he'd* known.

The whole visit had been... problematical in a variety of ways.

But given the amount of magick he'd had to expend, the quality of the food hadn't been a minor concern. And by now, Damien would have just about *killed* for roasts and lightly steamed vegetables and milder cheeses and cakes. Even those yeasted breads that he had been – discreetly – trying to phase out of popularity.

Ironically, he actually enjoyed the *taste* of yeasted breads, but having the dying yeast screaming as his wakeup call every morning – and at the pre-dawn hour that the Castle and City bakers put their loaves into the oven – had been worth learning a different preference. And as went the king, so went the commoners...

At least he could – now – eat meat and plants that had been killed sufficiently far away. And most cheeses, though the soft ones had to be specially treated. That he could was another credit to Adam – and Jason, though his *former* Champion had seemed rather baffled at Adam's *(successful)* plan to get Damien to eat. *(Baffled by the entire problem, actually, though he'd gone along with what Adam had decided was necessary, as he tended to go along with everything Adam proposed.)*

There was, after all, no place in the *Realm* where Damien could not feel every sparrow's fall. It was simply something he'd had to learn to deal with and set aside from his conscious mind after Ilseador had Bound him so tightly following their discovery of the Monarch's Blade...

Well, that or go mad.

That he hadn't... was again likely to Adam's credit. His Captain *(at the time)* hadn't revealed his own *empathy*, but he had always known how to guide Damien through these things. Exactly how the King had never noticed... made some rather embarrassing suggestions about his observational skills. Or maybe could more comfortably be laid at the former Captain's feet, since he'd been intentionally *avoiding* explaining himself.

Had Adam somehow used his projective *empathy* to divert Damien's attention?

The King glanced at his, erm, companion. Because he'd been thinking about all those odd past interactions. And because he really should make sure they were maintaining sufficient skin-to-skin contact for Adam's well-being. Not because he just wanted to look at the handsome man stretched out without even a blanket drawn over his muscled body.

How was it that Adam had already managed to tan that lovely golden color when Damien was still pale and white from Winter? They'd been outdoors together on all this riding... not that such a differential would explain how Adam was tanned so *uniformly*...

Adam was looking at the plate of stew with a certain wistfulness...

"I'd take this somewhere else if I could," Damien said apologetically.

Usually, the King was starved to death by the time they set up camp and made dinner; though at home, he often lasted until the time everyone else was ready for bed. Just the habitual effort of using his Earth-sense and helping the Realm along as they rode was... Well, *both* exhilarating *and* draining. Adding a Healing in only exacerbated things.

But they'd stopped so early this time – there was a niggling bit of the King that was still working with the Sapphire River, just as last night his attention had been on the Topaz. But it was a very small part.

Most of his current goal was to keep the water clean of the tinylife – like yeast, but different, there in the river – that would be inimical to his people camped here. They were, after all, blithely scooping up drinks with full trust in their King's ability to keep them healthy.

Both rivers – and the life within them – were much healthier anyways than their combination would be, far down on the plains. And certainly, by the time the waters made their way down to the sea through his city of Emeralsee.

(The tinylife deserved its own place, of course, but for the most part it – they – had no real need or desire to spend time inside of mammalian guts. Damien was more ambivalent about the few that **did** *need such an event to complete their lifecycles, but the rest really just tried to get out as quickly as they unhappily found themselves so confined. The human gut might be a great place for high-speed reproduction, but was arguably terrible for long-term prospects. For the others, he'd toyed with the idea of looking for volunteers to allow the others a turn of the lifecycle – not being able to properly control the system if he volunteered himself – but had reluctantly decided it wasn't feasible. Perhaps if he had leisure to do nothing but manage a herd of cattle for the purpose – keeping the incursions of the tinylife so minor as not to inconvenience the cattle... But until and unless that was feasible, they would just have to make do with wild creatures and with Damien constantly chasing them out to reside unproductively in soil and water...)*

The Champion's eyes flicked upwards from the enameled dish, and he smiled a little absently. "I know... and we really need to come up with at least some sort of temporary solution regardless. What goes in must come out after all."

True... and dragging Adam along for *that* was hardly romanti– um, appealin– Erm.

In good taste.

Adam sat up and a little away from Damien, his face set and grim as he tested the question.

"Well?" the King asked carefully after a moment.

The tall knight's expression stayed fairly grim, but one corner of his mouth quirked up in a sardonic smile. "It's talking to me. I confuse it, apparently."

"It? Elaarwen?" Damien frowned.

"It," Adam confirmed. "Or maybe *She*. This... *Being* doesn't seem to be a plural the way you described Ilseador."

Damien's frown deepened. *That* didn't fit with everything he understood about his Realm. Or thought he'd understood.

And if this – if *Elaarwen* – wasn't comfortable with *Adam,* then why wasn't it talking to *Damien?*

Because you are known, Ilseador explained wordlessly, and somehow apologetically. *This Other is not. I/We have tried to make it clear that this Other is known to* **Me/Us.** *But Elaarwen has a different Onus and must make Her Own decision as to his acceptability.*

It/They actually sounded rather... miffed at that. If a Being such as the Realm could be miffed.

What? Damien couldn't make heads nor tails of that 'explanation.'

Because you **belong,** Ilseador tried again, but the difference between their perspectives was too great. The Realm didn't seem to use the word 'belong' in the same way that Damien did. Perhaps it was just the closest word that approximated the desired meaning in Its/Their opinion? *Perhaps She will accept this Other once it is clear that* **he** *belongs to* **you,** *just as* **you** *belong to* **Her.** *And to Me/Us. Make it clear, My/Our King.*

"Can you tell what the, ah, confusion is?" Damien asked Adam, hoping to come at the matter from a different angle.

While the King communicated with his Realm regularly, rarely did It *(or They)* attempt to communicate in actual *words.* And never before so... ambivalently. Or ambiguously. Or... ambi-something-ly. Even finding the relevant description felt beyond him just now.

Damien was entirely nonplussed and unsure of how to proceed.

His Realm – or at least one province – was speaking to *Adam* and not to *him.*

Why?

"She says..." Adam looked bemused. "She says that I don't belong *anywhere*. So... She isn't sure why She doesn't know if I belong *here*."

He shook his head. "Is this how the Realm usually talks to you, Damien? Or... how Genevieve does, through your soul-bond? Do you ever get used to hearing words inside your mind that aren't yours?"

"Um..." Damien gave him a baffled look back. "Genevieve... sometimes. But you know how she can't do that if she's not meditating. Or touching me. The Realm... not so much. Once in a while. Usually it's more like the *empathy* – feelings, not words."

Though It/They *had* spoken to him. Just a moment ago.

"She wants to talk to you more directly," Adam said after frowning thoughtfully for a bit.

"All right," Damien composed himself to try to make contact.

Adam shook his head. "She says She *can't* talk to you. Not... not *yet*. Because you haven't... done *something*. I'm not sure what that something is."

The King – the *Bound King of Ilseador and Bound Duke-Consort of Elaarwen* – gave his Champion a look of frustration. "Then how come She can talk to *you?*"

Would the Being that was Elaarwen have been able to talk to *Genevieve?*

Curse it all, this was like being on the wrong side of trying to communicate with the ghost of his great-great-grandmother who haunted the Castle and advised her acknowledged descendants *(and in-laws)* whether they liked it or not. Though at least the ancient Queen's advice usually *was* worth listening to. If not always her manner of delivery.

"I'll try to ask." Adam's frown deepened, his eyes going unfocused as his attention fixed on the words coming into his mind. And then suddenly he gave his usual sardonic laugh. "She says She can talk to me because I *don't* belong."

That... made *no* sense.

"No, I misunderstood," Adam corrected himself. "It's because *I* belong *everywhere*. You... you don't belong quite *enough?* She's still saying you need to go somewhere and do... something. She's... giving me directions..."

Adam's eyes nearly crossed. "Damien? Paper?"

The King scrambled to his feet and dug quickly through one of his saddlebags. Bless Alanna for having had it brought in here. He was back quickly with a small notebook and a pencil.

Adam began scratching immediately on a blank page.

Damien watched as a... *shape*... emerged. It was like nothing he had ever seen before, and the King suddenly had a certain sympathy with Azella's efforts of some months back to decipher the notes he had made while making sense of her tomes on the various Elementals. Whatever it was that Adam was drawing made as much sense to Damien as his own notes had made to the evil sorceress.

After several minutes of this, the scratching stopped, and Adam seemed aware of Damien again.

"She says She's still not sure about me, but as long as you continue to claim me as *yours,* She'll let me proceed to this place."

Damien looked at the entirely unclear drawing. "That's a *map?*"

Adam blinked and looked at it in surprise. "Well, of course it is."

Damien just looked at him. "It's a good thing Elaarwen will let you come with me then, Adam, because *I* can't make heads nor tails of that."

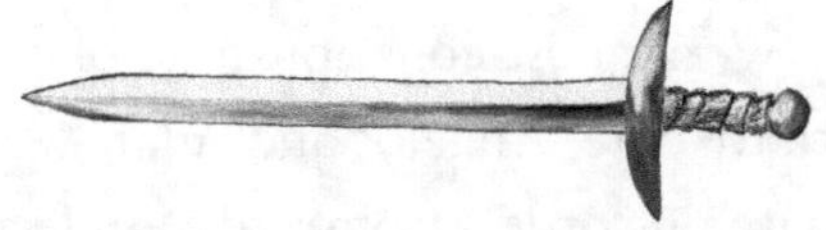

Chapter FOUR

Wishful Thinking

IT DIDN'T TAKE A GREAT deal more time to sort out the rest of what they needed *right now.*

The Being that was apparently Elaarwen agreed that, although Angelos 'belonged somewhere else,' he might travel so far as the 'place where earth kisses air.' A description which made no sense to Damien, but which Adam seemed to feel was sufficient for finding it.

She also made it rather clear – or at least *Adam* said She made it clear to *him* – exactly what She meant for Damien to do in order to 'claim Adam as his.' Since what *Adam said* Elaarwen meant by this was that the two of them were to 'sleep' together for the rest of the trip – or at least until they made it to the 'place' on the 'map' – Damien couldn't help thinking that Adam's accurate rendition of the communication might be... somewhat suspect.

On the other hand, it was entirely clear to his Healer's sense that Adam wasn't nauseous or dizzy any more, even when they weren't in physical, skin-to-skin contact. And getting dressed and going outside allowed the King to verify that Angelos was doing well now also. The young knight was even eating a late supper.

Alanna seemed very relieved, and not overtly skeptical that the invisible-but-somehow-manifest-consciousness of the province had been negotiated with to 'cure' Angelos and Adam. And that they had incomprehensible marching orders from said Manifest Consciousness.

Of course, she *had* seen her king fight a demon just over two months ago.

Maybe *anything* was believable right now.

"And just *how* are we supposed to make any plans if we don't know *where* we're going?" Damien demanded as the pair of them returned to his tent and the King thumped himself back down on his bedroll.

Fully dressed, one might note.

Their tent, the King somewhat sourly supposed he should consider it for the time being.

Not that this was particularly different than the way they'd *been* handling sleeping arrangements. The King's Champion was his by-default bodyguard, over and above the presence and capacity of the rest of the Royal Guard – Secret and Official both. Until they'd left the more populated areas, Adam had already been sleeping in the antechamber to Damien's tent or in the parlor of whatever room they'd had to inhabit at inns and castles.

Likely Damien hadn't needed to give Alanna that nonsense about how Elaarwen was nervous about Adam's magickal abilities and would only tolerate him if he stayed close to Damien himself. It wouldn't change any sleeping arrangements... though he had the uncomfortable sense that they might have to ride double tomorrow.

Though who knew? Maybe that even *was* the actual explanation.

"It could be worse," Adam said philosophically as he set the built-in wards.

It looked like the same setup as in the various warded rooms at the Castle back in Emeralsee – simple threads wound over hooks to engage the pre-set spells that Damien had imbued the tent with.

In reality, *this* spell had been much more complex. While the stones of Castle Alsterling were willing to consider themselves all parts of things called 'walls' and 'floors' and 'ceilings' and therefore to delimit spaces based on those definitions, the threads that the tent canvas was woven of each considered themselves to be separate and unique individuals.

Damien had spent more time and effort on enchanting the wards for this tent than he had on inventing the warding spells in the first place. He'd speculated to Adam – no one else being interested in the details of spell-casting – that the stones of his Castle had just been together for so long that they quite nearly saw themselves as having returned to their original and pre-cut state. The larger problem with the building stones was persuading them that *only* certain spaces were to be included and that such temporary things as wooden doors should also be used for delimiting the warded spaces.

Negotiating with the tent, by contrast, had been more like attempting collective bargaining with an entire guild of humans who were choosing to abjure having their guildmaster speak for them.

Honestly, the rats of Emeralsee had been more group-minded.

"Really?" Damien asked grumpily. "Worse *how?*"

Adam turned towards him with a wicked smile. "*She* could have demanded that you sleep with *Angelos* as well."

Damien glared at his – hmmn, maybe *former* best friend. "Not funny, Adam."

The tall, blonde knight chuckled and lowered himself to the adjacent bedroll. "Really? Because *I* think this is hilarious."

The King narrowed his eyes. "I only have your word on any of this, you know."

"True." Adam propped himself up on one elbow. "Quite true. We're all rather used to doing this the other way around, aren't we. A bit odd to have the shoe on the other foot."

"What are you talking about?" Damien frowned.

"Usually, it's *you* telling us all these otherwise-unverifiable things," Adam clarified. "And the rest of us having to take your word. Which we *do,*" he added a bit pointedly.

"I've never lied to you," Damien said, rather stung by the implication. "*Any* of you."

Though he'd occasionally left out pieces of information that might be... distracting.

"Nor have I," Adam retorted. "And you just implied that I have. That I *would*."

That... was fair.

Unfairly fair, since Adam was taking altogether too much delight in the situation. But... although he, too, had left the occasional item unsaid when it wouldn't be helpful, he'd never *lied* to Damien. *Never.*

"I'm sorry," Damien said, trying to sound penitent rather than... *frustrated* or *resentful* or *whiny*.

Particularly not *whiny*.

Bad enough that this man had seen him through far too many of his most awkward growing experiences to have any of the awe that a man *should* have for his king... Not that Damien had ever wanted to *be* king, except that doing so had meant he might actually survive.

And... normally he didn't think of Adam having been with him through any of those things as *bad*.

Having a best friend who knew you and cared for you and loved you despite having seen all the weak and whiny and dark places in your soul... that was surely a *good* thing, wasn't it?

Adam sighed. "My sweet prince. Are we going to go through this *every* time we go to bed?"

Damien swallowed down his very mixed emotions.

"Go through what?" he asked.

"You trying to figure out how to push me away."

Adam's expression wasn't *condescending*. And it wasn't *resigned*.

It was... *bordering on exasperation,* Damien decided was the right description.

"I don't know what you mean," he said, trying to pretend it was true. "We're in here, like you wanted, Adam. And supposedly we're under Divine Orders – or the next closest thing – to, ah, '*sleep*' together. Again, like you wanted."

He paused. "I hope that She's satisfied with us for tonight, though, because I can't imagine this is going to work else – *eeph–!*"

His words were cut off as Adam pulled him all the way down and rolled on top of him for a kiss that set all of Damien's nerves on fire. Again. And pressed close as they were, it was obvious that no part of *again* was going to be a 'problem.'

As, indeed, it wasn't.

"How did that work?" Damien asked somewhat – no, a *fair* bit – later, as they snuggled down to sleep at last. "I didn't think you *could*. I mean... Not so *soon*..."

Adam chuckled into his hair. "Jason mentioned that he'd forgotten – until the two of you took that little vacation in the grotto last Fall. Apparently, when one's lover is a Healer, you can make love all night long. Or as long as the Healer wants to, anyways. Jase says an *empath* is quite nearly as effective – you might remember he was... rather *interested* last Fall when you mentioned *I* was one."

The tall man's tone was... fairly smug. "I don't know that I ever got around to thanking you for outing me to him like that. It made last Winter... rather special."

"But you'd never told him yourself." Damien stated it, trying to block off the inevitable connections that were flooding into his mind at Adam's assertions. At Adam's *rather well-supported* assertions.

Exceedingly well-supported, given what else was again rather... *exceeding*. And how *Damien* was feeling... If one *empath* or Healer could have that effect, then *two*...

Adam gave a shrug that... did all sorts of interesting things. "It's a Loveress family secret. Mama didn't want it noised about during King Reginald's reign... and by the time you were crowned we'd been together for so long. There didn't seem to be any reason to stir things up."

There seemed to be something else the tall, blonde knight wasn't saying. But it wouldn't be anything important and relevant. After all, they'd just agreed that it wasn't a *thing* between them to keep important secrets from each other.

And all of that made sense. No one had willingly let it be known they had special abilities that might draw themselves to the notice of King Reginald or Lord Prydeen. Or Prince Oskar.

"And you had *your* projective *empathy* under control, so no reason Jason would ever notice," Damien added. "Any more than Grandfather did."

Adam ran a fingertip along Damien's jawline. "I made sure you had *yours* under control as well, my sweet prince. Genevieve never figured it out either, did she?"

"No... Or at least she attributed anything she did notice to my Healing magick," the dark-haired man agreed. And since said-magick had become manifest about the same time that Genevieve had appeared in his life to stay... she'd had no baseline for comparison. "Same with Jason, I suppose. I don't think it's so much that my *projections* are *under control,* Adam, as that they're just *shut down* most of the time."

"Safest thing to do with them," his Champion said philosophically. "Most of the time it's neither terribly useful nor ethical to be *projecting* emotions at people. And they certainly aren't shut down when you're with *me.*"

He kissed Damien's ear. "The which I *very* much appreciate."

And while Damien couldn't really disagree with that right now, either...

"There's downsides, Adam. I couldn't get *free* of you earlier. You almost had *me* vomiting."

There was a slight pause. Adam's roving hand stilled and Damien found himself regretting that. And what he'd said to stop... *that.*

"That... was my fault," the blonde man admitted quietly. "I haven't lost control like that since I was a child. Not even when I really *did* have food poisoning. Not even when..."

He stopped, but Damien could fill in, based on the feel of old rage, fear, remembered pain... *helplessness.* The words Adam didn't want to say was that it hadn't happened even when Harald of Siovale had briefly usurped the Throne and Adam had been beaten half to death after the invaders had managed to capture him while he tried to defend Castle Alsterling.

Harald's forces had taken it from within, subduing most of the would-be defenders before they'd even known there was anything to defend *against.* Harald had had Adam dragged out to serve as a handle on Jason – and Damien – and had him further injured when Jason had still been willing to sacrifice them both in the protection of his king and presumptive queen.

Jason had been unwilling to give up his king… but *Damien* had surrendered at that point, unable to let Adam die to prove a point. Or rather all of them, since even Jason – with himself and Genevieve as backup – couldn't even have escaped the Castle bailey with Harald's forty enchanted Siovalese men-at-arms and Lord Prydeen's score of thugs ranged around them.

They'd escaped the Castle that night and Damien and Genevieve – with the help of the Castle servants and Castle Guard – had retaken it the day after, in a masterful exhibition of his wife's strategic genius. Adam and Jason and the Royal Guardsmen who had escaped with them had missed all the excitement, riding into the Throneroom itself on drafthorses co-opted from a friendly farmer at the tail end of events.

Adam hadn't let his injuries stop him, though he'd forced Sir Tim – who had several broken ribs – to stay behind. He'd been nearly as much in need of Damien's newly revealed Healing Powers as the all-but-bled-out Duke Aldred by the time it was all over.

Adam had never faulted *Jason* for choosing Damien – and Genevieve – over himself.

But he'd never quite *forgiven* Damien for choosing Adam himself – or even Adam himself along with the rest of the Royal Guard and Secret Cadre – over Damien's own chance at freedom and safety, no matter how unlikely. Recent events had only increased the number of sardonic complaints about 'sacrificing himself.'

Sardonic… and *terrified,* the King now realized.

Damien ran a gentle hand up and behind himself to caress Adam's cheek and ease away some of that remembered tension and pain.

"No. Not even then. So, I have to assume this – what *Elaarwen* was doing to you – was a great deal worse. But there's other problems with me not having that projective *empathy* under conscious control. Especially if it… does what you're suggesting it does. Or rather *has done* for you and Jason."

And for the pair of *them.* Though which of them was instigating this particular evening's delights might be an open question. Apparently.

There... was a feeling of startlement as the old emotions were tucked away again. "Jase said it was *almost* as good as being with a Healer... which I assumed he knew what he was talking about, given you and... *Oskar*."

They both shuddered slightly at the thought of the dead prince who was missed only by Jason.

And only *'almost.'* Jason was terrible at lying but brutal honesty wasn't usually his style. Damien didn't really want to wonder what the two of them might have been doing to get that sort of a confession out of his... *other* oldest friend.

"A Healer needs receptive *empathy* to detect what's wrong," Damien pointed out. "The projective *empathy* is usually used consciously only for managing pain. And I still do all of that instinctively, of course, though all those books on anatomy and such that we've read have helped."

Adam had been the only person particularly interested in understanding Damien's magickal abilities these last five years. At least until Azella. Had it been because he was interested for himself and not merely to support his young sovereign, as he'd implied?

"The Healing itself," Damien went on, feeling rather nonplussed again, "showing the body *how* to fix things and helping it along where needed..."

He flushed. "I suppose I can see how it could help with increased, um, sexual stamina."

Damien was facing the other way and he'd used a wisp of magick to douse their lamps ages ago. Adam couldn't possibly tell that he was blushing at being so blunt. Even if Damien was trying to stick to medical-sounding terminology to make the discussion a bit less... lurid.

The way Adam was snuggling a little closer even with this overly-clinical description suggested that *lurid* was something the taller man rather *appreciated* just now.

Damien tried not to swallow too obviously hard. But damn him if he wasn't *responding*...

"But I suspect it's the projective *empathy* that makes the biggest difference, or *you* wouldn't be able to do... whatever it is... at all." The King paused, then added lightly, "Unless you've been holding out on me, Adam. Are you a Healer, like your brother Martin?"

Adam's honest, surprised laugh answered that one quickly. No, he wasn't.

Still, it *had* been a question he'd really wanted to know the answer to. Adam had sort of implied, last Fall, when Damien finally – *finally* – realized that the other man was an *empath,* that he hadn't *known* his own skills. Or... the name for them anyways. Hadn't *known* that the rest of his family was so supernally Talented with magick.

The fact that none of that was true had been... leaking out in conversations ever since. If Damien didn't have the unusual memory that he did, he'd likely never have picked up all those little hints.

And just now Adam had said it was the Baronetta, his mother, who had decided it was a 'Loveress family secret.'

Which was fine. Plenty of families had 'secrets' – probably even a number of them counting their own magickal Talents as such, as Angelos had just informed them regarding Damien's mother's family. There was no reason for a king to know all those secrets – no *good* reason, anyways. His grandfather had made a habit of ferreting such things out to hold over the heads of their keepers.

And, after all, none of those things were the *important* and *relevant* kinds of secrets that would be unfair to keep.

"You're upset, Damien," Adam said gently. "Why? Because I didn't tell you these things in the first place?"

Now Damien gave a laugh of his own. Shaky, but real. "What, when I was fourteen and terrified of everything? Or when I was seventeen and you kept helping me center myself by dumping me in the nearest horse trough? Or later when – no, it doesn't matter. It wasn't – no, it *was* important, but that was what you did with it, not the name for what you were doing or even whether or not you explained it to me."

"I... trained you the way *I* was trained." Adam sounded apologetic, but slightly confused. "We – my family – we don't teach the children *how* to use it. We teach them how *not* to."

That... made sense.

Mostly.

"I just..." Damien shook his head and pressed himself deeper into Adam's chest. He was deeply tempted to turn over so that he could burrow his face into the soft forest of Adam's chest hair and hide from the world. Likely his Champion would even let him do that and never ask again any more than he ever had.

Adam had been doing that since Damien was sixteen, after all. Though, back then, it had been with clothes on.

But if he couldn't talk to *Adam*...

And much as he didn't *want* to talk... it felt like it might be better if he *did*...

"I need to know *how* so that I can *decide*. On *when*. And... when *not* to."

"When *not* to..." Adam repeated thoughtfully.

He hadn't gone from swordmaster and safe harbor for Damien's heart to the King's chief advisor because he wasn't good at figuring things out. And observant as all get out.

"You're concerned that you somehow made it easier for the White Witch and her pretty-boy minion to prey on you. That you... essentially gave them *consent* to do so by unintentionally using your projective *empathy* to... hmmmn. Inspire their lustful interest in you."

It sounded... a little stupid when put so baldly, even with the attempt at a less painful euphemism.

But what else was he supposed to think? Damien had spent hours and days and *weeks* trying to persuade Azella that *he* wasn't interested. And she'd never given up. And apparently, she really *had* put the *sleep* spells on him that he'd suspected and then she'd had Jeremy – who had been Mikhail then and entirely her creature–

"It would be *my fault*, Adam," Damien said almost too softly to hear. "Or at least... less *hers*. *Theirs*. All because I let my dreams – of Genevieve and Jason and you, but mostly of *you* – out where they affected... *them*."

"Mostly of *me?*" Adam sounded – and *felt*, and oh dear Gods, was Damien doing it *again?* – both bemused and *interested*.

The King shrugged.

"I wanted – I *prayed* – for one of you to rescue me. Genevieve, mostly, probably because she had command of the Army. But when I was dreaming, it was always you. Probably because you already *had*."

Adam's hand smoothed the shorter man's hair back – unnecessarily because Damien was keeping it too short lately to get in his eyes – but it was a loving gesture. "I thought it was Jason that got the credit for that."

"And I thought *you* told me before that you could have gotten me out of the Library far faster than he did. If you'd been willing to lure me out *empathically* and let me be dependent on you." Damien paused. "I'm not faulting that decision, by the way. But I think I told you, once, that you've always made me feel *safe*. More than anyone else ever has."

More than the parents who had taken him from home and to his terrifying grandfather's huge, scary Castle filled with people who – to a very young *empath* – all seemed to want to *eat* each other. Greed of a different sort, he'd understood as he grew older. But Mother and Father and even Kandy had never understood why Damien had screaming terrors at night for the first year. Only at night, because that was when he couldn't cling to any of them to protect him.

Adam's arms pulled him gently closer again. "Oh, my sweet prince."

There was a moment of silence. "It still wasn't consent, Damien. Even if you *were* doing something that... aroused her – or *their* – interest. Not any more than it's *consent* to rape if a scantily-clad woman walks through the docks quarter of Emeralsee."

"Hmmn." Damien didn't – *couldn't* – say anything more.

But the knot inside that he managed to forget existed most of the time anymore... the knot that had *tightened* more and *more* the longer he was in Azella's Keep... loosened a little.

Several moments passed. Adam's breath was slow and even and Damien began to let himself drift towards sleep. Twice in one night should be sufficient to content anyone after all. No matter what Adam had implied, or what his body had suggested to Damien's.

"Is it... really that bad to... be *with* me like this?" Adam's voice was quiet. Wistful. Sad.

Oh...

Damien hadn't wanted to cause hurt. Not to anyone, but particularly not to *Adam* whom he owed... *everything* to.

"No," he replied just as softly. "And that's the whole problem."

"Ah..."

It was barely a syllable, more of a mere out-breath. But there was a world of understanding in it nonetheless.

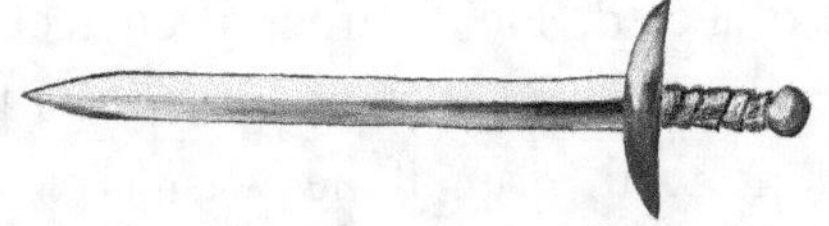

Chapter FIVE

Hints and Hopes

THE REST OF THE JOURNEY up to Castle Stellarine – which was located in what was referred to, by those who knew no better, as Elaarwen's 'city' – was fairly unremarkable.

The weather stayed more friendly than anyone had a right to expect in this part of the Realm in late Spring. The road was dry enough for good footing but not so much as to provoke clouds of dust. It was too early for mosquitoes, and not quite too late for some rather impressive displays of fireflies. The trees were in full leaf, providing scattered shade from a sun that rose high enough to make the afternoons a little uncomfortable for the men in chainmail just before it started to cool off again.

Angelos looked a little strained, but seemed otherwise fine. Damien kept more of an eye on his young cousin than he had done previously and began to wonder if the younger man's deference to Lady Alanna was solely a professional courtesy.

He mentioned as much when Adam shooed away their Guards – pointing out that a king who was in touch with every living thing

87

in the Realm was actually safer in the wilds of Elaarwen than in 'civilized Emeralsee' – and won his King a little privacy to wander freely in the forest nearby their camp one evening.

Damien hadn't objected. He'd rather been feeling the press of having been in the same company of people for so long, and Adam had likely felt that as well, even if he wasn't picking it up from Damien. Lynncrag was a bucolic little fief and *outdoors* was where Adam and his large, busy family had habitually gone to seek privacy.

Damien himself was really more of a city-boy, despite his early years at Ravenscroft. In his City or his Castle there was a constant flux of people around him. Different people, different needs, new problems to solve, less of a sense of being immersed in the personal dramas because they took themselves away before he was. Even Royal Guards had the dramas of their personal lives, after all, despite setting them aside professionally in favor of loyalty to King and Crown.

He loved Elaarwen, because it was part of Ilseador and part of Genevieve... but he *missed* Emeralsee. And he appreciated the mental and physical space from his Guards while somehow simultaneously *missing* the bustle and press of over half a million people in the combined City and province.

And of course, *he'd* known, after all, that for Adam this was more about the romance of a private stroll for the two of them amongst the fireflies than anything else.

"Angelos and Alanna?" Adam replied thoughtfully. "I can see how that might work. If *she's* interested. You've settled your retiring Guards with cottages of their own, and with Alanna being Commander of the Secret Cadre, I assume she'd be due a slightly larger one. And Angelos would be due the same when he's done. That could give any children they have a good start."

Damien shrugged. "I'll have to see what's available at that point. There's a limit to Crown lands."

Adam snorted. "But there's *always* that cottage you keep trying to pack me and Jase off to."

"I'm not trying to get rid of you Adam. Not either of you, I just..."

A warm arm came around his shoulders.

"It's '*complicated.*'" Adam's tone was humorous, if understanding.

Damien nodded, sighing and leaning his head into Adam's chest as they walked – slowly, because it was an awkward position, and walking wasn't really the point. They'd both done arms-practice this morning as always, after all, even if it had been an attenuated one during travel.

"It is. And it never won't be. You say this is what you want. Now. While all those children exist only in your *visions*. But in five years? Or ten? Or thirty? When Marli is all grown up and wedded and you can't claim your *grand*children?"

"'Marli'?" Adam's tone was still amused. And he seemed to be ignoring everything else Damien had said.

"I... it's what I've been calling her. In my head," the King admitted shyly. "Giendra Marlerite Stellarine Alsterling is... a little long."

Not to mention that it arguably left out a name to claim the father who had sired her. Though Jason seemed to be retaining the Solway name only out of respect for the stepfather and half-siblings that he was trying to build a relationship with. Not *rebuild*, because his grandmother and mother hadn't left him any foundations to do that with. Or... at least his grandmother. Jason's relationship with his mother – whom they'd all thought was his sister for over thirty years – was much more fraught.

Adam leaned in to kiss the top of Damien's head. "Marli. That's pretty. I like it."

And *that* conversation hadn't gone any farther in any particularly useful way... though the fireflies glimmering around them made the small excursion very memorable and unique. They *probably* even camouflaged the way Damien *glowed* afterwards – with *real* light, not just magick, and he'd been told anyone could see it. At least their fun didn't light up the rocks of the steep-sided hills around them the way the walls of their special grotto near Emeralsee would do.

The villages they stopped in occasionally overnight to make use of the wayfarer inns – to do laundry and let everyone get a hot bath in the bathhouse – might have made things a little awkward. There were no 'antechambers' or 'sitting rooms' in those tiny inns. Honestly, on the time or two that they'd had to make this trip closer to Winter, their Guards had needed to divvy up and sleep in front of the hearthfire in the various houses or risk frostbite; unmagickal tents were simply not enough up here and none of the inns could possibly fit their whole party.

But no one questioned Alanna's instructions to the innkeepers when she informed them that His Majesty's Champion would be placing his bedroll athwart the threshold of Damien's door – where anyone trying to push the door open would have to ram it through him to get in. Not that that was where Adam would *really* be sleeping... but hopefully even Alanna didn't realize that. And since she'd suggested that Adam should really have a cot moved in, rather than sleeping on the hard floor, it seemed she didn't.

The lack of the usual questions about what Damien had been doing all these months *(and why he and Genevieve hadn't come up to Elaarwen in over a year)* from the curious and folksy innkeepers and villagers was explained over dinner in the communal room of the first inn, the one situated where the Siovale Road merged with the one leading down to Emeralsee.

Apparently, the stories of what had happened to 'our Duke' since last Fall had made their way through even remote Elaarwen. Some of that seemed to be due to how the mountain-man mercenary, Darvin, had passed through and shared his story about meeting Damien in Azella's Keep.

Darvin – and his Sindallese companions, Franz and Rob – had passed through *en route* to Emeralsee at the side of 'the old Duke,' who had been "a-rushin' down to the lowlands to aid our good Duchess an' let 'er know ye was well, milor'."

There were a great many amused comments about how young Rob needed to grow those bushy sideburns of his into a proper beard... and then a few more about how Damien's was entirely too short. Adam's smooth chin had earned him a few teases and knowing glances as well – he was as familiar a figure after six years of visits as his King, after all. *(Or rather his **Duke**, since the people of Elaarwen put the local title higher in their perspective.)*

The three mercenaries had been caravan guards for a delivery of supplies to Azella's Keep and the sorceress had retained them for the Winter to eventually employ them as entertainment for Damien – arms-practice partners for the restless, frustrated, and *bored* captive King. All three were good people, and Darvin had recognized Damien right off as Genevieve's husband.

They had struck up a tentative friendship... and Darvin had agreed to try to get word to Genevieve – by way of her temporarily banished father, up in remote Cloudcroft, if necessary. Which it apparently had been.

However, the timing had been off. None of them had expected that Damien would be able to free himself and travel faster – by foot – than the mercenaries on their horses. The trio, along with Duke Aldred and his newborn son, had made it into Emeralsee shortly after Damien's battle with the demon.

The old man had wept actual tears of joy to see his son-in-law and admitted to his errors of judgment... Not that he could actually make amends for Genevieve's long-gone years of suffering, at Harald's hands, that he had known about but not acted on.

But Aldred *had* sworn to raise his infant son, Emmeren, without any ambitions for the throne.

(Though Damien still had his doubts. Aldred's change of heart appeared to have been inspired by a 'scolding' from the Realm Itself when Damien had finally Bound him via the Vassal's Oath. How well that would last – even with little 'reminders' from Ilseador – against a lifetime of habit and training... they would have to wait and see.)

Aldred and Ciriis – the baby's mother and the third member, with Jason and Adam, of the trio that had gotten Damien to his throne – were already pretending that she had died during the birth so that Aldred couldn't marry her to fully-legitimize his son. It was a rather gruesome solution that seemed unlikely to stand the test of time, but Cloudcroft was remote, so perhaps it could work.

Both Damien and Genevieve had pressed the pair to promise that they would tell the child the truth.

All of which had *helped,* and Damien – who adored all children – had genuinely enjoyed holding his brand-new brother-in-law. He didn't mention to Aldred – *or* Ciriis, or even Genevieve *(yet)* – that he fully intended to bring little Emmeren down to Emeralsee as soon as he was weaned, as well as bringing Marli – and the rest, when they were born – up to Cloudcroft for visits. The boy would be raised as a sibling to Damien's own children if the King had any say in it.

Damien still *loved* his father-in-law... But he no longer trusted Aldred's parenting skills and Ciriis – who had, after all, been his own first lover – had always been sly.

And of the three mercenaries – Damien's sparring partners and friends-in-peril from Azella's Keep... Darvin, of course, had taken his inclusion in Aldred's party as given. There weren't sharp divisions between nobles and commoners here in the Elaarwen mountains and Darvin might well be Genevieve's cousin at some removes. Franz and Rob, however, had amused the locals along the way by being overwhelmed at the exalted nature of their companions... and of 'that odd, scruffy fellow they'd practiced with what turned out to be a sorcerer.'

And a king, though they hadn't known *that* until Darvin dragged them up to Cloudcroft and they were introduced to Lord Aldred. By contrast, they'd seen Damien start *glowing* right in front of them after he re-connected to the Realm.

Elaarwen-folk knew their dukes and duchesses intimately – the province was too sparse and rustic to even consider putting on airs, no matter how closely the Stellarines were linked to 'that there throne down in the flatlands.' Damien's fancier titles meant nothing to these mountain people – he was The Lassie's husband and their Duke and everyone had a solid, supportive swat on the shoulder for him, from the stablehands to the farmer come up from furrowing his terraces and still with the rich, black soil of Elaarwen covering his boots and trousers.

Genevieve's people – who were now also *his,* of course – were *proud* of him.

It was... more deeply satisfying in some ways than the adulation of the masses had been in Emeralsee. Only the Army and Royal Guards – and Siovalese men-at-arms – had actually *seen* the outcome of Duke Tomas' insurrection, of course, since Damien's City Guard and Army had done their best to get all the civilians out of the way. But the soldiers had been happy to spread the word of how their King had slain the treasonous duke and then immediately launched himself into a battle with a demon. And won.

Adam came in for some good-natured ribbing over all that as well, of course, given that the first part of that resolution had involved single-combat between the tall Champion and the bespelled Queen – their own Duchess. He took it in good part, noting that if Tomas of Siovale had allowed Genevieve's hair to be properly bound back in braids and pinned up, the way she *usually* wore it when fighting, he might well not have managed. Thank all the Gods for Tomas' idiocy and the errant breeze that had blown her hair into her face, for he was Their Graces' true knight and could never have actually harmed his beloved Queen.

*(Damien kept silent when that topic came up. He had never told even Adam, and never intended to, that he'd had sylphs blow Genevieve's hair into her face to allow Adam the chance to disarm her safely. Safely for **both** of them.)*

The hail-fellow-and-well-met attitude of the villagers – and of the mountain-folk who came down to regale their Duke with their opinions – rather grated on Damien's Royal Guards, he knew. In Emeralsee, the people were never allowed such casual access to their monarch – and for good reason. But here in the mountains – in *Elaarwen* – it was different.

"You look pleased," Adam commented as they left the last village before Elaarwen's 'city.' They were riding their own horses again, though Damien had been right and they'd had to ride double for the first day heading uplands from the Sapphire River.

Damien shrugged, trying to tone his face back down to his usual expression – the one that he hoped conveyed serenity and confidence. "I just... These people see me as *theirs*, Adam. In a way that no one ever seems to at home. In Emeralsee, I'm the king and I did my job to protect everyone and they're *impressed* and they're *grateful*. But here..."

Sir Angelos had just dropped his horse back beside the pair of them as Damien said that, and gave his King a wry look. "Home-boy makes good, sir?"

"I suppose so..." The King felt a little silly when he put it *that* way...

"You'd have that if you came home to Elderwyld, too," Angelos told him. "You're *ours* in a way that... well, there's just too many people in the city. And we – the Guards – don't really give the commonfolk a chance to get close to you like here. Or if you came home."

"Well, except for when he sat on that pier for close to an hour when he came back from the White Witch's Keep," Adam said dryly. "*Anyone* could have taken him out then."

"The rats had my back," Damien said peacefully, "and no one really knew who I was, anyways, with that mountain-man's tangle of a beard I was sporting at the time."

Not to mention all his own protective spells.

Adam snorted. "Hardly. The dockworkers knew enough to send up to the Castle for me, after all."

Damien rolled his eyes and looked back at the patient young knight riding beside him. "Did you have something to tell me, Angelos?"

The young man's eyes crinkled with a smile. "You mean, besides trying to persuade you to come home for a visit? Actually, yes," he hurried on as Damien's expression doubtless matched the *shuttered* feeling that came over him at those uncomfortably welcoming words. "Milady would like to know if you wanted to put on a bit of a show for coming into Elaarwen's city."

"Pennons flying and shields and fancy gowns much in evidence?" Adam snorted again. "I'll just bet she did. Tell me, Angelos. Did the words 'show these local yokels what a *king* looks like' happen to turn up in her comments?"

Damien gave his Champion a raised eyebrow. Alanna had never given him the impression that she took the people of Elaarwen anything but seriously. He looked ahead to where the young woman was leading the troupe. She was as elegantly dressed and coiffed as ever, in a brocaded riding habit of forest green that marked her position as a lady-in-waiting to the Queen by its very sumptuousness. Her seat on her pale roan palfrey – that had warhorse lines not too far back in its lineage and had been chosen and trained as such – was as sure and easy as ever.

Her back was... perhaps somewhat overly stiff.

But Angelos was flushing a bit. "Not... not *exactly*, sir."

Adam's look of skeptical amusement said everything he might have wanted to. "Perhaps it's a good thing we don't have trumpets with us."

Angelos looked... *extremely* uncomfortable.

Well, there was a middleground to everything.

"Tell Alanna we'll stop at the bridge over Berryripple stream," Damien told his young knight. "She can get my flag out and have you carry it in, if she likes. And anyone else can do whatever they'd like in order to prepare. Keeping in mind that we'll probably end up walking halfway through the town if past experience is any guide."

Which should discourage any nonsense of full-plate armor for those who had brought it, or floor-brushing gowns. After all, the King's retinue could hardly stay mounted if *he* was walking.

"Or possibly the *whole* way," Adam suggested. "Given that Genevieve isn't here to do most of the gladhanding and Damien will let people hold onto him far longer than she will."

"I don't want them to think I don't take them seriously just because I'm from Emeralsee, Adam."

"That doesn't really seem to be a problem anymore, Damien. Not that I'm sure it ever was. They seem to have adopted you as one of their own pretty thoroughly – what is it, Angelos?"

The young knight was giving them both a rather... curious look.

"I noticed this the last time we were up here as well. You *never* refer to the King and Queen by their names except in Elaarwen. Not even when we were on the road without anyone else around." Angelos paused, then added a *little* too quickly, "Well, I would assume you do that in private also. Given that everyone knows you and Prince Jason were His Majesty's closest, um, friends long before he was crowned."

"My mentors and teachers," Damien corrected, with a wry smile, and hoping he'd misinterpreted that quick fix. "And eventually my friends, too, of course."

And pray all the Gods that whatever *else* they were to each other – and to Genevieve – *now,* might be subsumed in public perception by the knowledge of how close the four of them had *always been.*

Adam shrugged. "We tried being more formal the first time Genevieve brought us all up here, shortly after she was crowned. Not only did the people here take it rather amiss, but *she* laughed at us the whole time."

"We're not *the King and Queen* in Elaarwen, Angelos," Damien explained more helpfully. "We're Duchess Genevieve and her consort. And the population of the whole province of Elaarwen is... maybe a tenth that of just the *city* of Emeralsee. The only times anyone here uses titles for the Stellarines – or any of their other nobles, for that matter – it's to show off for lowlanders."

"But the Royal Guards – including the Secret Cadre – still use the royal titles while we're here," Angelos pointed out.

"And they – the people – are calling Lord Aldred 'the old Duke'," he added a little uncomfortably. "Despite the fact that you, um..."

Damien nodded. He'd thought that might come up. "So, they are. And I'm not going to correct them on that. Nor are any of you – and you may pass that word as my command."

Likely he should have sat everyone down before they even entered the province and explained things. And certainly, when they'd stopped for lunch the day after that first inn.

Being... *distracted* by the unexplained map and instructions from Elaarwen Manifest *(and no, not by Adam,* **that** *wasn't it at all)* wasn't a very good excuse for not dealing with this situation pre-emptively and leaving his people in an awkward spot.

Well, done was done. There wasn't really time to do so now, even when they stopped at the stream to 'freshen up' and meet Alanna's need for pomp and ceremony. After all, anyone might happen along the road and hear what was likely to become a rather contentious discussion if Damien did it himself instead of passing it down the chain-of-command.

None of his Guards – of either ilk – weren't *clever*, after all. They knew the political situation and the implications of little Emmeren's birth – most of them knew Ciriis rather well also. They all felt fairly protective of himself and Genevieve – and Adam and Jason – and likely felt more than a bit betrayed on behalf of their charges. They would accept his word and mind their well-bred manners, but they would also voice their – ah – *concerns* and *dismay* if given the opportunity.

Which, granted, was just how Damien – and Genevieve – wanted it. And Adam as well, for that matter. Royal Guards heard things that the royals themselves wouldn't, and often made excellent advisors. It was a part of their purview to guard the royals' *political* well-being as well, after all. *(Which was a part of why Angelos was being considered as a replacement for the rather ham-handed Marcus...)*

The King frowned thoughtfully. *"That's* what has Alanna's dander up, isn't it? And why you wanted to talk to me?"

Angelos ducked his head a little. "It's not my place to criticize my commanding officer..."

"And she didn't listen very well when you tried, did she?" Adam sighed. "You did the right thing, Angelos. Both with talking to her first, and then with talking to *us* before she bursts out with something we'll all regret."

"Captain..." Angelos was twisting his reins in his hands and... rather looked like he wanted to pace or twitch or at least *wriggle* the way Damien knew *he* often did. Was that particular need of his something inherited from his Eldridge family? "It's just that milady is... very fond of... of *all* of you, and–"

"I'll talk to her, Angelos," Damien interrupted the young man's discomfiture. He gave Adam a mischievous look out of the corner of his eye. *"His Highness, Prince-Consort Adam,* and I will *both* talk to her."

Angelos' look of increased dismay was almost as amusing as Adam's reaction.

The young man's dark eyes fastened on Adam. "I'm so sorry, Your Highness. I didn't mean not to give you your due respect..."

He stopped as Adam waved a hand at this while giving Damien a bit of a dirty look.

"I've no *objection* to wearing the title granted me by *His Royal Majesty, Defender of Emeralsee and Ilseador* and by my Goddess-Blessed marriage," the tall man replied. "But I'd just as soon use the one I *earned.*"

He rolled his eyes at Damien. "Or at least the one I was awarded for the *skills* I earned."

Adam's golden-hazel gaze was more amused than irritated, however. The close *empathic* connection that he shared with Damien wasn't enough to send words across. But somehow it still conveyed that Adam remembered quite well that the King had told him – him and Jason both, actually, though under separate circumstances – that his appointment had nothing to do with his martial skills and everything to do with how he had found a lonely, hopeless boy hiding in a library and given him a heart to call home.

The Champion – of Damien's whole world – smiled kindly at the young knight from Elderwyld. "And I take it as an honor that some of you still call me 'Captain'."

Angelos gave him a reassured, if still somewhat nervous, smile back.

"And we won't mention that it was you who brought the problem to our attention," Adam added, and that brought a flood of relief into the young knight's eyes.

"Thank you, sir, ah, Your Highness, ah–" Angelos flushed a little.

"We wouldn't want Alanna to suspect you of sharing intimate confidences," Damien suggested, and panic surged in his young cousin's eyes again.

"I wouldn't – I mean, I didn't – I mean, there's nothing to–"

Adam reached out and bopped his king lightly on the head. "Stop that, Damien. Apologize."

"Sorry, Angelos," Damien said automatically, and laughed as the young knight's eyes widened. "What? He's been *my* swordmaster longer than he's been *yours.* Don't tell me you didn't recognize that 'disappointed swordmaster' tone in Adam's voice. Or that you wouldn't react exactly the same."

Angelos looked like he was trying to squirm again...

Adam shook his head. "I assume Alanna sent you back to check that we aren't leaving stragglers behind."

The young knight bobbed his head quickly. "Um, yes, sir. We can't see the tail of the train – and the wagons with His Ma– um, Damien's – um, His Grace's tent while we're traveling through all these canyons. And I'm to keep track of it all until we're at Castle Stellarine."

She really *was* irritated, then. Guarding the tail of a train of wagons and horses – the 'dust-eater' position – was honorable work... But it was also a clear sign of disgrace when assigned to the Official Commander of the troupe. Not to mention whatever else might be happening between the two younger people.

"Go on then," Adam gestured, and Angelos turned his horse and headed on his errand with a look of relief. He'd clearly rather eat dust than deal with Alanna just now.

"You need to stop teasing that boy, Damien," the Champion commented, turning in his saddle to do a visual check of the outriders and the rest of their column for himself. "You're switching back and forth between treating him like a favorite cousin and 'just another' Royal Guard. He doesn't know what to do with it."

"I do that with *you* all the time," the King pointed out a little defensively.

"*I'm* used to it. *He's* not."

Damien sighed. "And what *else* am I supposed to do, Adam? He *is* one of my Guards. *Our* Guards. Your *Highness*." He snickered slightly.

Adam glowered at him halfheartedly. "Perhaps we *should* have the Guards follow local custom as well. Clearly, all this formality has gotten out of hand."

Which, unfortunately, was a reminder of the new problem at hand.

Damien sighed. "*Should* we both talk to Alanna? Or should it just be you?"

Adam looked ahead at the stiff back of the young woman riding point. "*Neither* of us right now, not if we really do want to keep Angelos' name out of it. It's fairly obvious that she sent him off because he was trying to talk her down a bit. And that he stopped to talk to us. Though I suppose that does mean I'd better apprise her that you're fine with stopping at the stream for some gussying up."

Damien waved a hand to indicate he knew that. "Fine. But later? And... we probably need to find out just how much she, ah, *knows.*"

He paused.

"About *us,*" he clarified, just in case there was any question.

Adam gave him a dry look. "Looking forwards to conversations with Aryllis and Tim when we get home?"

Because Alanna reported to Aryllis and Angelos reported to Tim... And Aryllis and Tim were married, so what one knew the other tended to anyways. Which made for more efficient Royal Guards *(of both types)* but wasn't particularly helpful for keeping secrets.

The King winced. "Definitely *not.* But it would be nice to know just *what* those conversations are going to be *about.* Both of them – and our higher-potential Guards, like Alanna – are surely aware of the problems inherent with Emmeren's birth. If it's possible for *that* to be the only topic..."

"Alanna... *and* Angelos," Adam noted. "And the rest of the others we brought along on this traveling circus. We recruit them for their intelligence and loyalty, *then* train for the physical and observational skills. And he's *your* cousin, which should tell us something, even if we hadn't already seen evidence for how clever that boy is."

That was... fair.

And something Damien wasn't really ready to deal with right now.

Not when there were other things to worry about.

"She's been running interference for us at the inns, Adam. If she's figured out *why–*"

"You gave her a perfectly reasonable explanation that first night, Damien," Adam said with... possibly misplaced equanimity. "And a perfectly *true* one, even if incomplete. Elaarwen-Manifest *did* tell me to stay close to you."

"Adam..."

"And I'm your Champion. Which *usually* goes with the duties of a bodyguard."

"At least since Queen Marian's day," Damien muttered. "Not that Grandfather usually had *his* Champions serve that role."

Adam gave him an amused nod. "And we'd all rather you follow *her* example than his. In anything."

The King gave him an unnerved look. "Adam... you *know* what Queen Marian says *she* used the position of Champion for."

The ghost of Damien's great-great-grandmother had been quite blunt. Though whether she had named her lovers to the position or had simply made lovers of those who earned the title fairly... Damien had never really wanted to ask for clarifications on. Especially once she started twitting him about Jason. And then Adam.

His own Champion rolled his eyes. "I *do* talk to the old biddy myself now, Damien. And she's not exactly shy or subtle. So, yes. But that was nearly a century ago. No one remembers details like that now."

"Hmmmn." Damien fixed his eyes on... Alanna's stiff back. "Where I was *originally* going with this was that we've been up here before. You have permanent separate quarters here, just as I do."

And that suite had been designated for *him* and *Jason* to share – and at the initiative of Genevieve's people and not at her order, she had told them. It had been a gift of acceptance that had nearly brought the cynical Adam to tears. They had been designated those rooms years before Damien had dared to suggest he would support them making their relationship into a marriage.

Elaarwen really was a very different place than Emeralsee. Or Siovale.

"We've only been barely able to get away with having you 'sleep across my threshold' in the villages without offending anyone," Damien forged on. "Alanna's 'explanations' about magick they can't see hasn't been what they care about. They've been kindhearted about letting you all look paranoid because of everything that's happened in the last year – but there's no way that's going to fly in Castle Stellarine."

"It's not really that big of a problem, Damien."

The King pursed his lips and avoided looking at his Champion. "I'm sure that's what you'll think when *Elaarwen-Manifest* decides again that you don't *belong–*"

"Damien..." Adam's tone was chastising. "We're not *alone.*"

Which was true. Even if their Guards were following their standing orders and staying out of earshot of a quiet conversation. After all, they weren't supposed to be privy to every policy discussion between the King and his closest advisor.

"Don't belong *here,* was what I was going to say," Damien threw his... *friend...* a dry look. "Because, as we've told Alanna and she's told everyone else, that *was* why you and Angelos became sick. And that *he* didn't need my closer attention because – as even he says – he just doesn't have all that much magick."

Adam gave him a disconcerted look. "Neither do I."

It was Damien's turn to roll his eyes. Why Adam felt that *this* was the hill he had to die on, the King had no idea, but it wasn't really all that important.

"Whatever. Somehow, I doubt *Elaarwen-Manifest* is sufficiently convinced, but if *you* want to test the question... Not that I can see what *else* we can do while we're staying in Castle Stellarine."

Which he did have to do for at least a few days, no matter if the Soul of the Province wanted him – them – to hurry on to this 'earth-kisses-sky' place, wherever it might be. Genevieve hadn't been home to Elaarwen in over a year, nor was she likely to make it up here for awhile yet, given her pregnancy and that she'd then have a nursing babe.

And there were certain things that *couldn't* legally be resolved by the Stellarine cousin who was her chatelaine and steward. Things like new – or resurgent – blood-feuds, for example, or certain matters of inheritance.

But Damien, as her Duke-Consort, *could* see to those matters in her place.

Not to mention that the people *missed* their 'Lassie.' And in a more than sentimental fashion.

The Bound ruler of a place had to maintain a certain level of connection to it – usually by being in residence for a significant amount of time. If they didn't, the Land and the people *and* the ruler would all begin to sicken.

But Damien could stand in for her here magickally, too. And stand for Elaarwen to Genevieve.

"It's still not a problem, Damien," Adam asserted. "You can just *Vanish* yourself over to my quarters once you have the door to your own suite locked. It's not as if you usually make use of valets or have the servants bring you breakfast in bed or anything, so no one will even notice."

Well, yes, and that *had* occurred to Damien.

"*Alanna* is going to wonder," he pointed out. "Especially when we have to move on because you still insist on following that map-that-isn't-a-map off to Gods-know-where."

Though, properly, that was a separate question.

He'd looked over Adam's sketch numerous times by now, including with copious and incomprehensible 'explanations' over his shoulder from Adam.

Granted, he *might* have been a tad distracted at least *some* of those times by Adam's warm breath on his ear. Followed by kisses along his shoulders and the rather abruptly urgent need to set the 'map' down somewhere safely while it was still possible to do so.

The slightly smug look on Adam's face just now suggested he was remembering the same things Damien was.

"You keep calling it that," the Champion commented. "The thing is plain as day to read."

It was *not*.

The '*map*' had strange swirling strokes that circled and eddied around gaps that might have been lakes in the sorts of maps that Damien was used to interpreting. But there weren't any lakes of those sizes in Elaarwen, let alone ones that numerous, and Adam insisted that the Entity had told him the '*map*' was of somewhere in the province.

Eddies...

Swirling...

Interpretable by *Adam,* but not by Damien, who was Bound to the Earth here...

The King frowned. He felt like he was on the edges of figuring this out, but there was some critical piece that he didn't...

No, he had the sense that he knew what it was, but... he hadn't looked at it in the right way yet?

Why did it feel more as if he was *refusing* to realize what he needed to make sense of it all?

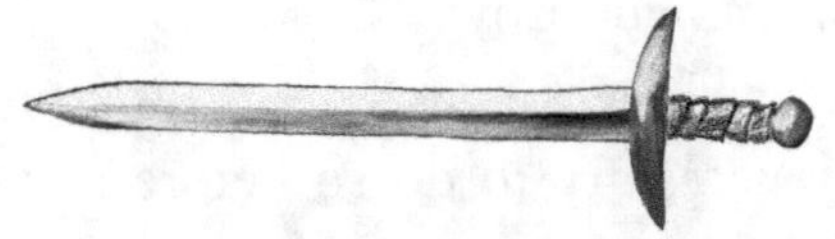

Chapter SIX

Possibilities

"**I** THINK IT'S BEEN LONG enough," Adam announced. "I'm going to go have a word with Alanna. Keep your eyes on the road, Damien, even if your head *is* in the clouds. That poor horse of yours can only do so much if you're wool-gathering. And it would be a little embarrassing if you fell off. Even if you *can* trounce all of your Guards in the practice-ring."

The King gave him an affectionately annoyed look at the backhanded compliment, and waved the tall Champion away. As if he'd *ever* fallen off a horse, even in those early days when Adam had been teaching him to ride.

Adam chuckled and moved his horse up to a trot to catch up to Alanna on hers. It was... briefly distracting to Damien to watch Adam posting easily along. The man looked... altogether too enchanting with his rear bobbing along just out of his saddle like that, the edges of the uniform jacket he still wore despite no longer being a Royal Guard not quite covering all that interesting musculature and his dark blonde hair flopping a bit as it picked up brighter highlights in the afternoon sunshine. By the end of Summer, Adam's hair would be bleached nearly as pale as Jason's more golden locks, but right now it was on the edges of a light brown.

It was hard to tear his eyes away.

And completely necessary to do so before anyone else noticed his... avid attention to details he shouldn't even be noticing.

Damien had, he thought rather guiltily, grown entirely too comfortable with this state of affairs that had Adam sleeping with him every night. He was... *happy,* unquestionably. And, erm, *satisfied.* And it *was* working to keep Elaarwen-Manifest from harassing the other man.

For the short-run – provided they were able to keep their clever, observant Royal Guards (of both ilks) from noticing – it was a ... fairly *wonderful* solution.

But it was doing nothing to make the inevitable, critical, *essential* dissevering of this facet of their, um, *friendship* any easier in the long-run. Rather the opposite, if anything.

Damien *probably* should be spending some thought on the long-term problem. It required a creative, thoughtful, *kind* resolution that would work for Adam, Jason, Genevieve, their future children, the people of Ilseador... and maybe even himself. Something that *didn't* require living a life half in shadows and lies.

And nevermind that it was hard to fight down his current sense of happiness and perfect well-being to concentrate on the *problem* that he knew this mess was. Intellectually, anyways.

Damien *should* be trying to come up with that solution.

But instead of being able to focus on solving any of that, one of the phrases his... *friend*... had used kept coming back to Damien: 'head in the clouds.'

It was just such an... *Adam* thing to say. He'd used it much more often on Damien back when he had prised the young prince out of the Royal Library and taken him out of doors – in a courtyard within Castle Alsterling – to learn swordwork and riding, but the phrase was still incredibly familiar.

The whole, huge world – and especially the open *sky* – had been quite overwhelming to the young prince back then, after nearly seven years immured in the Royal Library. Sometimes Damien had spent half their practice sessions staring in humbled awe at the open sky above him. To be fair, the usually-brusque Adam had always seemed to understand Damien's need to absorb all that sky... and had diverted any impatience on the part of the usually imperturbable Jason.

In fact, Jason hadn't taken on the bulk of Damien's training until the prince had gotten used to the sky and quit staring at it so much that he couldn't focus on anything else. That... was a detail that Damien had been aware of, but never really thought about before.

How much of Adam's 'impatience' was an act? How much of Jason's 'patience' was really to Adam's credit instead, setting up a situation of contrast to make Jason appear so? And was Jason aware that he was being shepherded into always presenting that contrast in behavior to Adam? *(Not that it worked in all situations, though. Damien wasn't the only student they'd trained who found Adam easier to confide in, despite the former Captain's prickly exterior.)*

Nonetheless, the phrase 'head in the clouds' had been reasonably appropriate to describe the younger Damien. Even when he wasn't staring at the sky, he'd been quiet and distractable, absorbing all of the things he'd had so little exposure to in the Library and that Adam and Jason and Ciriis had been so determined to embed him into.

Adam had used the phrase 'wool-gathering' frequently as well. And the latter had somehow seemed less to do with sheep, when Adam used it on Damien, and more of a reference to the fluffier clouds...

Sifwisa, the Goddess of the Trade-Winds Who had rescued Damien from the conundrum he had found himself in during his battle with Azella's demon, had referred to Adam as belonging to Her.

Adam... with all that near-blinding *blaze* of magick that he refused to admit to possessing...

Adam... whose *empathy* was ridiculously strong for someone who wasn't a Healer...

Adam... whose entire *family* seemed quite *Gifted*...

Could it be that Adam was – or at least had the potential to be – an actual Elemental *mage*? Like Damien himself, but with a natural affinity for *Air* instead of for Earth?

That... might explain what Adam had relayed as Elaarwen's confusion that he 'didn't belong anywhere.'

Air didn't after all – it belonged everywhere and nowhere. And while that was probably perfectly natural for *actual* air, the 'Element' as manifest in a single, individual *human* might well seem strange to a Being that was all the Land Itself.

*Her*self, Adam had said. Elaarwen apparently considered *Her*self to be female. Or at least feminine in some sense.

Not that any of this explained why *She* couldn't, or wouldn't, talk to Damien directly.

He'd tried, a day or two after that first romantic, firefly-lit walk with Adam, to make contact with Elaarwen as distinct from the rest of the Realm.

Damien's retinue had camped that evening at the mouth of one of the innumerable canyons that carved their way up from the feet of the mountains. This one was an older canyon, the stream which had smoothed those granite walls over the eons of its efforts was already down to a single, clear trickle – though boulders and uprooted trees and the fresh, dark scars where one or both had impacted the walls in the Spring floods made it clear that this little brook wasn't *tamed*, but only *resting*.

This time it had been Damien's idea to wander away from their guards. Just a *little* away from the others, and Adam had been there to protect him if his magickal protections should somehow fail in the attempt. Not that there had been any sense of other people – such as bandits – anywhere nearby, nor even bears or wolves or mountain lions. Adam's argument of their previous private expedition had worked again, of course, as far as Alanna and the rest were concerned.

The King needed quiet and privacy to try this... thing that didn't make sense to him. The idea of trying to talk to *just* Elaarwen, felt like trying to have a conversation with Adam's hand alone. Not that Adam's hands couldn't be quite... eloquent at times...

Damien had first removed his boots and stockings to let his feet make contact with the cool, soft earth. That was Elaarwen, right? The living soil, the network of moss and roots and mycelia that connected plant-life everywhere...

It hadn't worked.

Elaarwen's soil was rich and dark, but it was still only a thin, scanty layer over the timeless masses of ancient bedrock. There were too many bare spots where soil had eroded away with wind or water – or simply never existed. The soil and the life it contained weren't *contiguous*, the way they were in Siovale or Reyensweir – or even Emeralsee with its thoroughly overbuilt and cobbled city.

So, Damien had thought that perhaps it was *rock* he needed to make contact with instead.

They'd wandered on a little farther, to the water-smoothed wall of cliff that defined the small side-canyon. Damien had splayed his bare hands against the weathered rock, standing close to let his toes make contact with it as well.

And when none of *that* had worked more than to give him anything besides an inaudible, nonverbal *hummm* that suggested the province was *happy* and *healthy* – which he already knew – the increasingly frustrated King had shed his shirt and jacket, hoping that still *greater* contact would make real communication possible.

And then his pants, to Adam's *amusement*... But after all, Elaarwen thought of Herself as female, so was it possible that Genevieve was somehow Her embodiment as Bound Duchess? And therefore, mightn't She expect Damien to come to Her as he did to Genevieve?

Perhaps not, though he made himself thoroughly, uncomfortably cold in places that shouldn't ever really get chilled like that. He'd resisted being sensible and giving up until Adam had started shivering with *Damien's* chill and had yanked him away from the canyon wall to warm him up.

And *that* had ended the way he might have guessed had he been thinking about anything other than not being *left out* by Land to which he was *Bound,* for crying out loud. And that had been lovely, too, and there had definitely been *communication,* but not with Elaarwen.

Though he'd rather thought that the Land had seemed a little frustrated Itself as well. *Herself.*

Why was this so hard? He communicated with *Ilseador* just fine. Though usually not in words.

It is because you are not Complete, came another, strangely verbose answer from his Realm that had usually been so quiescent since It/They had made Its/Their peace with Damien remaining outside of the fabric of magick rather than melding wholly with it. *You* **belong** *to Me/Us, but to Elaarwen only at a remove thusfar.*

Or... it was another *attempt* at an answer, since this one made about as much sense to Damien as Its/Their previous tries.

So Elaarwen could talk to **Genevieve***?* Damien tried to ask.

Perhaps... The Realm seemed doubtful. *The Other who stands between you and Elaarwen is also Incomplete. Although she is a little closer to Completion? The situation is !*!&!*

The concept that the Realm was trying to convey seemed to be a combination of quicksand and muddy water... and of skies and rivers thick with smoke and ash.

Murky? Damien suggested, and had his definition turned over thoughtfully a few times before it was approved.

Yes. 'Murky.' You are both very close to Complete. And neither one of you is properly Anchored yet. Though she – Our/My Queen – has managed to Anchor you on her own through sheer Will in the past.

Which was a rather oblique reference to how the Realm had tried to *eat* Damien every time he sat on the Throne these last several years, and how Genevieve had stopped It/Them. Not to mention that he was *talking* to the very Being who had tried to *eat* him...

But you have grown, and she is unlikely to be able to do so again and survive.

Well... *that* was a chilling pronouncement. Though Damien had also managed to sit the Throne all on his own, without Genevieve's protective presence. since returning from Azella's Keep with his improved trove of knowledge. So, maybe it wasn't as bad as all that... but he'd still rather not test the question.

What do you mean by 'Anchor'? Damien asked.

Not that he couldn't at least hazard a guess. The still all-too-recent memories of the Realm trying to suck him bodily into Its/Their Own magickal fabric still woke him with occasional nightmares. Or maybe It/They had only been after his soul; Damien had been a bit too preoccupied with trying to get free to tell. The last time had only been last Fall, after all.

It/They seemed to realize he was remembering those not-always-agreeable parts of their relationship... and maybe feeling a tad... *guilty?* Was that why It/They was trying so hard to explain what seemed to be unexplainable? The Realm had never before been so direct, for all that half of what It/They was 'saying' still made no sense to him.

But there *was* a question that he should ask, for all that he wasn't sure he wanted the answer.

Is... is that why she couldn't carry a baby to term? Or... was it because she didn't bide her pregnancies here in Elaarwen? Damien had begged her to do so, when it became clear that none of their other ideas were working.

That idea seemed startling to the Realm. Or perhaps even amusing.

There was a definite sense of negation.

The opposite, if anything. It is because she is so close to being Complete that **this** *baby will survive. The others were lost because she was not Anchored. The ones that were begun in Elaarwen even moreso.*

Damien hadn't even been aware that Genevieve had miscarried in Elaarwen. He couldn't even remember her having *visited* Elaarwen when they knew she was pregnant... which was odd, now that he thought about it. Had *she* known about this problem on some level? Or... did this finally explain why she hadn't conceived a child by Harald in eight years of marriage as far as anyone had ever been able to tell?

Just how *many* miscarriages had his strong, wonderful wife suffered? Did even she know, if they had been very early ones as the Realm seemed to suggest? She'd told him shortly before they were wed – in a brief paroxysm of self-doubt such as he'd never seen before or since – that she wasn't sure if she *could* bear a child because her courses had always been so erratic.

Had her courses been erratic because she had been miscarrying repeatedly as the province that she loved literally devoured her unborn children? Damien had never thought to inquire if Genevieve's monthly courses had been more regular *before* she married Harald. Or... after.

He tried not to ask about those days unless she brought it up first, after all.

As to what it is to be Anchored... The Realm seemed perplexed on how to clarify what was so obvious to It/Them. *Anchoring is what happens when you are Complete.*

And how can I tell when I have become Complete? Damien tried to tackle the problem from the other side.

You will know because you are Anchored, the Realm replied, giving Damien a sense that it was just as baffled with his incomprehension as he was himself.

"I thought I told you *not* to have your head in the clouds while you're riding."

Adam had returned and was re-aligning his steed with Damien's palfrey. His teasing tone chased away Damien's sense of the Realm. There was a sense that the Realm felt he should give his attention to his Champion – rather the way one can tell when someone else is relieved to escape an uncomfortable conversation.

Likely It/They would not be so forthcoming even if Adam went away again.

And 'Champion' wasn't exactly the way the Realm seemed to think of Adam... He was, after all, the one who had taken It/Them most seriously when Damien was sequestered in Azella's Keep.

It/They seemed to consider the tall, blonde knight nearly as precious to Itself as Damien.

Which was more than confusing, it was almost... upsetting.

It also was what it was and he might as well make the best of things.

"How's Alanna?"

That easy expression that Adam had been wearing so much more these last several days went sardonic again. "She's being stubborn. But she'll be sensible in the end."

Damien looked ahead at the young woman. Her posture was still quite correct... but there was that hint of hunching in that often followed a younger person's 'improving' conversation with Adam channeling his persona of swordmaster.

"Did you figure out why she's reacting so strongly?" Damien asked. His Champion sounded acerbic and always gave out some rather pointed suggestions in these sorts of conversations... but he actually listened more than he spoke and usually could figure out the sources of a young person's problems. Gods knew, he'd done so for Damien enough times over the years.

Adam sighed. "It's... complicated. She won't tell me everything, but a part of it *is* what Angelos suggested – she's upset with Aldred for putting you and Genevieve in a dangerous position, and she's conflating him with the province."

That made sense as much as such things ever did. But...

"Only part?"

A nod. "Her family had a baronetcy in Cedarwen, but they fled to Siovale some twenty years ago. I'm gathering that she's feeling... disconnected. As if she *should* belong in Elaarwen, but... doesn't."

"That's hardly surprising," Damien commented, though Alanna had also seemed perfectly fine the *last* time they'd been here. "She would have been what? five? six? when her family fled? I was *eight* when we left Ravenscroft and I don't have much of a connection there. And you were eleven and your mother's Named Heir, but you clearly aren't all that attached to Lynncrag, given that you've spent the last half year trying to get Baronetta Linda to divest you of it."

Adam gave him an odd look, but another nod.

"True. And actually," Adam winced slightly, "that's been one of my arguments to Mama about why she should Name Desirée. It's not just that she's spent her whole life there and I've been home for maybe a total of three months in the last twenty-two years. It's that Siri is *connected* to Lynncrag in a way I don't think I ever could be.

"I *do* love it there," he added candidly. "It's home in many ways and always will be. But so is Emeralsee. And even Elaarwen. I don't need to *live* in Lynncrag. If I never went there again it wouldn't hurt me any. Although that's not an ideal end, in my opinion."

Adam was quiet for a moment, and Damien was left to ruminate over the notion that Adam didn't feel any call to go back home. It seemed... a rather alien idea.

"I think Jason feels more or less the same about Brindlewell," the Champion added at last. "Though I think *place* matters more to him than it does to me. I honestly don't care *where* I am – provided it's not some sort of hellhole like the Emeralsee docks district or Minglemere in *most* seasons–" he rolled his eyes in memory of their one visit to the fief that always seemed to be half flooded and entirely muddy "– so long as he and Genevieve and *you* are there most of the time. And the children, eventually. Of course."

"And your family, I assume," Damien said, still trying to wrap his head around this. Not that he could really disagree with how Adam was describing himself *or* Jason. But it would never have occurred to him on his own to even think about that as a distinction.

A brief smile swept Adam's face. "Yes. I don't want to lose them. Again. Though if I *had* to choose..."

Well, they all knew whom he would choose. Whom he *had*.

Though Angelos' revelations of the other day suggested that... that might not have been what any of them thought it was at the time.

"And there are a fair number of friends I'd prefer to keep contact with," Adam was going on. "Tim and Aryllis and so on. My former students, like Alanna and Angelos and even that idiot Marcos."

He gave Damien a wry look. "At this point I think I've trained something like half the knights in this Realm."

It was only a slight exaggeration.

"But we were talking about Alanna," Adam returned to the original issue. "I think... she's another like you. Or maybe more like Genevieve. *Place* is important to her. And since Cedarwen swears to Brindlewell, and Brindlewell is *supposed* to swear to Elaarwen... she feels like she *should* belong here... and she doesn't. Quite. It's making her feel unsettled and... grumpy."

"I've been trying to figure out a good time to give Brindlewell and its vassals back to Elaarwen," Damien commented. "Having Alexa's oath directly made... political sense. But Genevieve and I have both been uncomfortable about it."

He sighed, looking over his shoulder as if he could see back along the winding road and intervening mountains to the county where Jason had been born and where his grandmother, Countess Alexa Solway, was immured for the rest of her days. Likely not all *that* immured, given that Damien hadn't said she couldn't still rule the place, just that she couldn't leave the county.

Because his head was turned, he missed the thoughtful, measuring look Adam gave him.

"I suppose it's a matter between Jason and Genevieve now," the King added as he turned back. "And I can't imagine *he'll* want to take Alexa's oath, so that should get properly resolved. At last."

Not that that was likely to do Alanna any good, since she'd still be a transplant with her parents in Siovale and herself mostly in Emeralsee. Assuming that was the problem at all. Damien had never noticed any particular abundance of magick about, well, *any* of his guards.

He tried looking at the commander of his Guards to see her magick. But it was close to noon, and whatever aura she might have had beyond the normal amount that kept everyone alive was swamped out by the bright, physical light of the sun.

"No, probably not," Jason's husband agreed, then heaved a sigh. "*I* wouldn't mind never having to see that... *woman* again myself. But I imagine we'll have to go back home that way. To see Raphael in Cedarwen, at least."

And they probably *should* check to make sure Alexa didn't have some inordinate amount of sympathy from her people that might result in her breaking her banishment. Though when it came to politics the woman had always been a follower, not a leader, she'd been a decent liege-lady to anyone outside of her immediate family.

"The day we crossed the Sapphire, Angelos said Alanna was mildly affected by... whatever happened to him. And you," Damien noted. There wasn't really anything else to be said about Countess Solway, after all.

"So, he did." Adam hesitated. "I'm... actually wondering if the attraction between them – which she admitted isn't all just on his side, although she was fairly elliptical about it – is more that Angelos is connected enough to Elderwyld that he carries a certain sense of the *place* with him. And given that Alanna's – grandmother, I think it was – was an Eldridge... perhaps she feels enough of an affinity *through* him..."

The King had heard enough comments from various nobles that they found it bemusing to discover that the young knights and squires and ladies and gentlemen found their sharp and cynical former Captain to be a sympathetic ear for their confidences. The cheerful Duke Zachary of Dalziallest had found the whole idea hilarious, and Duke Quillian of Reyensweir had given Adam odd looks for an entire week when the topic had come up in discussion. Even Genevieve had been startled – though that was years ago, of course. *Damien* knew the prickly exterior was a shelter for Adam's overly-sensitive heart, but then he'd known Adam for half their lives.

"So, it might not be true love everlasting?" Damien said softly and with a slight hint of sarcasm. "That's... a little sad."

Though it rarely was at that age, not that most young nobles had the opportunity to discover that the hard way given arranged marriages and other parental expectations. Adam's brother Lorenzo and Angelos's sister Julietta apparently notwithstanding.

Adam gave him a wry look. "It might *grow* into something more – but not if Alanna discovers she *needs* to go back to the family's holding in Cedarwen. Because I think Angelos isn't going to want to – or maybe be *able* to – settle anywhere else than Elderwyld if I'm reading *him* right."

Damien winced. "Their *former* holding in Cedarwen. When the family fled, Grandfather gave it over to one of his favorites. Over Baron Anvliyar's protests, I might add."

"Raphael's father, that would have been," Adam nodded. Raphael Anvliyar... who should have been Damien's brother-in-law – or possibly even King by now, at the side of Damien's sister. "And I suppose *that* fellow's oath held? The one who replaced Alanna's family?"

Damien shrugged uncomfortably. "Raphael's did. Not that I really ever doubted *him*. I haven't Bound most of the baronets, as you know."

Such as Adam's mother.

Adam sighed. "Well, let's hope that Alanna doesn't feel particularly *drawn* to be there then. Or that she can re-define her *home* in a more welcoming location, as Genevieve has seemed able to do. I can't imagine that a man who was a favorite of King Reginald's enough to be awarded a fief would exactly welcome her as a daughter."

Damien winced again. "But if she's – I suppose you're implying that she has some affinity for Earth-magery, even if she hasn't enough to really use it for anything. Then she might very well *be* connected to the place where she was born. Whether or not she wants to be."

"She *can* make a different choice, Damien," Adam told him firmly. "Birth isn't destiny."

"*Can* she, though?" the King asked sadly. "*I* can't really imagine not returning to Emeralsee's City. And no matter that I'm Bound to the entire Realm. At least," he added with a sigh, "at least *now* I can *leave* occasionally."

Adam was giving him that odd look again. "Damien... *you* were born in Ravenscroft, in the barony of Elderwyld. Not in the City."

The King looked away from that wise, golden-hazel gaze. Adam had found him when he was fourteen because of his nightmares, he'd said. Had worked to alter the lost young prince's dreams into better ones. If Adam hadn't recognized the place that the *good* dreams happened in... well, Damien wasn't going to enlighten him.

It wasn't as if Damien *could* go back to Ravenscroft for any length of time, after all. And his mother's next-younger brother's family was overflowing the place, her five still-younger-siblings having taken themselves off to find their own homes and fortunes as the 'cottage' filled up. He couldn't – well, *wouldn't* – kick his numerous cousins out of *their* home just to have the place as his own.

And the Castle – and City – really *were* the place he belonged. Even the Realm agreed.

"It's likely different for me. Because of the Sword. And the Throne."

"Hmmmn." Adam didn't *actually* disagree, but he sounded – and *felt,* as Damien's not-completely-unwillingly-entangled *empathy* informed him – altogether too *thoughtful.*

"We're approaching the stream," the King noted to distract them both. "Time to get gussied up for all the mountain-folk who won't care."

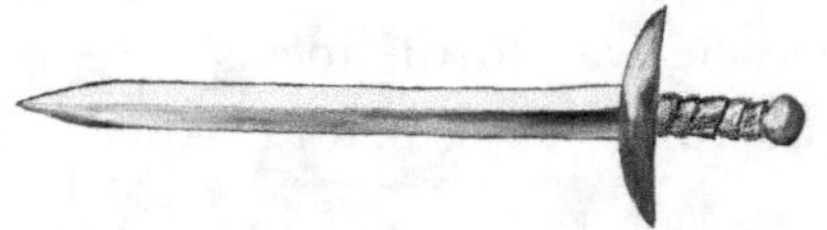

Chapter SEVEN

Confidences

I T TOOK AN HOUR OR SO to get everyone prettied up to Alanna's standards.

Which *did* include Angelos riding along ahead of everyone with the Royal Standard flying over his head from a pole jammed into his stirrup. Not that the young knight looked like the small discomfort bothered him in the slightest – and certainly not by comparison to the way his eyes lit up when Alanna told him to take point and ride at her side as advance guard for Damien and Adam.

It took another hour of riding the last dozen miles of the winding road up from Emeralsee to reach the edges of 'Elaarwen's city.'

It took all the *rest* of the afternoon to make it the couple of miles from the edges of Elaarwen's 'city' to the gates of Castle Stellarine.

Everyone in the grandiosely-labeled small town had to turn out to see Damien, from the smallest babe and busiest farmer to the oldest granny, carried out on her chair by a pair of strong young lads. And as he'd predicted, Damien ended up dismounting so that he could greet everyone individually. It drove his Royal Guards a little crazy, he knew, but he still felt it was the Right Thing to do.

Adam, at least, was used to this by now. He stayed at Damien's heel and – known as he was to the locals here as much as in the wayside inns along the road – came in for his own measure of friendly welcome.

As did the others who had been up here before, including Alanna and Angelos. It clearly touched the young knight's heart as much as it dismayed his lovely commander. As best Damien could tell while engrossed with his own set of greetings, Angelos spent the distance running interference for the increasingly unhappy Alanna.

By the time they made it under the castle's barbican and Genevieve's chatelaine and steward, Adsel Topasirre – a cousin from her mother's side – had charge of the entire troupe, it was clear that the young woman needed a break.

Damien barely needed a glance at Adam to communicate a plan. The King offered his arm to Lady Alanna and had her walk with him while Adam took charge of working with Lord Adsel to see all the knights and ladies and gentlemen properly housed.

They'd done this sort of thing before after all.

Though thank goodness *Elaarwen-Manifest* was giving him and Adam a long enough leash to actually be able to do so.

Angelos was distracted by having to fill his place as Official Commander, but Damien made sure to give the young knight a small nod before whisking the... not-quite-as-young woman out of the way.

"Do you want to talk, Alanna?" the King asked as he guided her through the stone rabbit-warren that was Castle Stellarine. He'd been here enough times in the last five years to know his way around – even if he hadn't memorized the floorplans when he was twelve or so in his eternal – *and* ultimately fruitful – pursuit of all-things-Genevieve.

Just now, he was taking the unhappy young woman out to the lists – the jousting and arms-practice area that legend said had been installed by Duke Siegfrid to please his wife, the Grand Duchess Alicia. Genevieve's grandparents... there was a post out there covered in slashes that supposedly commemorated each one of Duchess Alicia's jousting victories.

The place was unlikely to be in use at this time of day, and it was fairly private.

Actually, Damien mused as he found the pair of them seats in the bleachers looking down over the jousting grounds, the area was probably unused most of the time when he wasn't here. Adam would have their whole troupe out here at practice shortly after dawn, if he was running true to form. The Elaarwen men-at-arms who were off-duty would likely join them then, and again in the hours before dinner. And likely Damien along with them, at least one of those times – *he* needed to stay in fighting-trim at least as much as the men and women who were tasked to protect him, after all.

But the Elaarwen men-at-arms – tough and formidable mountain-folk that they were – usually had other, more urgent, tasks when their duke and duchess weren't in residence. They were hunters and fishermen and farmers and smiths and served in the Castle Guard on a rotating schedule that had to be planned around all those other commitments. Elaarwen simply wasn't prosperous or populous enough to maintain a set of people who had to do nothing else but train when there wasn't anyone around to need them regularly.

Luckily, with the province so far interior to Ilseador – and surrounded by almost-impassable mountains on the other sides – there was little need for any permanent armed force. The tiny mountain-communities largely policed themselves and their neighbors and reached out to the ducal seat when a problem was beyond their capacity – which it rarely was.

Outlawry happened, of course, but there was a sort of unspoken agreement that the outlaws shouldn't prey upon their own people. It made the problem of bandits in the foothill margins – in Siovale and Brindlewell and Dalziallest – worse, but any bandit who turned on the mountain-folk quickly found themselves at the sharp end of... rather a lot of their kinfolk's sharp, pointy objects.

Genevieve's patron Goddess – as much as she had any such thing – was the nameless Maiden of the Hunt, in token of her obligation to take the lead on dealing with any such offenders. And in silent affirmation of just what she was expected to *do* with such offenders, though presumably the offenses would have to be pretty damned dire before that issue came into play.

Elaarwen's poor relations with the neighboring fiefs and provinces – in addition to its poverty and paucity of people – had been the reason why the birth of the Rebellion had taken King Reginald by surprise. The idea that Siovale would actually *ally* with the source of most of its usual troubles had seemed rather inconceivable.

Rosa's father's – and grandmother's and *great*-grandmother's – refusal to ally County Zialest with Elaarwen had made perfect sense at the time. Even Rosa herself might not have made the alliance, despite her personal 'admiration' for Genevieve and her sympathies for the Rebellion... if not for Prince Oskar having used the night before her wedding to slaughter her family and claim *droit d'signeur.*

To this day, Genevieve refused to admit that she should have done anything other than suffer through her abusive marriage to Harald of Siovale to maintain Elaarwen's alliance. And although he would never admit to agreeing with that, Damien had studied the history of the situation enough to see her point.

"I'm sorry, Your Majesty," Alanna began stiffly. "I'm afraid I don't know what you mean."

She had withdrawn her hand from Damien's arm as soon as he settled her in her seat, and now fidgeted with the brocaded skirts of her dark green riding habit, avoiding his eye.

Damien half-perched on the balustrade separating the bleachered viewing stand from the practice-area and folded his arms, not letting his own gaze waver.

"Come now, Alanna," he said, letting the faintest hint of 'disappointed swordmaster' into *his* voice but keeping his tone mostly compassionate. "You know that Adam and I talk all the time."

The young woman dared a glare up at him. She was only slightly older than Jason's sister Elaina, but had lived a far harsher life, including having bloodied her sword years earlier in some of the Rebellion's bloodiest skirmishes against Crown troops.

Well, harsher save for Elaina's constant exposure to her grandmother-and-liege-lady.

Alanna's family was kind and caring and supportive as best Damien had been able to determine.

"He's not the Captain anymore," Alanna half-complained. "He's not in charge of us. He's one of the ones *we're* supposed to look after, so it goes the other way, if anything. And the rest of them *still* hop the instant he says to, or tuck their tails between their legs and act like small children caught with their hands in the cookie jar. Even *Angelos,*" she added, her gray-green eyes flashing with her aggrieved tone.

Probably she'd have liked to toss her auburn hair to emphasize the point, but she'd put it up in an elaborate chignon instead of her usual functional ponytail to impress... well, certainly not the people of Elaarwen.

Damien gave the young woman a wry look. "That's only natural, I suppose. He trained most of them – and Angelos is less than a full two years out from earning his shield, after all. You're the exception, you and Aaron and the rest who came to us from Genevieve's retinue."

"Babies, all of them," Alanna muttered. "Never seen a real battle. Never likely to – begging Your Majesty's pardon," she added a little belatedly.

The King gave a dismissive little wave of his hand. "That wasn't a *battle,* two months back, so you're right. Though I'd as soon none of those 'babies' ever *need* to learn what it's like to be in one for real."

Alanna made an uncomfortable *'hmmn,'* kind of noise, likely remembering that her King had been at Genevieve's side when the Queen retook the Castle from her former husband's coup. At least, that was the phrasing Damien had overheard some of Genevieve's former Rebels using in describing the incident.

Which was... rather understating his own involvement, for all that he'd yielded to Genevieve as the superior – and experienced – strategist.

Just now he raised an eyebrow at the young woman who... wasn't really as young as she should be, given her years. Killing another human aged you in ways that didn't usually show on the outside.

"Are you suggesting that you think one of them – Angelos, say – *should* have to learn what that's like?"

She gave him a shocked look. "No, sir! I mean, Your Majesty..."

Damien chuckled and sat down in the chair beside her. "It's just the two of us chatting here, Alanna. 'Damien' is fine for now."

Alanna gave him an uncertain look, then straightened up with that *stiff* look to her again. "No, *Damien*. And that's why I don't think it's wise to have all these people brushing up close to you like they've done since we came into Elaarwen. If any one of them means you harm, there's no other option *but* a pitched battle in that case, if we're to have any chance to get you and the Capt– Prince Adam out safely."

"A fair point," Damien conceded. "Though personally, I'm more concerned about any of my Guards or subjects being injured. You saw the enchantment I used to protect Jason two months ago. Adam and I are similarly protected."

She gave him a stubborn look. "And Genevieve, I assume. But it can't be a completely impervious protection or you wouldn't have worried when she faced off with Sir Adam. And you did."

The King nodded. "True. Though mostly that was because of the enchantments on the Monarch's Blade." He tapped the hilt of the Sword that was slung at his hip in reminder. "Which is why I didn't dare face her myself."

Because it had been Genevieve wielding the Monarch's Blade. Whether the Sword could understand that she had been *enspelled* to fight her husband and king – or whether it would even *care* – Damien still didn't know. The Sword's function, after all, was both to 'speak' for rightful heirs to the Throne and to cut off the heads of those who attempted to claim it in pursuit of a coup.

"Tim and Aryllis said that *they* knew that you and Genevieve were protected like that," Alanna's tone was accusing now. "But not Jason. Or Adam. And none of the *rest* of us knew."

Damien closed his eyes with the pain of that. "It's... like the existence of the Secret Cadre, Alanna. The more who know what your real role is, the less effective you'll be – and the more likely someone who means ill will find a way to circumvent *you,* specifically." He paused. "That said, it is to my everlasting regret that Aaron didn't know."

And to his everlasting regret that, when the Siovalese man-at-arms had lopped off Aaron's hand, Damien himself hadn't been in a position to do more than magickally cauterize the wound. In a different time and place he could have reattached the hand – though how much use of it Aaron would have had after, it was impossible to say.

He opened his eyes to see Alanna's shoulders had slumped a little.

"He'd have done it anyways," she said to her lap. "It... was less about saving Prince Jason than trying to stop Arabella from implicating herself as a willing traitor."

"I know," Damien said softly. He could have imagined trying the same thing himself.

They sat in silence for a moment.

"I just..." the young woman began at last, "I keep *seeing* that happening. Over and over and over. Which is... *silly,* is the only word I have for it. I saw much worse things happen on the battlefield. I *did* much worse things."

It came out in a rush, as if she couldn't quite bear to say the words, and couldn't quite bear *not* to.

Damien shivered. "You, too, then?"

He gave his – well, technically his *wife's* – lady-in-waiting a shaky nod as her gaze met his in startlement. It wasn't his imagination that a certain tension flowed away from her face when he did so.

"I've... done some horrible things," the King told her. "Not on a battlefield – the closest I've been to that was when we retook the Castle, and for the most part Genevieve and the rest kept me from getting involved in the actual fighting." He tried for a wry grin that... probably only partially succeeded. "You heard about 'pretty little Maree,' I imagine."

Alanna's automatic snicker – so she *had* heard the story – disappeared back into that... look of deeply hidden trauma all too quickly.

It was a look that Damien was all too familiar with seeing in the eyes of the people around him. *Eighty-three years* of his grandfather's increasingly corrupt and corrupting rule... The survivors were all damaged and he could only hope that that would change over time. The kind of Healing they needed was beyond the magick that he possessed.

Just like Genevieve, though *her* scars came from Harald's abuse rather than anything directly to do with King Reginald. And Jason's scars seemed to have come from his grandmother more than anything that had happened to him in the City.

Gods knew, Damien probably had those shadows in his own eyes, given the nightmares that still plagued him.

"I think..." Damien went on, "I think that Genevieve – all of them – were trying to protect me. They all seemed to have this idea that they wanted a king who was... *pure. Unsullied.*"

"Well, there was a reason for that," Alanna spoke up to defend the Queen she had adored since childhood. "After all those years of King Reginald's rule..."

She hesitated. Alanna was one of the people who were close enough to the royal set that she had likely heard Damien refer to the tyrannical Evil Wizard who had been his predecessor as 'Grandfather.' It was... no more than the truth, but it was a hard one for most people to swallow.

King Reginald had required his grandchildren to call him that – possibly being aware of what worse terms they might arrive at, else. Damien had intentionally kept up the habit. Partly to remind himself never to forget how he had ended up as king himself... of what he owed those more-worthy cousins and aunts and uncles – and his father and sister – who had never had the chance.

And partly to keep anyone else from forgetting his origins either.

If only someone had acted *sooner* to stop his grandfather...

"I know," Damien answered the brave young woman. "I knew it then, too. But it didn't really help. Not when I still had to deal with the traitors afterwards."

Nailing them up alive on Traitor's Wall... Damien always set the first nail, not sparing himself by handing off the dire necessity to anyone else.

Alanna looked... almost as greenish beneath the beginnings of a Summer tan as Adam had done when they crossed over the Sapphire some ten days ago. "I've never known what to think about that. That you... do that. You're such a gentle person, but..."

It was impossible to hold her gaze.

It would be incredibly wrong to look away.

"I can't ask someone else to do what I won't do myself," Damien said softly. "Though... I can't make myself do more than the one nail. Genevieve insisted. She thought I was going to faint and pitch myself off the scaffolding we were standing on." He winced. "I was too sick to make *her* stop. With Harald. I think I heard she set *three* nails before... before Tomas took a turn."

Alanna broke their gaze, swallowing hard. "She... that's what I heard, too. One for herself. One for Duke Aldred. And... one for you."

That made... a certain horrible sense.

Though he *really* hadn't needed to know that.

"It's... easier on the battlefield, I think," Alanna volunteered after a moment. "There's... no time to *think*. No time to second-guess yourself. You... just do what you have to in order to survive and move on. You don't... keep count or... or anything."

"I've heard there are some who do," Damien said a little dryly. "I'm rather glad you're not one of them."

Alanna shook her head. "No. Never. And... no, I don't want An– *any* of the others to have the chance to do that, either."

Adam had been convinced that the problem had been Alanna's connection to the Earth... That might still be a piece of things, but it wasn't the main part at all. Damien resisted the urge to feel a little smug that *he'd* gotten this out of her when *Adam* hadn't.

"How old were you, the first time you took the field, Alanna?" Damien asked.

She sighed a little. "Sixteen. At Deepenfeld. They said I was too young. But we needed more people and... I'd been training. I knew how to fight. It... it didn't feel *right* to let other people – people I *knew* and *cared for* – go out there and fight while I stayed back. One more sword, after all... If there was any chance I might make a difference..."

"I read the reports on that battle," the King told her. "You might have done."

He shook his head at her skeptical look. "No, I'm serious. It was... one of the closer ones."

Unsurprisingly, Alanna didn't look reassured.

Though... *mollified,* perhaps.

On the verge of tears... *definitely.*

"How can I ever go on?" the young woman asked, her tone hopeless. "I have all these... memories. I was older at nineteen than... any of those knights in your service. I'd been fighting for my life and the lives of those I loved – on *battlefields* – for three *years* by then. They seem so *young*... and that's... that's a *good* thing..."

"It is," Damien agreed, but didn't add anything. He could *feel* that Alanna had more she needed to say. And perhaps even to admit why she'd chosen *nineteen* as the age she'd compared. She was twenty-three now – so that was a year after his ascension to the Throne and marriage to Genevieve had ended the need for a Rebellion. Her claim of three years was... a bit overstated.

But Angelos wasn't quite twenty now...

If it came to that, Damien wasn't quite thirty himself. Not all that much older than Alanna.

He'd been about nineteen when she had begun her career on the battlefield. It had been the year that he'd finally let Adam and Jason and Ciriis persuade him to take permanent quarters outside of the Royal Library – the same isolated, securable suite in one of the Castle's towers that he and Genevieve still used now.

"Genevieve fought on battlefields," Alanna said after a very long moment. "And... *you* didn't. How do you...?" She flushed and looked down.

But it was obvious what she wanted to ask.

"How do *we* make it work?" Damien gave her a brief smile. "I gather you've been around both of us long enough to know that the soul-bond doesn't solve everything."

Alanna shook her head but didn't look up. "She... she said once that it just means you don't have a choice about finding a solution." And now the young woman *did* look up, with a rather wry expression. "She also said that you put her on such a pedestal that disagreements usually resolve without a great deal of effort on her part."

"And in her favor?" the King chuckled. "That's not because I adore her as a person, Alanna. It's because she's a very wise and thoughtful person and if she's actually willing to argue with me about something there's usually a very good reason behind it. One that she's thought through more carefully than I have.

"I have rather a multitude of things to keep track of," he pointed out. "It's only natural that I'll get some of them wrong – that's what a king's advisors are *for.*"

"Hmmn." That clearly didn't address Alanna's concerns. "And... the Captain? I mean, Sir Adam? *Prince* Adam? And Prince Jason?"

Damien felt his insides go... very still. He wasn't sure what she was asking – all that his *empathy* was picking up was the young woman's inner turmoil.

He wasn't used to using this skill so *intentionally* anyways, so he might be misreading... well, anything. As part of his Healing, or subconsciously to pick up clues that helped him sort out the people around him... it all came naturally.

But these last few days – as he'd become so close with Adam – the *empathy* seemed to be jumping out in front of him and making him much more mindful of his use of it. Which would be a good thing – eventually – once he got used to it.

Right now, it was just confusing.

"The two of them – Prince Jason was never on a battlefield either, was he?" Alanna elaborated, and Damien relaxed again.

"No," the King agreed. "He wasn't."

And it wasn't – or *shouldn't* be – within his ability to explain or even understand what sorts of nightmares Adam dealt with from his own time on the battlefield. Scars of the soul... though different ones than those that haunted Genevieve or Jason... or Damien.

Closer to what Alanna was dealing with, actually. Though it should be Adam who discussed that with her.

The young woman was still looking at her lap. At her hands, lying there, fidgeting with the brocade of her gown... no, her *left* hand was doing that. Her *right* was wrapped around her left wrist... covering the place where Aaron's hand had been severed from his arm.

"I... I could still... in your service..." She swallowed, then added fiercely, "And I *would*. I would do *anything* to protect you and Genevieve."

"I know you would," Damien said as she gave him that same *fierce* glare. It was interesting how easy she was with his Queen's name, and how uncomfortable she was with using his – or even Adam's. "It's why Ciriis chose you to replace Kamauri – and why Aryllis then chose you as her Second."

It didn't really surprise him when those names made her tense up again.

"They... they all have *children*... Even Ciriis, and she's as old as Genevieve." Alanna flushed. She was one of the ones who knew the truth, but it still shouldn't be spoken aloud more than necessary. Even here in Elaarwen, where it was surely going to be an entirely *open* secret before terribly long.

He waited a beat. "And Genevieve is also having a child. Do *you* want children, Alanna?"

The young woman looked away again. "I don't know. I think... maybe... if the right person..."

Her right hand tightened around her left wrist, and her left hand tightened into a fist so tight that her knuckles went white. "But how could I? Even with the right person. With someone who would... would *understand*. Who could handle the times when I... when I..."

"When you can't see or hear what's around you because you're stuck in the past?" Damien suggested, and when her gray-green eyes came up in shock to meet his, he knew they were hitting the mark.

"I know that you and the others who deal with this talk about these things," he added gently. "To ensure that you don't leave gaps in our security when one of you is having a difficult moment."

"Or hour, or day, yes," Alanna agreed, her eyes still wide. "It's gotten... harder to talk about but less of an issue in making sure there's proper coverage as the younger ones have come into the Guards."

The ones like Angelos – or even Tim's current Second, Marcus – who had never seen actual battle.

"Does... does Genevieve have... *flashbacks?* Or... or the Captain?"

"That's a conversation you should have with them," Damien demurred. "I wouldn't presume to share their stories for them." Though that *was* practically a 'yes.' "I *can* tell you that *I* do. Though not of the battlefield, obviously."

Alanna gave him a dubious look... no, that was a *compassionate* look. A *relieved* look.

"Then... then *you* understand."

Damien shrugged a little uncomfortably. "I... understand the basic problem of not being able to adequately address the current situation when caught in a *flashback*. I'm not sure if I could fairly say that mine compare to yours."

Likely not. His own had centered around his parents' murder for more years than he wanted to think about. And then been partially replaced by the executions of the traitors he'd had to sentence. And most recently involved a mix of things from Azella's Keep and his battle with the demon.

And they were less *flashbacks* that blotted out his sense of time and place in the middle of the day – anymore. More often – now – they were nightmares that startled him out of sleep in utter, abject terror or... to his horrified embarrassment, in a state of unhappy arousal.

Though after all the *compulsion* spell games Azella had played on him, perhaps that last wasn't unexpected... not that he'd wanted Genevieve to notice.

Adam... had noticed immediately, of course, long before they'd had that awkward conversation on the bank of the Sapphire River a week or so ago. And he was helping the King figure out how to cope and move on, just as he'd always done for Damien. Though it had never been this much, ah, *fun* before.

"They're... they're all *older* than you," Alanna asked after a moment. "Genevieve and Adam and Jason. How... how does *that* work?"

Had she... really just asked what he thought she had?

"I'm not sure what you mean," Damien said cautiously.

"You're... you're the *king*," Alanna said, sounding frustrated and... far too *helpless* for this strong, independent young woman. "How can you be – all the things we all need you to be when... when people you love and listen to are... so much..."

Dear Gods, she was *blushing*.

So much for hoping this was a question about how Damien could manage to order around his former mentors and his wife. Not that he really *did*. Or at least not very *often*.

It had probably been foolishness to try to keep secrets from Aryllis' Second. As Adam had mentioned, Alanna had been chosen for the Secret Cadre for her loyalty and intelligence and then trained to be even more astute. Her skill in all areas had led to Aryllis picking her.

As had Angelos', as one of the *official* Royal Guards and Tim's presumptive Second. Which meant there was likely another awkward conversation to be anticipated with his young cousin in the future.

Somehow, Damien didn't really think that Marcus had any clue.

Was it better to ask the question openly?

Did he really have any *choice*?

"Is this really about how I manage *my* life, Alanna?" Damien asked, trying to be kind and not crisp, "Or is this about you figuring out how to manage *yours*?"

The young woman had the grace to look embarrassed beyond her red cheeks. "You... can't have imagined we didn't... *notice*. Your Majesty. You're... very *easy* with both, um, the Captain and Prince Jason."

Damien rolled his eyes. "Of course, I am. They practically raised me."

Perhaps this was still salvageable...

Alanna rolled her own eyes. "There's easy and then there's *easy*, Your Majesty."

Was she calling *him*...?

Well, it wasn't as if it was any great secret that he'd had all of the first twelve of his Secret Cadre of ladies as lovers before he'd married Genevieve. Not that any of it had been his idea – but he hadn't exactly *objected* to it either. Not that he imagined a great many *other* young men would complain about having a series of beautiful, fierce, caring women fill *their* beds, either.

For the first time, he couldn't help but wonder exactly what his original twelve ladies had actually *told* the young women who took their places as they began to retire and marry. None of the *new ones* had ever even flirted with him outside of their official duties, even when Genevieve was gone for months on end for *her* official duties.

And, good grief, now there was that handful of 'gentlemen-of-the-chamber.'

What might *they* have been told?

Genevieve had insisted on adding men to the Secret Cadre so that there would always be someone available to guard Damien. None of *them* had flirted with him either, with the exception of Lord Aaron before the coup – and the bright young assassin had flirted with *everyone*, seeming to take a cheerily lascivious approach to life in general.

A couple of the *knights* of his Royal Guard had propositioned him. *They* were all men, his grandfather having refused to allow women to earn their shields for the last half-century or so – a matter which they were in the long process of rectifying. And until last Fall there shouldn't have been any reason to expect that *he* might have been receptive to such interest. He hadn't really known that *himself*, after all.

"I... see," Damien said a little faintly.

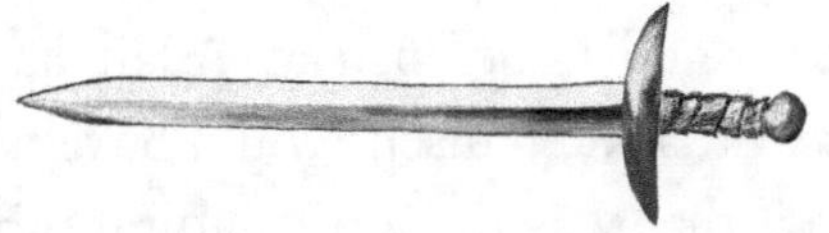

Chapter EIGHT

Seeing Sylphs

"A ND *THEN* SHE WENT ON to tell me that it was *easier* on everyone if *we* knew that *they* know," Damien told Adam that night.

The awkward conversation with Alanna had been followed by a relatively *non*-awkward dinner where Damien sat in Genevieve's usual seat and played the part of Duke-Consort. It mostly meant that he sat at the head table and conversed with Lord Adsel and his wife and the handful of other Elaarwen nobility that were in town – and with whomever else decided to wander up and chat with him, given the decidedly informal atmosphere over dinners in Castle Stellarine.

The entire castle staff and nobles ate together in one giant hall, with the servers getting fed before everyone else. Anyone in the 'city' was welcome to come up for a meal or to visit with the duke or duchess, though it was the men and women of rank – clan-chiefs, master craftsmen, particularly notable warriors or hunters and such – who actually tended to do so.

His Guards weren't terribly thrilled with *that*, either.

Lady Alanna had served as his hostess when they were dealing with the nobles in Farivera, but here in Elaarwen it would have been poorly done to seat her at his side. Instead, Adam had been put at his left hand – in the seat that he himself would have used if Genevieve had been there – as if that was the most natural thing in the world. *(Though maybe it was. By order of precedence, Jason had usually sat to Damien's left, and then Adam beyond him. There was no real reason to leave empty chairs for their missing spouses... It felt like someone* **knew** *their secret, but that* **might** *merely have been his guilty conscience...)*

Damien had felt utterly bemused by, well... *everything.*

"Did you ever get an answer out of her about Angelos?" Adam asked curiously, as he watched his King pace up and down the sitting room of the suite that he and Jason had been given four years ago by the castle's staff.

The King stopped and glared at his Champion. "Is *that* all you got out of everything I told you?"

The tall blonde knight had leaned back in his chair, fingers laced behind his head, long legs stretched out under the low table and crossed at the ankles. He raised one sardonic eyebrow.

"You more or less answered anything *else* I might have asked about."

Damien threw up his hands in exasperation and tossed himself into another chair. "She's interested. She's worried that he's too young for her. Too innocent. Too... undamaged."

Adam snorted. "Sounds like all the things Genevieve said about *you.*"

Damien gave a brief nod. "It's almost even the same age gap."

His Champion chuckled. "You clever, handsome Eldridge men are pretty attractive. I can't exactly blame her myself."

The King rolled his eyes. "Adam..."

He bounced up and started pacing again.

The tall man opened up his arms. "Come here, Damien. All that pacing is going to wear a track, and I happen to like that carpet."

"You're making light of everything," Damien grumbled, but he came close, then eyed Adam's chair dubiously when the tall man reached a hand up to tug him down. "That chair is going to collapse if I'm in your lap."

Adam snorted. "Not hardly. Jason and I are both big men. Can you seriously imagine that we'd have anything in our private quarters that hadn't proven itself able to stand up to a certain amount of... are you *blushing*, Damien?"

"Damn straight," the King muttered, but he didn't object any further as Adam pulled him down into his arms. Onto his lap.

Damien pulled his legs up and hung them over the arm of the chair as he snuggled into Adam's chest. He would think about finding that *better, permanent* solution for all of them some other time.

And there was nothing *lurid* about this. He'd been snuggling into Adam's chest for comfort and safety since he was... not quite sixteen.

Of course, it might have been a bit more lurid even then from *Adam's* point of view, given that he'd had all those *visions*. 'For parenting,' he'd described them to Damien, and while he'd certainly done a great deal to help the terrified young prince grow into a confident and skilled man and king... a number of the *visions* he'd described hadn't sounded like they were about *parenting* at all. Which was sort of confusing and weird all on its own.

And just *now* it got a great deal more... hmmmn, *lurid* didn't seem *quite* the right term... almost immediately as Adam tilted Damien's chin up for a kiss and then began unbuttoning his shirt to access the skin beneath. They'd both draped their jackets over the backs of chairs on entering the room *(though Damien had 'entered' moments later, having **Vanished** himself from his own quarters)*, and removed their boots as well – to Damien's surprise. He often wandered about barefoot himself – another relic of his Library days – but Adam usually put his own on at dawn and pried them off only when he went to bed.

Oh.

Hmmn.

"Alanna seems to have a certain amount of hero-worship going on with respect to Genevieve," Damien mentioned, not *exactly* as a distraction.

"Mmmmn. Perhaps another reason she finds Angelos attractive. And again, I can't fault her."

Those kisses were migrating all over his face... and neck... and... rather hampering further efforts at unbuttoning. Well, of unbuttoning *Damien,* anyways. His own fingers were busy at Adam's fasteners as he tried to breathe enough – in between all those lovely kisses.

Seated where he was, Damien could easily tell just *how* much Adam was enjoying kissing him.

It was completely natural to slide his hands up around the taller man's neck to pull him closer... Which, not-so-coincidentally also hindered Adam's efforts with the buttons and freed his hand to move where *he* could feel how much *Damien* was enjoying the kissing...

It was *wonderful.*

And... it was only what they had to do, right? What Elaarwen was *making* them do. It was only returning the care that Adam had given *him* when he'd come home both more broken and stronger than he'd ever been before, and so desperately needed the security of a heart that loved him without question... and to be told in no uncertain terms that what he had done in Azella's Keep hadn't destroyed his worth as a person.

It was... probably wrong to *enjoy* it this much, though.

Surely.

"Adam...!" He broke off the latest kiss guiltily, his hands sliding down to the front of Adam's broad, muscular shoulders that felt so *good* under his fingers to make a little space between them.

The tall knight straightened up a little with a wry expression. "Damien, playing at this is all very well and good, but you're giving me very much mixed messages. Do you want me to *stop?*"

"No..." slipped out before ears and brain had completely connected, and the dark-haired man looked away. "No. I mean, it's not like that's even an *option* right now, after all."

There was a long pause...

A pause that was really *too* still...

He looked back up to see Adam biting his lip. Seeing his King's gaze on him, the tall man slowly let out the breath he'd been holding.

"Damien…" The *interested* look in Adam's eyes faded a bit – and some of the serene confidence that the man had been showing faltered, cheerful lust giving way to loving concern. No… a touch of *anxiety*. A certain level of… *hurt?* "I thought you were okay with this now. With *us.*"

"I know." The King swallowed hard.

"I know," he went on in a more metered tone. "Me, too. But it's still not going to work out in the long run. And… I've caused you and Jason enough hardship already. And…"

It wasn't like anything was about to change right *now*. Not with the Soul of the province looking over their shoulders as it were. Damien didn't need to feel like his heart was breaking *now*.

He didn't need to dispute any of this, *now*.

Adam just watched him for a long moment, then – astonishingly – he chuckled.

"How many times have I told you to deal with *one* thing at a time? You're getting yourself all worked up and putting the cart before the horse again. The answers will be there when you're ready to see them."

That was all true – and it was a fair description of how Damien's mind worked. Which Adam should know, if anyone did. But…

"Adam, you're making light of things again."

"No," the tall man disagreed. "I'm putting aside things that can't be dealt with yet. Entirely different."

He scooped his free hand – the one he'd been using on Damien's buttons… and nipples – under the shorter man's knees, and his muscles bunched…

"Adam!" The King's arms immediately went back around his friend's neck to steady himself. "What are you doing?"

"Taking us to bed, my sweet prince. I have only until our provincial Goddess releases us to convince you to see things my way, after all."

Adam's arms were like bands of metal around Damien's back and under his thighs as the powerful man managed to stand up while holding his King. Sturdy and powerful and... rather narrow to have supporting one's entire weight.

The bedroom wasn't *that* far... But Damien was a heavily muscled warrior himself...

"Adam, you'll hurt yourself!"

Not to mention that being carried, 'bridal-fashion,' like this *looked* romantic, but was rather painful for the person being carried. Adam's hard, muscled arms cut off circulation in Damien's legs and practically bruised a strip of flesh across his back.

"Then you'll just have to *fix* me, won't you my Healer-King," Adam's expression was still amused, although the strain of the effort was evident in the taut tendons standing out in his neck. And he hadn't taken a step yet, apparently still figuring out how to balance his unwilling load.

Unwilling, but not struggling. The younger man neither wanted to fall a good four and a half feet to the stone floor *(carpeted or not)* nor did he want Adam to pull muscles in trying to contain his efforts.

"Adam..." Damien began worriedly.

And then... the rockhard muscles of Adam's arms weren't pressing so painfully into Damien's back and legs. And the look of strain was disappearing from Adam's face... though the amusement was rapidly being replaced with *be*musement as he began to carry his King to his bedroom almost easily.

"Thank you, thank you..." the tall knight muttered distractedly as he walked.

"Adam...?" Damien asked carefully.

And got that bemused look turned on him for an instant.

"There are a... rather lot of beautiful – and translucent – ladies here, Damien. That are helping me carry you. And, um, they're floating."

The King blinked in surprise, then activated his magickal *sight*.

And, yes, there they were, just as Adam had described. Quite a flock of them, actually, some of them with large, lovely wings but others not bothering to manifest such 'explanations' of their ability to fly.

Most were giggling, though some seemed shy. One cheeky creature winked at the King and gave him a patently fake flirty wave before adding a significant look and then directing his attention back to Adam. She was behind the Champion's shoulder, so that was apparently a message just for Damien.

"They're sylphs," he told his, ah, *friend*.

"I know *that*," Adam noted as he laid Damien gently on top of his bedspread. The bed that the thoughtful castle staff had provided so long ago was as generously proportioned and, ah, *sturdy* as any of the other furniture meant for a pair of such 'big men.' Damien's own bed across the hall – usually shared with Genevieve – was actually slightly smaller, despite being intended for their ruling duchess. "What I don't understand is why they decided to reveal themselves to me right *now*."

"They might tell you if *you* ask," Damien noted dryly. Rather like Elaarwen... though *She* hadn't been able to explain Herself in a way that had made sense.

The King watched with his own amused bemusement as Adam attempted to shoo the bevy of ethereal beauties out of the bedchamber with a great many 'thank you, ladies,' and 'I very much appreciate your assistance' kinds of comments. Anyone else would have seen the second-most-redoubtable knight in the Realm talking to empty air.

The King decided not to mention the sylphs who darted up on top of the bed's canopy or behind the floor-lamp or under the bed as Adam closed the rest of their sisters out and sealed the door with a relieved sigh. Nor would he mention to the exasperated knight that there was certainly enough of a gap under that door to allow any sylph to come back in if she so chose.

It was... *interesting*... that none of them did.

In fact, a couple of the ones who had hidden were sneaking *out*, and trying not to let Adam see them...

Perhaps they could use a little help.

Damien opened his arms to his forever-Champion, and Adam's face lit up with a smile as he came to bed.

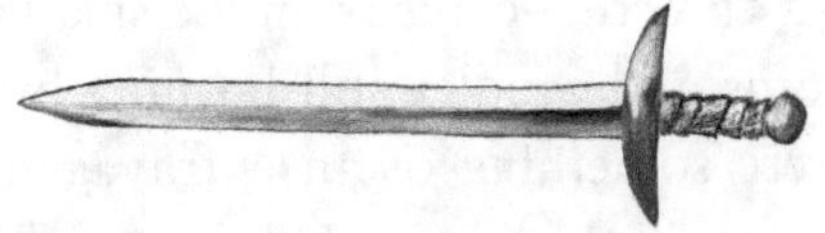

Chapter NINE

Surprises

"I COULDN'T HEAR WHAT ANY of those sylphs were saying," Damien murmured teasingly into Adam's ear a little later. "Were they trying to *entice* you, love?"

Because if such appeals should fall upon deaf ears and blind eyes anywhere, surely...

Damien had used a touch of magick to turn down the lamps a while back, but Adam's blush was evident in the warmth of his neck as Damien teased him with soft kisses. And in the rather disgruntled non-verbal sound the tall knight made.

"Oh, ho. Maybe I should be asking if they *succeeded*," Damien suggested with a grin as Adam turned towards him with another growl, one strong arm scooping under Damien. He sprawled over Adam's chest, feeling entirely loved and protected and peaceful. "I thought you didn't lean that way at *all.*"

Adam's hands came in from both sides to tug him up higher for a proper kiss.

"And now you're just trying to distract me from the fact that you called me 'love,'" Adam said when he was done.

His eyes were just barely visible as faint gleams in the slight glow from the window – a glow that came from the small number of *other* windows with lanterns and candles still burning brightly for Gods-knew-why. Both were something of an extravagance in Elaarwen, even in Castle Stellarine; in the 'city' below it would be entirely dark.

It was hard to imagine what might be so urgent as to have anyone spending lamp-oil this late at night out here. Though perhaps it was actually light from the couple of taverns... After all, Damien had brought in half a dozen ladies and gentlemen who might be too much of snooty lowlander nobles to carouse in the local taverns and brothels – but the dozen knights he also had along and the mountain-folk come in to see their duke likely weren't so prim.

It was never this dark in Emeralsee, where the dockside taverns would still be buzzing yet for hours and street-lamps lit the constant slight haze of smoke and mist that rose up from the Emerald River and Emeralsee Bay.

A brief pang of homesickness for the City that held his Court and Castle struck the King – for all that Damien had once thought that it was impossible for him to be homesick for any *place* while he was within Ilseador's borders.

"I've told you that I love you for years," Damien protested. "The first time was when I was seventeen and you told me you were taking me to Lynncrag."

"Fair," Adam conceded. "But you said '*I love you*' all those times. You haven't *called* me 'love' before."

"I did so," Damien retorted, before thinking better of it. No one else had as clear a memory as he did, and sometimes that was good. Or at least *wise*...

"Oh?" Adam raised an eyebrow. "*When?*"

The King sighed and laid his head down, tucking it under Adam's chin. The tall Champion had shaved just before dinner, so the slight stubble of the last few hours didn't catch much in the thick waves of Damien's black hair.

"It was right before you fought Genevieve. I was terrified I was going to lose you both."

"Ah." Adam's breath flowed softly over Damien's naked back. "It might take threat of mortal peril, but... The truth will out."

"Adam, it's not that this – that *you* – isn't what I *want...*"

"It's that you've convinced yourself it's not the *responsible* thing to do. Fool king."

That last was, as usual, a uniquely *Adam* endearment. Not that he'd ever heard the man call *Jason* anything but 'Jason' or perhaps 'Jase.' Not even when he'd slept with – er, *spent his nights tucked in safely between* – the pair of them after Tomas' attempted coup.

"It's *not*." The Sorcerer-King of Ilseador, Defender of the Realm, Father of Giendra Marlerite Stellarine Alsterling closed his eyes tightly, not lying to himself that it was for any reason other than to hold back tears. "The people–"

"Damien, my darling," Adam interrupted, "the *people* are so grateful to have *you* on the Throne that they would accept just about anything you threw at them."

"They haven't accepted same-gendered marriages so kindly as all that," Damien disagreed, though this newest appellation made him tremble at the awfulness of having to push Adam away. He'd seen the reports on violence faced by those who were following Adam and Jason's example.

"Let me re-phrase. They'll accept anything about *you* that you throw at them."

Damien winced. He didn't want to throw it at Adam that *his* marriage was the one that 'normalized' all the others. First, Adam would point out that Duchess Laura's marriage – and the freedom to wed as one pleased that Alpinsward had picked up during its over four decades-defection to Mercasia – had *really* paved the way.

And second... he'd likely add that the whole point of Damien sanctioning same-gendered marriages was to make people more whole and free to be themselves. So how was this – whatever *this* was – any different?

"Fine. The nobles, then."

"*They're* all terrified of you."

"They won't be once they realize *they* all have magick to use now, too."

"You still have more than they do, my sweet prince," Adam said with great equanimity. "It will all be all right."

Damien had fully expected to have this conversation with Adam at some point.

His decision to wake the magick of almost all of his bound nobles had been a desperation move, since he *hadn't* had the Power – then – to tell all the people in the whole Realm to get under shelter before the ice-storm. Not and try to do anything about the intensity of the ice-storm itself, anyways.

Damien had been aware when he did it that he was potentially loosing a future wave of magickal miscreants on Ilseador – and the neighboring Realms or even the known *world*. But the alternative would have been thousands upon thousands of deaths...

And it was usually Adam's place to point out these 'little problems' with Damien's ideas. He hadn't had a chance to do that pre-emptively because it had been a crisis, and Damien had been in a meeting of his Council of Peers and Vassals the morning after Adam and Jason's wedding.

So, yes, Damien had known that they were going to have to discuss this at some point. Presumably it hadn't happened before now only because of the press of events that really were far more urgent.

But.

The King had always assumed that when they *did* have this conversation, it would be *Adam* telling *him* off about what a stupid idea it had been and going on about the repercussions. And *himself* trying to point out the necessity and claiming that he *could* manage the inevitable repercussions with his own Power.

Not... the other way around.

Nor with the two of them naked and in bed with each other.

Damien wasn't prepared to field *this* side of the argument.

Better to turn this around again.

Instead, he laced his fingers across Adam's broad chest, enjoying the feel of the powerful muscles under the soft, well-furred skin, and propped his chin on the backs of his hands.

"So. Is this the first time you've seen sylphs?"

Not entirely to his surprise, Adam's arms came around him and he found himself spilled rather gently to one side and covered with what were obviously intended to be highly distracting kisses. What *were* highly distracting kisses, to be honest.

"Adam... tell me about the sylphs," Damien said after... well, not exactly *fighting* his way free. "When did you first start seeing them?"

The tall knight heaved a sigh. "Why is it that you can't keep your mind on one thing for a dozen minutes straight half the time and then other times you can't let one inconsequential tidbit go?"

Damien snickered. "*Tidbit* makes it sound *much* more interesting."

He felt his nose tweaked, though how Adam could be sure he was doing *that* in this darkness, instead of poking out his King's eye... was perhaps better left unquestioned.

"Hardly. When I was a boy, I thought they were fairies. I know better *now,*" he added before Damien could say anything. "But what was I supposed to think? Beautiful ladies that could change size and fly – and some of them have *wings–*"

"And most of them don't bother manifesting *clothes,*" Damien teased, but then a thought occurred to him. "Wait. Sylphs don't have inherent gender. They're sort of... well, *manifestations* – though we're using that word a lot lately – of the Air itself. Why didn't they manifest as males to show themselves to you?"

He could almost *hear* Adam's frown. The other man's body was now blocking even that faint gleam from outside, so there were no visual cues at all. "I assume they have some inherent preference for the female form. Aren't they always seen as females? Why should they care which way *I* 'lean'?"

"Because all those stories about lascivious Elementals – and other Fae folk – aren't just tales," Damien tried to keep his tone from conveying his embarrassment. It was yet another thing he'd learned from Azella's library. "I'm not sure if they just prefer humans for some reason – they don't seem to destroy their partners the way demons do – or if there's some other reason. They tend to manifest as male when encountering a woman... so I would have assumed..."

Adam snorted. "I suppose I can guess that *you* see them as women, then."

If *that* wasn't blushworthy... Damien slid his hand up and around the back of Adam's neck, considering his own offering of distracting kisses. Except... he really *did* want to know the answers to this.

"So far, yes. Not that I've seen all that many of any of them. I tend to deal with the Land in a... broader sense, maybe?" And... it hadn't been a year yet since his rather vague, boyish crush on his mentors had become reality. If the sylphs were relying on the imagination of the person looking at them to determine how to *manifest* themselves... though he'd seen rather *more* Elemental Fae since his unwilling sojourn in Azella's Keep and that had been *after*...

"But you said *you've* been seeing them since you were a boy? Did your brothers and sisters see them, too?"

That got him a shrug. "Not that I'm aware of. Mama and Papa seemed rather disturbed when I was small and kept talking about the pretty ladies that they couldn't see. So, I... stopped. *Talking* about them, that is."

Damien slid his other hand up and around Adam's neck from the other side, twiddling slightly with the knight's short hair. It was longer than his own, but tended to lie rather flatter – and at collar-length and free of the brief queue in which he usually wore it, was soft and alluring to the touch.

"Adam... you keep denying that you have magick..."

"Besides *empathy*," Adam agreed, his tone wary now.

"Besides *empathy*," Damien repeated faithfully. "But you *have* admitted there are Gifts scattered throughout the Loveress family. Marianna is a Spellbreaker. Martin is a Healer. Desirée and your mother have *visions,* like you do, and you told me Desirée has a *connection* to the fief at Lynncrag. Fontaine was a novice priestess – and I've still never heard why she quit. Charley's tracking skills are far beyond the average – I checked. And Lorrie..."

"What about him?" Adam sounded half-curious, half-unhappy with the conversation's direction.

Damien gave his own shrug. "I haven't figured him out, but he seems to attract women rather more than even *he* wants to. It's probably a surprise that he's only had the two marriages. My impression – after talking to him – was that those happened more because he was hoping it would keep the others off than out of any deep and abiding love."

"Don't mention that notion to Angelos," Adam warned with a certain dark humor.

"I hadn't planned to. But your father knew he had to come all the way across Ilseador to find your mother – and *you* knew you needed to come to the City to find Jason."

"And *you*," Adam added with a sort of... desperate attempt at distraction.

The other parts of that 'desperate attempt' were rather interesting in and of themselves. And definitely distracting.

"Adam, my love," Damien finally found a chance to say, adding his own distractions, "if you really don't want to tell me about your family, don't. Though I can guess that your mother and Desirée both have an affinity for the magickal Element of Earth. But your own magick is something we *have* to deal with. It's leaking out of you everywhere and you need more than that trained, reactive response you use to keep your *projections* under control."

"Damien..."

"You said it yourself earlier, Adam. They trained you *not* to use it. You probably don't even know when it *is* leaking out unintentionally." He looked up into the near total darkness hoping that Adam's night vision was enough better than his to let him see Damien's earnest expression. "You're walking around with an unsheathed sword that you don't know how to use. And your eyes closed."

"Hmmn." Adam's tone was heavily skeptical. "I don't suppose you have any examples of these 'leaks'?"

Well, maybe it was better to hope Adam *couldn't* see his fierce blush. "There was that... *thing* you did. Um, earlier. When we..."

"What *thing?*"

Irritated-Adam was a known quantity, Damien reminded himself.

Bu there wasn't any particularly *easy* way to put this.

"You put a *compulsion* spell on me. To keep me from, um, finishing until you were done."

A year ago, Damien might not even have noticed, but he was hypersensitive to such things as even rather minor *compulsion* spells right now. Not that he'd particularly *minded* this one... it had been light enough that he could have batted it away without half thinking about it, so it hadn't been a worry. And it had been from *Adam,* so he'd rather thought he'd see where it went... and hadn't minded then either, when he'd found out what the spell was for.

Unexpectedly, that elicited a chuckle. "Oh, you noticed that, did you. Damien, my sweet prince, there wasn't anything *un*intentional about *that.*"

Damien... guessed his own face was entirely... flabbergasted. That was probably the safest word.

"Where did you learn to do *that?*" He answered his own question immediately. "Jason, of cour–"

"It was Edmund actually," Adam interrupted him. "He... liked to keep his sheets clean."

"Oh."

If this wasn't the most awkward thing *ever*... and *that* was saying something, all things considered...

But apparently Adam wasn't just going to let that statement sit there.

"I told you how he was my first," the tall man went on, and Damien was torn between desperately wanting to see his face and being desperately glad that the darkness made that impossible. *Empathy* was much more effective at conveying single emotions. Or ones that were... simple combinations.

Adam's feelings were... definitely not simple.

"You don't have to explain anything to me," Damien said quickly.

There was a soft sigh, a softer kiss, and then... "I think maybe I do. This *idea* you have of me as being some sort of 'pure and perfect' person – not that I really want you to think less of me–"

"I wouldn't," Damien protested. "And you *are* special like that, and–"

"Hush." He abruptly wasn't in control of his lips again. "Damien. I've... had to do a great deal of growing this last Winter while we tried to fix the Realm and each other and pray that you were safe and would make it back to us whole."

Perhaps Adam just needed to talk this out to a sympathetic ear... much as Jason had needed to finally have someone *listen* last Fall to his long-held grief and positive memories of Prince Oskar.

150

"Not just me, of course," Adam added as Damien wriggled underneath him, uncomfortable with the memory of the mess he'd left them with when he surrendered himself to Azella to save the City and his loved ones. "Genevieve had to learn the whole administrative side of ruling the Realm – you'll have noticed that she's much more appreciative of what you do, now."

Actually... Damien rather had.

In the past, Genevieve's attitude about what her husband did while *she* was off negotiating the return of the Lost Provinces with the Army at her back had been slightly... dismissive. Even condescending. She'd listened to Damien telling her about his struggles and practically patted him on the head and told him it wasn't so hard as all that once you got the hang of it.

If she hadn't followed those sorts of comments up with... Well. Those conversations about his frustrations and travails and concerns had usually occurred in the day or two after she got home, and only ever in the safe privacy of their bedchamber. Where else could a king admit to his own incompetence after all?

And there were always better things to do there – and then – than to try to explain to his confident wife that there were rather large differences between ruling tiny, sparsely-populated Elaarwen which had been so lightly touched even by King Reginald's *magickal* depredations, let alone his more visible tyrannies... than administering even just the province of Emeralsee, which hosted one of the largest cities in the known world. Not to mention managing the rest of the Realm.

"I... did notice that," Damien admitted. Almost absently, he sent out a tendril of magick to turn up one of the lamps so that he could see Adam's face.

He wasn't sure if it was just the natural result of having spent so long without real human interaction in the Royal Library during his formative years *(though he'd **observed** plenty of other people's interactions, even during that time)* or whether it was something intrinsic to himself, but Damien tended to need all the clues to understanding other people that he could get. Perhaps his *empathy* wasn't so much a natural gift as an underutilized human capacity that he had developed more than most out of self-protection. It was said blind people's hearing sharpened, after all.

His... friend *(no, he should be honest, at least in his own thoughts, his lover)* winced slightly at the increased light. Or perhaps at the idea of speaking of such intimate and difficult things without the cover of darkness. Though he didn't object.

"It wasn't just Genevieve, of course," Adam went on. "Jason tried to help her out at first, of course, which annoyed the hell out of her, because he knew even less than she did about the whole mess."

He rolled his eyes, but there was something slightly... evasive about the movement. It was only distinctive because the Champion was usually such a forthright person – he kept secrets, certainly, but his usual way of keeping people from noticing was to be acerbic, not evasive.

"Hmmn," Damien commented. "And you?"

Adam snorted *"I'm* not an idiot. I stood back and waited until Tomas stepped in and 'kindly suggested' that Count Antonin could use Jason's help. Not that that was really true at first, but it got Jase out of Genevieve's hair."

The Count of Emeralsee City was Jason's first and most important vassal since he'd been made duke of the province last Fall. He was also a squirrely old fellow, who had been quietly embezzling from the public coffers since long before Damien was born. King Reginald hadn't seemed to care, so long as the city's taxes were paid and his luxuries continued to come in via the trade ships that so appreciated their well-protected harbor. The Royal Exchequer was in pretty much the same position with regards to the Royal Treasury, likely in collaboration with Count Antonin.

Damien had known what was going on from his earliest days as king. He'd spent about six months reading through the financial records of the Realm when he was thirteen, then gone back to review them and look over the ones for the City when he was eighteen and it seemed possible that he might actually have a chance to make some positive changes someday. He had all the *data*.

What he *didn't* have was the skills needed to prove their wrongdoing in such a way that he could easily dismiss the Royal Exchequer – who was well-connected and Damien's nobles were restive enough with all the other changes he'd been making. And

Count Antonin's Oath of Vassalage had held, which suggested he wasn't so much a *bad* man as an opportunistic one – and might do well if he was properly reined in.

Not that Damien had had leisure to do that, either, given all the other problems of dealing with eighty-three years of neglect to the Realm, a *(barely)* defunct Rebellion, new and uncontrolled magickal powers...

"Out of Genevieve's hair and into Antonin's," the King agreed, unable to find a great deal of sympathy for the *opportunistic* old man. "Though he already knew he was going to have to teach Jason about how everything works. We'd been talking about *that* for two months." He cocked his head slightly, quizzically. "*You* were there with me for all of those discussions, Adam. Why didn't *you* tell Jason?"

"I *was* there for those conversations," Adam agreed. "But I could also see that Jase wasn't going to take suggestions from *me* any better than he was from Genevieve."

He snickered as Damien contemplated that Jason's and Adam's wedding vows would have been less than a week old at that point. He couldn't fault his Champion for deciding that they didn't need that added stress on their marriage on top of everything else.

"Not that *her* suggestions had been anything that deserved the name for about two days by then," Adam added, still grinning.

Damien winced. "More along the lines of 'get out of my way and try to see if you can find something *useful* to do with yourself'?"

"With not-so-muttered additions like 'if you can find anyone who'll put up with you.'" Adam snickered again. "Well, 'tis an ill wind indeed, as they say. There was absolutely *no one* who would have guessed that the pair of them have a soul-bond after watching *that* go on. Not after seeing how lovey-dovey she was with *you* when the first one happened."

That was... a deeply *weird* thing to say given how Damien was snuggled up naked with *Adam* right now... but this was still a story of what had gone on during his absence that he hadn't yet heard. Things he should probably know – all the more so because the discussion was pointing up how reticent everyone had been about what exactly had gone on in Ilseador while the King had been immured in the sorceress' Keep.

And it was *still* a less-awkward discussion than what Damien had *thought* Adam was going to insist on discussing a moment ago. Though he was going to have to circle them back around to that at *some* point, because Adam's magick really *did* need some training.

"So, Jason went off to Count Antonin's tutelage and you – and Tomas – taught Genevieve what she needed to know," Damien summarized.

Dammit, but the Duke of Siovale's treason still hurt to think of. Damien had thought of him as nearly as dear a friend as... well, Zachary and Rosa.

"Me, more than Tomas," Adam said rather pointedly. "Siovale is a great deal more prosperous and populous than Elaarwen, but it's still small-potatoes compared to Emeralsee. And I've been at your elbow almost constantly for the last five years."

"Of course." It had been Adam that Damien had wanted to name his Heir, and for just that reason. But politics had made it impossible to name the son of a mere baronetta the Heir to the Realm, no matter how capable he was. The son of a countess had been... just barely possible, and only because everyone knew it was a legal fiction... Well, until the Sword spoke for Jason and it suddenly wasn't one.

He'd actually considered Tomas, given that the man was both a duke *and* competent. Not that anyone would have accepted Harald-the-Traitor-King's half-brother as Heir to the Realm.

Nor, apparently, should they have.

"So, Genevieve listened to you?" Damien asked,

Adam snorted again. "Eventually. She spent another few days making a mess of things on her own, then reluctantly accepted a few kernels of advice from His Grace of Siovale as her peer. It took several semi-major crises happening at once to get *Tomas* to accept that it was more than he could deal with."

"*Several* 'semi'-major...?" Damien was beginning to feel this wasn't really something he could literally take lying down and wriggled himself free to scoot up and lean against the headboard. "I know I didn't have a chance to read the reports, but why didn't any of you *tell*–"

Adam sighed as he sat up as well. "Well, there was a... certain amount of embarrassment. On all of our parts. And since we *did* get things to work out, it wasn't really relevant by the time you came home."

The King glared at his Champion, then shook his head and sighed, running a hand over his face until he had his expression under control. Hopefully, anyways. "All right. That's... fair. Or it *was*. At the time. Tell me what happened."

"Antonin had Jason dealing with the recuperation of the province from the ice-storm," Adam told him a little warily. "Which actually *was* useful once Jase figured out what he could do. Took about half the load off of Antonin... The old man didn't even complain about David taking over dealing with the docks, which tells you something right there."

Indeed, and it did. While Lord David Metreedi Solway was undoubtedly the best choice to sort out the removal of the ships that the pirates had sunk that were clogging the harbor, he tended to be a little... high-handed. David was also rather insufferably honest – Damien had had a taste of that when he'd made Jason's stepfather a member of his Royal Council and the man had immediately confronted his Lord Exchequer about keeping two sets of books on the Royal Treasury.

Adam was also well aware that Count Antonin was lining his own pockets, so... the fact that Antonin had managed to get along with David was... significant.

Still...

"These 'semi-major' crises, Adam," Damien said a little impatiently.

His Champion nodded. "The first one was the flood of requests for help from outside of Emeralsee. Dalziallest, of course. Rosa and Zachary were gone by then, so they were accepting those pleas as they headed home... and forwarding them on to Genevieve, since it was clearly going to be beyond their own emergency funds."

Damien closed his eyes. "And Reyensweir. The same thing, I imagine."

"There were offers of help from Alpinsward, Embervest. Tomas volunteered Siovale–"

"You had Embervest send aid to Dalziallest, Alpinsward to Emeralsee, and Siovale to Reyensweir?" Damien broke in to ask.

Adam rolled his eyes again. "And from Elaarwen to Reyensweir as well. Genevieve knew to do *that,* Damien. She wasn't familiar with the bureaucracy we've been rebuilding, but redirecting material assistance to build more distant connections rather than unduly strengthening local ties is more strategy than anything."

Local ties, such as those between Siovale and Elaarwen or Elaarwen and Dalziallest that had been the birthing-ground of the Rebellion. There was a fine line for a monarch to maintain between supporting a sense of nationhood for everyone and keeping potentially fractious nobility from forming actual factions. If anyone should understand that, it would be his strategy-minded wife. Who, after all, had benefited from the other side of the equation as the Rebel Duchess.

"Oh, right, of course," the King subsided. "So, a flood of requests for help. What else?"

"Well, it was more of a slowly building problem than a *crisis,* precisely," Adam went on, "but Jason was having to mediate between Count Antonin and Lord David – and Mistress Lenore, who seems to think of David as being fairly high-handed as well–"

"Lenore *Metreedi?*" Damien frowned as Adam nodded. "But isn't she David's cousin or something?"

"Cousin at some removes," Adam agreed. "But I gather there are some *distinctions* within the ever-so-unitary Metreedi clan. Lenore was muttering under her breath about *'those damned core-House cousins from Wave.'*" He smirked. "I rather wish she hadn't noticed I had come close enough to hear her. An inside view on the Metreedis would be... handy."

"To put it mildly," Damien tried not to sound quite as eager as he was at that idea.

One of the things that he'd gotten out of his grandfather's notes, and then confirmed with the ghostly Queen Marian, was that there was something very secretive about the Metreedis. Every ruler of

Ilseador – and Queen Marian had confirmed that she'd had some very private correspondence with the Jeweled Queen of Vindalia and a few of their other close neighboring monarchs on the topic as well – since Suzannah Alsterling herself had apparently tried to ferret out the mystery.

It wasn't any secret that the current people who claimed the name were descended from the hereditary administrative branch of the old Turquoise Empire, of course. Until a thousand years ago, when the Empire finally collapsed into itself and the Last Empress had given her daughter and Heir in marriage to an unimportant inland king on the eastern continent and accepted fealty to the combined nation resulting therefrom, the Head of House Metreedi had been the Emperor/Empress' Prime Minister.

The entire House had been known as the Hands of the Empire and anyone who showed any administrative talent anywhere was brought into their fold by marriage – within a generation, if not immediately. Supposedly the legendary – and perhaps mythical – secret order of spies, thieves, and assassins, the Tirgessi *(also called the **Eyes** of the Empire),* had also answered to the Head of House Metreedi.

When the Empire had collapsed, the Metreedis had seemingly bent their knee to destiny and turned their attentions to trade. It was hardly any surprise – with all of that collection of administrative talent – that the family had done stunningly well at that as well.

But the entire family walked as if they were... still something more special than merely the descendants of those who had once run an empire. And none that Damien had met did so more than Adam's father-in-law Lord David Solway – the former *Captain Daffyd Metreedi.*

It was... possibly currently irrelevant, but unavoidably fascinating, to discover that Lenore – who was Head of their own local branch of the House – found David just as... *high-handed* as did Damien's own nobles. At least since the man had emerged from his self-imposed hidden-in-plain-sight role as the meek-mannered son-in-law of the irascible Countess of Brindlewell.

Definitely irrelevant to the current discussion, though Damien had to admire Adam's verve in attempting yet another *distraction.*

"I would imagine dealing with those three... personalities would have absorbed Jason," the King said mildly. "He's practically famous for hating confrontation in any form other than the dueling field."

"The practice-ring," Adam corrected. "Jase has never *actually* dueled anyone. He tried to drag *me* into sorting all of that out, but since no one but me knew all the details of what *you'd* been doing for the *Realm* – and where all the relevant reports were on that mess of your desk – our sweet and mild Genevieve had me fetching and carrying all day."

He put on a pious expression. "Abandoning our Queen to that desk of yours was too much for even Jason to ask."

Damien narrowed his eyes at his Champion. "And I imagine you didn't bother to enlighten anyone that you also had copies of every one of those reports – in alphabetical order or something, knowing you."

Adam's pious look grew rather wicked. "After all the effort Genevieve had gone to in getting rid of the spell you'd placed over the entire mess when we had all those children hiding in there during the pirate attack? That was how we *first* discovered Marianna is a natural Spellbreaker, actually. Besides which," he added, "technically all those reports were for the office of the Captain of the Royal Guard, so I didn't have access to them anymore."

Damien rolled his eyes. "You got copies of the reports as Captain because *you* happened to be the captain. Not the other way around. I have no objection to Tim – and Aryllis, though I believe she has her own set – having those handy. But there's no reason why he would have kept you – *or* Genevieve – from accessing them either."

The King frowned. "In fact, why didn't he *offer* to do that? I know full well that *your* office wasn't a mess, and that you made sure he knew where everything was before he took over."

Adam snickered. "Well... let's just say that Tim and I were in agreement that there wasn't any great benefit in Genevieve and Tomas flailing around any longer than necessary."

"Ah." Damien winced. "They were *both* doing that 'I have been ruling for a dozen years, I know better than you' thing?"

Adam shrugged. "Well, seven for Genevieve in Elaarwen. Sixteen or seventeen for Tomas. So, it averages out to about there. No reason for either of them to pay attention to those of us who *aren't* the rulers of our home fiefs."

Damien scrubbed at his face again. "And Antonin was too busy with Jason and all of Emeralsee – even if they'd have listened to *him*. Given that he's *only* a count. I didn't think Genevieve would fall for that nonsense. Elaarwen is so egalitarian it's practically horizontal."

"Except for the mountains, yes," Adam chuckled. "And our plainslanders – like Tomas – tend to be the ones who stand on their titles." He shook his head. "I don't know. I'd like to say that it was that Tomas was laying some sort of groundwork for that *compulsion* spell he used to draw her away from the Castle later on, but... honestly, I think she was just overwhelmed and trying to use her rank and title – and supposed expertise – to keep the bucking beast from throwing her."

"It could have been both," Damien sighed. "My poor love. She's usually so sensible about things. She *knew* how much I rely on the Royal Council. And on *you,* particularly." He focused on his... closest advisor. "So, you made sure that the 'bucking beast' actually *did* throw her. Didn't you."

Adam shrugged again. "I didn't really have to. And I *was* giving her as much support as I could, Damien. As much as she'd *accept,* anyways."

"Except for those reports."

Another shrug. "That was only a day or two. And if she wouldn't accept *my* advice, do you think she would have taken any from Tim? She wasn't even listening to Aryllis much... though she couldn't brush her Spymistress off entirely, so Tim and I managed to sneak a few things through to her that way."

Damien scrubbed at his face. "So, what happened to change things?"

"The sewers in the tannery district exploded."

The King blinked. "What."

Adam's usual sardonic look was more of a smirk. "The sewers exploded. Genevieve and Tomas had all but camped in your office – Jason and I had to pry her out of there to eat or sleep, and I would send for Mark and Arabella to get their father to take a rest.

"Mark and I were in the middle of doing that for luncheon, about two weeks after you were gone, when we heard a huge booming sound. The reports started coming back about a quarter-hour later.

"First, it was word from the Castle walls – a plume of thick, black smoke followed the noise, and an absolutely horrendous odor as the wind started dispersing the smoke. Then reports began to come in from the City Guards, beginning with a really panicked fellow covered in soot and stinking to high heaven. Apparently, he'd been close enough to actually see... something. Not enough to give us a good explanation as to what had *happened,* but it narrowed down things enough to start pulling out the more detailed maps of the area.

"Jason was already down in the City at Antonin's manor – before Genevieve and Tomas had even managed to send their own runner out to get more information, we had a message from Antonin saying that they were evacuating that part of the City and everything downwind. No one could breathe for the smoke and tannery fumes.

"It took a few hours more to discover that it was the sewers that were the source of the trouble."

Damien was picturing the layout of his city. "This was daytime, yes? So, the wind would have been coming in from the bay – and the tanneries are already located near the edge of the outer city and to the northwest... That's not so bad..." He gave Adam an alarmed look. "Please tell me that the smoke settled before the air flow reversed for the night and you had to evacuate everyone *east* all the way down to the docks...?"

Adam's expression was too entertained for it to have been the disaster that Damien was imagining...

"It did," the Champion agreed. "Antonin used our usual approach, of sending for any minor Earth-witch with a hint of Elemental magick to pull the smoke particles out of the air. That worked excellently, so then all they were left with was the flooding. Normally that's a bigger problem–"

"I'm aware," Damien shuddered.

The Emeralsee sewers had been on his never-quite-urgent-enough list for the last five years. He'd been dealing with problems as they occurred, working with Count Antonin to patch the ancient, leaky system rather than doing the complete rebuild that was really needed. There were places – not always in the poorer districts, either – where the smell in Summertime was nearly enough to make your eyes water. And two years ago, when they'd had an exceptionally *dry* Summer after Damien had messed up in trying to magickally mitigate the annual flooding in Cedarwen, the smell had reached epic proportions and driven a minor relocation of parts of the population.

Unfortunately, it was all too obvious that the problem would not be solved by building new parts of the City farther out into the Emeralsee plains and extending the overburdened sewer system even farther. Though likely that had to be *part* of the solution while Damien and Antonin – and now Jason – had buildings razed and rebuilt and the hodge-podge of gutters and catacombs that dated back before the Fall of the Turquoise Empire was reconstructed. More than a thousand years of filth...

Damien had finally found a way to bypass the other needs that the Royal Council had allocated funds for by presenting the monies directly to Jason as a gift from the Crown to his new Duke. The work was supposed to have begun... oh. The week following the coronation and wedding. Likely the start had been delayed by the ice-storm and everything that went with it.

"I thought the new program of convincing people not to throw every damned thing down the sewers was beginning to work," he said guiltily.

Adam shrugged far too nonchalantly for a man describing a rather stunning human disaster.

"It may have helped. The system is just too old, but the new system is going in with a great deal less complaining than we'd been anticipating. And there seems to be a great deal of civic engagement now in the idea of *not* using the sewers as a catch-all for every kind of trash. So perhaps it will help the new system as we put it in place," the Champion noted. "And the disaster did some *other* good."

He snickered. "As the reports of the damage started pouring in, you could just see Genevieve turning to Tomas hopefully. Neither this castle of hers here in Elaarwen, nor the town below us, has more than a settling cistern and leaching fields to deal with any kind of waste – and gutters in the town for direct run-off. So, *she* had no idea what to do, poor girl–"

"Woman," Damien corrected absently. "And Siovale's towns aren't much bigger – nor do they have more advanced infrastructure," he commented as Adam rolled his eyes.

"No," the tall knight agreed, "they don't. Tomas looked nearly as flummoxed as Genevieve. Eventually they stopped staring at each other in bafflement and realized that Tim and I had the map of the city out, with markers to indicate the site of the explosion and the evacuation routes. By then, I'd sent word to General Direlien to get the army ready to host the refugees for a few nights. Aryllis and Tim were coordinating with Captain Seldebard of the City Guard over having the damage surveyed for survivors – she has informers down there in the catacombs, so she knew where they might find people who could navigate down there. We had all the first responses to the crisis well in hand."

Damien breathed a sigh of relief. "Of course you did."

Adam gave him a wry look. "I think I was working on the Royal Contract for the Guild of Structural Engineers to go in and check the integrity of everything when Genevieve thought to ask what we were doing. She... didn't know there *was* a Guild of Structural Engineers."

The King laughed. "You don't have to sugar-coat it, Adam. I doubt she knew what a structural engineer *was*. Not Tomas either. There's simply no *need* for those things outside of Emeralsee."

"I think they have guildhouses in Cedarwen and Reyenrald," Adam said a little pedantically.

Those were the two next-largest cities in the Realm – and possibly the only ones large enough to really merit the title.

"So... I suppose that was the point at which she started listening to you," Damien noted.

The King shook his head ruefully. He'd known it would be a mess when Azella took him away, but he hadn't anticipated Genevieve trying to do everything... well, the way he did it himself. She was always twitting him about his too-perfect recall for seemingly-unrelated facts after all; it should have been obvious that what worked for him wouldn't for anyone else. Damien only did it that way himself because he'd been so woefully unprepared to *be* a king, after all – he'd had no idea *how* to delegate, let alone whom he could trust to delegate things *to*. At the time, after all, the handful of people he could trust had been as ignorant of administration as he was himself.

"You'd think," Adam said dryly, "but no. And..." he added with some embarrassment as Damien looked at him incredulously, "looking back, I can see why. Genevieve and I... weren't on the best of terms right then. And that was probably my fault more than hers."

The tall knight winced. "I... was feeling very *torn* about our whole... situation. And I was probably being – no, I *was* being rather insufferable about knowing more about how what was purportedly *her* government ran than she did."

"Ah." Damien didn't really know what else to say. "I... thought the two of you were getting along beautifully."

Actually, after Adam's initial – and rather vehement – rejection of the idea of Jason siring Genevieve's first child as the prophecy demanded, the two of them had been getting on almost *too* well.

Adam winced again, then sighed. "Yes, well. Both of us – Genevieve and I – seem to have made being the Person Who Doesn't Get Ruffled a core part of our self-image. Jason always seemed to need me to be that person, and, um..."

"So did I." Damien gave him a wry nod. For some reason this seemed much more awkward than all the other weird aspects of this that kept wopping them in the nose.

Legally, Damien had been just months shy of his first majority when Adam found him – he'd actually been a legal adult *(though not a **full** adult until his second majority five years later, of course)* by the time Jason had begun carefully taming him with crumbs of patiently proffered affection and attention. The young prince's *emotional* development, however, had been partially arrested at the time of his parents' murder, and his near-entire lack of human social contact had served to isolate him from any further growth even as his heart – had not so much *healed* as *scarred over.*

He'd needed Jason's unconditional acceptance to dare to come out of the Library, certainly.

But he'd needed Adam's unrelenting expectations and confidence to be able to *mature.*

Which of them had needed more patience might be a matter of debate.

Adam gave him a half-smile. "Yes, well. *That* had sort of been falling apart all Fall anyways. Between you and your 'crazy scheme,'" he actually made air-quotes with his fingers, "and discovering that Jase had been communicating with my family behind my back – and that it was a *good* thing – to suddenly losing the position I'd designed for myself in order to take care of you. And *then* realizing what was between Jason and Genevieve... and between Jason and *you*... And then what was between..."

Adam's voice trailed off and he actually looked slightly nervous for once.

"Between you and *me*..." Damien cocked his head. "But... you keep telling me... those *visions*..."

Adam sighed. "Damien, my darling... I hadn't had any of *those visions* in nearly ten years. I'd... made myself forget them as much as I could. To make a place for Jason and me. To avoid being so damned inappropriately *jealous* every time another one of your Guardswomen went to your bed..."

He gave a sort of painful smile at the King's startled look.

"But actually, Damien, a moment ago I wasn't going to say anything about what was between *you* and me. For all that that brings its own set of complications, a part of me has always just been waiting for *that*. No, I was *going* to say 'what was between me and Genevieve.'"

That... could *not* mean what it sounded like.

Adam, of all people?

No. And better not even to imply Damien had considered such an idea.

"So... you had to grow a bit to get used to all the changes," Damien tried to say it slowly, thoughtfully, so that it didn't sound like he was speaking quickly to cover up... any other thoughts. "And so did Genevieve, I'll imagine. She had a great many of the same challenges," he pointed out, "or, hmmn, *anti*-parallel ones I suppose, like losing the support of her father."

Adam let it go *(thank the Gods)*. "Exactly. And it was complicated enough while *you* were there to act as ballast and leavening for all of us – to mix a metaphor. Once you were gone... it was like we were all... a kite without a tail."

"I had a kite when I was very small," Damien mused. "In Ravenscroft. I remember wondering what the tail was *for.*"

"Balance," Adam replied instantly. "Papa loved to have us play with kites in Lynncrag. They don't fly hardly at all without a tail. Without you there... well, it wasn't just the three of *us,* it was the whole Realm that seemed off-kilter. Jason and I had to figure out how to anchor Genevieve enough to cope... and it meant we had to actually *talk* to each other about some of the things that made us who we are.

"We spent a great many long nights up in that bedroom of yours," he added candidly. "Talking, more than anything else."

"That must have been hard on you," Damien ventured. "Given that they have their soul-bond."

His knight chuckled. "You'd think so, wouldn't you? And they've been friends for even longer than I've known Jase..."

"Not *much* longer."

"No," Adam agreed. "And he and I have so many more shared experiences. But Genevieve gets to see a side of Jason that I don't think he's showed anyone else."

Damien reached out and caressed Adam's cheek. "The side of him that *could* have been her Duke-Consort. That has to be hard for you. It's hard for *me.* And I *am* her Duke-Consort."

Adam caught his fingers and kissed them. "It was... and it wasn't. But it gave all three of us a chance to understand each other. To get past the things we *thought* we knew about each other simply because we've spent so much time together. Of course, that was more true for me and Jason – or for the two of them."

This was all very interesting... and probably very *good* for all of them...

But it hardly had anything to do with Adam's refusal to accept that *he* had magick.

Which *was* where they had started this very strange conversation.

"Fair enough," the King acknowledged. "Self-understanding is always good. And it should make it much easier for you to train *your magick* so it won't get away from you, like..."

No, he couldn't use *that* example again.

Adam gave him an odd look. "I haven't been trying to distract you, Damien. I've been trying to get this conversation to the place where I could explain properly. Jason and Genevieve insisted that *I* be the one to tell you – when you seemed like you might be ready to hear it."

Nothing *good* ever had a lead in like that.

Damien regarded his friend and mentor and *lover* warily. "All right."

"That sewer problem? Jason and Genevieve cleaned it up. *Together.*" Adam gave the last word a peculiar emphasis.

Damien frowned. "Well, she's the Queen and he's the Duke of Emeralsee. I would assume they'd have to work *together* to get that sort of a mess cleaned up."

Adam shook his head. "No, my sweet prince. I thought – like you did – that that crisis would be the one that would make Genevieve get over herself and listen to me. Not that I'm sure I had things to say worth hearing..." He winced again.

"No, I'm trying to tell you that when Genevieve insisted on riding out to see the actual damage herself, and Jason came up to her and took her hand – and he *swears* that he was going to remonstrate with her for bringing herself and the baby into reach of those nasty fumes... Well, *I* was back in the Castle handling logistics for the disaster instead of at her side as I *should* have been..."

Damien was frowning hard. It wasn't like Adam to weasel around something like this... like he'd apparently been doing for this *whole conversation*.

"Adam, spit it out. What are you trying to tell me?"

The King's Champion *(and lover)* sighed.

"When they joined hands, they both suddenly realized what they could do. They dried up the flood waters and... Genevieve tells me *sterilized* the muck that coated everything. It was still a mess to clean up, and there were nasty things in it – chemicals from the tanneries that weren't supposed to have been dumped, mostly – but it was do-able."

That... sounded like...

"Your wife is an incredibly Powerful Fire-mage, Damien. And my husband is a Powerful Water-mage."

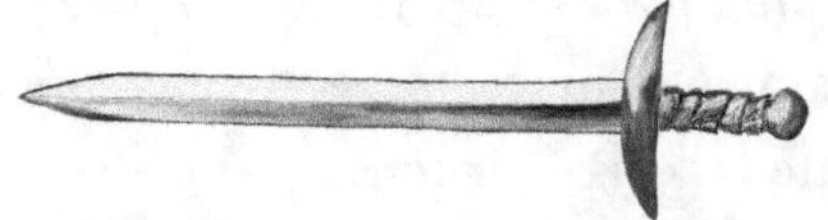

Chapter TEN

Marching Orders

A SCANT HANDFUL OF DAYS later, the gentle kiss on his temple woke Damien more effectively than the brave rays of sunlight straggling through gaps in the drapes. Those rays were, after all, fairly high up on the wall, not falling across his face. Jason and Adam's bedroom window faced the northeast more directly than the far-less-heavily draped one in his own suite.

"I'm going down to practice," Adam said in the hushed voice people tend to use before dawn.

Or, well, the hushed voice one used in the *bedroom* before dawn. Damien would likely be able to hear Adam's parade-ground roar out on the practice-court even with the windows closed and drapes drawn – from anywhere in Castle Stellarine.

He reached a hand up to catch Adam's.

"Come back to bed, love," he said half-pleadingly. "Surely the children can practice without you for *one* day."

Adam's expression didn't so much *soften* as become slightly *malicious.*

"You're just hoping I won't get *you* out of bed to practice."

"That, too," Damien admitted artlessly. It was also that they had stayed up *far* too late talking... *again*...

It surely had nothing to do with the way he'd been having a devil of a time sleeping ever since Adam's stunning revelation.

He'd known, after all, that Genevieve had a certain affinity for Fire. Red hair wasn't exactly a predictor for that, despite common belief, but there *was* a correlation. And he'd known that Genevieve had far more magick than she'd ever wanted or admitted – or tried to use. It had become unlocked for her when she'd taken her oath as his vassal, and then opened up still further when she was Crowned Queen. But Genevieve had made a conscious decision *not* to make use of magick save in support of her husband.

Damien had known about Jason's potential as well, having had a sense that it was lurking there beneath his *(former)* Champion's serene exterior before he'd ever handed him the Heir's Ring. Azella had even referred to Jason as his 'Apprentice' when she'd caught them travelling incorporeally to evaluate the ice-bound City and do what they could to free the starving and asphyxiating inhabitants. Jason had been a bit more willing to use what he had, in the desperation of the crisis, but he'd seemed to have a far greater inherent distaste for even the *idea* of magick.

Likely the second soul-bond had been the final key to unlock their abilities. The sewer crisis had happened barely two weeks after the bond formed.

But now...

Even after mulling over it *(Adam had used far less attractive terms like 'brooding' and 'sulking')* for three days since Adam's convoluted explanation, Damien wasn't sure if he was more discommoded that it had apparently taken his absence to spur them to accept this 'new' facet of themselves... or if it was that he was so deeply dismayed that he had *more* 'Evil Wizard bait' to try to protect.

Not that their awoken magick should make much of a difference in the latter case. An unawoken mage of high potential might – for all Damien knew – be even more attractive. And as his spouse and dearest friend, they'd already been at risk of being kidnapped as levers on his heart and his own Powers, both magickal and secular.

Had actually *been* so kidnapped for that very purpose, not three months agone.

Nothing had really *changed*... But it felt like the ground had shaken under Damien's feet.

His Champion snorted. "Those *children* practiced without either one of us for over a week when our Lady Province wouldn't let me stray from your side by inches. At *our* age, *we* can't afford to miss so much practice-time. And watching you at practice these last three days, it *shows*. Get yourself out of bed, my sweet prince."

"Adam..."

"*You*, particularly, get more benefit from arms-practice up here in Elaarwen, since you can actually practice with everyone else openly. These mountain-folk don't talk to the lowlanders and there's no one here who'll spill on how good you are with a blade to the curious ears of potential assassins."

Nothing Damien didn't know already. He just hated getting up at the hour that Adam deemed appropriate, especially after another night filled with dreams of dark and terrible things happening to his nearest and dearest. Dark dreams that had woken the ever-patient Adam up as well, but *he* hadn't spoken a word of complaint for the long minutes spent soothing his King back to sleep.

Damien sighed. "All right..."

He sat up, finger-combing his thick hair back – it was almost in his eyes, time to get it cut again – and stretching a bit. The blankets fell away to just over his knees...

...and Adam turned abruptly away.

"Don't forget to *Vanish* yourself over to your *own* suite to get dressed, Your Majesty," he said with what *almost* sounded like his usual sardonic tone...

Damien grinned to himself and slipped off the bed to come over and slide his arms around the taller man from behind.

"Of course, love." He let his hands roam over Adam's torso... and lower... It was less about what *could* be felt through all the layers of cotton and linen and wool – and even leather, though the tall knight hadn't put his light armor on yet, perhaps to spare his then-sleeping monarch the jingle and clatter and strong metallic scent.

Less about what could be *felt,* and more about what the imagination might make of what *would* be felt *without* all those intervening layers...

Adam's growl was all the warning there was before he turned in place and took his unsurprised sovereign in his arms... capturing Damien's willing lips in a possessive kiss.

"You... are *impossible,*" the taller man murmured. "One moment you're pushing me away, the next you're trying to entice me back into bed with you."

"Would you prefer we go back to the other way?" Damien asked a bit archly.

Adam rolled his eyes. "Not hardly."

He punctuated that with another breathtaking kiss.

"Now. Can you *please Vanish* yourself off to your own quarters, my *love,* so that I can manage to get out of these rooms and do my *job?*" Adam demanded after that. "And if Your Highness could be *bothered* to come down and see if you still remember which end of a sword is which–"

Damien laughed. "Oh, I think I can remember which end of *your* sword I'm supposed to hold on to."

He wriggled his naked body a little closer and then *Vanished* himself to the ducal bedchamber before Adam had barely had time to say his name in that enticed and exasperated tone. *Again.*

He rumpled the sheets and blankets and punched the pillow a few times to give the room a slept-in look, then opened the windows and glanced down at the lists located below. The castle's servants knew that their Duke liked to have the breeze whenever possible.

A bright blue songbird flitted over and perched on the top edge of the casement to regale him with a cheery, lilting melody. Damien amused himself with the thought that it was probably a love song composed for its mate. He didn't understand birds, but his *empathy* informed him that this one was very pleased with his acquisition of a prime territory and an attractive mate. He'd built his pretty hen a nest and she was already warming their first set of eggs. A clever little cock with everything in his own little world to sing about.

With a smile on his face, the King *reached* across the hall to retrieve the clothing – and, most particularly, his *boots* – that he'd left scattered in Adam's rooms the night before. He had others to wear, of course, since the servants would have unpacked his things as usual, but it wouldn't do for someone to come in to freshen up Adam's suite and find Damien's discarded clothing.

He was still smiling as he found a similar set of rough clothes to those that Adam had been wearing and headed into the washroom for a quick sponge-bath and his other morning ablutions. The facilities here were much more modest than the luxurious, sunken tub that he *still* couldn't explain the existence of in his tower-top room at home, but they got the job done.

As predicted, he could hear Adam's voice already cracking like a whip over the not-so-idle efforts of their Guards when he came back into his bedchamber. It was a comfortable piece of familiarity.

Unlike this revelation about Jason and Genevieve. Apparently, Adam's dispensation – or direction – to explain the whole thing to Damien was supposed to have been more along the lines of a description of why it couldn't possibly happen *again*.

Unwillingly, his mind went back to revisit the trails it had tread most of the night – most of the last *two* nights. Neither Queen nor Crown Prince wanted anything to do with magick. In fact, Adam claimed that they were both still denying that they had actually accomplished what they had.

That despite having performed a piece of magery that most Elemental mages would drool over *(all right, maybe not **literally**. It was sewage, after all)* both Jason and Genevieve seemed convinced that it had somehow been a fluke. That the Realm had somehow stepped in and *used* them to do what needed to be done.

In the process of putting on his second sock, Damien paused thoughtfully, toes half into the tube.

That idea might be worth pursuing.

Likely the Realm *had* taken a certain amount of initiative, possibly because It/They was frustrated with how neither Its/Their Bound Queen and Heir weren't using the Power that was theirs to do what needed to be done. Possibly It/They even saw this as a teaching technique.

He'd have to ask, if the opportunity to actually speak with the Realm in actual words ever arose again.

The technique might even have worked – if both his wife and his... Heir... weren't so damned unwilling to believe they had Power.

Damien realized his toes were getting cold and his back and leg weren't enjoying this cramped position with his knee tucked up and his toes half into his stocking. He went back to getting dressed.

It probably wasn't even all that startling that it had been the physical contact between the two of them that had sparked this new ability. Physical contact *was* a significant part of soul-bonds, after all. There was probably some of the same amplification effect Damien himself had *felt* when in contact with Genevieve. Adam had said that they had refused to touch each other for nearly a week after that incident, fearing a repeat... and that *that* hadn't done any good for either of their states of mind.

...a soul-bond denied...

Damien knew the painful routes *that* could take for himself.

Adam had also *implied* that no one else seemed to realize who had effected the 'miracle.'

Not the people themselves – there had apparently been a minor religious revival and then some altercations between those claiming Divine Intervention and those positing some impossibly distant action by their absent King.

Not the Guards, City or Royal – though they'd been rather too busy doing their actual jobs to bother about the Queen and the Crown Prince disagreeing over something.

And not Tomas Elsevier, who had apparently dismissed both Jason and Genevieve as 'merely warriors' – capable of creating battlefield strategies, but not of managing the refined and vicious politics of the Court or the intricate and corrupt paper-trails of a bureaucracy.

Well, that last was probably just as well. Though perhaps Tomas wouldn't have abducted Genevieve – and Jason as well, if unintentionally – if he'd realized he was taking a pair of puissant wizards hostage. Not that they'd proved themselves to be such while he held them... and surely *training* of such vast native Power would have helped protect them, though they still might have fallen to Tomas' – and Azella's – schemes.

A thread of unavoidable jealousy wound its way through Damien's heart as he did up his pants.

Genevieve's Power had manifested for *Jason.* Not *himself,* though *he'd* given her all the support and adoration it was possible to do for five *years.*

And Jason's had manifested for Genevieve. And he hadn't *shutdown* emotionally when confronted with all these new challenges as Damien had watched the tall knight do every time for the last fifteen years. Even in response to his partner and beloved proposing a marriage supported by their King. It was as if Genevieve was the sun, warming the cool serenity and carefully quiet depths of Jason's personality into something much more... roiling and active.

On the other hand, Damien told himself, trying to be fair, he'd practically turned cartwheels for Jason himself over the years. And he'd blossomed like a flower in the warmth of Genevieve's regard. That they should have the same effect on each other as they each had on *him* was, perhaps, inevitable.

It didn't really help.

None of it really helped.

Even up here in easy-going Elaarwen, where Harald's infidelities to Genevieve had almost seemed to distress her more for his rudeness in throwing them in her face over dinner with her father – and for her own barrenness – than for the fact that he'd done such things at all...

...even *here,* this... whatever it was that was between the four of them...

It couldn't *work.*

Even Adam – with his weirdly peaceful Acceptance of All Things Heretofore Unimaginable – hadn't suggested that Damien sleep openly in his room.

A lifetime of such subterfuges stretched, miserably ahead of Damien.

Lying to his friends.

Lying to his children.

Lying to the *people*.

It was...

A sharp pain – and then a blankness that was almost as sharp in the sudden cessation of sensation across a bond the King hadn't fully realized was there.

Damien *Vanished* himself to the practice-yard without stopping to think.

Well, almost.

He had sufficient focus to remember to appear in one of the shadowy doorways that let in to the lists his grandfather-in-law had installed here for the delight of Genevieve's grandmother.

The Royal Guards standing duty on his door all knew by now about their King's ability to *Vanish* himself from place to place – he could return on foot without confusing them or causing a fuss – but he tried not to do anything obvious or flashy in front of the people of Elaarwen. The mountain-folk treated Damien as if he were 'just The Lassie's husband' with 'that there fancy lowlander title' and he wanted to keep it that was as long as possible. Not to mention that *Genevieve* preferred it that way.

But it meant he had to push his way past the concerned young Guards – and bushy-bearded and wild-haired Elaarwen men- and women-at-arms – clustering around Adam, and Damien briefly regretted not just *pulling* himself to his love's side. Though what he could have *done*, even *then*...

"He seemed fine, and then he just, just *collapsed*," one of the newer Guards blurted as Damien shoved him out of the way to get to Adam's unconscious form. "You'll make the Captain all right, won't you, sir?"

For once, Damien didn't bother to pay attention to the young knight's name or answer his concerned – no, *terrified* – query.

He was too busy fighting with himself not to throw himself down and try to revive Adam with kisses... or to pull the prone man's head onto his lap and weep with worry and frustration.

Neither of those were *useful* things to do.

Neither of them respected Adam's dignity – nor his own need to maintain the authority of a king.

Neither did they *solve* Adam's *crisis*.

For *crisis* it was.

The tall Champion was more than unconscious – he wasn't even *breathing*. And his heart was stuttering to a stop as the air that nourished *it* diminished past usefulness.

Damn you, Elaarwen, Damien raged silently as he threw all his Power into forcing air into his love's lungs and the tall man's heart to beat. *Damn you! We've* **done** *what you instructed. Why are you doing this to him?*

It had to be Elaarwen – there was no detectable reason for Adam's sudden collapse.

His attention was so focused on the fallen knight that the King was entirely unaware of the humans around him – and hardly more aware of the rather disgruntled discussion that he could sense between the Realm and... something else.

Adam's breath began to even out. His heart began to find its rhythm again. Color began to fill cheeks that Damien hadn't even taken time to notice were pale as death. The *feel* of Adam's mind began to resemble the drifting of sleep, rather than the deeper-than-unconscious quiet that had nearly paralyzed Damien with terror. He had *emotions* again to Damien's *empathy*.

The King straightened up and sat back on his heels, taking care to keep his hands on Adam's skin and only now noticing that his back was cramped. He took a deep breath, and wrinkled his nose at the sharp, unpleasant aroma of fear-sweat surrounding him. A trickle of liquid made its way down his back *(so some of that smell was his own)*, tracing an icy, zigzaggy line alongside his spine.

Really icy.

Damien blinked in surprise to discover that he was wearing pants and socks – and nothing else – just as Alanna bustled up anxiously to ask him if the Captain was stabilized enough to move him indoors. The King nodded absently, and she started directing the men-at-arms to fetch supplies for a stretcher.

"And a cloak or something for His Majesty."

Almost before the last words were out of her mouth, something warm dropped over Damien's shoulders and back, cutting off the light wind that... That hadn't been there at all when the King arrived in the lists. The air had been utterly still when he *Vanished* himself in, Damien suddenly realized – *dead* still.

He didn't want to waste energy engaging his magickal *sight,* but somehow the King didn't doubt that if he did, he'd see the practice-area crowded with worried sylphs.

Hopefully they would make themselves useful and make it easier to lift Adam on the stretcher that was being assembled by the Elaawen men-at-arms.

Angelos and a few other rather shaken-looking young knights came forwards, when the stretcher was ready, to help shift Adam onto it. Damien focused on keeping the skin-to-skin contact that he didn't dare test by losing... but it wasn't just Adam at risk...

"Angelos?" he asked. "How are you doing?"

The young man was definitely far too pale. "Mostly worried about the Captain, sir."

It looked like it was more than that, but if that was how he wanted to play it...

Damien nodded, looking quickly around the courtyard that was now drenched with the light of early morning. His knights were mostly in little huddles here and there – *all* of them, and *all* of the Secret Cadre that he had with him were out here doing the same, which wasn't standard protocol. There was *always* someone left on duty at the doors to their private suites.

Master Derrick and Lord Lewis and Lady Emily – the older members of his current retinue, and the ones who had joined up from Genevieve's Rebels – were moving from huddle to huddle. Alanna was managing her own small group of knights, a hand on Angelos's shoulder.

They were all the ones who hadn't begun their careers as squires, or even pages, under Adam's tutelage, the King suddenly realized. The ones who saw his Champion as a man, and not an invulnerable icon. The ones who weren't shaken down to their boots by seeing Adam collapse for seemingly no reason.

There wasn't time to think about what a problem *this* was, because Alanna had the whole group with the stretcher moving. Damien had to rearrange himself to maintain contact as they all walked. Clever Alanna had commandeered a handful of other weepy-looking knights to hold doors, but the King had to sidle through each doorframe and walk sideways as they climbed the awkward, curving stair that led up to the row of private suites.

An overly-pale lady-in-waiting – Tasha – skittered out of Adam's rooms just as they arrived, giving her commanders a quick nod. Alanna had sent her on ahead to check the unguarded rooms. She followed back in after the men with the stretcher.

There didn't seem to be any real way to move Adam off the stretcher and onto the bed without Damien letting go... none that weren't too intimate or awkward that they wouldn't beg comment from the locals, anyways. The King tried not to look too obviously anxious while Angelos helped the two burly Elaarwen men-at-arms transfer his... Champion.

"Thank you, Istvan, Albin," the King told them, trying to bide peacefully until they were out of the way and he could go to Adam's side. His beloved knight was still breathing easily, so no one would understand... but Damien had needed to go back to forcing Adam's heart to beat in its proper rhythm.

"The Captain's near as dear to us as you and Genevieve, milord," Istvan told him as they wrestled the stretcher out of the room. "Seein' both as how he's dear to her and how he takes such care of all of ye."

"Aye," Albin added. "And yer own lads and lassies weren't in much shape to handle things. Savin' the handful of 'em."

He jutted his beard to the window where Alanna now had an arm around Angelos, who was visibly shaking. The drapes were tied back now, and the bed had been made and the covers turned down, either by servants or by Tasha, who had headed out again with the knights after the transfer.

Istvan paused at the door into the bedchamber. Albin already had the other half of the stretcher out in the sitting room. "That there's... a fair problem, milord. Sir Adam isn't immortal any more than you are yourself – no matter what wild stories we hear comin' up from the lowlands."

"Just Damien," the King said absently, his focus on his prone lover. "You're right, but we'll deal with that – later."

"Alanna?" Istvan asked, his voice full of concern, and presumably got some response that reassured him, because he picked up the stretcher again and left the suite with Albin.

Damien had sat down on the bed again and placed both his chilled hands alongside Adam's cheeks. His eyes searched his love's expression for any change, despite his *empathy* telling him there wouldn't be any. At least he was able to relax his Healing magick – Adam's heart and breath had stabilized again at his touch.

"Wake up, *please,*" he whispered, biting his tongue on the word 'love.' He didn't dare say that with others present...

...which reminded him...

"Alanna, is Angelos doing all right? Is this... the problem we were dealing with before?"

The woman sighed. "Some, I think. Not so much as all that. I'm..."

She hesitated, and it seemed so odd that Damien looked up to see her blushing. In his experience, Lady Alanna didn't *blush* at very much. Of course, she now had *both* arms around the young knight and Angelos had his face buried in her no-longer-so-perfectly-coiffed hair.

"Angelos?" he asked.

His young cousin looked up from Alanna's auburn locks to... look rather embarrassed himself.

"Elaarwen... seems willing to accept milady as a... surrogate of sorts for... for Herself," Angelos half-explained. "Because she was born in Cedarwen, we think. We, ah... Milady was, um, willing to take your example..."

Alanna rolled her eyes, but lifted her chin a little defiantly in Damien's direction.

Damien stared at them blankly, trying to pull his mind out of Adam's state in order to comprehend what they were telling him. It was just too hard. This had been far too close in his opinion.

"I... I was hoping you'd speak to Alanna's father for me," Angelos added, his cheeks brightening further as the silence stretched on.

Alanna rolled her eyes again and commented that she was far past the age for that to be an issue.

"Um, what??" Damien managed intelligently. "Why?"

Angelos buried his face in Alanna's hair again, and even the rarely-ruffled Alanna looked a bit flummoxed.

"For pity's sake, Damien," Adam moved under his hands, pulling the King's full attention back instantly. "Don't make them explain it in detail."

"Adam!"

Forget protocol and dignity and... he threw himself onto the older man's chest, shaking as hard as Angelos had been doing a moment earlier. No, harder.

The Champion made hushing noises as one arm came around Damien's back.

"Of course, we'll speak for you to anyone who believes you need more of a reference than Alanna's word," Adam told the younger pair. "Or that and your position as Second-in-Command of the Royal Guard. And cousin to His weepy Majesty here."

Clearly Adam *was* back to normal if he could turn this into a joke.

"Thank you, sir." Angelos's voice. "And... you are... you are..."

"I'm fine," Adam said dryly. "Except for getting saltwater on my chainmail. Damien, would you *please* get up?"

Chainmail? Oh. Yes. Adam had been practicing.

Reluctantly, the King sat up. Maintaining skin-to-skin contact wasn't a problem, since Adam had his hands on Damien's bare back. Or, hand rather, and it slid along his waist rather too alluringly for the younger man's ability to cope in the backwash of emotions from nearly watching his love *die*.

Adam's other hand was outstretched to Angelos, who had let go of Alanna to lean across the very wide bed and grip it. Well, grip it and weep over it.

"Are the rest of the girls and boys in this same state, Alanna?" Adam asked.

The commander of their Guards folded her arms and nodded wryly. "Well, except for Derrick, Lewis, Emily, and I. As you doubtless expected. The other three are holding the fort, as it were."

"Hmmn." Adam heaved a sigh. "Well, *this* won't do. But... maybe you can go reassure the rest of them now? And we'll figure out a more robust solution when..."

"When you're feeling more *robust?*" Alanna suggested, and Damien realized how *weak* Adam's return chuckle sounded.

He looked sharply at his Champion – Adam looked and *felt* so much better than he had a few moments ago. But he was still far too pale, and he wasn't even *trying* to sit up.

Getting that chainmail off of him was going to be a challenge.

"Thank you, Alanna," Damien said quietly, shoving down the panic that was starting to bubble up in him at last. There hadn't been *time* for panic earlier...

She gave him a long-suffering look. "Get this sorted out, please, Your Majesty. I'll go deal with our troops, but we can't have *you* falling apart like this in addition or it'll all be for naught."

Adam raised his eyebrows. "Seeing to things when *the King* falls apart is their *job,* Lady Alanna. Bad enough that they can't handle seeing *me* collapse. If they can't handle Damien doing the same, we need to replace them all. And seriously rethink our training."

He glowered up at Damien. "And *you* need to keep a level head, too."

Alanna inclined her head as the King flushed a bit himself. "*He* did, actually. He even managed not to *Vanish* himself directly to your side – at least I *assume* that was how you arrived so quickly, Your Majesty?"

Damien nodded, not quite trusting himself to speak yet. The shakes were starting to subside, and all he really wanted to do was curl up into Adam's side. Preferably after shelling him of his armor, but either way would do right now.

"He came out of one of the shadowed doorways," Angelos said quietly. He seemed to have recovered himself somewhat.

"Good," Adam said firmly. "We haven't lost five years of convincing the people here that you aren't the terrifying scion of your grandfather."

"Would it be so bad as all that?" Angelos asked. He'd let go of Adam's hand and sat up. His other hand reached backwards for Alanna's and she took it without comment. "We know – down in Emeralsee – what Dami– I mean, the King, can do."

Damien managed to give his young cousin a watery smile. "It's still private enough to call me Damien, Angelos. Just family, I think? Just me and Adam, and you and... your fiancée?"

Alanna shrugged a little uncomfortably as Angelos turned glowing eyes up to her. "We haven't discussed that yet. Getting him in and out of Elaarwen seemed... enough for now."

As the young man's face fell, she squeezed his hand and added, "For *now*."

Angelos perked up again a bit and she shook her head in exasperation and looked over at Adam. "If I ever wondered why you never tell His Majesty 'no'..." Her gaze slid to the King, "Though how *you* managed to fight that demon with Sir Adam lying there on the ground... If I'd seen this *first,* I would never have guessed you could."

Damien dropped his eyes, swallowing hard to fight down *that* remembered terror. There hadn't been time *then* until afterwards either, to let himself realize how scared he'd been.

"I didn't have any choice," he said softly. "Neither time, actually. It was *act* or Adam would... would die."

He was marginally pleased with himself that he kept from emphasizing that last word. Adam's hand on his waist squeezed slightly, but his voice was as usual: steady and ironic, if a bit gentler than normal. Or was that *weaker?*

"Well, it worked out. Both times. Go tell the rest of our loyal troops that I'm fine," Adam commanded the younger two. "I'll be down for lunch, so there's no need for some sort of sobbing parade to come visit me on my death-bed, either."

He paused. "And Alanna? Tell everyone to pack up their stuff. We'll be leaving directly after lunch."

Damien frowned at that, but kept quiet. If Adam was making this decision without consulting him, that meant he had some sort of information that the King didn't. Something that couldn't wait on a debate.

Given the timing, it probably meant that Elaarwen-Manifest had been communicating with him again.

Alanna's gaze flickered between the two of them, but since Damien didn't object, she simply nodded and tugged Angelos to follow her out of their – out of *Adam's* – bedchamber. The young knight paused to give the older men an almost mischievous look as he let himself be tugged, but there was a look of lingering worry. Adam waved him off, and the pair disappeared, closing the doors quietly behind them.

"I like that boy," Adam commented. "He reminds me a great deal of you at that age."

"Was I ever that relaxed and confident?" Damien sighed.

"Occasionally. And by nineteen or twenty you did a pretty good job of faking it around..." Adam chuckled and squeezed his King's bare waist – this time with both hands. "Around pretty much everyone but me, I suspect. And I had the advantage there, given that I *knew* what you were actually feeling."

Damien laid down next to his Champion, draping his arm over Adam's chest, notwithstanding all the sharp and pinchy bits of metal encasing him. The older man's arm curled snugly around Damien's bare back, his hand caressing the soft dip between ribs and hip.

"And that was about the time you decided to try to repress your *visions* of being with me like this," Damien noted. "Or so you told me."

It came out a little accusingly, not that he meant it to.

Just... right now the thought of losing Adam before they'd ever even had a chance to find out how important they could be to each other was... devastating.

Adam sighed. "Ah, love. I also told you that I was trying to make a life with Jason. And trying to take it in stride that you were, well, *not*-sleeping with every woman Ciriis added to your Secret Cadre."

His arm tightened around his King, somehow still careful not to poke with any of the edges of vambraces and pauldrons. "Most of my *visions* about you by that point had... gone away anyways. There had always been so many more that worked to alert me to when I needed to rescue you from a state dinner. Say, when Prince Oskar or Lord Prydeen or some of your grandfather's sycophants were going to harass you. Or when you were likely to have a meltdown in the middle of arms-practice and I should make sure the horse-trough was clean and full. Or when I was pushing you too hard.

"The ones of *later* were... flashes, really." Adam brought his other hand across to bury in Damien's short beard. "It was almost hard to identify the incredibly sexy and handsome, bearded *man* I was *seeing* as the devastatingly beautiful *boy* I'd helped grow up.

"It was... pretty confusing, you know," he added. "I practically acted in *loco parentis* to you for five years. It seemed... well, *wrong* to even be *able* to think about you as a lover."

Damien shivered and tucked his chin in, snuggling closer despite the sharp, metallic tang that assaulted his nostrils, the hard, pokey chainlinks and edges of the breastplate... and the fact that Adam certainly couldn't feel him clinging.

"It seems wrong *now*. For different reasons." One with fiercely red hair and one with pale blonde, both back in Emeralsee. And for a throne that needed an Heir.

"I don't love Jason any less, you know," Adam said softly. "I don't imagine that *you* love *Genevieve* any less."

He paused, then said *"Do you?"* and laughed aloud at Damien's indignant refusal.

The King – and oh, how he wished he didn't have to be 'the King' all the time, but it was what it was – pulled himself up and looked into those laughing, golden-hazel eyes that held no trace of cynicism or irony for once.

"I know you believe we can make this work, Adam. And... I *want* to. Gods only know how much I *want* it to."

He didn't need to actually *say* that such beliefs and hopes were nothing more than wishful fantasies.

Adam smiled gently. "Well, we have the length of this trip that Elaarwen is insisting we make for me to convince you it will."

Damien rolled his eyes. "Yes, this *trip* that apparently you – and Elaarwen – have decided we need to leave for *today*. You do know that I haven't gotten through half the things Adsel wanted me to look over?"

If Adam was feeling well enough to go back to joking about *that,* then it meant Damien needed to go back to pretending he wasn't still shaky with fear and that things were *normal.*

"You've gotten through the big things," Adam said. "Except for getting the Landsfell and Eybird clans down to discuss their problems. And it's likely that even if they *come,* they won't get anything accomplished until Genevieve herself is here. You're The Lassie's husband and stand-in when they want you–"

"–and 'that lowlander fellow' when they don't want to listen," Damien sighed. "Yes, I know. So, where are we going anyways? We'll need a direction."

"It's right there on the map, Damien."

"Which we've agreed I can't read," the King retorted. "Where are we going, Adam? And is Her Provincialness going to insist we ride double again?"

That sounded delightful, actually, though a bit too *open* if they had to ride out of the castle and Elaarwen's 'city' that way. And rather physically chancy to accomplish, unless they were heading back down towards Cedarwen and Brindlewell and Emeralsee; the 'roads' in any other direction from here were little better than game-trails half the time. Or goat-trails, even.

"I don't *think* so," Adam said thoughtfully. And we're going southeast. To Cloudcroft, if I understand Her instructions properly."

Damien looked at him in dismay.

Cloudcroft wasn't an easy trip, though at the end of Spring it was probably as good as it was ever going to get. Goat-trails indeed.

But of all the places to have to try to hide what was blooming between the two of them – in front of the sharp-eyed *(if hypothetically deceased)* Ciriis Celavell and Genevieve's banished-and-restored *father...*

This might be the worst place of all for them to have to go.

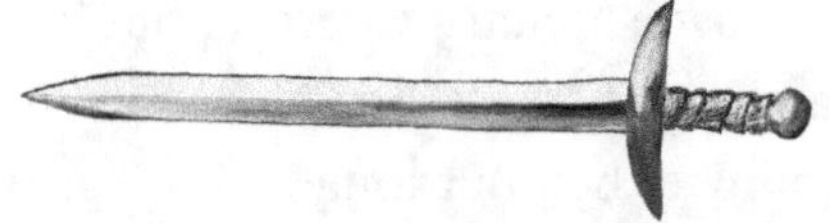

Chapter ELEVEN

Elemental, My Dear Champion

"**Y**OU MIGHT AT LEAST *LOOK* a little discommoded," Damien complained as they rode the last stretch of the road towards Cloudcroft where it was even possible to ride side-by-side.

The first day of travel had been relatively easy. The road was regularly used by wagons coming in to the 'city' and the only complication was that the grade was much steeper than the royal riders and their steeds were used to. As usual on this trip, they made a far shorter distance each day – measured as the crow flew – so as not to overstress the horses.

Damien's Sunset was Elaarwen-bred, but the elegant bay mare had spent nearly her entire life in the lowlands. She had the lungs for it, but her legs were in no better shape for mountain-climbing than anyone else's. The others had horses of Siovalese breeding; Damien's knights and Secret Cadre had been slightly offended when he sighed deeply as they all refused to switch over to locally-available mountain-ponies for the trip.

Adam, at least, had known what he was getting himself into. Alanna and Angelos and a few others – Derrick, Lewis, and Emily – had made the trip to Castle Stellarine before, but only the Champion had come all the way up to Cloudcroft. Not that *he* had been willing to switch over to a pony either, but long as his legs were, that wasn't really an option for the incredibly tall man.

On the second day, they'd crossed the ever-rickety bridge over the canyon that contained this part of the Sapphire River. The waterway was just a small stream right now, but the deep, jagged walls of the chasm marked with fresh, dark scars were a reminder that the Spring floods brought the water as high as within arms-reach of the top of the crevasse; it was at least fifty feet deeper than that now.

The trail – it really didn't deserve the title of 'road' – had become narrower as the grade became steeper still. Every branching that led to another village or homestead made the 'main' trail a little smaller.

"You worry too much, Damien," Adam said with unreasonable equanimity. "We're doing what we're supposed to be doing. It will turn out all right."

"I thought you believed in free-will."

Adam gave him a dry look. "My sweet prince, I'm following the dictates of a fragment of your Realm that will talk only to *me* where no one else can hear so that I can make the *visions* I've been granted of the future come true. What part of that suggests that I *want* to exercise free-will to change things?"

Damien growled and kicked Sunset to move up to a position behind Alanna's beast. The last branching of the 'roadway' before the trail that led only to Cloudcroft was less than a hundred yards ahead; after that they would have to ride single-file anyways.

He wasn't really in the mood to appreciate the vistas that opened up as they made their slow, careful way up the mountains... but it *was* incredibly beautiful.

Elaarwen in late Spring – nearly Summer – was green with those shades that come only from newly-leafed or -needled trees. It was easy to look out and see the tapestry of fresh greens as they traveled along cliffs or hillsides so steep and rocky that even grasses seemed to have trouble finding purchase. Deep, dark shades for the conifers, reddish ones for patches of sugar-maples. The palest shades were reserved for the stands of birches and weeping willows lining streams that glimmered like threads of gold when they caught the sunlight at just the right angle.

Stark sweeps of black showed where the Spring melt had initiated landslides, and the occasional scraggly silhouette of spidery branches against a brilliantly blue sky showed where one of the tough mountain-trees had finally given up fighting the weather.

They were above many of the other mountains by now, and it was possible to see hawks and eagles circling lower peaks or returning to rest in their sharp-cornered aeries tucked in the interstices of rocky precipices. The novelty of looking *down* into the nests of such magnificent birds of prey to see their scrawny, fuzzy-looking young ones absolutely riveted a number of the King's retinue – and Damien himself couldn't pretend to be jaded at the sight when his young knights begged him to come look.

He'd only been up to Cloudcroft twice before, after all. It was nearly as new to him as to them.

And the mountains called his name with the pride and abandon of things – like the eagles – that would never be tamed. Elaarwen's mountains were old and wise and full of strength.

For his own part, Adam seemed to be seeing the mountains with new eyes. He seemed reinvigorated, filled with sparkle, and relaxed in a way that Damien couldn't *ever* remember having seen his friend.

Although... when could he have?

Adam had come to King Reginald's Court at the age of eleven, fallen in love – *twice at once,* he now claimed – and realized he couldn't act upon or reveal that love till at least adulthood. He was his mother's Heir and the eldest of seven children – he'd helped care for his younger siblings as soon as they were born. Damien had heard Baronetta Linda mentioning that her eldest had changed Charley's diapers, and Charley was only two years younger than Adam.

And then a lost young prince had reached out to him in his dreams and Adam had been set upon the path of placing that prince on the throne. And then advising and protecting him.

When, exactly, could *Adam* ever have been carefree?

"Stop that," his Champion told him when they camped for the night in one of the few places along the trail where a flat enough space large enough to hold everyone *(including the horses)* offered itself. It was early for stopping, but their map – the regular one, not Adam's incomprehensible mess of chicken-scratches – indicated this as the last possible campsite they could reach without traveling by dark and no one was foolish enough to do that in the mountains.

"Stop what?" Damien asked. He was standing, feeling more than slightly useless, off to one side. The tents had been left behind at the castle, but he apparently wasn't even to be allowed to lay out his own bedroll.

Nor to help with dinner, though that was likely to all of their benefit.

"You're obsessing about something," Adam told him. "I don't know what it is, given that I can't actually *hear* your thoughts, but I know it has something to do with me. And considering what circles you've been going in for the last few weeks..."

The King sighed and shook his head, wandering farther away from the camp and the picketed horses and dinner preparations, and towards the cliff edge that lined the trail.

"It's not that, really. You just... seem really *happy* here. *Relaxed,* in a way I've never seen before. It occurred to me that we – all of us – put too much responsibility on you from the very beginning."

He looked down at the drop-off nearly at his toes, but he could practically hear Adam's eyebrow rising.

"I'd say I *took* more responsibility than I maybe had a right to... but it was my choice. All of it."

"Was it?" Damien squatted down and picked up a twig, idly drawing in the dust. "You saw things that needed doing and did them. Because other, older, people who *should* have been doing them... *weren't.*"

He heard a snort. "Mama was telling you that story about Charley, wasn't she? Was he there, too, when she did? Honestly, I'm not sure which one of us gets more embarrassed–"

Damien waved his free hand. "Not that. Or, well, yes, I guess that, too. It's... Someone should be taking care of *you,* Adam. You shouldn't have to feel that the whole world will collapse without you there to fix everything."

That occasioned another snort, and his Champion settled down next to him, actually dangling his lower legs over the edge of the cliff and nevermind the hundred-fifty-foot drop below.

Damien's mouth went dry watching as Adam shook his head. "Given what happened a few days ago, perhaps I'm not wrong. And *you're* a one to talk."

"The Sword and the Realm kind of don't give me a choice about that," Damien said almost absently. "And it was sit the Throne or death for *me*, so... Adam, can you move back from that edge, please?"

Adam gave him a very sardonic look. "I only sat down here, fool king, so that I could try to catch *you* if something startled you out of that squat and *you* started to fall. That is *not* a stable position," he added disapprovingly.

Damien gave him back ironic for sardonic. "I actually *flew* when that demon knocked you unconscious, you know."

"So, I have heard. Repeatedly. However, you had planned for that. I'm talking about what might happen if you fell over by..."

Adam's words trailed off and he was focusing... at a distance where there didn't appear to *be* anything to look at.

Open, empty air...

Oh.

Damien engaged his magickal *sight* and suddenly the space around them was filled with sylphs. He couldn't make out what they were saying, but they were clearly chattering up a storm.

"Nevermind," Adam told him with a brief, wry glance, "the ladies here say they won't let either of us fall. Not the horses or all those children either, apparently. As a favor to *us*."

He paused. "Oh. Not *us*. To *me*."

The tall knight blinked and ran a hand through his dark-blonde hair with a rather bemused expression.

*We won't let **you** fall either,* Sorcerer-King, said a chorus of feminine voices that was somehow light and cheery and deep and meaningful and, um, *suggestive,* all at the same time. *Our cousins won't have anything to do because **we** will keep all of you safe.*

A lovely girl was... resting her elbows on top of the cliff-edge and giving Damien a knowing smile. Her skin was the color of fresh-turned earth and her eyes were a determined slate-grey. Her hair hung down straight and thick, and...

Oh. She wasn't somehow dangling from her folded arms over the side of the cliff. She was coming up *out* of the cliff...

Damien startled, just as Adam had feared, but he moved backwards not forwards, landing on his rump in a puff of dust.

"Oreads now?" Adam asked. The pretty, dark-skinned female Elemental winked at him.

"I guess we're... good, then," Damien said, half to the oread and half to Adam.

Indeed, the Elemental replied, still sounding like a chorus all speaking together. *You may tell that female that she can stop worrying about the trail being washed out. This is an important pathway, and we will never let that happen.*

"Alanna will be relieved," Damien replied. "Thank you."

Actually, Alanna – assuming she decided to believe him – would be more than 'relieved.' The woman had stayed out ahead of the rest, watching for any sign of instability in the trail before allowing her King and Prince and colleagues to venture onto it. She had been a sweating, shaking mess when they stopped, and was letting Angelos take care of things for once.

"Alanna will be relieved about what?" Adam demanded. "I can't hear this lady at all."

Damien gave him a curious look. "I can't hear the sylphs. She said the trail is good ahead and we don't have to worry." And that had been bothering him, too. He'd been able to communicate with sylphs – and even Sifwisa of the Trade-Winds – just fine a couple of months ago.

Adam snorted. "I don't think Alanna will take anyone's word on that."

The oread shrugged. *Perhaps the male can convince her. He is of the Earth – like you, Sorcerer-King – though he belongs elsewhere. He seems a good fellow, kin and kind of yours, so he can be tolerated. The female is of Fire, like our Duchess, and she* **almost** *belongs here. A good pairing, though not so strong as to require more.*

"Um... thank you?" Damien responded, unsure what the Elemental maiden wanted of him.

That thought got him a hoot of laughter.

*'Maiden!' Not the way you think of such things, certainly! And you'd know what I **wanted** of you, were you not so well-set already. You need balance, anyways, not more of what you have already, and the other one wants nothing but you, more's the pity. I could balance **him**.*

The oread slid a sly and knowing glance over to Adam.

You bring the Duchess with you in spirit, and he brings the... the oread frowned. *The Duke? Not **our** duke, surely, since that is either you or the old one. The Prince? Whatever. It would be better if they were here more fully, but this has been delayed too long already. The Heart has been awaiting you.*

"For me?" Damien asked, confused. "What's been delayed too long? What is the Heart?"

Adam looked at him sharply.

The Heart is the Heart, the oread's 'explanations were about as useful as Ilseador's... though she seemed a great deal more chatty. *And the delay has been... problematic. The old one never joined with the Heart. Nor did the one that preceded him. The female that birthed that one was from far away and did not understand.*

"*I* don't understand!" Damien exclaimed with frustration.

You will, the oread assured him with annoying confidence, *when you are come to the Heart.*

"And where is this 'Heart'?" he tried, hoping to get something *useful* out of the creature.

The other one knows, he was told. *But be sure you bring **only** the other one with you past the point where earth-kisses-sky. The Heart is not meant for all. Only the true guardians may approach it.*

"And *I'm* a true guardian of this thing?" Damien felt like he was being a bit crabby about it, but couldn't help himself. Nothing but riddles...

Adam's warm arm circled him and tugged him comfortingly close as the oread chortled. *Not you alone, of course, Sorcerer-King. This other one and the Duchess and the Prince will aid you, of course. Amongst all of you there is enough to Anchor properly. The foreign blood that runs through you and the Duchess is diluted now and lends you only its strength.*

"The sylphs want me to mention that in the 'olden times' we brought 'foreign breath' into the line on a regular basis. To keep it fresh and strong," Adam said. "I gather that they can hear your oread and this has something to do with what *she* has been telling you."

"I suppose so..."

The oread had turned her head and was now directing her comments only to the sylphs, who were fluttering about in a dramatic display of consternation and disagreement.

Damien looked at Adam, who shrugged. "At least they're pretty."

The Elemental dispute ended with the oread making what would be a rather rude gesture for a human and disappearing into the cliff-edge. The sylphs likewise flounced off in a display of temper.

Damien sighed and disengaged his magickal *sight* before leaning his head on Adam's shoulder. "I want to believe I learned something useful out of all that... but I couldn't make heads nor tails of any of it. She mentioned something about an Anchor – which the Realm did as well, back when we crossed the Sapphire.

"The first time," he added, as he realized that, technically, they were again in the land between the rivers. The stream that had cut the canyon they crossed that first day was the headwaters of what later became the river.

"So... nothing new then?" Adam asked.

Damien shrugged. "She seemed to have trouble with names, so I'm not sure. But I *think* she said that we have to do something that hasn't been done since Genevieve's... *great*-grandfather was duke. Something *necessary*, but..." He shook his head. "Duke Emmeren's wife was Lady Shalla Elemandros of Wave. There seemed a suggestion that Duke Siegfrid – her son – *couldn't* do whatever-it-is because of his foreign blood."

"And that would be what the sylphs objected to," Adam noted. He gave a low, impressed whistle. "I didn't think Elaarwen had ever rated a Turquoise Princess marrying into the line. When would Duke Emmeren ever have even met her?"

Damien shook his head. "No idea. The oread seemed to think that Genevieve is sufficiently *not* foreign now to do this thing..."

"'Whatever-it-is,'" Adam nodded. "And presumably you count, as her husband and Duke-Consort. And *you're* sufficiently not-foreign? Despite Queen Rena?"

Damien's grandmother had been a princess of Dawil.

The King spread his hands. "I told you – I told *her* – I don't understand any of it. The oread did say it would be better if Jason and Genevieve were here. But apparently they're with us in spirit – so that's why it's supposed to work. Whatever-it-is."

"Hmmn." Adam looked at him thoughtfully.

"And she also said that – whatever-it-is – you and I are going to have to go on and do it alone. That this Heart-thing is only meant to be approached by its 'true guardians.'" Damien sighed again. "I suppose Cloudcroft has to be this 'earth-kisses-sky' place that is as far as we're allowed to bring Alanna and the rest."

Adam's chuckle rumbled though Damien as well. "'Earth-kisses-sky'? That sounds... romantic."

Damien rolled his eyes, but didn't move away. "Yes, very romantic. With my father-in-law and Ciriis and all their servants there in that teeny-tiny house."

Another chuckle. "It's not *that* small, Damien. It's just not a castle like you're used to."

"Or a proper manorhouse like your parents have," Damien countered. "Or like Rave–"

"Like Ravenscroft," Adam finished for him when Damien bit his own words off. "That sort of sprawling compound with a grand and elegant manorhouse to greet visitors of rank is the way things are built in *Emeralsee*. We have a much more forgiving climate after all. Cloudcroft is just *compact*."

"Hunh." Damien couldn't really disagree, but... they would see *compact* when good Lord Aldred had to stuff nearly two dozen extra people into his holding for... who knew how long.

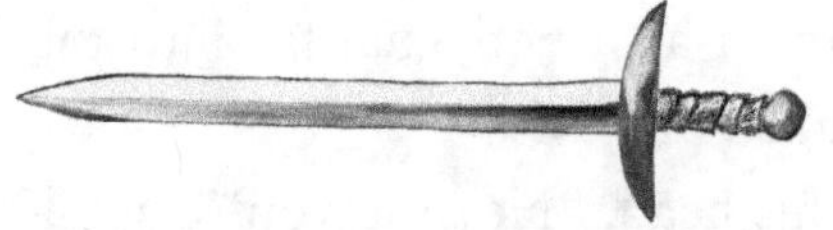

Chapter TWELVE

Troubling Hints

THEY ARRIVED AT CLOUDCROFT BEFORE noon the next day.

There wasn't a huge amount of flat space around the 'cottage,' but the half-dozen acres that comprised the high plateau was enough to allow for a paddock that they could turn the horses into. The man-of-all-work who opened it up for them to do so noted that it would be a bit crowded come evening, when the flock of sheep and herd of milch-goats was brought in from the lower pastures where they grazed during the day.

But fortunately the weather was mild, so they didn't have to try to get all the animals into the barn and stables. Angelos and Adam weren't the only coastal-bred members of the party who shivered a little at that offhanded qualification. Cloudcroft's temperatures weren't *mild* by their reckoning.

Aldred came out to greet them, moving well despite his age and the heart condition that Damien discreetly checked him for every time they met or parted.

"We had no idea you'd come up so far, Son," the old man noted as he escorted Damien and Adam – and by default, Alanna, who was staying with them as a bodyguard – into the house. "Tell me Genevieve hasn't taken poorly."

Damien shook his head. "No, and you've actually seen her more recently than I. You knew we were coming up to Elaarwen after checking on Farivera and Siovale."

Aldred nodded as they made their way into the central room of the structure – the hearthroom that had been the original one-room cottage when his parents had accidentally wintered there. As Adam had said, the place was far more built up now, having slowly grown into multiple stories of a sprawling, random structure that defied the term 'architecture' even before Genevieve's little remodeling project of a few years ago.

Though it was still relatively 'compact' for a nobleman's residence.

"Aye, up to the city and my– the castle. But all the way up *here?*"

Damien shrugged. "The Realm asks me to do odd things on occasion, Papa. Though it wouldn't have been a proper trip to Elaarwen without a visit to you and Ciriis and the baby."

"Hmmn." The old man looked both curious and skeptical, but turned and greeted Adam with pleasure as well, and was re-introduced to Alanna, who had once served in his Rebel forces under Genevieve. Alanna was rather more stiff and formal than usual, which Damien wondered at. He would have thought she'd be *more* comfortable in the presence of her former liege-lord and commander.

"What a lovely young woman," the old man said approvingly as he seated himself in the worn, leather-upholstered chair that had clearly been his for long enough that it had molded to the curves of his body.

Damien recalled seeing it in Castle Stellarine during his last visit and winced internally at the effort it must have taken to haul the tired old piece of furniture up that hazardous trail. Clearly Aldred wasn't really suffering a great deal for having acceded to Damien's very brief banishment of him last Fall.

"I see you're taking your full Court about with you, even when Genevieve isn't along," Aldred added, gesturing genially at the other comfortably mismatched seating.

"Just enough to maintain appearances," Damien replied, settling himself in another chair. "Count Marsham – did you know him? – was much more accommodating when there was a lady of quality pouring out and serving as hostess."

He gave Alanna – who had remained standing in her role as bodyguard – a small nod of thanks.

Adam snorted a little at that, and Aldred frowned at him.

"Marsham... Felix Marsham? Or was that the father...?"

"The current Count is Felix," Damien said. "His father, Nathaniel, was the Count when Farivera was Lost. Felix is about your age, is my guess," he added a bit ingenuously. Adam's amusement was easily detectable across what Damien had decided to call their *'empathic bond.'*

"Can't say as I did. Son of a minor noble from another province, after all. No reason I should have done." Aldred shook his head, though a certain glint in his eye suggested he remembered the former Count Marsham's eldest son rather well.

Given that the current Count Marsham had deeply enjoyed some of the fine Wavian and Dalizelli vintages that his isolated fief hadn't had access to during the Lost years, Damien had gotten a great deal more detail out of the man than he'd really been hoping for. According to Felix Marsham, he and the then-Ducal-Prince of Elaarwen had been roustabouts together at King Reginald's Court, fighting duels of honor, frequenting the rowdier taverns of Emeralsee, and lifting the skirts of every girl they could, no matter her rank or state.

It had given the bemused King a rather... *different* perspective on his father-in-law.

Adam snorted at this 'lack of memory' as well, but didn't make any actual comment.

"So, where's my brother-in-law?" Damien asked, as Aldred tried to get Alanna to come sit down and she rather stiffly declined.

The old man blinked, then brightened up. "Ciriis is putting the lad down for a nap. I'm sure she'll be down to greet you herself as soon as she's done."

"Does he sleep well then?" Adam asked.

"What? The babe?" Aldred seemed a little confused by the question. "Oh, aye, I suppose so. Ciriis sees that he doesn't wake me, anyways."

He apparently took Adam's rather stunned silence for disapproval, for he hastened to add, "The babe sleeps at her side, of course. 'Tis too cold up here to put him in his own cradle, and no room for a proper nurse to keep him as we had for Genevieve down in the castle."

Damien could *feel* Adam's mingled irritation and sorrow that Aldred thought that was how things *should* be. Marianna had been six when Damien had visited Lynncrag, and while the sweet-natured child *had* possessed her own bed, she never spent a night in it as far as Damien had been able to tell. She'd even snuggled in with *him* one night, to his utterly baffled enchantment.

"Well, we'll see Emmeren later then, I suppose," Damien said quickly. "I don't suppose you've come up with a nickname for him yet?"

With the shock of dark red hair that the newborn had already sported when Aldred had brought him down to the capitol two months ago, he was likely to get stuck being called 'Red' if they didn't give him something else soon enough. Or perhaps even if they did. Adam had passingly mentioned that he'd had to put a stop to that among the pages a few years ago, when one lad was particularly dismayed.

Aldred looked a bit startled. "A nickname for Emmeren? But that was my grandfather's name. Whatever would we shorten it for?"

"It's a bit of a mouthful to shout when you're trying to stop him from climbing into the sugar bowl or jumping off a fencepost," Adam suggested. "What did you call Genevieve when she was small?"

The old man looked baffled. "We called her Genevieve." He paused thoughtfully. "I suppose her nurse may have called her something else. And Giendra called her 'sweetie' until I asked her to stop – not really appropriate for a future warrior-Duchess – or Queen, after all."

Damien reached out to put a hand on Adam's shoulder before the other man could express what was rapidly segueing from sympathy for the new baby to outrage for what was starting to sound like Genevieve's stolen childhood. She'd turned out fine, after all.

"To each their own. We called my sister 'Kandy,'" he told Aldred, "But I was always just Damien. And Adam was always Adam if Baronetta Linda and his father are to be believed."

With a look of relief, Aldred leaned back in his chair. "Ah, yes, Linda Loveress. She was a fine-looking lassie in her youth. Sweetest girl at Court, too. Always seemed to have a kind word for everyone, and that wasn't common in those days."

Maybe that wasn't a look of *relief,* but of *memory...*

Adam shot Damien a look of alarm, clearly remembering Felix Marsham's *memories.*

"Um, yes," Damien agreed. "The Baronetta is a lovely person. Very, um, *motherly.* Though I suppose that's natural, given that she has seven children. She all but adopted me as well when Adam and Ciriis took me out to Lynncrag when I was seventeen."

Aldred looked wistful. "*Seven* children. And that damned Reginald had *thirty.* And my sweet Giendra couldn't manage but the one."

He shook his head. "I used to think perhaps I'd erred and should have wedded Alexa Solway after all, given that she'd birthed two. Now, of course..." He sighed. "Well, now we know *she* only managed one either. Though her daughter has had *five,* even with starting so young. That ruins a woman for later bearing, often," the old man noted wisely. "A pity none of us knew about that at the time."

Adam looked about ready to choke. *That* was why Aldred no longer regretted not having married Alexa Solway? And he couldn't *really* be implying that *he* should have married Megan after – presumably *after* – his wife had passed away when his daughter was still so young. Were Genevieve's usual soliloquies about her parents' great romantic love... a bit off-base?

Not to mention how *awkward* it would have been for her soul-bond with Jason to have arisen if the two of them had been raised as uncle and niece. Or brother and sister.

"Grandfather had over twice that number of offspring, if you count the illegitimate ones," Damien said, for lack of any better ideas.

Aldred waved this aside. "You can't count those, boy. We all have a few of those hidden about here and there." He looked over at the suffused Adam with a wry smile. "Well, not you, I suppose. And not young Jason."

"Not me either," Damien said firmly as the old man's thoughtful gaze came back to him.

"No? Well, I imagine that's a relief to my daughter," Aldred noted, though his tone suggested he didn't entirely believe the assertion. "Not that a bastard can inherit anyways, no matter what that fool Harald tried to claim when he was outed."

There was a flash of hatred across the old man's face when he mentioned his former son-in-law... who had kidnapped him and let Genevieve think them both dead for two years. Harald had worked with Lord Prydeen – if not King Reginald himself – to claim the throne on the strength of his claim to being King Reginald's bastard child by Duchess Lydia of Siovale.

Those two years of captivity had destroyed Aldred's health. And the final confrontation with Prydeen – with Harald in chains at Damien's feet – had nearly ended Aldred's life when the sorcerer's bullyboys had cut the former duke's wrists. Damien had saved him – discovering his own latent Healing Talent in the bargain.

It was entirely understandable that Aldred would–

"To think I let my only child, my *Heir* marry a *bastard*," Aldred was complaining.

And it was immediately clear that he meant legitimacy and not quality of character, for he added, "I should have known that *Hector* could never have kept his family tree clean. Lydia was always at Court, even when he wasn't, for all that everyone knew better than that in those days. And she pranced around in gowns that would make any *decent* wife blush, acting like she thought herself better than the queens, for all that she was no better than any other whore. Though she turned up her nose at men from the mountains."

Himself, presumably.

He snorted. "Lowlander women. No better than they should be, I suppose. Excepting your lady mother, Damien," he added quickly. "Miria was as modest as a princess-by-marriage should be. And your sister was always in full military uniform when I saw her. Not that Eric was particularly openminded about, well, *anything.*"

Damien felt his eyes going wide as he tried to figure out what expression could possibly make sense to wear and how to compose his face into whatever that might be. He could *feel* Adam struggling with the same problem. Pray Gods that his love would assume that Aldred's omission of his own mother in that 'exception' was simply out of the old man's rush to cover his own *faux pas.*

Was it possible that Genevieve's father was starting to go senile? He'd heard there were people who simply stopped filtering what words they would say as they grew older and simply said whatever came to mind...

"You'll raise your own daughters to be proper mountain-maidens, of course," Aldred added. "Like this lass here."

He indicated Alanna, standing by the wall and looking like she would rather be anywhere else.

"You're Elwood and Liliana's youngest, aren't you?" Aldred asked her. "You've the look of the Widdenwood clan, though you've your mother's hair. Cousin of Giendra's, wasn't she? Damn shame how Reginald gave over your lands to that fellow of his. Merwin Saltenshire, wasn't it? Why haven't you gotten around to fixing that, Damien?"

The King winced as he glanced at Alanna. "It's not as simple as that, Papa."

Aldred *harumphed.* "Well, it should be. The Fathelirres have been true vassals to Elaarwen since time immemorial. Speaking of which, why is *Brindlewell* still under Crown vassalage? Rebellion's over, isn't it?"

Damien sighed. "It didn't really seem to matter before, since Genevieve is both Queen and Duchess. Doubtless we'll be readjusting things now that Jason is Duke of Emeralsee."

That got him a snort. "That's a legal fiction, isn't it, boy? Until my grandchild is old enough to carry the title?"

Damien winced again. "Yes and no. The Sword has spoken for Jason. He really is the Heir and Crown Prince and Duke of Emeralsee. And he's doing the *work* that goes with those titles. I'm not changing that around for an infant until the Sword speaks for him or her."

Until and *unless,* but Aldred didn't know about Prydeen's prophecy.

"A few more months then," the old man said confidently.

Damien forced himself not to grind his teeth. "I'm not even *trying* the Sword out on my child until she's old enough to walk and talk. And I'm not removing Jason's titles until she's legally of age to rule."

Aldred waved this aside. "She – or he – will be a Stellarine. The Sword spoke for Genevieve. Mama said it spoke for *me* as a babe, though Grandmother Alexandria spirited it away before I can remember that for myself. It will speak for my grandchild."

Well. That answered the question as to whether the old man had known that the Sword had considered him a candidate for the Throne – and a more legitimate one, presumably, than the king who held the seat and whom the Sword had rejected. Had that been on the younger Aldred's mind when he came down to his cousin's Court as 'merely' the Heir to Elaarwen?

Aldred looked briefly annoyed at having to mention that his grandmother had taken the Sword away before he could have taken possession of it. His eyes flickered down briefly to the scabbarded Blade that now resided at Damien's side.

"We'll see what happens when it does," the King said firmly.

"Of course, lad," Aldred agreed. "But a Stellarine is meant to be on the Throne, not a Solway."

"An *Alsterling,* either way," Damien pointed out. *"Jason* is an Alsterling. And so will be any child of *mine."*

And since Jason was the eldest-and-only-child of the eldest-and-only-child of King Reginald's eldest child... himself the eldest child of Prince Anthony, himself the eldest child of Queen Marian... who was the last ruler that everyone had been able to agree upon... Arguably Jason's claim to the Throne – not that he wanted it, any more than any rational person – was better than *Damien's.*

Aldred gave him a smug smile. "Of course. But the *people* will be reassured to have a descendant of Princess Alexandria on the Throne."

Even Genevieve hadn't been sure what her father had known or what seeds of ambition her erratic and irascible grandmother, the Grand Duchess Alicia, might have planted in her son's mind. Though there had been little doubt that Alicia's mother, the Princess Alexandria, had spirited the Sword away to prevent her reckless daughter from embedding Elaarwen in a rebellion it could not then have hoped to win.

Genevieve had repeatedly assured Damien that *she* had never been told that the Throne would someday be hers... though she'd admitted that she was well aware that it would be if the Rebellion succeeded.

Her lineage was as good as Damien's, after all. Better, if one considered descent through the King Reginald to be a tainted line.

"As, indeed, there already is," the King said, hoping his tone was final enough to quell even his seemingly irrepressible father-in-law. "Given that Genevieve is Queen."

Queen Marian's ghost – who had some mysterious communication with the Sword – had insisted that the thing had 'spoken' for only one person between herself and Damien. It had become obvious that must have been Aldred, when the Sword had required Damien to Heal him. *(Though the ancient Queen also claimed that she had a sense that the Sword* **would** *have spoken for* **Damien's** *father as well, had it ever had the chance... Damien had always suspected that she was saying that only to make him feel better.)*

Damien had made sure that the entire Realm – or at least those attending Jason's coronation, which had *not* included the recently disgraced Lord Aldred – had seen that the Sword spoke most brilliantly for himself, then Genevieve, then Jason. Least for Jason, but still undeniably and distinctly.

Not that *he* wanted his Throne either, but somebody had to do the job.

"Of course," Aldred said again in that smug tone, and Damien looked helplessly at Adam, hoping *he* could somehow redirect the conversation. He completely deserved the sardonic look of acknowledgment that he got in return.

"Lord Aldred," Adam began a bit hesitantly, and clearly trying to come up with something on the fly – Damien's Champion as he always had been.

"Just 'Aldred,'" the old man corrected him with genial smile. "Or 'Papa' when it's just family. You're as dear to me as Genevieve and Damien, after all, you and Jason," he added.

Adam's sense of shock peaked at the first part of that, began to subside a touch at the second...

"After all, we all know that there's no possible way she'd be carrying this baby if it weren't for the two of you."

A newer, *much* higher peak of anxiety...

"I never *could* get that girl to just take a proper rest when she needed it," the old man added, with a proud shake of the head. "Not even when she was a little lass. She always had to show that she was ready to be my Heir and Second. So, I don't blame you, son," this was directed to Damien, "I'm not a bit surprised that it took all three of you to keep her from wearing herself out further. And it was worth it, no matter how odd the whole thing looked from the outside. She's well again, and *I'll* have a grandchild."

He leaned forwards eagerly, elbows on knees and hands clasped, as Adam started to breathe again. "Maybe even a second one, later? For Elaarwen? My little lad can't inherit, as I promised you, since Ciriis supposedly didn't survive to wed me. But I don't want to see my seat go to a collateral line."

Not that he *would,* since presumably that would happen long years into the future.

Nor was it *his* seat anymore. Genevieve had been Duchess for seven years and Bound to the province for five.

"Um," Damien had to force himself not to look at Adam, *will* himself not to think of four beautiful children... "We'll have to wait and see how she does with this one. I don't want to risk Genevieve's life for some hypothetical future child."

"Of course, of course." Aldred leaned back again, looking a little disappointed.

It was beyond difficult not to speak aloud the dark truth that Tomas of Siovale had given Damien shortly before he'd ripped his own throat open on Damien's sword. That not only had Aldred known and ignored the abuse Tomas' half-brother, Harald, had heaped upon Genevieve during the eight years of their marriage, but that his alternative to saving her had been to consider re-marrying to breed himself another Heir.

As indeed, he'd actually *done* so recently... only recanting his actions when Damien had finally made him take the Vassal's Oath and allowed the Land Itself *(Themself)* to rebuke the old man for his temerity. Which It *(They)* had done, since no one needed alternate claimants to the Throne after two Siovalese attempts to usurp, the Rebellion before that, and the eighty-three years of his grandfather's tyrannical rule. And hence this crazy pretense of Ciriis' death in childbirth.

Poor baby to get stuck with all this history before he was even born.

"Genevieve's a bit old to start having passels of children," Adam pointed out. "You wouldn't want to risk Ciriis, I assume. They're the same exact age."

"Wouldn't want to risk me for what?" Ciriis Celavell demanded as she came into the room, and Damien had to take a quick breath as he saw her.

She was...

...as beautiful as the day – some dozen years ago – that she had seduced a heartbroken, lonely young prince into her bed.

...as terrifying as the day – three years before *that* – when she'd 'discovered' him in the Royal Library.

...and as intimidating as all the years between and after when she schemed to put him on his throne... and keep him there.

He was on his feet and bowing over her hand before he even thought about it, straightening up to see a look of deepest irony on Aldred's face. He didn't dare look at Adam's expression.

"Well, aren't you still a dear boy," Ciriis reached up – Damien was only a hair above middling height, but she was as tiny as she was terrible – and pulled the King down to kiss his cheek.

Her eyes flickered appraisingly to Alanna, silent at her post, then to the King's Champion.

"Adam."

"Ciriis."

There had always been that odd, alert, wariness in the way they greeted each other. Respect, even friendship... but always the sense that they were rivals in some sense.

Damien had never understood that before.

He thought he might understand it a bit, now.

Adam's face was serene, but held just the hint – something about the eyes – of a self-satisfied smirk. Ciriis was just as unfazed, but was there a sort of wry acknowledgment?

"We were just talking about how my Genevieve's life isn't worth another baby, my dear," Aldred told her, his own sharp eyes taking in all the parts of the scene. "Nor yours either, of course."

His Genevieve...

And that last bit was clearly a tag onto the end of his thought, to judge by the deepening irony in Ciriis' eyes.

"Of course," she said, and somehow the lack of overt emphasis implied a world of irony.

She had placed one king on a Throne... and schemed to try for a second. Now she was stuck in the web of her own machinations, tied to a man too old for his ambitions and a babe who no longer had any real prospects, in a place remote from any of the power she had manipulated so well and for so long. And now, having faked her own death, there was no real way to come back from the bed she had made and would be forced to lie in.

Damien fixed a pleasant expression on his face as he reseated himself. "How's my new brother-in-law, Ciriis?"

She made a face and flopped into a chair with far less of her usual elegance and far more exhaustion than Damien had ever seen, even in the marathon of work that had fallen so suddenly upon them all when his grandfather passed away. Her dark hair was pinned into an chignon that was far too fashionable for such an isolated outpost of humanity – and slightly askew, as if she had neither a lady's-maid nor a mirror to aid in assembling it… or had managed it in a hurry, say following their unexpected arrival and laying her son down for a nap. And her gown was of fine wool – lovely and well-fitted even for a woman just months past her pregnancy – but it was a far cry from the satins and brocades she had once sported even for riding clothes.

"Asleep. At *last*. If he doesn't get a nap in the afternoon, he's up half the night, but I swear – he hates going to sleep like cats hate water. Every time I set him down, he starts crying *again*. I'd leave him to cry himself out," she added with tired frustration, "the way the midwife said works. But he just gets louder and louder and…" she gestured around the house, beginning and ending with Aldred, "… it's a small place. You can *hear* him screaming unless you go outside. And a *ways* outside."

Well… Ciriis had never seemed like a *motherly* sort of person to Damien. Predestined *empathic* connections aside, it really wasn't a mystery why he'd cleaved to the patient Jason and the protective Adam, rather than the terrifying Ciriis when they'd lured him out of the Library. Even if Ciriis *did* bear a cursory resemblance to his own mother and likely could have gotten him out faster had she bothered to mute her own sharpness even a little.

"Some babies need to be held to sleep," Adam said in what sounded to Damien like an attempt to sound neutral and not judgmental. "Fontaine was like that. She'd sleep easily so long as she was held. We all took turns. Even me, and I wasn't ten when she was born."

"Well, that must have been nice for *your* mother." Ciriis glared at him. "Everyone *here* has *jobs* to do, so the babe is *my* problem. As has been made clear to me."

She didn't quite throw Aldred a dark look, aware as she was of which side her bread was buttered on. Presumably the former duke had heard enough of her rant before to not take umbrage so long as she didn't directly cast blame on him for the failure of their combined scheme.

"I'm going half *mad* with never being able to put the… my son down while he's *awake*, Adam. If I can't get at least a few minutes to myself while he's *asleep* I probably will start raving. And *I've* got a job here, too, you know," she added, clearly dismissing the problems of motherhood. "Cloudcroft isn't large enough to keep a chatelaine on.

"Speaking of which," she went on, turning to Aldred, "Do you have any idea *where* we're going to *put* all those Guards they brought in with them? Or what we're going to *feed* them? We haven't gotten but the one supply caravan up from your 'city' since the New Year."

The quotes around the word were clear in city-bred Ciriis' voice. She was a cousin of Rosa's and had spent her Summers in Zialest at Rose Lake, but the Celavell family were city-dwellers and made their home in Reyenrald, which the Dukes of Reyensweir considered their 'second capitol.'

Alanna cleared her throat. "Begging milady's pardon, but we brought a train of packhorses with extra supplies. His Majesty was most adamant that we not impinge on Cloudcroft's hospitality."

"Hmmph." Ciriis narrowed her eyes at the Guardswoman, clearly sending her a reminder that she was supposed to be a fly on the wall, then looked at Damien. "And how long *will* you be staying for?"

Damien glanced at Adam. Who shrugged.

The King winced. "I'm not sure. And... actually, *Adam* and I won't be staying long at all, but our Guards will."

His former Spymistress and founder of the Secret Cadre sat up with a frown at that.

"What are you talking about, Damien? Where you go, they go. That's how this works."

Well, it was nice to see she still cared about *him* as well as her collapsed scheme to replace him.

Which, to be fair, wouldn't have been for twenty years or so, unless he and Genevieve really did *die* of the needs of the Realm and the soul-bond.

The King shook his head. "Not this time, Ciriis. There's something... *magickal* that the Realm is asking me to do. I've had it made clear to me that I am *not* to bring along a whole troupe of Guards. I *am* bringing Adam," he added, hoping to mollify her.

Needless to say, it didn't work.

"I didn't build you up an entire cadre of *Secret* guards so that you could flounce off without anyone but Adam," Ciriis told him.

She pinned Alanna with another glare. "What are *you* thinking to allow this?"

To do her credit, Alanna didn't wilt under the disapproval of the Architect of the King's Reign.

"It's my place to *serve,* Lady Ciriis, not to question His Majesty."

"It's your place to obey *Aryllis,*" Ciriis corrected. "And Tim, I suppose. Do you think *they* would permit Damien to go wandering off on his lonesome? With *one* bodyguard? Even Adam needs to sleep."

Damien met Alanna's wry gaze and willed himself not to blush. Used his *Healing magick* to cool his cheeks and neck, actually.

Thank the Gods that Adam and Alanna both had a sense of humor...

"I'm aware," Alanna replied. "But His Majesty is still my ultimate commander-in-chief. His decree overrules even my Captains."

Ciriis looked like she was seething, but didn't have a ready comeback for that one. Alanna had been much more meek during the brief overlap of their tenures in the Secret Cadre and she hadn't expected the young woman to push back.

Angelos poked his head in at that moment, smiling at Damien, but his whole self seeming to light up at sight of Alanna.

"There you are, my lady," the young knight said, addressing her quite properly as the King's temporary hostess, though Damien guessed that 'my' was meant rather more personally and possessively. "Your Majesty, Your Highness. We've turned over the supplies to milord Aldred's cook, who also helped us sort out where everyone will bed down tonight."

Damien caught Adam giving Ciriis a lifted eyebrow – so much for her claim to serve as chatelaine – and Ciriis' complete ignoring of him.

"Thank you, Angelos," the King said. "Aldred, I don't believe you've met my cousin before. Sir Angelos Eldridge. He's in charge of Our knights whilst on this trip, and will be formally confirmed as Timothy Ancellius' Second when we return to Emeralsee."

"I saw him around the castle when we were down a few months ago," Aldred gave the young man a nod. "I'm all for helping out relatives, but he's a little young for the post of Second, isn't he?"

"Tim and the rest were that age when we first formed Damien's Guards," Ciriis snapped back at her... lover.

"Jason and Ciriis and I were a little older," Adam agreed. "But most of the rest still had paint drying on their shields. Angelos isn't being chosen for nepotism, but because he's demonstrated competence, intelligence, and discretion in his duties."

"And a sense of humor," Alanna muttered, almost too low to be heard. "Which is an absolute *requirement* in this job."

Damien flashed her a quick grin.

"*I* trained *Aryllis*," Ciriis noted sharply. "She wouldn't be party to choosing someone who wasn't suited. How Marcus Dunsteador ever managed to end up as Second is beyond me."

Adam winced. "Marcus is loyal, scrupulous, and a fine hand on a blade. Never mislays a piece of paperwork... There were reasons at the time, Ciriis."

She looked down her nose at him. "Clearly not *good* ones, if you're replacing him so soon."

"Or it's possible Angelos is just that *good*," Adam suggested, and Ciriis looked skeptical.

Angelos looked extremely uncomfortable, but he managed a Court-perfect bow in her direction with utter suavity. "I certainly cannot lay claim to such qualities, but can only hope to please."

"Add humility to his list," Adam noted dryly, and Angelos's eyes twinkled.

"I actually came in because Mistress Zelda – Cloudcroft's cook," he explained for the benefit of the other newcomers, "decided that in order to fit everyone, a couple of us need to sleep in this room. And that you and the baby will need to share Lord Aldred's room, Lady Ciriis. If that's acceptable."

Ciriis and Aldred eyed each other.

"His Majesty and Prince Adam should stay in here," Alanna said immediately. "It's clearly the most defensible spot in the entire compound."

That was fair, since there were two doors, but no windows and the rest of the structure had been built surrounding what had originally been a one-room stone-walled peasant cottage. Though why anyone had decided to build up here at all, in this Gods-forsaken place, was still a mystery to Damien.

Hardly 'Gods-forsaken,' the Realm rebuked him unexpectedly. *I/We and Elaarwen forsake no part of Ourselves. And this place where Earth-kisses-Sky is an important one. It is the final guardian of the Heart.*

What do you mean? Damien tried to ask, but the Realm went back to not answering.

"I'll have knights at the entrances, of course," Angelos added.

"You say you and Adam are leaving tomorrow?" Ciriis addressed the King again.

Damien nodded, noting how Angelos hid his flicker of surprise quite well. And that the young knight looked not to Adam, but to Alanna for confirmation.

Alanna's own face was... only grim if you knew what to look for.

The tiny, fierce woman heaved herself up from her chair with a sigh. "We can make it work for a night. I'll go move the things I need."

Angelos politely offered her his arm and his assistance, and Ciriis' stiff and irritated posture eased just a hair as she went out of the room with the good-looking young man. Aldred followed after a moment, saying something about clearing some space for her and the babe.

Damien sighed and slumped back into his chair, scrubbing both hands over his face once the door closed. At least there were doors hung in most of the frames here – the better to keep warm air where it was wanted, though the corridors were icy at night as he recalled. Even at high Summer, which this time of year most assuredly was *not*.

But it did make for more privacy.

He opened his eyes to see Alanna and Adam regarding each other.

"I would request that Your Majesty give me a *little* prior knowledge of your planned movements," the Secret Guardswoman said with a tone nearly as icy as the hallways.

"That would be *my* fault, Alanna," Adam told her. "For whatever reason, Elaarwen is giving *me* these instructions instead of Damien."

The young woman gave him a very brief nod. "I'll assume you had your reasons then, sir. I'll just go see to having your packs brought in here. And make sure that your steeds are given some extra care so they're ready for more travel by morning."

She wasn't any less unhappy, but she apparently wasn't going to question *Adam*.

"Thank you, Alanna," Damien nodded a dismissal, and she also left.

The King stood up to stretch the muscles that had gotten too used to sitting and began to wander around restlessly.

"That was... fairly uncomfortable," Adam commented. He'd stretched out his long legs, crossing his booted ankles, and leaned back with his fingers laced behind his head.

"Things... aren't right here," Damien said, fairly unnecessarily.

"The walls have ears, my King," Adam reminded him, but Damien shook his head.

"No. There aren't so many people here that I can't place every one of them. No one's listening." He sighed heavily. "No one's even near this part of the house."

"Well then."

Adam stood up in a movement far too smooth for a man who'd slept on hard ground the last three nights and ridden the rest of the day – and then sat for the last hour. Before Damien could complain about the unfairness of his ability to do that, the tall knight had taken the two strides across the room and pulled the King into a fairly wonderful kiss.

"Gods, but I've wanted to do that for the last four days," Adam said when he was done.

Damien snuggled into the taller man's embrace. "*Only* that long?"

"Of course not," Adam kissed his hair. "But it's hours yet till everyone *else* goes to bed, and it will be far too obvious if you ward this room right now."

Damien sighed. "And... this is where we are again."

Adam's fingers combed through his hair. "I'd rather be here than any of the other possibilities."

"True..." Damien hesitated. "Do you... think that Aldred *knows?*"

He looked up to see Adam shake his head thoughtfully. "No. If he did, Ciriis would as well, and *she* would never have let it go like that. It would have been clear that *she* knows from the moment she entered the room."

Damien relaxed a trifle. "She might just have been waiting to talk to us without an audience."

Adam shook his head again. "She'd assume that if *she* knows, so would at very least the commander of our Guards. Alanna's presence wouldn't have sealed her lips."

Likely true... but what about Aldred's? After what he'd just seen, Damien wasn't so sure that the co-conspirators were sharing any secrets at this point.

"Aldred... doesn't seem like himself," Damien said, sadly, into his Champion's chest.

"Or perhaps this is what he's like when Genevieve isn't around," Adam's tone was sardonic. "She puts him up on a pedestal as much as you do her. And, I'll just say, I think she deserves it far more than he does, if half of what Felix Marsham told us is true."

Damien tipped his head to look up at Adam again. "Count Marsham's stories are over forty years old, Adam. People change."

And Gods, but how he wanted to believe Aldred had changed.

They said the love of a good woman could change a man... Damien certainly felt Genevieve had changed *him*. And no one had ever said anything but good things about Duchess Giendra... though granted, the woman had been dead for over twenty years.

"They do," Adam agreed. "And they don't. You noticed, I'm sure, that he didn't make an exception for *my* mother in naming all lowland women as whores."

"Adam..."

"Doubtless *he* was a 'fine figure' of a young *man* in his twenties as well," Adam said dryly. "I wouldn't blame my mother for having had a fling with the Ducal-Prince of Elaarwen before she met my father. It's more the... lack of respectfulness that bothers me."

Adam's arms tightened a little. "That and that poor baby."

Damien wriggled a hand out to run it down Adam's cheek. "I hadn't mentioned it before, except to Genevieve, but I don't plan to leave Ren up here any longer than necessary."

"'Ren'?" Adam smiled. "I guess that's one 'problem' solved. How do you plan to get him away?"

Damien shrugged. "It's clear that neither of them really wanted a *baby*. They wanted another Heir to Elaarwen... and the Realm. I doubt they'll mind leaving him in Emeralsee when they come down after Genevieve gives birth. We'll have nurses and everything they think is necessary after all, and at nearly six months old, he can technically be weaned. Or a wet-nurse hired as well."

"Damien..."

The black-haired man squeezed his Champion with the arm he still had around Adam's waist. "Of course, *we* won't leave Ren to nurses any more than we will Marli. If Genevieve doesn't want to nurse two – and I can help her manage it if she does, but I suspect we'll want a wet-nurse for Marli anyways, since Genevieve isn't, um..."

"The type to sit around glorying in her baby any more than Ciriis is?" Adam suggested sardonically.

"Oh, quite a bit more than Ciriis," Damien disagreed. "But... not to the degree that your mother did. Or... my mother."

Adam's embrace somehow became warm and protective without twitching a muscle. "And Jase is still terrified of being a parent. But you and I... we can do that part of things. Four of us... should be enough to provide all the different kinds of love and encouragement for any number of children."

Damien smiled at the thought that Adam considered *him* to be capable of nurturing like that. He wasn't so sure himself... "You've been practicing already, after all, with the pages and squires."

Then he sighed.

"We'll... have to bring Ren back up here as often as is feasible," Damien pointed out. "They *are* his parents. And Cloudcroft *will* be his someday..."

"And we want his roots to be so deep here that no one ever drags him into Emeralsee politics unwilling," Adam nodded.

The tall man sighed then as well. "I'm sure they love him in their own ways. Perhaps once they can see him as a small *person,* rather than just the symbol of why they ended up stuck here in the back of beyond..."

"Perhaps they can even fix their own relationship," Damien suggested, then gave a rueful chuckle as Adam raised an eyebrow. "No, I suppose not. They made a bid for a Throne and ended up with Cloudcroft... and Ren. There wasn't anything more than ambition to tie the two of them together. Or maybe that and some good old-fashioned lust."

He nudged Adam to release him. There was someone heading in this direction with a feeling of *intention,* so they likely they were about to be interrupted.

"Maybe something can *grow,*" Adam said, though his words were clearly to make Damien feel better than any real belief. A downside of this *empathic* link was the inability to give each other these little white lies.

"They're both intelligent, interesting people," Adam added a little more believably. "Lifelong marriages have been built on less. If they respect each other – which they must, in order to have been willing to work together on their scheme."

He winced as Damien took a turn to raise an eyebrow. "All right, I'm grasping at straws. But I love them both – *we* love them both and I'd hope for something better for each of them than a lifetime of misery."

"Fair," Damien agreed. "But it's up to them to decide. And up to us to make sure Ren has all that *we* can give him. And right now..."

He paused as one of his knights stuck their head in to inform them that lunch was ready.

"Right now, we have to get through lunch."

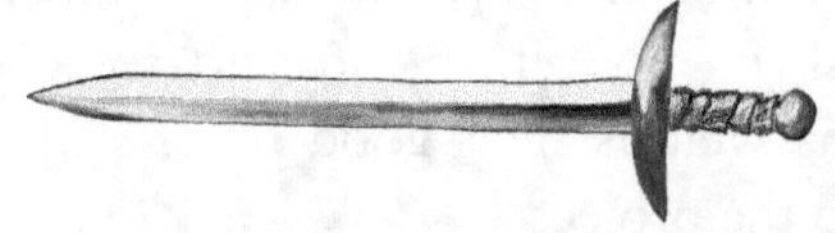

Chapter THIRTEEN

A Taste of Treason

LUNCH WAS... MORE OR LESS fine.

The rest of the King's Guards were apprised that His Majesty and Prince Adam were leaving in the morning – without an escort. There was the predictable kerfuffle, put down with a stern look from Alanna and an apologetic one from Angelos.

The kerfuffle started up again when Adam volunteered their Guards to start building another outbuilding for Cloudcroft. It was mortally obvious that the tiny holding would have to grow a bit in the years to come, with Aldred living up here year-round and Ren to inherit it someday. It was also mortally obvious that the place had outgrown its infrastructure already.

The former Rebels – all in the Secret Cadre – sat back and watched with amusement as their younger colleagues protested being put to such labors. Angelos stayed silent, uneasy at dismissing his fellow knights' objections, but clearly unwilling to let his King – or possibly Alanna – see him as anything less than responsible and capable after Adam had listed out his virtues earlier.

Damien put an end to it all by making it a Royal Decree – and adding some commentary about how serving the people, let alone the Queen's father, should be embraced by any member of his Guards. And that he hoped, on his return, both to see good progress on the new building as well as hear good reports on the energy and enthusiasm put into the project.

Which only led to questions of just *when* they would return... and neither he nor Adam had any particularly good answers.

The afternoon was taken up by walking over Aldred's acreage followed by a sullen group of young people, all working not to be *noticed* as being sullen.

The putative Lord of Cloudcroft wandered around with them, looking rather bemused – Castle Stellarine hadn't been added onto in decades, if not centuries, aside from the lists added for his mother's amusement – and that had been more of a repurposing and walling-in of an adjacent outdoor space than a major addition. Aldred had spent his tenure as Duke planning and then executing a Rebellion, not worrying about such plebian details as where to store a Winter's worth of food or how to house all the laborers and servants needed to run a working farmstead.

The location for the new building was marked out *(by Adam)*, and its purpose decided *(also by Adam)* – a bigger barn, with partitions for storage of hay and grain. *(Aldred objected, suggesting that the humans needed more space before 'mere animals' and was shot down with incredulous glances from anyone from a farming background... as well as Damien. Ciriis just looked on sardonically, then went back inside to see to the baby.)*

Damien then stood out in the middle of the planned space and *looked* to see whether the base was solid enough to withstand the weight of stone walls *(everything up here had to be built of stone to withstand the Winters)*.

Cloudcroft was also dependent on its nearly acre-sized, shallow pond, filled annually with melt from the jagged peaks that surrounded them and the occasional Summer rainfall. The homestead plateau was in a bit of a bowl amongst taller peaks that cut off enough of the wind to allow a small grove of conifers to grow straight and tall, and those trees provided shade, small amounts of kindling, pine-nuts, and a number of other benefits.

Having just seen the result of denuding of forests in Farivera, Damien was more than usually alert to the importance of trees. But trees needed a steady supply of water even more than the humans and animals, given that the latter could – however inconveniently – walk to other sources.

Having seen the wonders of Azella's unnatural Keep, Damien explored the possibility of bringing up water from below to supplement the supply – and mitigate any risk of contamination. The local oreads and undines were amenable, so he directed them to create a new stream that spilled from a nook on one of those jagged peaks, allowing a trickle to refresh the pond.

The oreads lined the new streambed with freshly made sand and fine gravel, and then prepared a runoff streambed to take overflow and prevent flooding out onto the rest of Cloudcroft's relatively flat plateau.

Damien was actually somewhat startled by just *how* amenable the local Elemental sprites were to this fairly extensive and unnatural addition. They seemed as enthusiastic about keeping humans here as the humans were *(incomprehensibly)* enthusiastic about staying, and suggested adding a secondary hot spring in addition *(Damien decided to wait on that one until he could have the appropriate human infrastructure built to support it. Hot baths were all very nice… if an indoor bathing room and drainage system was prepared in advance.)*

There was also a certain *feel* to the local rocks that Damien identified as 'having been touched before by Earth-magick.' *Human-directed* Earth-magick as well, so not the work of Elementals.

And it was *old* work. At least as old as his Throne and Castle in Emeralsee, that had been designed to *concentrate* the flows of magick and allow the Bound Monarch better access. As, indeed, he suspected that the entire City of Emeralsee had been so designed.

The work here seemed to have been oriented around making it possible for humans to live in Cloudcroft at all, rather than those more abstract purposes. Though who would ever have decided to make Cloudcroft habitable was as open a question as why they had bothered to do so.

Not that it had been all *that* habitable until Genevieve's renovations a few years ago, and she had only had the tiny stone cottage kept as the core of the manorhouse out of sentiment and family history. That romantic tale of her grandmother, Alicia, the princess-at-one-remove who'd been raised an outlaw in Elaarwen's forests, kidnapping Ducal-Prince Siegfrid of Elaarwen when he tried to protect the province's taxes *en route* to Emeralsee... the two of them getting trapped up here all Winter... then falling in love and conceiving their son, Aldred...

Ah, well, there were many mysteries from the past.

(Damien's impression was that Duke Siegfrid ahd expanded the cottage into a real, multi-room house and added the stables. Genevieve's additions had been more practical and included the barn and an expanded kitchen and laundry. Who had seen to having the cold-cellar dug in the King wasn't certain of – it might even have been Duke Emmeren, in reaction after his son and daughter-in-law all but starved up here... or planning ahead for a place to stash his son's inconveniently royal wife and son and mother-in-law should need arise.)

*(**Retreat** didn't seem to have been a potential outcome for the Rebellion in Aldred's eyes, based on the comments he was making now.)*

Next, the King used his own magick to reach for reasonable-sized rocks all over the nearby mountains and pile them near, but not *on,* the building location.

It was Angelos who noticed the streams of rocks arcing through the sky and got everyone out of the way. Well, everyone other than Adam, who settled himself at Damien's feet and waited out the strange rain.

And who was also there when the 'rain' petered out and the King began to wobble on his feet.

"I don't know why you won't *sit down* when you do these things," Adam complained after catching Damien and lowering him to sit cross-legged on the ground.

Damien turned his head from where he was holding it up with elbows braced on knees, too weary even to sit up slumped. "People need to see something impressive, Adam. Laying down flat would actually make the most sense – and I could do all of it comfortably from a proper bed indoors. But if they don't *see* me doing something... they won't respect the result. Or me."

And he really didn't want to have to deal with the results of his people not taking him seriously. The Power he controlled was much easier to use for redirecting major floods than for nudging a fruitfly off of a slice of cut apple. He was exhausted now, less from the *amount* of Power expended than from the incredible focus he'd needed to manage the fine-control while he brought in those several tons of rocks.

Adam thought about that. "This is something else you learned from Azella, isn't it, Damien?"

The King twitched his shoulders in what might have been a shrug if there had been any energy to it. "More from what her master left behind for her, I think. I don't think she appreciates how much of her ability to impress others is her surroundings."

Adam snorted. "She was damned impressive when she showed up in Emeralsee."

"Pirates," Damien's head drooped a little lower. "Ice. Night-time."

"Hmmn." He felt Adam moving around and then pulling the King into his arms. "Speaking of impressing people who need some of that. The sylphs are helping me again," he reassured his King as Damien moved feebly to object to his Champion killing his back for no real need.

Dinner... was a great deal quieter.

The young knights had all, in training, had to learn how to carry a fallen comrade. Several of them had contributed to carrying Adam into Castle Stellarine after his collapse less than a week ago. They were also all aware that Damien could – and regularly *did* – trounce any one of them in the practice-ring, and what those two facts put together meant in terms of their King's muscle mass compared to their former Captain's.

They'd also all spent the last few hours of daylight shifting a handful of those rocks that he'd brought flying into the clearing in what was virtually a reversed waterfall of stone.

Most of them had gone home regularly as squires for Spring planting or Fall harvests, or both, and were familiar with picking rocks ranging up to the size of a man's head out of the newly turned fields. Since that was the size of the *smallest* rocks Damien had brought in, they'd had small doubt of the weight they were being asked to move. A few of them had been heard to remark, resentfully, that if His Majesty could fly in so many damned rocks, why couldn't he just build the damned barn while he was at it? And what kind of idiots lived in a place that needed *stone* barns, anyways?

A reminder of the King's attempts at architectural readjustments in Castle Alsterling settled the first group. It had taken weeks to mend the rather spectacular hole that had stranded a solid dozen people in one of the towers – though luckily Damien had been able to extract *them* in a matter of hours.

Damien's query to Lord Aldred about the origins of the stone cottage around which everything else was built sparked enough of an update on not-so-recent Stellarine history that the other group busied themselves with their food and their tired muscles. The cottage had apparently 'always been' a part of the family's private holdings. Tradition and history were enough of an explanation for most of that subsection of tired young knights.

The *King's* curiosity, however, wasn't so easily settled. He felt entirely refreshed after a short nap, and the words of the oread on the cliffside kept him probing for more detail.

"Was there any tradition of the family coming up here, then?" Damien asked his father-in-law.

Aldred shrugged. He wasn't terribly interested in his son-in-law's latest odd obsession. He likely still remembered the year that Damien had spent every minute during his and Genevieve's annual visit learning to *spin*, of all the useless things for a ruler to know. Or the visit when Damien had insisted on measuring the thickness of every glazed window. Including the ones in the city, so absolutely *everyone* had to see just what an odd duck Genevieve had chosen to marry.

Or the year she had tried to teach him to hunt... and he'd somehow chased off *every animal in the province* with that magick of his. That had been more serious, of course, it being late Spring and long before even the first crops were coming in. Though at least the strange young King had sent food up from the lowlands so Aldred's people hadn't all starved.

Damien tried not to wince as those memories all clearly washed across his father-in-law's face.

There was no use in explaining how he'd used his knowledge of spinning thread to trap the demon that Azella had sent two months hence.

Nor that understanding how glass was a fluid and a solid at the same time had contributed to the studies that had let him make glass fragments to attack the pirates – and had helped him pull together Azella's 'lessons.'

Nor that Damien hadn't had any control over his reaction to Genevieve aiming her bow at a fawn. She'd wanted the fawnskin to wrap their own much-hoped-for baby in, she'd half-explained, half-apologized to him later. But Damien, who'd practiced his archery skills under her tutelage at painted targets up to that point had only seen a baby that needed to be protected.

He hadn't understood then – or even later, really – how he'd managed to tell not only the fawn and its mother to flee... but all the rest of the province's wildlife. And, um, the domesticated animals *(ot that they'd been able to do much besides batter themselves against coops and barn-doors or get stuck in – or half over – fences...).*

Projective *empathy,* he knew now.

And he'd gone home to Emeralsee in shame, intending to at least make things right by sending aid... which *Genevieve* had done, with his blessing... But he'd discovered that he couldn't eat... well, almost *anything,* so he wasn't a great deal of help to her.

The incident with the fawn had opened him up to being able to sense *everything* that died in his Realm. Humans. Animals, of course, but even those all the way down to lice and ladybugs. Plants. Even the tinylife that lived in dust and made bread rise and no one else even seemed to believe existed.

He'd nearly gone mad with the pain of it all – just the dying 'screams' of yeast from the morning's baking had made him weep.

Eating had been utterly impossible. *Every* food had life in it, no matter how well-cooked, even if it was only from dust-motes settling during the journey from pot to plate.

He'd starved himself half to death until Adam and Jason had taken him down to the grotto and forced him to practice with a sword until he was too exhausted to sense anything... and too hungry to object to anything edible that they'd put in front of him. Not his own Sword; holding *that* just exacerbated the problem by connecting him to the Realm more deeply and replenishing his flagging energies enough to continue sensing things... without, unfortunately, abating his inability to consume nourishment.

It had taken a solid *week* just to get Damien to the point where he could tolerate plants that had just been cooked, honey, the cores of certain very hard cheeses, eggs from hens that had no roosters – Jason had been utterly baffled by how he could always tell the source of the eggs. Adam had been frustrated, but unerring in his ideas of what foods to try their young king on.

It had taken a whole year after *that* for Damien to re-acquire his taste for other foods. Or, really, to learn to ignore the tinylife in the dust-motes in favor of the hungry tinylives on his own skin and in his own gut.

Aldred had never understood.

"Did your parents bring you up here?" Damien tried again. "Did your grandfather ever say anything about it?" The oread on the cliffside trail had implied that might be true, after all.

Aldred sighed and gave in to his son-in-law's famous inability to be diverted. "Grandpapa – Duke Emmeren, that was – I think he might've done. I think Papa said *his* grandfather had taken him up every Summer, which was how he was able to direct Mama up here when she captured him. He said he left a number of signs that he thought Grandpapa would recognize to realize where Mama had taken him to."

He chuckled. "Papa did suggest us coming up here a couple of times, but Mama just said she'd seen enough of this place that Winter to last her a lifetime."

Damien frowned thoughtfully to himself, but Adam was curious now and looked up from where he'd been tickling the baby in his lap.

"Duchess Alicia asked her captive to find them a hide-out? That seems a little odd."

Aldred sighed. "You had to know my mother for it to make sense, Adam. She could be... incredibly persuasive when she wanted to be. For all that the rest of the time she could be a hot-tempered, ah..."

He winced. "Well, Papa had moments when he was rather fed up with her, let's just say. Grandpapa was forever complaining that Papa would get irritated with Mama and go storming off and leave her home with him and Grandmama. And Grandmother Alexandria."

"A Stellarine with a temper," Ciriis drawled. "Who would *ever* have guessed."

She was half-turned away from him, her elbow propped on the back of her chair and what must have been her third glass of wine dangling from her fingertips. Apparently, she was making up for the midwife's injunction not to partake of spirits while she was pregnant. Occasionally, she was casting disconcerted glances at her son cooing happily in Adam's lap and the tall knight's entirely enchanted expression.

"Mama was an Alsterling," Aldred pointed out a little stiffly, and clearly avoiding a look at Damien.

"Where did Prince Siegfrid go?" Adam asked before Ciriis had a chance to point out that it was Aldred's *father* she was referring to. "Up here, since he knew his wife wouldn't follow?"

Aldred snorted. "Not hardly. Papa went down to Court. I went with him, once I was old enough." He rolled his eyes. "Mama asked me if I'd seen *her* mother every time I came home. As if I'd even have remembered what the old woman looked like. She left with the Sword when I was all of three."

Damien was seated to his father-in-law's righthand, so it was easy for Aldred's eyes to mark the presence of the Blade that... *hadn't* changed his life. Though it had *saved* it.

"Much more interesting place the Court," Aldred noted. "Grandpapa seemed to think we should prefer it up here, the both of us, but Cloudcroft compared to Emeralsee? I've never understood what he was thinking. Or why Grandmama let him hide her away in the mountains like that."

He drained his own wine and frowned into the empty cup. His gaze moved between the flagon of wine and ewer of water set out on the table, then to his slightly soused mistress at his left hand. And then to the Sword that had never been his.

"I thought Princess Alexandria had chosen to secret herself in the mountains," Alanna mentioned, though the words looked to have been dragged out of her.

She was seated beside Ciriis, though she'd been edging a little farther to her left until she was almost in Angelos' not-unwelcoming lap. Damien couldn't really blame the young woman for wanting to get away from her erstwhile superior, given the aggressive and unhappy mood Ciriis was in.

Most of the rest of the young knights had needed to fill their plates and find places to sit elsewhere in the house, although the Secret Cadre had all been seated at table in a nod to their decorative as well as defensive role. Lady Emily was on Adam's other side from Damien, and looking rather bemused at his fascination with baby Ren. Derrick and Lewis faced each other at the far end, with Tasha facing Aldred down the length of the table in the seat that, arguably, Damien should have been offered. It had seemed more politic to act the polite son-in-law and accept the more humble position at Aldred's right hand.

Aldred looked up at Alanna with a great deal of interest. "Oh, not my *mother's* mother. My *father's* mother. Duchess Shalla. She was a Turquoise Princess of Wave, you know. I could never understand how *she* could bear to be stuck in Elaarwen when she'd grown up in the largest city in the world."

"How interesting," Lady Emily volunteered, flipping the tail of rich brown hair that fell gracefully down from her updo over her shoulder. She was wearing a Court gown that was lower cut than was common in Elaarwen, as were the other two ladies, and Damien had no idea how the fabric had survived the trip in such good order. "I didn't know that. However did they meet, my lord?"

Aldred gave her a rather *interested* smile as well, while Ciriis smiled sourly into her cup and Damien tried to tell himself to interpret his father-in-law in the best possible way, always. For Genevieve's sake if nothing else.

The royal ladies-in-waiting were chosen for their intelligence, loyalty, discretion and *beauty,* after all. And then trained to develop the skills they needed to defend their sovereigns – and themselves – in all situations. It would take a strong man indeed, not to notice their physical charms and lovely manners.

"Why do you know, I don't know the whole tale of it?" Aldred informed Emily. "I know that he was sent to Wave for some reason – and came back home with Grandmama. But exactly why he went, or how he won her hand? I've no idea."

"So, you – and Her Majesty – are cousins to the Lord of Wave, then?" Miss Tasha asked from the far end of the table, and Aldred oriented his *interest* on the buxom, platinum-haired beauty.

"We are," Aldred smiled at her. "I don't believe we've any claim to *that* throne, however. Legend has it that the Sea-Queen will only Choose a scion of the Elemandros family who has never set foot across the sea."

Ciriis snorted. "Legends aren't law. Though I'll admit, *Damien's* claim to the throne of *Dawil* is probably better. Didn't King Eldrig name one of his nieces to follow him?"

Damien gave her a tight smile. "Crown Princess Emmerine, yes. I sent her congratulations on her recent treaty-marriage to the Sethivali prince just before leaving Emeralsee."

"And she's your first cousin, isn't she?" Ciriis persisted.

"Half-first cousin, once removed," Damien recited. "Her mother, Princess Livette was from King Ezerial's second Queen, my grandmother and King Eldrig were the children of Queen Marlerite. Crown Princess Emmerine is about the same age as Lady Alanna here."

Alanna looked a bit like a hunted animal as all eyes naturally turned to her, and Damien would have kicked himself for drawing attention back to her... Adam actually *did* kick him under the table as he lifted the baby up to his shoulder.

"That Sethivali prince is barely an adult, isn't he, Damien?" Adam commented. "The announcement they sent mentioned that the marriage is to complete the treaty they signed after that war they ended five years ago, but didn't they hold off on the marriage then because the prince was still a child?"

Gossiping about the relatives he'd never met across the ocean was *probably* better than the other alternatives, Damien thought to himself with a sigh.

The rest of the meal wasn't particularly enlightening. Or pleasant.

Adam and Damien took turns with the baby while Ciriis got herself thoroughly sauced. Aldred looked more and more interested in Damien's ladies-in-waiting, who tossed the conversational ball around to keep him from focusing on any one of them. Angelos, Derrick, and Lewis did their best to add to the distraction effort, but neither Aldred nor Ciriis seemed to pay any of the men much mind.

Aldred looked amused when Angelos finally put a possessive arm around Alanna, but that was all.

Adam finally announced that the baby needed a diaper and declined to turn him over to the grouchy Ciriis. She'd always held her liquor well, and it was hard to tell from her movements whether she was as tipsy as the several glasses of wine might suggest.

Aldred declined to take his son as long as Adam had the baby in hand.

Ciriis ended up leading Adam to the room she was – apparently – now sharing with her lover to take care of the baby. Angelos handed his lady out of her chair and guided her out of the room as the rest of the Secret Cadre also quickly emptied from their seats at Damien's nod.

It wasn't precisely protocol, but Cloudcroft was a small place. They'd more than doubled the population, and all the additions were people sworn to keep their king safe.

Which left Aldred and Damien at the dinner table and no easy way for the King to escape his father-in-law.

"So, am I still in your poor graces, my King?" Aldred asked quietly. The doors were closed and they were as private as might be. It suddenly struck Damien how very little of a mountain-accent was ever in Aldred's voice. The old man could have lived all his life in the Court in Emeralsee by the tone and timber of his tongue, save for when he was clearly affecting a mountain lilt for some effect.

Genevieve sounded more like a mountain-woman when she was trying hard *not* to.

Damien shook his head. "Of course not. I rescinded your banishment months ago."

"Yes... so the mercenary fellow, Darvin, told me." Aldred swirled the latest contents of his wine glass, looking into them as deeply as if he sought for oracles. "A bit roundabout, that, though I suppose there weren't a great many options available to you then."

"No." Damien agreed. "I wasn't even sure Darvin would make it this far. I thought he promised to try, but... we had to speak in – how did you put it? – a roundabout fashion while we were in the sorceress' Keep."

"Hmmn," Aldred took a small sip and swirled some more, still looking into the shallow depths of the sparkling liquid. "There were... *some* as said I should wait to hear from you more directly before we went down to Court. Not that I would listen to them, when it was my Genevieve as might need help," he added.

"I see," Damien said neutrally. He rather wanted to fidget with something himself, but Ciriis had long ago taught him the power in *not* doing so. Besides which, the only thing available to fidget with *elegantly* would be his own wine glass, and that would make it look like he was copying Aldred.

"There were some as *still* think I should wait to hear an apology from you," the old man went on after a moment. "Seeing as how I was treated as a man should never be by the son-in-law he's all but named as his own son."

"Hmmn," Damien kept even the sound as noncommittal as he could.

"There's even *some* who think that *apology* should be as public as the shaming that preceded it," Aldred added, looking up at last to meet the King's eyes. "Seeing as how any possible *contention* between the two of us should have been resolved by Emmeren's poor mother dying in labor, as it were."

Damien raised an eyebrow at that. "Did she now? And yet there's a lady who looks a great deal like her who was at dinner with us just now. And who has a great many kinfolk scattered about the Realm who might be able to identify her such that a certain... *gentlemanly agreement* might be revealed as the scam it is."

Aldred purported to look shocked. "Surely you're not suggesting that we make the story *real...?*"

The King snorted. "Of course not. I would like nothing better than to see my father-in-law and one of my dearest friends retire in happily – well, not *wedded* bliss, I suppose... Genevieve and I would *both* like to welcome you back into our lives. And we've been assuming you'll come down when *our* baby is born – as I had invited you to do even when we had our... *disagreement* last Fall."

This having to talk around things to satisfy both manners and politics was... more than mildly annoying. Damien had always put Aldred in the category of people with whom he could simply be himself. Or at least he had until last Fall.

Aldred frowned at him. "I'm a simple mountain-man, Damien–"

Hardly, but best to see what hen the old fox was going to try to scare out of the coop.

"–so, I'll be blunt."

Damien would believe *that* when he saw it. He'd come to realize lately that everything Aldred had ever said or done had layers upon layers...

"You shamed me terribly in front of all of Emeralsee," Aldred told the King. "And after all I've done for you these last five years. The whole world sees me as a laughingstock I discovered when we came down to Genevieve's aid – and found that you had somehow 'escaped' your 'captivity' and beaten us there. You need to make it clear that I am rehabilitated and restored to my place."

Those quotes around *escaped* and *captivity* were all too audible.

"Your place?" Damien knew where this was going, but inclined his head with gentle curiosity. Let the man dig himself deeper...

"*My place,*" Aldred said firmly, "as Duke of Elaarwen. And as your honored father."

Apparently, he realized he'd gone a touch too far with that, based on the sudden, frightened look in those blue-green eyes that matched the ones the King loved so well.

"I see," Damien said again. "And how, exactly does the Land feel about this? You should be able to tell now that you have your own connection, since the Realm Bound you with your Vassal's Oath."

The old man scowled at him. "And am I supposed to believe in the authenticity of *feelings* engendered by some ridiculously powerful *compulsion* spell you placed upon me when you made me swear – practically at swordpoint!"

Damien gave the man he called 'Papa' a disappointed look. "Do you know, that's almost exactly what Tomas Elsevier accused me of? While Genevieve fought a Champion's duel against Adam?"

Aldred's beard obscured whether he was pursing his mouth or sneering.

"Are you or aren't you going to do this for me, Damien? For *Genevieve?*"

The King leaned back in his straight-backed chair.

"Well, that's the thing, isn't it, Aldred?" he asked, deliberately using the old man's name rather than a title of rank or endearment. "*My* Genevieve has been Duchess of Elaarwen for seven years. Two as a Rebel, and then five as my vassal, Bound and Sworn. And she's done a damned good job of looking after Elaarwen. I can't very well take away what is hers – and mine only by marriage."

Aldred frowned. "You're the king, Damien. You can do anything you damned well please, I should think. And it's not as if it won't come back to Genevieve when I've *really* passed on."

And... this was why the Sword probably would *not* speak for Aldred anymore. No matter how much it loved him. No matter that it had spoken for him as a child of three. That early potential had clearly been eroded away through a lifetime of privilege and ambition and, yes, hard work and well-intentioned effort.

But now...

This was quite nearly the same thing Aldred would have him do in Cedarwen to return Alanna's family to their ancestral lands by taking them away from a qualified and competent caretaker. As Damien had *not* done to Alexa Solway despite her crimes and cruelty against her own family – and his – because she was also a good ruler in the estimation of the Land.

Damien sighed and let some of the tension drain away.

"A King is more Bound than anyone else, Aldred. I have restored you as much as I'm going to do."

The old man looked desperate now. "Not even for the sake of your child – my grandchild? He shouldn't have to grow up with such a cloud as this over our fami– what are you laughing at, young man?"

It hadn't been intentional, but... Damien picked up his dinner napkin to dab at his eyes. "I'm sorry, Aldred. But the idea that a... a *disagreement* between her father and her grandfather is the worst 'cloud over her family' that my daughter will have to live with... well... I'm sure *my* grandfather would have found the notion quite nearly as amusing as I do."

The former Duke of Elaarwen looked... mortally offended to have been compared to the former tyrant king... but really, he had done it to himself.

"I value your support from the days when I was learning to rule," Damien said after a moment, leaning back again, this time with folded arms. "I respect and cherish the love and care you have given me then and since – but it is up to *you* to recognize what you have been given and decide its value to *you*.

"Had you been anyone else, I would not have given you a *third* chance. To re-prove your loyalty to the Crown. To *my* Crown."

"It should have been *my* Crown," the old man muttered fiercely. "Your whole line is a-tainted."

Damien shook his head. "No, it shouldn't have. Queen Marian says that while the Sword did indeed speak for you once, it wouldn't do so now. She *also* says that she's fairly sure that it *would* have spoken for *my* father, had it ever had the chance."

He leaned forwards. "And *your* line is now *my* line, old man. Genevieve is my wife and the mother of my future children. The Stellarine and Alsterling lines are *one*."

There was the odd feeling of... almost of a *bell* ringing when Damien said those words.

As if it was something so *right* and so *true* that the very universe needed to acknowledge it being said aloud.

Aldred blinked, as if he, too, had heard that bell-like tone that was neither a bell nor a sound.

"So, we're back where we started," he said in a voice that was suddenly almost too weary to be believed.

"We never left," Damien told him as gently as he could. "Although I would rather go back a little ways to where I call you 'Papa.'"

Aldred sighed. "I suppose that's all I have left, isn't it?"

Damien closed his eyes. "I... had hoped it would be enough."

There was a long silence, broken only by the sounds of Aldred rising from the table and leaving the room.

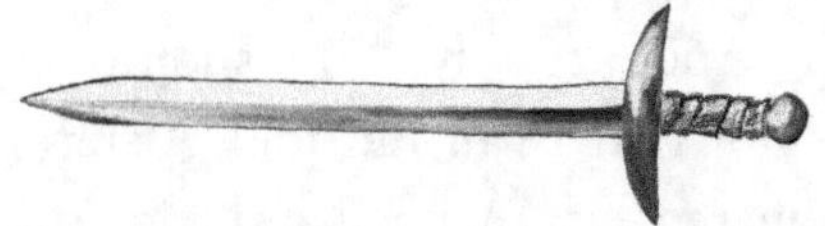

Chapter FOURTEEN

A Bit of Palate Clearing

ADAM FOUND HIM THERE A few minutes later, apparently homing in on the feeling of a broken heart. As he'd done from the very beginning.

And as he'd also done from the very beginning, he didn't offer sweet sympathies, but rather chivvied his sorrowful King out of his chair and down the hall to the hearth-room where Sir Rodney and Sir Mikal already stood Guard at this entrance. And then out again and to the washroom to take a turn before bed. With a warm hug and no questions in between.

And then, at last, they were alone before the glow of the banked fire, wards up to guard both life and privacy. Adam looked sad, but not incredibly surprised, at Damien's description of his chat with Lord Aldred.

The tall knight sighed at the end. "I suppose it could have been worse. He didn't actually suggest trotting Ciriis out and marrying her to legitimate the baby. Or that he'd sue to have Ren legitimized posthumously. That's been done before, too, after all."

Damien dropped at last into a chair – Aldred's chair, actually – and stretched his stockinged toes towards the fire. "Rarely, but yes. For Jason's father, among others."

Adam snorted. "And actually, you should probably do that officially for *Jason*, not that Evan Eldridge Alsterling is *dead*... But since he and Megan were never married and Evan's marriage to Alexa was clearly a farce–"

Damien winced. "I hope it was. I rather suspect it wasn't."

Adam looked a bit sick at that as well. The dates lined up for that wedding to have taken place just after Evan's fifteenth birthday, as they both knew – only even legal because King Reginald, as Evan's grandsire and natural liege-lord had given his permission.

David might be planning to rescue Megan from Evan for her sake – and entirely fairly...

But who could ever possibly rescue *Evan?*

"Just so," Adam said after a moment. "Your Heir shouldn't have any taint of illegitimacy about him."

"Or her."

Adam gave him a stern look. "Marli won't be your Heir. You know that. It'll be that black-haired little boy, or one of the twins."

"The older twin, then, if one of them," Damien said morosely. Because the younger would be Lord Prydeen's 'true Heir,' presumably meaning that he or she would be an Evil Wizard.

He shook his head and looked back at Adam. "I should ask how things went with Ciriis. Was she actually sober enough to take care of the baby?"

Adam sighed heavily. "Yes... though I stayed a while to be sure. It gave us a chance to talk, so I suppose that was worthwhile..."

Damien leaned his head against the high back of the chair and closed his eyes. "Really? She seems... in even worse state than Aldred."

"It's... a mix," Adam admitted. He sounded compassionate... and sad. It was a side of him that Damien wasn't sure he even let Jason see very often. "She's sneaky and sly, but a very upstanding person in her own way. She always has been. She'd have jumped through fire to put you on the throne – or to find someone else who would have the moral fiber to do right by the Realm."

He sounded like he was describing himself, actually. But he'd known Ciriis longer than anyone else, so presumably he knew her better.

"She'll take it farther than I would, though," Adam went on, acknowledging the ironic look Damien opened his eyes to give him. "I... can only compromise my morals so far in pursuit of a goal. Perhaps it's the *empathy...*" He shrugged.

"Perhaps it's having a stronger moral compass in the first place," Damien suggested.

Adam looked uncomfortable with that assessment, but didn't argue. "She says – and the one positive thing about imbibing too much, from an *empathic* point of view anyways, is that it leaves all the emotions bare and honest. I'm a veritable Truthfinder around drunk people."

He rolled his eyes. Damien noted that the tall man's lashes were... overly glisteny. He'd had to shut down his own *empathy* fairly hard to get through that awful dinner, but he could imagine...

"So, you're saying Ciriis' emotions were consistent with her words," Damien interpreted. "And you believe her."

His Champion nodded. "Consistent with her words now *and* what I know of her from the past. She joined Aldred's scheme to create an alternative Heir to the Realm to *avoid* another civil war, not to start one. And to save Genevieve's life, and yours. She says that old as he is – and this is her ruthless side showing up again – that she figured Aldred wouldn't live terribly much longer and that it would be natural for you and Genevieve to adopt the child and raise him as your own. And if you didn't wish to... well, she figured that she'd already raised one king. She could raise another to save the Realm again."

Damien snorted slightly. "*You* raised me. You and Jason."

Adam shrugged. "Her words. And we only helped you into adulthood if it comes down to it. Your parents – and your sister – made you the kind of person who *could* be a good man. And a great king."

Damien sighed. "My parents, my sister... and my Eldridge grandparents and aunts and uncles, I suppose. My memories of Ravenscroft are... jumbled," he admitted at last. "Not because they aren't *clear,* but because a small child doesn't really place things in a timeline. I could tell you *what* happened, and probably in what order, if you really pressed me. But I'd be extrapolating."

And presumably also from a child's perspective... which might or might not make sense when recalled presently. Damien hadn't been able to connect any of the adults he remembered from his childhood to Baron Eugenio when he'd met him, for example. And his memories were unquestionably colored with both the over-gentle rosiness of his happiness before everything went sour... as well as his lingering bitterness at his grandparents' rejection.

It wasn't often that the King admitted to the lapses or limits to his perfect recall.

Adam took the statement as the pearl of trust that it was.

Then he nodded and set it aside. "She's... not entirely *wrong,* you know. Given the information available to her."

Meaning, without knowing about Prydeen's prophecy.

Damien sighed. "I wish I could believe that Aldred's motives were as pure. But I think he pretty much cured me of that illusion."

Adam laughed mirthlessly. "Oh, I wouldn't say Ciriis' motives were *pure.* She would dearly love to be the power behind the throne, though *you* know that after she tried to drive that wedge between you and Genevieve, back at the beginning. If she'd succeeded *then,* she wouldn't have needed to try to become Queen-Mother-Regent *now.*"

"If she'd 'succeeded' then, I wouldn't be here to be having this discussion," Damien told him dryly. "And you'd be dealing with that civil war that she claims she wants to avoid. A two-way one between Lord Prydeen and Harald against... I don't know. Rosa leading the remnants of the Rebellion, I suppose. New fractures in the Realm..." he muttered, losing track of the conversation as he imagined the likely fallouts of such a scenario.

"Not exactly what I meant," Adam commented. "I was trying to say that Ciriis supports a stable and prosperous Realm first, and everything else at a very distant second, even personal power. She deeply regrets having ended up in this situation – she never planned to get stuck in Elaarwen for the rest of her life and certainly not in *Cloudcroft*. You know how she loves her comforts, and this is as close to the opposite as she could get without having to join the peasantry."

Damien tucked a hand behind his head, relaxing a bit more against the high back of the upholstered chair. "That's fair, I guess. Though Court has been... *easier* since she's been gone. Aryllis manages the Secret Cadre and the spy network with a great deal less drama."

"You're telling *me.*" Adam rolled his eyes. "I've had to work with both of them, kindly recall."

The King gave a small snort of dry amusement. "At least Ciriis didn't try to 'test' you every now and then. Just in case that wasn't *really* a soul-bond. She always accepted you and Jason as a pair."

Adam looked slightly disconcerted. "Yes, she – what? She did *what* to you?"

Damien tucked his other hand behind his head and let his expression go wry. "I did have to talk to Aldred eventually, but I'd planned to put it off until our return trip from whatever-we're-doing. In case it went as poorly as... well. As it did. I considered following you and Ciriis out – claiming I wanted to learn how to change a diaper before *our* baby is born, perhaps. But with Ciriis as... *sauced* as she was, it didn't seem like a good idea. She hasn't tried to vamp me in front of *other* people since I was eighteen, but unhappy and drunk... I wasn't so sure."

"How did I never notice...?" Adam was stunned.

"Because you assumed a soul-bonded man was inviolate," Damien told him. Well, until recently anyways. And Damien had more or less set himself up for *that*. "And like I said, *you* have a stronger moral compass. It's why... I miss Ciriis in some ways, but I'm not entirely displeased that I can't let her come back to Court. As herself, anyways, though it's probably better if she doesn't even come down with Aldred," he added. "After this next trip, I suppose. Since we want them to bring us the baby."

There was a moment of silence.

"Sometimes," Adam said slowly, "I forget how ruthless *you* can be. My sweet prince."

Damien gave him a pained look. "I'm not really that right now, I know."

Means before ends... it was still destroying him on the inside, what he'd had to do in Azella's Keep.

That look of compassion was almost too much...

"You will always be my sweet prince, Damien. And I will always be here to hold you when you need to recover from having to be ruthless."

Damien closed his eyes and swallowed. Hard. He couldn't really bear to talk about... *that* right now. Not while still working their way through... *this.* "Unfortunately, Aldred *is* going to be a part of my Court until he's too old to make the trip. As Genevieve's father... that temporary banishment last Fall is about as far as I can take it. And *he* shows no signs of remorse. Rather the opposite, if anything."

He paused, and the tears he'd been trying to hold back finally trickled out of the corners of his eyes.

"Damien..."

"Dammit, Adam, I really *loved* that old man. I *want* to love him, for the sake of Genevieve and the children... *including* Ren..."

A familiar sigh. "I know what you mean."

"But he'd take my Throne in an instant," Damien said it out loud because he needed to hear the words to really believe them. "He'd take Elaarwen back from Genevieve – for his *own* pride and rank, rather than being proud of what *she's* done with the province. And I have small doubt that the moment I'm not watching closely enough, he'll reveal Ciriis as being alive and legitimate Ren. And then we're back where we were last Fall, but even... messier."

Because Aldred would make it clear that Ciriis' 'death' had been to appease the unreasonable and paranoid 'young' king. And which side Ciriis would come down if faced with ending her own likely-permanent exile to Cloudcroft... Adam might think she put the Realm before all else, but Damien wasn't so sure she couldn't talk herself around into believing that Aldred's plan *was* best for the Realm.

Her own son would surely make the *best* future king, wouldn't he? And she respected, but had never particularly *liked* Genevieve – for taking what she saw as her own 'proper place' at Damien's side as much as some other sort of private competition that seemed to be about *which* woman had *actually* Saved the Realm... Ciriis wouldn't mind dispossessing Genevieve at *all*...

"I wish I could disagree," Adam's voice was reluctant. "But we know he's a sly old fox. And that he's willing to break oaths that inconvenience him. Elaarwen was barely touched by Reginald's reign–"

"And it wasn't likely out of some deep sense of *morals* that he decided to found the Rebellion," Damien kept his eyes closed, his head tilted back. "Duchess – *Grand* Duchess Alicia–" giving the woman her royal title in this instance made more sense than the one she'd married into, "–had been filling his head with stories of how the Sword had spoken for him as a toddler. And apparently, *he* liked being at Court very much as a young man... Did I mention that he contrived to look completely shocked when he pretended that *I* had suggested that Ciriis be killed to make their story *real?*"

"Gods. No. You hadn't."

Damien opened his eyes to see Adam looking... entirely green, now.

"You don't think he was asking for *permission?*" the Champion asked faintly.

Damien gave a bitter laugh. "No, of course not. Ciriis being alive and available is his only tool to possibly legitimate Ren. And he's well aware that the servants he has up here have all been vetted by Aryllis and know which side their bread is buttered on – long-term. He can't *claim* they've been wed, posthumously, because we'll have too many witnesses that would say otherwise. Just as there were down at Castle Stellarine."

He gave a slightly more real laugh. "Thank the Gods for these straightforward, honest, *clever* mountain-folk."

Though if Aldred wasn't too old to sire *one* baby, he might manage a second. And with a more biddable and less politically problematical woman. One of those mountain-girls, so naïve of 'lowlander ways'? Unless the Land took a stronger hand with the chastisement It had given him when he was sworn – and that Aldred now seemed determined to ignore away – and simply granted him a level of fertility more appropriate to his years... would It do even do such a thing?

"Hmmn." Adam looked thoughtful. "I think they might lie for Genevieve. But not for Aldred."

Damien frowned in surprise. "Really?"

Adam gave a one-shouldered shrug. "It's just a feeling I have. She's... been more their own than he has in some ways."

"You think? Even though she's spent most of every year elsewhere since we married?"

Adam gave him a one-sided smile that was sad more than sardonic. "She's also brought her royal flatlander husband home to be her humble, affable Duke-Consort.

"And when you were captured, it was to one of *their* people that you turned for help. Befriending that fellow, Darvin, may have been the best thing you've done in Elaarwen. Well, that and giving them as much of your ear as *anyone* could possibly want."

He rolled his eyes, and Damien felt it necessary to protest, feebly.

Adam brushed that aside. "And everyone knows that she's out doing Big Important Things for the Realm and showing Elaarwen off to advantage. *Aldred* seems to have fled down to Court just to have fun. And left his mountain-bred lady-wife here on her own, but with no real authority."

Damien winced. "So, you've picked up on that, too? Genevieve always seems to see it as her father gathering valuable intelligence."

Adam snorted.

There didn't seem to be anything else to say.

The tall knight stood up from his own chair and stretched, then started unbuttoning his shirt. "Ready for bed, love? I imagine our good Lady Elaarwen is going to want us on the road at the earliest possible hour."

Damien nodded and stood up as well, but stepped across the intervening space and into Adam's arms instead of beginning to undress. "I'm glad you're here, Adam. And... I'm glad Genevieve and Jason *aren't*."

Adam sighed and embraced his King as well. "If she'd been here, either Aldred would have put off making his demands or–"

"Or else he'd have used her as a lever," Damien pointed out. "And if Jason were here..."

The King shook his head. "I love him. You know I do. But... *he* wouldn't have gotten what you did out of Ciriis. *I* probably wouldn't have, for that matter. And *he'd* hate dealing with all of this even more than... than I do."

"Than *we* do," Adam corrected gently.

Damien nodded. "But you can hate it and still... still keep doing the work. Still keep me *stable.*"

Adam forced a chuckle. "We keep *each other* stable. It's occurred to me that Aldred... used to be a great deal more subtle. And this – all of this mess he's created – might simply be a result of... age."

"Well, age mixed with o'erweening ambition," Damien agreed. "And he's no less dangerous for all that."

"More, if anything," Adam noted. "But you've done what you had to. Can you put it all aside to sleep? Tomorrow is going to be a long day. There's a fog coming in, among other things."

The King made a face, but didn't question how Adam knew about the fog. It *might* simply have been that one of the locals had mentioned it, after all. "Mountain-riding in fog – at least I *assume* we're riding to wherever. Those oreads and sylphs will have their work cut out for them, keeping us on solid ground."

The Champion snickered. "Well, they seemed to want to help... come to bed, love. We haven't had any privacy for four days."

Damien laughed, but cringed inwardly.

They were in his father-in-law's house; no matter how many wards he'd set, this still felt... *awkward.*

On the other hand, they'd had no indication that *Elaarwen-Manifest* was willing to give them any wiggle-room on Her requirements. After Adam's collapse in Castle Stellarine, they hadn't even tried testing the question beyond riding separate horses... and they'd stayed side-by-side for the first half-day of riding, just in case.

That had meant getting rather... *creative* while they had to sleep just feet away from everyone else on the trail. It wasn't as if Damien could cast wards on the air, after all. While that might be theoretically possible, the stuff just moved around so much as to make it impracticable.

Or at least *he* thought so. Adam had gotten a very... *thoughtful* look on his face when they'd discussed the problem. Perhaps it was that nascent connection of his to Elemental Air that was becoming so much less *nascent* lately.

"Tired of having to be 'creative'?" Damien teased to distract himself from their location as he tugged off his shirt. He eyed his socks warily, wondering whether it was worth the feeling of constriction that sleeping in socks always gave him to not have his toes come in direct contact with the chill stone floor.

Adam's arms came around him from behind, hindering further progress. "With you? Never."

An interesting phrasing... who *was* he tired of having to be creative with? Jason would be the obvious answer, and by Adam's own admission they'd been trying *new things* since last Fall. Had Jason and his rather extensive experience from his years with Prince Oskar been pushing Adam's boundaries a bit farther than he was really happy with?

It wasn't his place to ask, Damien told himself as Adam's hands made it hard to focus on such abstractions. His *hands*... and his *lips* on Damien's *neck*...

"I love you, my sweet prince," Adam murmured between kisses that made the black-haired man's knees melt like... like... like paper in a rainstorm. Paper with *love-poetry* written on it...

Just a few more days, Damien thought helplessly as he yielded – again – to what his heart wanted. A few more days and they would resolve whatever-it-was that Elaarwen needed of him. And then they could work on figuring out what their future would look like.

It had to be something that didn't hurt so badly.

Something that they could live around others.

Something sustainable.

Something...

But in the meantime, there *were* the next few days. This was *necessary*. Surely there wasn't anything wrong with enjoying what was *necessary?*

And given that there *were* likely to be only a few days...

He turned slowly in Adam's arms.

"Adam? May I... try something?" Damien asked rather shyly.

Adam looked up curiously from migrating his kisses around from Damien's neck. "Of course."

No question asked... that was a *trust* that the younger man hoped he would always live up to.

"All right..."

Damien took a breath, and looked down. Adam had been quicker with his disrobing and stood there entirely bare, proud and tall in so many ways. And beautiful in so many ways.

The tall knight shuddered a little and closed his eyes with a smile as Damien caressed him, gently... gently...

"Tighter, please," Adam murmured, and gasped happily as Damien complied.

One more thing...

Damien dropped to one knee on the hearthrug, and *tasted*...

Adam's sharp intake of breath was as affirming as... as the tall man's sudden, if slow, drop to his own knees was confusing. Had Damien done it *wrong?*

Strong, callused hands lifted the King's chin for a deep, *claiming* kiss as they knelt, facing each other, both breathing rather quickly.

"Did... didn't you like... what I was doing?" Damien asked when he had a chance.

Adam smiled. "I did, love. Very much."

"Then... why?"

"Because *my King* should never be on his knees for *anyone*," Adam said firmly.

Damien looked at him for a moment with disappointment, then down in shame as unavoidable memories pressed against him. Again. He was right, of course. Adam was always right. "Too late for that, I'm afraid."

Adam's hands tilted his face again. His expression was resigned. "The White Witch again? Or was it her minion this time?"

He couldn't turn his head to look away. Instead, Damien closed his eyes. "Her."

"A *compulsion* spell, I assume."

Damien's eyes fluttered open in surprise. "How did you – oh. Because of all the other ones I told you she used."

"Because I know *you*," Adam corrected. "And I know that you wouldn't stand on your own dignity, but you would never have knelt for that bitch because you are *our King*. Because you represent Ilseador."

Damien swallowed hard. Adam's *trust* was sometimes too great burden to be borne. "Adam... she forced me to my knees with a *compulsion* spell, true. But what I did once I was there – she commanded, but didn't *compel*."

Adam's smile grew a bit wry. "Damien, my love, we've already covered this. You were doing what you had to in order to make her fall in love with you. So that she would give you access to what you needed to protect us all. I'm sure you made that little *compulsion* spell well worth her while."

The King blushed. "I... did my best."

A nod. "After all your *experience* in the bedroom with all those ladies that Ciriis – and I – sent in to sleep with you, I'd imagine that your *best* is... *very good* indeed."

"Adam..."

"Damien. I told you that I will always be here when you need me hold you and help you recover from having to be ruthless. I know you're still healing–"

"Adam, I *enjoyed* it!"

He pulled away as Adam looked startled at that admission, and turned away, hugging himself.

When Damien had come back to Emeralsee, Adam had recognized that he'd fallen in love with the pale sorceress of Farivera... and had forgiven him. It had been the first step for the King to forgive himself.

He... *pitied* Azella now.

And he despised *himself* for what he had done to win her – well, not her trust, as she had none to give, nor her heart, since that was still bound up with her former master whom she'd slain – but her... continuing *fascination* at least.

And... he hated that there were still some moments of... beauty amidst the ugliness of his captivity. That day after she had given him the books on salamandres... and he'd wandered out to find her in her office... The *compulsion* spell had been cast first to protect him before he touched her dangerous-even-to-touch books on demons. What had followed from there had been... playful. A sparkle of real joy.

A sparkle that had been quickly buried – it had been only a day later that she had tortured Mikhail... no, *Jeremy*... and...

"Damien." Adam's touch on his bare back was as gentle as a breeze – as searing as cold wind on an open wound.

"Adam, stop. You can't. You *shouldn't*. What's between us... it can't *last*. It *shouldn't*. Even if things were such that we didn't need to hide every moment... I'm... I'm this *broken thing* that *enjoyed* having weird sex with an Evil Sorceress. I can't protect Genevieve. The soul-bond... She's stuck with me as I am. But you..."

"I'm not some *innocent*, Damien." That tone of exasperation was perhaps to be expected.

He shook his head. "I'm not saying that. You've seen things – *done* things – that I can't even imagine. As Alanna reminded me, *I've* never been on a battlefield. That's... that's something you and Genevieve share, I suppose. But I was going to say, you're only linked to me through Jason's soul-bond to Genevieve. You don't have to, to *taint* yourself."

"*Taint* myself?"

The King bent over his knees, stomach hurting in way that had nothing to do with anything physical. The King bent over his knees, stomach hurting in way that had nothing to do with anything physical. Like Adam had dealt with when they entered Elaarwen, though Damien's bellyache wasn't being imposed by any supernatural Being. Just by his own unworthiness and lack of moral character.

"By association with my grandfather's line. We're *all* tainted, Aldred said. Me, Oskar. *Kandy* and *Father.* Even Jason, I suppose, though he's another generation distant, so mayb–"

"Damien, for the love of– I am going to give that old man a piece of my mind for setting this off."

The King felt himself tugged out of his hunched position, down to the padded surface that Angelos had gotten laid out for them in front of the fire. More layers than they'd had out on the trail, and warmer with the fire right there – and proper pillows. But the floor was harder and colder than dirt beneath those layers.

"There is nothing *tainted* about you, my sweet prince," Adam said, wrapping himself around Damien's back and caressing his side and chest in the warm, soothing way he'd done for fifteen years now – just with clothes on. "And there's nothing *terrible* about finding some fragments of humanity left in your White Witch. Of course, you enjoyed making love to her. It likely brought those fragments closer to the surface – and gave you reasons why you wanted so badly to make her whole."

The tall man paused his words, but his caresses only hesitated for an instant. "And there's beauty and pleasure in sex itself, after all. Even when it's not with someone you... well, *want* to love at all. Especially for an *empath,* as we both are. Simply knowing that you are giving the other person *pleasure* can be a joy as... as addictive as any drug. Even when that is all *they* give *you...*"

There seemed... a depth to that comment...

And old, old pain with a hint of self-disgust that was tantalizingly familiar...

Damien tried to claw himself up out of his own misery to answer that... that *need to be understood* that Adam was radiating. To help and Heal and...

"That's what I mean," Adam said gently, if rather breathlessly, as Damien turned in his arms and offered comfort in the way that seemed most natural, hands returning caresses and lips seeking... "From everything you've told me, I don't doubt that she's an entire bottomless *pit* of emotional need. There is no way you couldn't respond to that. Nor to the pleasure you brought her that even temporarily made her feel human again."

That old pain and self-disgust and all the depth that went with it was... neatly packed up and tucked away again. And Damien could breathe and blink and push slightly away. Adam gave him the space.

"What... what was *that* from?" the younger man asked after a moment.

It was Adam's turn to lower his gaze. But his sigh was less of a self-castigation and more of an old regret than that... that *memory* of an emotion.

"That... was from my time with Edmund," Adam explained. "He was using me, and I knew it. He never loved me – and he made it abundantly clear that he honestly didn't care how I felt. About anything."

"*'Clean sheets'*..." Damien remembered. He looked up into Adam's face, but the tall knight's eyes were still turned away. "He took his pleasure of you and... sent you away *wanting*? And... you came *back* to him after that? Was he even..."

Should he even ask this? But it was *Adam,* and Damien felt fiercely protective...

"...was he even, um, *kind* the first time you, um...?"

"The first time he had sex with me?" Adam shook his head. "No. He'd been... well, *feeling me up* whenever he got the chance for a month or two. And he was a knight and I was a final-year squire, so he could *make* plenty of 'chances.' It was just after Jason had been made Prince Oskar's bodyguard... and lover. I don't know if anyone else knew, but..."

"But you did," Damien nodded. Of course, Adam would have known.

That got him a glance and a slight smile. "Yes. I did. And – I think I told you some of this before. Tell me to stop if..."

"If you repeat yourself?" Damien shook his head and snuggled closer. "How many times have you listened to me saying the same things now?"

A smile ghosted across Adam's face, and then he sighed, acquiescing. "I'd told Jason how I felt less than a month before he was knighted. *Before* Oskar chose him as Champion. Jason had been... not as receptive as I'd hoped. As I'd dreamed. But he'd been willing

– after he thought about it for a week or so – to try a few kisses. To try... *touching* me a little. In quiet nooks, nowhere terribly private, nothing too very... *intimate*. I... had thought he liked it, though he wasn't ready for me to touch *him,* not more than to put my arms around his neck for a kiss anyways, and even *that* took a few days–"

"But that's just Jason," Damien pointed out. "You'd been close friends for years by then. You must have known how he reacts to change."

Adam smiled sadly and traced a line along Damien's jawline with one finger. "You can *know* something and it still.... *hurts,* Damien. And Jason was... well, he was being much more tentative and subtle than Edmund was a little later, but I'd been dreaming about him for *years*. I was... incredibly horny, to put it bluntly."

He chuckled at the younger man's sudden, fierce blush. "All that experience, and *you're* the one blushing. Anyways, it was – horribly shocking to find that Jason had apparently dealt with that resistance to *change* so much more effectively... so much more *quickly,* when it came to Oskar. *They* were in *bed* together the very first night he was the prince's Champion."

"Did... Oskar *force* him?" Damien asked – more to suggest the possibility and ease Adam's heart than because he thought it likely. Though on the other hand... they knew that Oskar had had some access to his own inborn magickal potential...

Adam made a face. "Jase told me – when we finally talked a little about it this Winter. He said there was a great deal of spirits involved. Oskar claimed that he wanted to celebrate having a Champion – something about it being an indicator that he would last as Heir, unlike all the rest. And Jason – you know he doesn't usually drink a great deal. But it was his first posting and to the *Crown Prince*. He said he felt like he needed to make a good impression."

"Hmmn." Damien didn't want to say it, but everything Adam and Jason had told him about his late uncle this last year suggested that...

Adam snorted slightly. "I'm not a fool, Damien. I'm aware that there *was* probably a bit of a *compulsion* spell involved. Whether to loosen Jason's inhibitions by getting him to drink too much or thereafter, to get him into bed... or both."

"So, you... you *felt* it when they..." Damien knew he was blushing again.

"I did." Adam sighed. "He was so *happy*. So perfectly *blissful* and happy. He felt so *good* that it was almost enough for *me*... and all I *really* wanted – or so I told myself – was for *Jason* to be happy. But..."

He shrugged. "I suppose it was impossible for anyone not to notice how I was moping around and finding excuses to be where I could watch Jase. And Oskar, since they were always together. Certainly, *Edmund* noticed, and that was when he began his campaign to get me into *his* bed. It was his suggestion that maybe I could make Jason jealous, I think."

Adam shook his head. "And when I finally agreed... well, being able to *feel* Jason's first time had given me an entirely unrealistic expectation. I didn't imagine it could *hurt,* for one thing."

Damien frowned. "Wait, but it didn't for Jason?"

Adam blinked away the fog of memory to focus on Damien blankly for a moment.

"Oh." He gave a chuckle that sounded half like a sob. "You're imagining things a little differently than they happened. I... don't think Jason has ever been... underneath. Not by choice anyways."

Well, if *that* didn't upend the mental pictures that Damien had never wanted to have about his horrible uncle... Not that *Jason's* confidences hadn't begun painting pictures in his unwilling head...

"Um. So... you didn't particularly enjoy your first time... but you felt Edmund's pleasure enough to... want to come back?" It didn't make sense to Damien.

Well, it did and it didn't.

"That was it," Adam agreed. "Well, that and having to *feel* Jason enjoying himself with Oskar otherwise. If I could time things right... the nearer-by sensations blocked that out for me."

He cuddled Damien a little closer. "It was... horrible in a lot of ways. Edmund certainly didn't care about me. He'd mostly do as he pleased and then send me off to... do for myself as it were. If he were feeling particularly generous, he might sit behind me at the edge of his bed when he was done and help me out... But then he'd make me scrub the floor clean afterwards. Naked."

"Adam, that sounds..." Damien couldn't find kind words to voice his thought.

To his surprise, Adam chuckled.

And kissed him on the forehead.

"It was stupid, yes. But I had myself convinced that if I gave Edmund what he wanted – *whatever* he wanted – that I could be happy with him. Even though he never wanted me to so much as stay the night." He brushed his fingers through Damien's hair. "It was... what I needed at the time, I suppose. And he found it amusing to play with my emotions for a few months. And then... he was done."

"Done?" Damien blinked.

"Done," Adam repeated. "He found some other lad more interesting – one that was still a bit of a challenge, rather than one who bent to whatever he wanted."

"What... what did you do?" the younger man asked.

"I cried a bit," Adam admitted candidly. "And I raged a bit. In my room when I was alone. I still had the problem of being able to *feel* everything Jason was, though I'd learned to wall myself off... a bit. But there was still too much. And then I started having these nightmares about being *alone* and *terrified* and–"

"I'm sorry." Damien knew where *those* had come from.

"Don't be," Adam told him firmly. "Your dreams were *very* effective at blocking the things I didn't want to *feel*. And... you *needed* me. I wasn't sure who you *were* until Ciriis actually found you, but I knew that I *knew* you. And that we were meant to be together."

He sighed and ran his fingers down Damien's side, stopping as they hitched up on the waistband of Damien's pants. "If I'd actually found you *then*... well, *I* was a legal adult, but *you* weren't. But I don't know if that would have stopped me when you... *needed* me so much. I'd have gotten you out of that damned Library and away from that damned Lady Theresa, even if I'd had to secret you in my room in the squires' barracks. And once you were fully of age... I don't know if I would have even *noticed* when Oskar discarded Jason the way Edmund discarded me."

Which would have been mere months...

Damien turned his head to lay it on Adam's chest. "I... wanted to say, 'oh, yes, please,' when you were talking about getting me out of the Library when I was fourteen. But Jason needed you later."

"You can dream about it happening that way," Adam commented as he worked his fingers under Damien's waistband. "It doesn't change what actually did. *I've* dreamed about rescuing you at that point, too. And how I would have protected you – and what I would have done with you once you were old enough..."

The explorations of his fingers kept that from needing any further description.

The tall man gave another wistful sigh. "It's all fantasy, of course. King Reginald *might* have let me take you out of there, but he *wouldn't* likely have let me hide you under my bed during room inspections. You'd have had your own suite of rooms and servants and all... *years* before I was ready and able to protect you."

"Mmmmn," Damien said, though that was at least as much of a comment on Adam's fingers as on his words. "Did you... do you *hate* Edmund?"

Adam's fingers stilled. "At the time... I oscillated. One moment yes, the next no. I'd've gone back to him if he'd taken me – at least until after the Battle of Siovale. I... learned that I had worth of my own out there. And I knew Ciriis was counting on me to come back and help her get you out of the Library."

"And when you all got back, that was when Prince Oskar discarded Jason," Damien continued the timeline.

Adam nodded. His fingers withdrew to fiddle instead with Damien's belt and the buttons on his pants. "And Oskar took Edmund as his Champion. For reasons that *I* wouldn't have cared about – except that Jason *did*. Jase had that broken heart that I didn't want to acknowledge *and* he was hurting for being replaced by a man of such vastly lesser talents than himself."

"But one who – ah – shared more of Oskar's interests, you said." Damien obligingly rolled onto his back, and Adam propped himself up on one elbow so he could see what he was doing. "It still baffles me that *you* could have fallen for a man like that."

Adam snickered. "Sometimes, Damien, *you* still seem like the innocent. Do you remember what Edmund Railston looked like?"

"Um.... no?" He'd spent most of his time trying to stay *out* of his Uncle Oskar's way. "Good?"

"Very good. Nearly as good as Jason. And I've heard enough talk to know that I wasn't the only one who thought that."

"Hmmn. You don't sound like you hate him *now*," Damien noted. He wracked his memory instead of trying to imagine *his Adam* as being callow and anxious enough to be interested in a man solely for his looks. "What happened to him, anyways? I... can't remember seeing his name on any of the lists of where knights were posted..."

Adam shrugged. "I have no idea. He was with Oskar at Zialest and seems to have vanished thereafter. Like most of the others who were with the prince. I can't imagine any of them wanted to be the one to have to come back and report what happened to King Reginald."

Damien sighed. "Grandfather *usually* spared the messenger but... yes. I can see their point."

He lifted his hips obediently as Adam helped slip his pants off of him. They had a brief debate about socks, which Adam – who was on the side of removing them – won by pointing out that keeping them on would keep Damien tossing and turning all night in an half-conscious effort to escape the constraints. And that neither of them would get much rest that way.

"If I'm going to lose sleep, I'd rather it be for more entertaining reasons," Adam had said firmly, and then chuckled and worked on kissing away Damien's blushes before pulling off his socks.

They lay quietly together under the covers for several minutes after that before Adam cleared his throat a little awkwardly.

"I didn't want to push you away earlier, Damien."

The King – who was far too awake for the hour – nodded. "I know. And, well, you were right, but..."

In a truly unprecedented display of... *shyness?* Adam cleared his throat again. "You're not kneeling now, love."

Damien's head popped up off Adam's shoulder, his silvery gaze seeking out Adam's golden-hazel. "Do you mean...?"

It was impossible to tell, by sight alone, in the ruddy light of the banked fire, whether Adam was blushing. Though it surely *felt* like he was. "If you still want to."

Damien surged up to kiss lips that *were* rather overly warm before proceeding with the, ah, *experiment*.

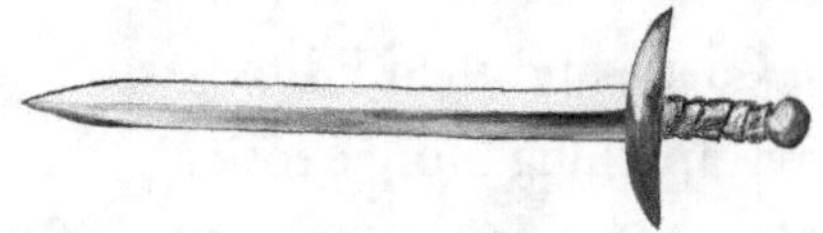

Chapter FIFTEEN

A Flavor of the Future?

"Т HAT WAS... LOVELY," ADAM SAID peacefully a little later. "It... seems odd to say 'thank you,' but..."

"You're welcome." Damien stretched up from where his head was nestled on Adam's shoulder to kiss his... well, his jawline, given where they both were.

"It was..." Adam's voice was... oddly shy and embarrassed again. "That was the first time anyone has ever done... *that* for me."

Damien rolled a bit so he could put a hand on Adam's chest and prop his chin on it. "I suppose that makes sense. Given what you've told me about Edmund. And what I know about Jason for myself. Just for the record, that was the first time *I've* ever done that either. For a man anyways."

And hopefully the ruddy light from the hearth masked *his* blushes, though Adam could likely *feel* them through their *empathic bond* much as Damien could do the same. A little... lowering after all, for a man to feel so shy with as much 'experience' as he had.

259

"Really?" Adam asked curiously. "After a whole *week* in the grotto with Jase?"

Damien gave him a bemused look. "I actually *slept* through most of that, Adam. I thought Jason had told you. We made love and I *called* food from the Castle and then I'd fall asleep again. I think he was too worried to try anything more exotic."

He chuckled. "He was worried enough that if the grotto hadn't lit up like the main ballroom on a festival night every time we made love, I don't know if he'd have been willing to do *that*. But I suppose being able to actually see that spillover of magickal energy helped him understand that I needed the loving as much as the sleep."

"He... told me a little," Adam said slowly. "Neither of us was ready to talk about it much then. And later..." He gave a rather *contented* sigh. "We've had a great many *other* things to talk about. It's been good, getting some of this stuff aired out. Things we didn't even realize had formed walls between us."

"Me, mostly, I suppose," Damien's sigh was a great deal less contented as he laid his head down sideways to listen to Adam's heart and breath. "I've gotten in your way from the very earliest days."

Adam's chuckle startled him with its rumbling depth. His large, callused hand made long, gentle strokes from the top of Damien's head down his back and... as far as he could reach. Which was... pretty far, with those long arms of his. "Don't give yourself *too* many airs, my sweet prince. We had plenty of our own problems to talk through that had absolutely *nothing* to do with you."

He paused. "And probably still do. Both kinds, actually. I've never mentioned to *Jason* how jealous I was of all your other lovers. And... I don't really plan to."

What could Damien possibly say to that?

"Did I mention how that weirded *Azella* out?" the King asked after a moment. "That I'd had *seventeen* lovers before her? It never bothered Genevieve. At least not that she's mentioned."

Although if *Adam* and *Jason* had so many things they'd never discussed...

Adam's hand continued those long, lovely caresses. "Seventeen? I suppose... Ciriis, the other twelve ladies of your first Secret Cadre. Genevieve. Jason. *Me.* So you slept with Azella's minion first, then?"

He didn't usually use the sorceress' name. Was he... trying to let her be a human instead of an icon of evil and cruelty for this brief, peaceful moment? It definitely made it easier to talk about her...

Though he still wasn't using *Jeremy's* name.

"I did," Damien admitted. He didn't really want to talk about how that hadn't gone so well, Azella having bound him up with compulsions that prevented him from having any real release that didn't involve *her.*

She'd managed to place those *compulsions* while Damien had still been reeling from Azella's near-severing of his connection to the Realm and to Genevieve – which he hadn't even thought to try defending against, since he'd been so confident it couldn't be done. He'd felt half-blind, half-deaf, and all but entirely numb to the world... and then she had denied him food and clothing and made him sleep in her bed with her naked and crawling all over him. What little energy and focus he'd been able to claim under all of that he'd used to prevent himself from reacting to her highly unsubtle attempts at seduction.

So, she'd sent the innocent-seeming Jeremy in to lure Damien to yield in a different way.

Adam... couldn't possibly be jealous of *Jeremy*?

Could he?

He'd said he wasn't before... or, no, he'd said he wasn't *threatened* by Jerem's continued proximity. That... wasn't exactly the same thing.

Dammit, but *empathy* should really be more useful in sorting this out. And it might have done, if Adam hadn't closed himself away rather effectively. Or closed this *part* of his emotions away somehow. His love for Damien was still abundantly detectable.

Perhaps it was time to discuss this. Some things needed words, as it appeared Jason and Adam had been discovering this last Winter.

As Damien and Genevieve had discovered almost immediately, given that they knew nothing of each other besides what was publicly available to know – and what their respective spies had ferreted out. Which had been rather more for Damien, given that he'd been actively searching out information about the Rebel Duchess for years, whereas *he* hadn't particularly come to *Genevieve's* attention until shortly before his coronation.

"Azella was having me teach him to play chess," Damien volunteered a little hesitantly. How he could possibly explain why he'd yielded to Jeremy's blandishments when he'd managed to resist Azella's without having to detail those humiliations...

"I... discovered that I like teaching," he offered, planning to connect that to how he'd enjoyed teaching Franz and Rob – and even Darvin – to improve their swordskills.

"I can see that," Adam said, a hint of truculence in his voice. "Though from what I've gathered of how an Evil Wizard has her bed-slaves trained, I imagine *he* was schooling *you*. Outside of chess, anyways."

Well... and Jeremy had, in some ways. More about how a pair of wide eyes of an almost unreal blue could hide a soul that wavered between potential worth and utter depravity than anything else.

But that wasn't what Adam meant.

Damien reached a hand up to touch Adam's cheek. His fingers came away damp.

"Love..."

"I suppose you didn't kneel for *him,* given what you just told me." That wasn't *truculent,* that was *bitter. Hurt.* And with a hint of a desperate effort at *understanding.* "I know that none of it was your idea. I'd rather you have... *enjoyed* it. Rather than be broken by... it."

Damien closed his eyes for a moment. Seventeen lovers or not, he really wasn't comfortable *talking* about these things. But it needed to be done. And, quite possibly, he was going to have to have some variation of this chat with Genevieve eventually.

She hadn't *asked* him anything about his time in captivity. Yet.

But she'd seemed more comfortable with Jason than with him. Damien had attributed it to the newness of her soul-bond to Jason and the strains that Azella's various spells had placed on the one she had with *him*. And on the demands of her growing pregnancy.

But likely there was emotional Healing that they needed to suffer through as well.

A pity he'd never found anyone with a magickal talent that covered that. Or damage to the soul, either. His own skills were limited to the physical form, as were those of the other Healers he'd met or heard of, though he seemed to have greater capacity than others, perhaps because most of his work was bent upon Healing the *Realm* and people were just so much *smaller*...

...though not necessarily less *complex*.

"Do you remember what you told me about Jason and... and my uncle Oskar?" Damien said. "There are only you and Jason whom I would willingly allow to love me like that. What happened with Jeremy... was about trying to control what little was available for me to control as... anything else."

His ear was still flat to Adam's chest, so there was no way he could miss the little "oh" of an indrawn breath. And it seemed that might have helped...

Not that it felt terribly good to have to admit to that aloud. Jeremy had been a slave and possessed as little *control* over their interactions and circumstances as Damien did. And Damien's own repeated assertions that *he* was *not* a slave had only been... as true as Azella permitted them to be. For a time anyways. Until he had been able to learn enough to make it worth checking her spells and determining that, yes, he *could* free himself when he decided to.

In those early days... he'd taken advantage of Jeremy's too-willing self. And he couldn't – even now that he was sure what had been done to him under cover of *sleep* spells – feel justified about his actions in any way. Even if Jeremy had enjoyed their time together *(whether or not Damien had been awake to agree to it)*. Jeremy hadn't had the *agency* to say 'no.'

It had been for all of that – as much as the King's honest fondness for the hopefully-salvageable would-be young Evil Wizard – that had made him free the boy and find a way to bring him back to Ilseador to build a new life. He... owed Jeremy an... *indemnity* of sorts. And one that could never really be paid off.

But... "None of that was exactly *willing,* Damien. Or so you said."

Not even the slightest extra emphasis on the last word. An... *attempt* to convey the information without more of an accusation than minimally necessary.

Not necessarily a terribly *successful* attempt.

"It wasn't," Damien agreed. "But I was so mazed with hunger and sleep-deprivation and the spells Azella had on me then... I was... desperate for what seemed like a caring, human touch. One that wasn't *hers.*"

"I see." Adam was silent for a moment. "So... he was... *your* first then? Like *that?*"

It seemed like more to be saying something, not wanting to just leave things in that rather awkward state than to really be asking the question. It still made Damien laugh, which helped more with the tension between them than Adam's hesitant query.

"Oh, Adam my love. It's not just *men* who like it that way, you know."

He propped up his head again to look into Adam's eyes and laughed again – though this time through a vague mist of tears that blurred his vision. Adam's expression was... beyond embarrassed.

"Oh. Um. I... guess I never really thought about that."

To see *Adam* so completely nonplussed was entertaining, but Damien laid his head back down to spare them both.

"I've never felt it was right to talk about it, but... my first twelve Ladies... you said you helped Ciriis pick them out and send them to my bed?" And how *odd* and *painful* that must have been for Adam, given the revelations of these last few weeks... "You knew how... *damaged* they each were, I assume."

"Some," Adam admitted. "I think Ciriis made sure I didn't hear details. *They* certainly didn't talk about their experiences with... with your grandfather or Lord Prydeen while I was around. Or Oskar."

Damien nodded, feeling the wiry fur around Adam's nipple teasing his nose as he did so. "I got the feeling that most of them didn't tell Ciriis either. At least not *before*. She made it clear to *me* that each lady was a test – I had no power to fix anyone or anything, but I could help these women recover. A little anyways. They... told me their stories eventually. Though I imagine they spared me some details."

"I should hope so," Adam sounded... worried, and Damien chuckled a little sadly.

"Still worried about my innocence, Adam? Every one of their stories was... the most powerful argument – beyond personal survival – as to why I had to become king."

And mere survival could have been accomplished by running away, after all. To the Rebellion, which might have protected him and where his heart knew Genevieve was. Into obscurity in some grubby village in the back of beyond, though he – probably still, to be quite honest – couldn't quite imagine such a life. Or even past Ilseador's borders... though he now wondered if the Realm would have allowed him to leave, and he'd been aware even then that a foreign noble or monarch would have found the lost prince of Ilseador a valuable piece on the gameboard of politics.

But the stories of each of the women that he had fallen a little in love with – and more than a little with Lena and, well, Aryllis – had built a picture for him of wrongs that needed to be righted, not fled from. Of people who hadn't yet been harmed that he might one day be able to shield. Of a future where he wasn't himself a vulnerable, powerless boy, but a person – a *king* – who could make the world a better place.

It was the future that his three most vehement protectors had envisioned for him, guided and molded him for.

But it was his twelve Ladies who had made it one he was willing to reach for himself.

"Terellie was absolutely terrified of me," Damien said softly. He'd never been one to kiss and tell – though whom would he ever have told? "Ciriis had told her to be naked in the bed when I returned from dinner... I found her one of my shirts and she slept in that – and

I slept in pants – for a week before I woke up to find her weeping quietly on my shoulder. She let me kiss her after another week. And then it was just kisses for a... very long time."

He paused, tenderly remembering. Those kisses had eventually moved to some... rather interesting locations. Not that he'd ever dared try anything new until Terellie had giggled at what he was doing already. Or unless she initiated it herself.

"And then she... wanted to try everything either of us could think of," Damien went on after a moment. "She had a great many more ideas, of course, having been through... what grandfather had put her through. But she wanted to see if she could find... *fun* in any of it. *Pleasure.*"

"And, um, did she?" Adam ventured.

Damien chuckled. "Oh, yes. But the one thing she was never willing to do... well, I suppose she got over *that,* given that she and Leverett have those two adorable little girls."

"But not with you?" Adam sounded like he didn't really want to ask... and that he did, all at the same time.

Damien shook his head slightly. "Not with me. But she introduced me to how much I might enjoy... doing things the way I did with Jeremy."

Adam went still again.

"Sasha had some similar reactions," Damien went on after a moment. "They... all did, to one degree or another, I suppose. I always felt my job was just to love them in whatever way they needed until... until they could believe me when I told them that they were beautiful and perfect and deserving of all good things."

He sighed. "It was so... damned *hard* and so damned *wonderful* to see them find partners from among the knights you'd chosen for my official Guard. Men who saw them as equals and appreciated... everything about them. Men I could trust with their hearts... I'd've called out anyone who wasn't worthy of them, you know."

Adam's chuckle sounded a bit forced. "That would have been a bit of a mess. Challenges are hard to keep quiet. And we try so hard to keep just how good you are with a sword quiet."

The Champion paused, then added, "It did made things a little awkward running your Guards there for awhile, though. Tim, Lev – most of them, actually – were rather dismayed that you'd had all of their fiancées in bed before they did."

Damien's chuckle was entirely natural. "Oh, I know. All those dark looks... and then, each of them came to me and actually *thanked* me for helping their loves become whole again. I assume my ladies set them straight and told them to apologize..."

There was a change in the tension of chest muscles under Damien's cheek that suggested Adam was shaking his head. "I can't say for all of them, but Tim... said enough for me to put the pieces together. He'd been... angry with you at first, because Aryllis cried when they first slept together. Not cried because she was *hurt,* I gather, but because Tim told her how wonderful she was. He thought *you'd* broken her spirit – it took him some time to realize that she *had* a spirit because *you'd* helped her put it back together. And that you'd told her all those things yourself, but it wasn't until *he* did that she could really believe it. I assume because she thought you loved her too much to say anything else."

"He told *you* that?" Damien was skeptical. Because why Aryllis would have thought *Tim* would be more clear-eyed about anything to do with her than Damien...

Another shake. "No, I overheard him explaining to... I think it was Lev and Otto."

Damien caught his breath... "Otto... *Thielda*... Adam, without breaking confidences... just how much did you hear?"

His Champion's voice was very confused. "It was Tim talking, mostly. Why?"

Should he tell? Damien had managed to set aside this question for so long...

And yet... Thielda had asked him to find out certain things for her, then wanted to let the situation lie, stable as it seemed. But was that fair? Especially now that certain things they thought they knew to be true... had turned out not to be...?

Thielda had said it was over for her. What Damien had discovered for her had been all she needed to know. She didn't want anything more. With care... she *could* still be kept out of it. There were potentially dozens of other women who might have had that outcome, after all. Ciriis – and Adam – had only brought their young prince the discarded noblewomen who were *damaged,* but not *destroyed,* by their experience. Peasant women or much more shattered noblewomen... Prince Oskar hadn't kept *records* that Damien had been able to lay hands on. Not that he wanted to know more than he already did, but it was his obligation...

Gods, but this might open an entirely different bucket of worms...

"What *about* Thielda, Damien?" Adam pressed, his voice disconcerted. As if he already knew something he didn't want to? Or simply out of concern for their friends? The original members of Damien's Royal Guards were much more his peers and close friends than his protegées... "She and Otto seem happy. They have a son and were expecting another babe, last I knew. Is there... something that might taint their happiness?"

No, but it might yours, Damien thought, grateful that this *empathic bond* didn't transmit actual thoughts.

If this had been Genevieve he was snuggled up to... the soul-bond *did* transmit actual verbalized thoughts, and not always the ones he meant her to see. The King hadn't worked on refining what control he had over that – since they'd been together so rarely, the thoughts he had when touching his beloved wife hardly centered on anything other than his desire to make her as happy as he possibly could do.

But Adam wasn't likely to be put off this trail unless Damien explained...

"Thielda... had a terror of getting pregnant," he said after a moment to try to figure out how to put it such that the whole story wasn't immediately unraveled. Adam was clever enough to figure out most anything... unless he had no reason to. The trick was to make sure that Thielda's story seemed wrapped up with a bow at both ends and the tails of the bow trimmed tight. Nothing to be tugged on by an idealistic, clever, curious mind...

Tight, complete... and just awful enough to repulse random ponderings.

"I gather that... Prince Oskar preferred his... mistresses to be heavily pregnant," Damien said. "Or... with nursing babes. But he had no interest otherwise. Thielda... had two babes taken from her. I tracked them down, when she asked me to. I don't imagine *Oskar* cared, but someone on his staff saw that those babes were placed with stable peasant families out in the countryside."

"He *what?*" Adam was entirely shocked.

"What I said." Damien didn't want to have to speak the words again. "I don't know if there were others – though she implied that there were. I haven't found any records that were kept, and – as you mentioned with Sir Edmund and the retinue Prince Oskar took to Zialest – whatever servants and such that he employed vanished even more thoroughly than the ones that most closely served my grandfather and Lord Prydeen."

"Does... does *Otto* know?" Adam asked.

The King shook his head. "I have no idea. Thielda didn't want her... first children's lives disrupted. They seemed happy and well cared for. Loved. She said she didn't want to see them, didn't even want to know where they were or what names they'd been given. Didn't want them to know who *she* was and how they had come to be born if at all possible. What she shared with Otto... is between the two of them."

He waited a moment. "Aryllis knows, though. And she knows to keep an eye out for any other such 'orphans.'"

"Damien..." Adam's voice was troubled. "Oskar took his victims from every rank."

Accurate, but hopefully Adam minded his phrasing a bit more with Jason.

"Some of those children could start showing signs of magick. And if they were all placed in peasant families... they'll be amongst people who won't understand or be able to help them," the tall *empath* continued. "The way *I* helped *you.*"

Well... at least that wasn't the direction Damien had hoped to divert Adam from ruminating on. Though it sounded like he might not let this easily go... Children after all. Damien couldn't have let it go easily himself. *Hadn't* actually, which was half of why he'd brought Aryllis in. The other half being that she was the one who had the resources to watch for such children.

"Prince Oskar was about five years older than you and Jason, wasn't he?" Damien commented. He knew his uncle's age precisely, of course, so it wasn't really a question.

"I told you that there don't seem to be records, but assuming that he was nearing legal adulthood when he began his... depredations, we should have started hearing about people like that by now. They would be adults by the way commoners count things. And we haven't heard any such tales, though Aryllis *is* watching," he emphasized. "She can do a better job than you or I could. I have to trust her."

"I suppose..." Adam still sounded troubled. "And the women? The... mothers?"

"No records of them, either," Damien pointed out. "Not that he did this to every woman he... kept. Mirabelle and Licia and Elsa went through his hands as well, after all, and none of them had that experience. How *did* you and Ciriis find Thielda and the others?"

Adam sighed. "Ciriis did. I suppose we should ask her."

"I think Aryllis already did," Damien said a little mendaciously. He was simply assuming that the incredibly thorough Aryllis would have done.

Was there a way he could segue this back to...

"If there were any with particular sensitivities, I'm sure Aryllis would have found them by now," he added. "And you know that I scan crowds with magickal *sight* when I have the chance."

"As if you get out of the Castle enough to make that more than marginally useful," Adam groused.

"I've been doing it on *this* trip," Damien said a little pointedly, "and almost everyone in Emeralsee eventually comes in to the City for market days. And I usually overlook the main market." And some of the secondary markets when he *did* go out.

And even if Emeralsee – City and province together – didn't comprise nearly one-third of the population of the Realm, it seemed the outside of unlikely that Prince Oskar's harried servingman – whomever he had been – would have taken the time or trouble to go farther than necessary to place the babes.

"Whatever they have – if there *is* anything – it has to be fairly small and not terribly troubling to themselves or their families." Damien rolled his eyes. "Gods know, we're still turning up – well, I suppose it's mostly my illegitimate cousins, rather than aunts and uncles, at this point. And none of Grandfather's such scions have had any particular Gifts."

That had been a little surprising to Damien, honestly, given how the legitimate ones *had* been so Gifted. Perhaps more was owed to their maternal lines than to the Alsterling line after all... though even Harald – whose mother was a daughter of a long-established noblehouse – had been rather less than talented. Almost the opposite of talented if anything.

"If any of them were as Gifted as, say *Jeremy*, I'd have noticed."

Adam heaved a heavy sigh. "You *want* to talk about him, don't you, Damien."

The King folded his hands across Adam's chest to shield his love from the point of his bearded chin as he leaned across the taller man's chest again. Both to pin Adam down a bit so they could talk this out and get past this, and so that he could meet his love's eyes.

"He bothers you. More than Azella."

"*He* lives in Emeralsee now – in *Castle Alsterling,*" Adam retorted. "Unlike *Azella.*"

"Fair," Damien granted.

And waited.

"You freed him," Adam said after a long moment. "You freed him and gave him instructions to follow you to Emeralsee. Which he *did,* albeit with a *demon* inside him–"

"I made the path too difficult for him," Damien noted a little sadly. "In retrospect it would have been smarter to work on those points *after* I got him home, rather than giving him more reasons to leave the path and be vulnerable to Azella and her demon."

That at least won him a snort. "The Eightfold Path is hard for those who spend their whole *lives* working on it. And the boy seems to take the whole matter more seriously now. I suspect whatever lessons you tried to give him more gently would have slid right off before. Boys that age," Adam said a bit too pointedly, "don't take instruction on the deeper truths of life all that well."

Damien gave him a sweet smile. "Not in words, no, but by example. I was just lucky to have two such *fascinating* examples in front of me all the time."

He paused. "So *utterly* fascinating that I could hardly take my eyes off of you. Or dream of anything but you at night."

As he'd hoped, Adam's cheeks flushed again. This seemed to be the night for it.

"Damien..."

"I *still* can't keep my eyes off of you," Damien added softly. "No matter how hard I try."

Which *should* have earned him a *kiss,* but instead there was a flash of a different kind from Adam's golden-hazel eyes.

"Or off of *him.* Why *did* you bring him home, Damien?"

The question Adam needed answered... but it was still too painful for Damien to try to explain even to Adam. Partly because *Adam* would insist – as he did over how Damien had harmed Azella – that the King had been doing what he should, as a prisoner of war. Adam's own jealousy of the only other *male* – besides Jason – that Damien had ever expressed any interest in wouldn't allow the blonde knight to understand the difference between the sorceress and her 'minion.'

This... taking care of Jeremy and giving him a chance to find a future... was something he could actually *do* to fix the harm he'd done. He couldn't help Azella – nor the other Power-slaves she held in her foul Keep.

But he *could* help *Jeremy.*

The King sighed. "I'd've brought them *all* home if I could, Adam. The little boys especially. And Denisa who *might* have been spared two months ago if the demon wasn't lying about not getting its hands on her until after it defeated me. But even the other older boys, cruel and corrupt as they were. It's just... Jeremy was the only one I had time to *find.*"

Adam frowned. "What do you mean?"

Damien shrugged, trying to hide how much it hurt that he had abandoned *children* who were even more vulnerable and futureless than he had been himself at those ages.

"I don't know. They were always in the slave quarters the rest of the time that I was there. I have to assume that o*n that one day* she had them up on the roof – the battlements – doing some preparatory work for her *demon summoning.*" He laid his head sideways as the tears threatened to break free. "I... *think* I would have felt if she... had done anything dire to them. Then."

Given the amount of energy Azella had uselessly expended... it was an open question what she might have done to recoup her losses. Pain and death released so much energy, after all, and her 'Gift' was to collect all that was freed...

"Oh." Adam's hand caressed his hair and back again. "And I suppose you wouldn't be able to distinguish... anything that happened to them from Emeralsee."

"Or here," Damien agreed softly. "Or even when we stood near the southern border of Farivera and looked up at that unnatural escarpment beside the Tree-of-Life River. There's just... so much *other* life – and death – to be sensed. A handful of human children and young adults..."

Adam sighed just as softly. "Not that I *ever* envy you one bit of your power, Damien – secular or magickal. But sometimes I'm... very glad indeed that my *empathy* has... tighter bounds."

They'd established that Adam didn't sense anything beyond animals that had two feet or four – fish were beyond him and amphibians were a stretch. He also had a now-unsurprising, at least to Damien, affinity for *some (but not all)* flying insects, but even caterpillars and wingless ants didn't touch him.

Though the fireflies' return interest in Adam had made that night a couple weeks ago... very special indeed.

"The only thing I feel for Jeremy at this point is... pity," Damien said quietly. "He had tremendous magickal Power – and now he has nothing. The skills he was trained in from birth are useless..."

"Not entirely," Adam said dryly. "I suspect *Aaron* is making quite good use of some of them."

"Hmmn. Does... Aaron know why you..." Damien began hesitantly, "or, at least I assume it *was* you who introduced them?"

"Elaina, actually," Adam told him. "She needed something to do as well. Apparently, she and Arabella Elsevier had become... quite close."

Jason's sister, who had joined the Secret Cadre alongside Marianna Loveress and Arabella and Mark Elsevier. Damien had seen that the young woman had been in a terrible state, but had attributed it to her mother having been stolen away by the pirate-king.

"I had the impression she was sweet on Mark Elsevier," Damien commented. "I... wasn't looking forwards to explaining to her that he and Marianna are next-thing to engaged when we get home."

Adam shook his head, and sighed. "No. It might have been easier if she had been, though. Harder on her friendship with Mari, of course, but..." He winced. "Mari confided in me – and made me *swear* not to tell Jason, or even Lord David, but somehow didn't put *you* on that list – that Elaina and Arabella were... romantically involved. Sort of."

Damien blinked in surprise. Given Duke Tomas and Duchess Sildra's nearly rabid distaste for same-gendered pairings – and Countess Alexa's similar attitudes – that was, perhaps, the most unexpected thing...

On the other hand, *Jason* had been subjected to Countess Alexa as well...

"Jason didn't have to deal with Alexa for more than a handful of days a few times a year after he came to Emeralsee as a page," Adam pointed out, presumably guessing which way Damien's thoughts would have run. "Elaina never had more than a few days *away* from the old... witch... in twenty-two years. She's... possibly even more... *confused*... than he was."

Hmmn. Although Elaina *had* known from the beginning that the Countess was her grandmother, not her mother. And she'd had her father, Lord David Metreedi Solway, who *had* done what he could to give Elaina and her younger siblings an idea that there was a world out there beyond the Brindlewell that his mother-in-law ruled with an iron fist. Not to mention that David was from Wave, which was possibly the most liberal-minded city in the *world*.

And she'd had the example of Jason – her supposed 'uncle' – out there in front of her for most of her life, to say such loves were *possible*. Though he'd undoubtedly been held out as a *negative* example, given all the mess that was the Solway family...

"It can't have helped to have the girl she was in love with declared only not-guilty-of-treason because she's criminally insane," Damien said with a sigh.

He'd disliked the Elaina Solway who had seemed to be following in her grandmother's – and mother's – footsteps, and therefore continually snubbed his best friends. But he'd heard nothing but good things about the girl that had been surfacing from under that mask since the King had banished Countess Solway to her own estates the day before Jason and Adam's wedding. Likely she was at least as emotionally-fragile as her newly-revealed elder brother...

"If it helps any," Adam offered, "Mari was convinced that it wasn't a *healthy* relationship. For either of them."

Damien winced. "No, I wouldn't imagine so..."

Arabella Elsevier had been willing to try to cut off Jason's finger to claim the Heir's Ring. It had been done at her mother, Duchess Sildra's, behest and with her father's approval when the Ring couldn't otherwise be removed due to its own mysterious magick. The expression on Arabella's face when she'd tried – first Jason's finger and then his wrist, failing only because of Damien's spell protecting his Heir – had been one of... concentration. As if the fact that she was attempting to mutilate a living person hadn't been important at all.

It had been in his attempt to stop her that Lord Aaron had lost his hand. Not because he was trying to protect Jason – though he had been – but because he'd been friends with Mark and Arabella Elsevier since childhood and had hoped to save her from having to be declared a traitor.

"Mari... seemed to think that Aaron and Elaina would... be able to grieve together," Adam said softly.

Damien gave him a wry look, trying to shake off the chill that always filled him when he had to think about the people he'd had to condemn to a traitor's end. At least Arabella was still alive... though confined to the care of her aunt and uncle, the Duke and Duchess of Dalziallest, for the rest of her natural life.

"I'm almost surprised you – and Marianna – didn't try to matchmake for Elaina as well."

Adam snorted a little with humor, but shook his head. "She's... not ready for that. I don't think she was ready for *any* relationship, even before this all went sour, actually. It took Jason *years* to come out from under Alexa's dark cloud, and *he* had all the positive feedback of being the best squire in training, and then raising the next King."

He tweaked the tip of Damien's nose, then shook his head again. "Elaina... will likely need at least that much time to grow into herself. Though perhaps that will go faster once she and her father have that ship of theirs and can go hunt for Megan."

Hunt... not *find*. They all knew that even with all the vast resources of the Metreedi trading empire at his disposal, Lord David was unlikely to be able to locate and retrieve his wife. Jason's long-lost father – the pirate-king, Evan Eldridge Alsterling, who was also Angelos' uncle – considered Megan to be his *own* wife after all, and had spent thirty-five years working to find a way to reclaim her.

Which would be a far more romantic notion if he'd ever tried to send word to *Megan* that he was doing so or tried to contact *Jason*, who hadn't even known his father's name. Instead, Megan had *(eventually)* moved on, married David a quarter-century ago, and had four more children. She had *wanted* to be the Consort of the Pirate-King about as much as Damien had *wanted* to be Azella the Unpitying's apprentice and captive.

But since neither Evan nor Azella had been willing to take 'no' for an answer without destroying the city of Emeralsee – which held some three hundred thousand of Damien's subjects – and likely slaying most of the higher nobility in the land, trapped as everyone had been in the wake of Azella's ice-storm... Damien and Megan had given themselves up.

It made the King guilty every time he looked at Lord David or Elaina, the two younger ones who were serving now as page and squire... or Jason.

He had known he could most likely escape Azella – eventually – after all. As he had, in fact ended up doing, coming home with a wealth of new knowledge and improved skill with his magick.

Megan... was likely to live out the rest of her life in her captivity.

And it had been *his* decision, after all. And *his* royal command to Megan to come with him.

"*Not* your fault," Adam had followed his thoughts again, somehow. "You're *not a God,* Damien. You can't fix *everything.* You had a set of bad choices and did the best you could at the time."

"Did I?" Damien sighed.

Surely there had been *some* possible solution that didn't involve giving up Jason's mother. Not that they'd *known* Megan was his mother until moments before, when the Pirate-King demanded Damien turn over 'his Crown, his wife, and his son.' And named both Megan and Jason explicitly.

Poor Jason had reacted as he always did to sudden and unexpected changes; he'd shutdown as thoroughly as Damien had ever seen him do, barely able to speak, let alone add anything. Though he'd recovered himself a few minutes later – because Adam had hitched a ride when Damien *Vanished* himself and Megan down to the pirate-filled square before the Castle's gates. Jason had woken himself up enough to tell the Pirate-King that he could give up any thought of a reconciliation if he harmed so much as a hair of Adam's head.

Or Damien's, though that had clearly been added as an afterthought.

Adam sighed and sat up. "Honestly, Damien, if you want *my* opinion–" as if not hearing it was ever an option, "–and with all due respect to Megan," though that eye-roll suggested that Adam viewed her as a preferable mother-in-law only by comparison to the awful Alexa, "they're *all* better off without her."

Damien frowned, sitting up as well, and with the same precaution. "What are you talking about?"

Adam gave him one of his usual sardonic looks. "I know you tend to see the best in everyone, and I won't quibble that Megan – like Elaina – has probably had the worst time of it in dealing with Alexa Solway and her schemes. With the possible exception of Evan Eldridge Alsterling himself.

"But I have about as much *sympathy* for the woman as I do for Evan. What she let happen to my Jason – what she let him *think* about *himself* while he was growing up–"

"Adam, Alexa brainwashed her to believe that stuff herself–"

"Maybe." Adam shrugged, but the *empath* who had just admitted he had no sympathy for Lady Megan looked stubborn. "I've spent time with, well, all *four* of her surviving children this past Winter. Jason the most, of course. And he's starting to have memories surface of her *trying* to mother him when he was very small. And then just... *giving up* every time Alexa told her to stop."

"Which sugg–"

"It *broke his heart,* Damien," Adam pressed on. "I don't know if it would have been better if she'd never tried – but he was *her own son* and she *didn't* protect him."

"She probably didn't know such a thing was even possible," Damien commented. "Megan *was* under Alexa's thumb longer than anyone else. You said so yourself."

Not to mention that Megan had been all of fourteen when Jason was born. Less than a year younger than the boy she'd fallen in love with... and who had been forced to marry her mother.

"I've *also* spent time with Elaina and Roger and Esmerelda," Adam said tightly. "Both with *and* without David present. She didn't protect *them,* either. And by then she had David to help her see what a messed-up situation Brindlewell was in. And she wouldn't let *him* try to protect them either."

"Alexa was their liege-lady," Damien felt he had to point out. "She could have turned David out and then he wouldn't have had access to his children at all. She could have done the same to Megan for that matter and just named Elaina directly as Heir. Or one of the younger ones if she felt they were more malleable." He shook his own head. "Changing the laws that give a liege-lord or -lady such full and complete power over their scions has... been on my list of things to solve for a long while. Because of Jason. But it's where things are right now."

And it wasn't an *easy* problem, for all that it looked like one at first glance. A ruling lord or lady who couldn't control the upbringing and marriages of their potential heirs was leaving things open to someone claiming their seat who had no familiarity with or investment in the local situation. Or leaving the situation open to a long – and possibly bloody – dispute over that same seat.

Even if Damien could somehow persuade his nobles to support such a change – rather than suing for his own overthrow by being so high-handed – it would leave the Throne of Ilseador itself open to such troubles. And after a decade-long civil war and two insurrections, all within living memory...

This simply wasn't a change he could make lightly or without building in some serious safeguards. And since there were so many *other* problems claiming pride of place in urgency and importance, Damien just hadn't had the *time* to try to find the creative solution that would be a real fix.

Adam folded his arms, that stubborn expression still on his face. "Including these last five years? If Megan had come to you and asked you to declare Alexa incompetent on the grounds that she was endangering the children's wellbeing – wouldn't you have done it? Roger and Esmerelda were eight and six when you were crowned. Elaina was seventeen. You know for yourself how much someone can recover at age seventeen."

The dark-haired man wrapped his arms around himself to ward off the inner chill.

Of course he would have done. Not *fairly*, though, since Alexa Solway really was a competent ruler, except in the matter of her own family. Setting her aside and putting Megan in her place – might have been what was right for the Solway *family*, but whether it would have been the right thing for the people for Brindlewell... There had been no hint from the Land that Alexa's Oath was false, after all.

On the other hand, wasn't it the primary responsibility of each ruling lord or lady to ensure the health – mental and physical – of their Heirs? Damien had used that argument with Genevieve on why *her* father, Lord Aldred, wasn't fit to wear the Crown himself, despite Queen Marian's assertion that the Monarch's Blade had once 'spoken' for the former Duke of Elaarwen.

Aldred hadn't protected *Genevieve* from the abuse of her first husband. He had been more willing to try to breed himself *another* Heir than help her when she'd not managed to bear Harald of Siovale a child in eight years of wedded life.

If the man hadn't otherwise been such a good father to Genevieve – and a second father to Damien himself in so many ways... well.

Last Fall, the King had *decided* that he would let this part of the problem that was his otherwise-beloved father-in-law go. He had decided that *again* this evening. There were plenty of people who felt they had no choice but to ignore what went on in someone else's marriage, even when they *knew* things were wrong... and since Genevieve had never *asked* her father for help, it was impossible to say what the old man would have done.

Likely not even Aldred knew the answer to that one.

There was small question that Elaina was not emotionally equipped to be Heir.

Whether Megan was...

"I would have set Alexa aside," Damien admitted. "If Megan had asked me to."

Adam's nod was filled with vindication. "But Megan *didn't* come to you. I have it from David that *he'd* been trying to get her to do it since the day you were crowned. *He* knew Jason was his stepson, after all. And Megan wouldn't even let him tell Jason that. *She* knew how important Jason was to you and that you'd be inclined to do anything that would help him.

"What Alexa could possibly have held over her head to–"

But this one Damien had an answer to.

He reached a hand up to cup Adam's cheek, gently tracing the tight muscles along the older man's jaw.

"She had Megan's initial capitulation. The thirty-year – at that point – long lie. The fact that Jason was nearly as terrified of Megan as of Alexa herself, which surely couldn't stand Megan well in my eyes...

"And..."

The King – who had once been a terrified and orphaned young prince – gently touched the other side of Adam's face with the back of the same hand. "And if she managed to depose her mother... *Jason* might well still not have forgiven her."

He didn't add that Megan could easily have seen that *Adam* was unlikely to counsel reconciliation. She surely knew that that Adam had abandoned his own warm, loving family for Jason's sake after all.

Or for what he'd *thought* was Jason's sake, if Angelos' assertions were to be believed... For Damien's sake in that case.

Another stone to weigh down what was between them. That load now seemed heavier than all the tons of rocks that the King had *pulled* in earlier to build Cloudcroft's new barn.

Adam took a deep breath, that stubborn, fierce, angry expression still on his face...

... and let it out in one long sigh.

"And I suppose she likely felt there was no point in appealing to you *without* trying to make things right with Jason. It's only her own family that Alexa has done poorly by, not Brindlewell."

Damien nodded. Adam knew the other half of that argument – if he was setting it aside to begin to try forgiving Megan, the King could only do his best to aid in that effort. "And none of us saw anything in Elaina or the others that gave us cause to know what was going on. And..."

He hesitated, knowing that his fierce, gentle Adam still had trouble understanding this despite all he had seen and lived through with Jason and Damien both. It was all to the credit of the Baronetta and Lord George, of course, and Adam was likely to be the best parent amongst all four of them because of it...

Nor was Damien ready to tell even Adam all the details of why his nightmares had disturbed the older young man when he'd been trapped in Lady Theresa's 'care.'

"And it's mortally hard to separate yourself from an abuser who has trained you to depend on them," Damien decided to say.

Adam gave him a sharp look that turned into that almost-too-*compassionate*-to-be-borne expression. "I suppose you would know."

After Lady Theresa... yes.

The woman had been strung up as a traitor and Damien had himself set the first nail. Adam already knew that she had been cold and neglectful – knowing more would only make the kind man castigate himself for not having moved faster, somehow, to rescue his prince from Lady Theresa's 'guardianship.'

Damien was free of her *now,* and that was all that mattered. All that he would *allow* to matter.

And then the look became a little flavored with exasperation and Adam rolled his eyes. "King Reginald, of all people for you to have any empathy for, after all."

What? Oh. Yes. And somehow *that* still made for a less fraught discussion than Damien's feelings about the Dowager-and-deceased Lady of Cedarwen. Nonetheless, this wasn't the time for that, either.

"I suspect Megan could have appealed to Grandfather as well," the King said mildly. "On Jason's behalf, if not for the younger children. After all, *she* knew the truth... oh."

Adam was rolling his eyes as usual at the idea that King Reginald had had a soft spot for his last living grandsons, but he stopped and frowned at Damien's tone of realization.

"*That's* why she didn't do it, Adam," Damien said sadly. "It *is* my fault. She knew that Jason was another contender for the Throne... and she didn't trust me not to do as my grandfather had done and..."

He looked up from his... well, *latest* self-immolation in guilt at Adam's snort.

"It's all very well for you to try to find some worth in that woman, Damien, and I appreciate – for Jason's sake, if nothing else – that you'll try. But I still think Elaina and the younger ones have a better shot at becoming healthy adults with both Alexa locked away and Megan – just plain *away.*"

Adam paused. "*Elaina* would likely do better if she were young enough to try for her shield, like Roger and Esmerelda, than follow David around hunting pirates as well. *He's* a good man – but he's a little... *obsessed* and now that he doesn't have to pretend to be a meek and mild milquetoast, he's... well, as *dominating* a personality as you might expect a former Metreedi ship captain to be. You've met some of their current ones, I think. You know what I mean. Elaina will have to work as hard to come out of David's shadow as out from under that 'dark cloud' that Alexa put over the whole family."

Well... that was interesting.

Adam seemed to seriously appreciate his father-in-law – this was the first critical thing Damien had heard him say about the man since they had all discovered Jason was Megan's son and not Alexa's.

On the other hand, the King couldn't really disagree with any of that assessment.

"We need some new *names* in this country," Adam was grousing a bit randomly as he laid himself back down, tugging Damien with him. "*Your* grandparents were David and Alexa. *Jason's* stepfather and grandmother are David and Alexa. There's too many repetitions. It gets confusing."

"Well, I don't plan to name any of *our* children 'David' or 'Alexa'," Damien replied, relieved that they were moving to a different topic. "But we're using the names of Genevieve's mother and my great-grandmother for this baby."

As he'd hoped, Adam smiled. "And no changes possible there, O The Sorcerer-King of Ilseador, Defender of the Realm, Father of Giendra Marlerite Stellarine Alsterling."

The younger man had taken that admittedly long and unwieldy thing as the *true-name* that fit him even better than the one that his parents had given him, in order to break free of Azella's spells. The power of a *true-name* over its bearer was hard to escape – in fact, Azella had been utterly shocked that he had managed it, since she had never heard of *anyone* being able to do so.

The trick was to find a name that was *more true*. Evil Wizards did that by using a *nom de magique* and hiding the name they'd been given at birth. Damien… had needed to hunt deep within himself to find a *truer* name.

He'd accidentally given his original name – 'Damien' – to Jeremy early in their acquaintance, not knowing the power it would give the youth. He'd managed to avoid doing the same with Azella – who had only been able to control him – in that manner – through Jeremy, who hadn't wanted to abuse what he considered to be a gift… but who had feared Azella. Feared her quite fairly, considering that, as her Power-slave he had been *required* to *give* her his own *true-name* when she purchased him.

The King had told – had *given* – his *new* name only to Adam.

And promptly been chastised by Adam for doing so.

Not that Adam didn't understand why he had.

Damien smiled tentatively back. "'Marlerite' for *your* grandmother as well."

More or less anyways. They were using the Dawilm spelling and pronunciation. Adam's grandmother had been 'Marguerite,' but it wouldn't be discreet to give their daughter that name.

"I know." Adam sighed.

"I'm sorry..."

Golden-hazel eyes gave him a wry look. "What for? Giving me the chance to raise the child of my heart – alongside the people I love best?"

Damien couldn't quite sustain that gaze. "Forcing you to have a child you can never claim."

Another snort. "I've told you before. Jason wasn't keen on having a child when it was just the two of us. I think he doesn't trust me to be able to parent well enough with just him to help. But with *you* and *Genevieve* involved... well. You know for yourself that there wasn't any *forcing* involved."

"*Me?*" Damien exclaimed. "But I'm not..."

...'*going to be a good parent*' was what he didn't dare say.

How could he, when Adam, and apparently Jason and definitely Genevieve, were counting on him?

But how could his own hodge-podge, mixed-up, traumatic childhood actually give him what he needed to figure out *how* to be a good parent?

"You're not what?" Adam asked.

Damien snuggled deeper into Adam's shoulder, trying to shove his own sense of disquiet down below where his *empathic* friend could sense it.

"I'm not sure I can live up to all of that," he said dryly. Which was true, if a vast understatement.

Adam chuckled. "According to Desirée – and Mama – no one does."

That... was hardly a reassuring thought to fall asleep to.

Travel with Adam and Damien as they follow the
directions of Elaarwen and Ilseador Themselves...
and perhaps even sort out their own
hearts and souls
in
Book 2 of The Heart of Ilseador:

Piled Higher and Deeper

Available at all fine online retailers in
June2025
Place your pre-order now!
https://books2read.com/Heart-2-Chronicles-of-Ilseador

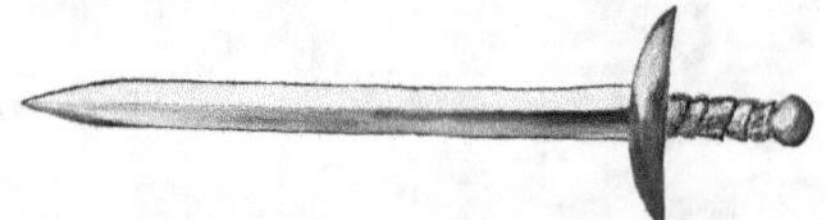

Family Trees

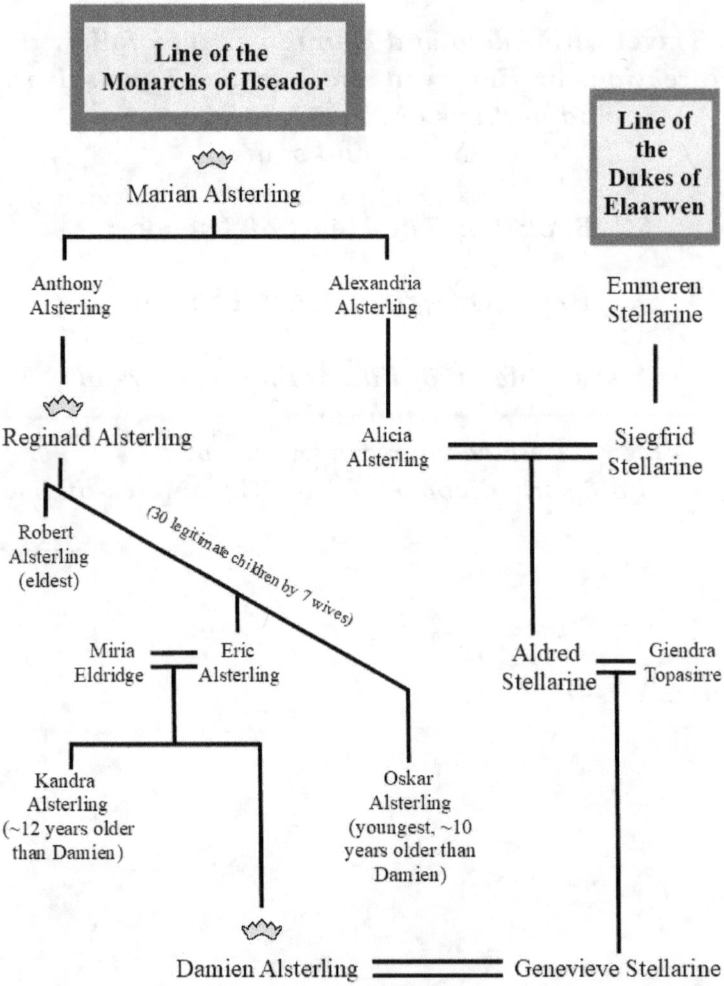

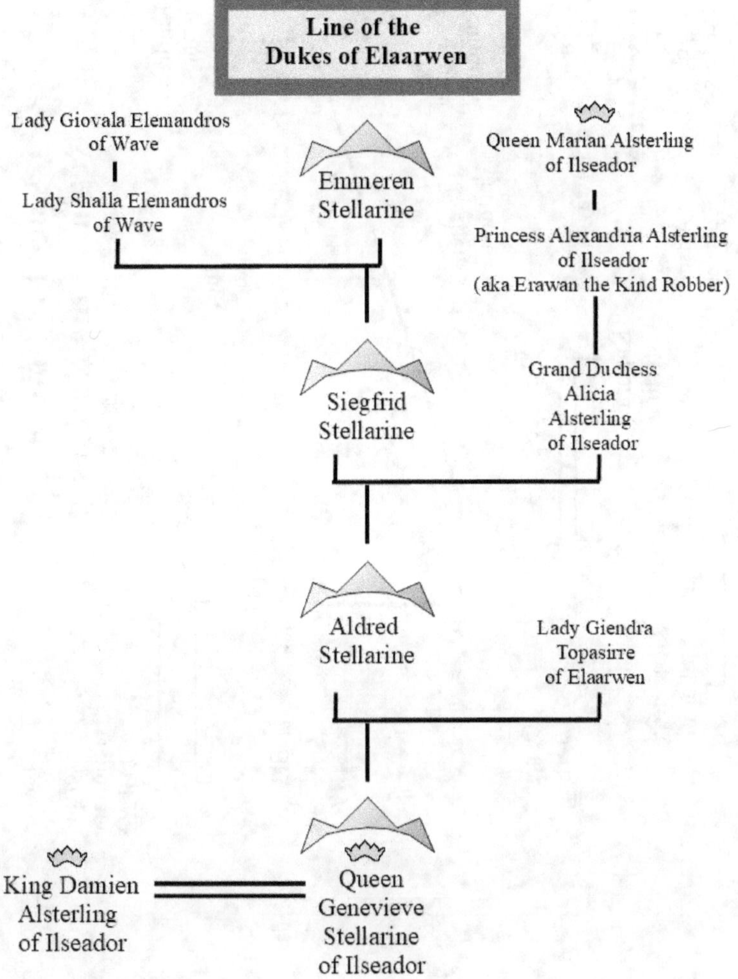

Line of the
Dukes of Elaarwen

Lady Giovala Elemandros
of Wave

Lady Shalla Elemandros
of Wave

Emmeren
Stellarine

Queen Marian Alsterling
of Ilseador

Princess Alexandria Alsterling
of Ilseador
(aka Erawan the Kind Robber)

Siegfrid
Stellarine

Grand Duchess
Alicia
Alsterling
of Ilseador

Aldred
Stellarine

Lady Giendra
Topasirre
of Elaarwen

King Damien
Alsterling
of Ilseador

Queen
Genevieve
Stellarine
of Ilseador

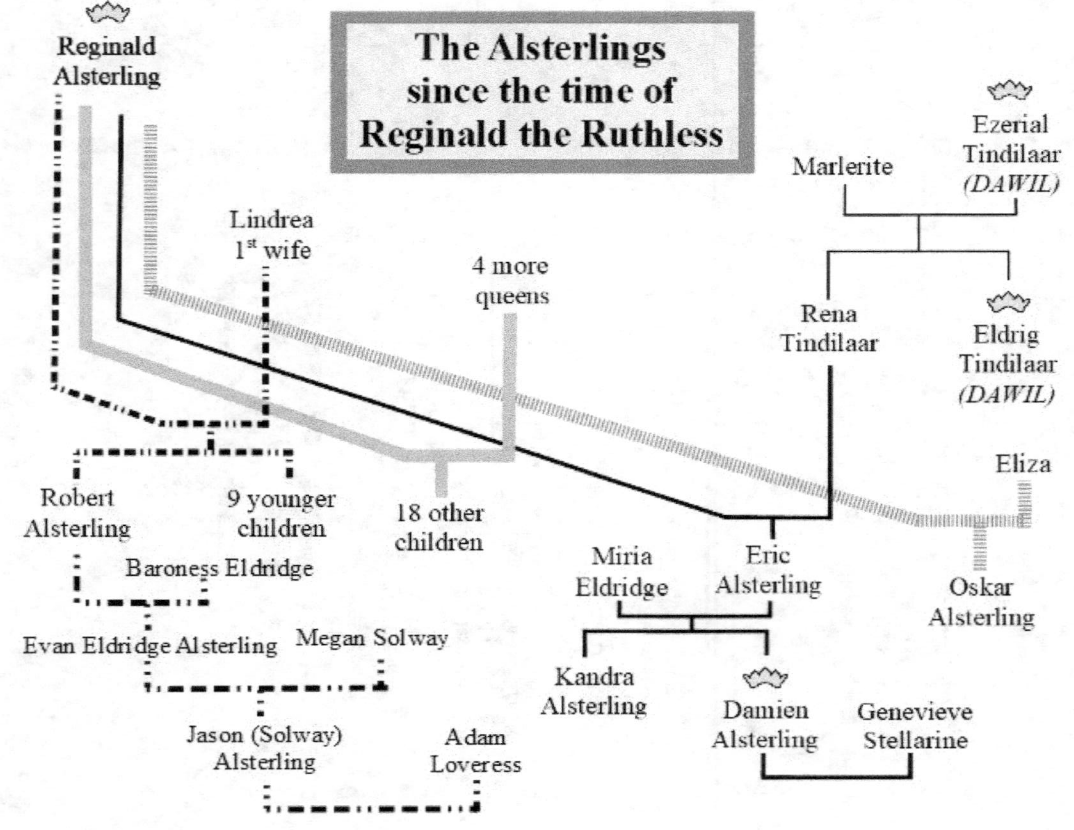

The Alsterlings since the time of Reginald the Ruthless
Reginald Alsterling
Lindrea 1st wife
4 more queens
Marlerite
Ezerial Tindilaar (DAWIL)
Rena Tindilaar
Eldrig Tindilaar (DAWIL)
Robert Alsterling
9 younger children
18 other children
Miria Eldridge
Eric Alsterling
Oskar Alsterling
Eliza
Baroness Eldridge
Evan Eldridge Alsterling
Megan Solway
Kandra Alsterling
Damien Alsterling
Genevieve Stellarine
Jason (Solway) Alsterling
Adam Loveress

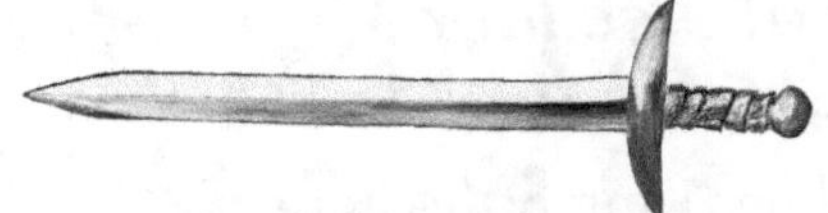

Index of Characters

Characters that appear in this book are <u>underlined</u>.
Characters that are referenced, but do not actually appear are in plain type.
Deceased characters are in italics.
Characters with speaking roles in this book are in **bold**.

The grandchildren of a reigning king or queen are officially grand dukes and grand duchesses in Ilseador, but are also referred to as princes and princesses when the question of their position in the line of succession is not in question.
Damien was Crown Prince after Oskar died.
Ages are given for the 6th year of Damien's reign.

Contents of the Index:

- **Royal Family of Ilseador**
- **Provinces of Ilseador** in order of precedence and relevant ruling family members
    - » **Emeralsee** contains the following fiefs among others: *Seasbourne, Cedarwen, Eldyrwyld, Lynncrag, Elmirscroft, Ravenscroft*
    - » **Elaarwen** contains the following fiefs among others: *Brindlewell, Cloudcroft*
    - » **Siovale**
    - » **Reyensweir** contains the following fiefs among others: *Zialest*
    - » **Embervest** contains the following fiefs among others: *Minglemere, Everfields*
    - » **Alpinsward** contains the following fiefs among others: Dalizell
    - » **Dalzialest**, duchy (contains *Flowerdell*)
    - » The Lost Provinces: **Alpinsward, Minglemere, Elendria, Farivera, Everfields**
- *Others of Note*

Royal Family of Ilseador
(and noted individuals in the Royal City and Province)

- **Damien Alsterling,** King of Ilseador
  - Queen Genevieve (Stellarine) Alsterling, Duchess of Elaarwen (a.k.a. 'the Rebel Duchess'), King Damien's wife; soul-bonded to King Damien and secretly also soul-bonded to Prince Jason
  - *Queen Marian Alsterling* (a.k.a. 'Marian the merciful'), King Damien and Queen Genevieve's great-great-grandmother (common ancestress)... currently a ghost in Castle Alsterling.
  - Crown Prince Jason (Solway) Alsterling, son of Evan Eldridge Alsterling, secretly soul-bonded to Queen Genevieve, husband of Prince Adam
  - **Prince Adam (Loveress) Alsterling,** husband of Prince Jason
  - Others of the Royal Family
    - » *Eric Alsterling,* son of old king Reginald Alsterling, former Crown Prince, King Damien's father
    - » *Queen Rena (Tindilaar) Alsterling,* a princess from Dawil; mother of Prince Eric Alsterling; grandmother of King Damien; sister to King Eldrig Tindilaar
    - » *Miria (Eldridge) Alsterling,* King Damien's and Princess Kandra's mother; wife of Prince Eric
    - » *Grand Duchess (or Princess) Kandra 'Kandy' Alsterling,* King Damien's sister.
    - » *King Reginald Alsterling* (aka 'the old king' or 'Reginald the Ruthless'); King Damien's grandfather
      - * *'Lord' Prydeen,* his Apprentice Evil Wizard
      - * *7 wives*
        - ◊ *1st Princess Lindrea Alsterling* (died before Reginald was crowned, still numbered as his first queen)
        - ◊ *2nd Queen*
        - ◊ *3rd Queen*
        - ◊ *4th Queen Rena (Tindilaar) Alsterling* of Dawil, *Prince Eric's* mother, King Damien's grandmother, outlived all but Queen Eliza
        - ◊ *5th Queen*
        - ◊ *6th Queen*
        - ◊ *7th Queen Eliza Alsterling* (Oskar's mother)

* Reginald's 30 legitimate children (all dead), including the following:
  ◊ *Crown Prince Robert Alsterling* (son of Princess Lindrea); he quietly married the widowed Baroness Dara Eldridge of Eldywyld and sired her youngest child, Evan Eldridge AlsterlingPrincess Selda Alsterling
  ◊ *Crown Prince Eric Alsterling* (son of Queen Rena), father of Damien
  ◊ *Crown Prince Oskar Alsterling* (son of Queen Eliza), youngest son of King Reginald
  ◊ Sir Jason Solway, Prince Oskar's bodyguard before Oskar was Heir, Oskar's Champion while Oskar was Heir
  ◊ Sir Edmund Railston, Prince Oskar's Champion and bodyguard at the time Ring was taken from *Prince Oskar* (also Adam Loveress' first lover)
* Reginald's ~100 legitimate grandchildren (all dead besides Damien and Evan) including the following:
  ◊ *Alric Alsterling*
  ◊ *Grand Duke Salleen Alsterling*
  ◊ *Grand Duchess Kandra Alsterling*
  ◊ Grand Duke Evan Eldridge Alsterling (son of Prince Robert), sire of Jason Solway Alsterling; King of the Pirates of the Merutian Sea
  ◊ **King Damien Alsterling**
* 1 legitimate surviving great-grandchild
  ◊ Crown Prince Sir Jason Solway Alsterling (son of Grand Duke Evan, husband of Adam Loveress)

- **Others of Note in His Majesty's Government**
  - General Direlien, **Commander-in-Chief** (under the King) of the Ilseadoran military, **Commander of the Home Guard**

  - **King Damien's Official Royal Guards**
    * **Champion: Sir Adam Loveress** aka Prince Adam Loveress Alsterling (shield is puce with a rose, argent, crossed by a black sword), a close advisor of King Damien
    * **Captain and Knight Commander of the Royal Guard:** Sir Timothy Ancellius (a.k.a. 'Tim'), Second-in-Command of the Royal Guard when Damien is crowned, marries Secret Cadre member Aryllis after Damien is crowned, has son Enrico (a.k.a. Rico)

» **Original Guards**
  * **Champion:** <u>Sir Jason Solway</u> (mother is Lady Megan Solway), a close advisor of King Damien's.
  * **Captain and Knight Commander of the Royal Guard:** <u>Sir Adam Loveress</u>
  * <u>Sir Timothy Ancellius</u>, marries Secret Cadre member Aryllia Ieldore
  * <u>Sir Leverett Childress</u> (a.k.a. 'Lev'), marries Secret Cadre member Terellie
  * <u>Sir Otto</u>, marries Secret Cadre member Thielda
  * Sir Randolph
  * (plus seven others not named)

- **Newer Guards members** (five years into Damien's reign)
  * <u>Sir Timothy Ancellius</u>, (**Captain and Knight-Commander**)
  * <u>Sir Marcus Dunsteador</u> (Second-in-Command)
  * Sir Mikal 'Mik'
  * Sir Rodney
  * Sir Everett Ladler
  * Sir Drake Milbourne
  * **<u>Sir Angelos Eldridge</u>**
  * (and five others not named)

- **The Secret Cadre of Royal Guards**

» **Original twelve King's Ladies:** the Secret Cadre of Royal Guards (all but Lena and Ciriis marry one of Damien's original Royal Guards following his coronation)
  * <u>Ciriis Celavell</u>: **Mistress of Protocol** and **Spymistress, Commander of the Secret Cadre** under Adam Loveress, later **King's Advisor** and then **Assistant to Duke** Aldred
  * <u>Lena Devergnon</u>: Poisoner/anti-poisoner, later **Assistant Royal Librarian**
  * <u>Aryllis (Ieldore) Ancellius</u>: marries Royal Guardsman Tim Ancellius; mother of Enrico Ancellius (a.k.a. Rico); becomes **Mistress of Protocol** and **Spymistress** and **commander of the Secret Cadre** under Adam Loveress
  * Felena
  * <u>Terellie</u>: marries Royal Guardsman Leverett Childress
  * Sasha
  * <u>Elsa</u>

* Emerie
* <u>Thielda:</u> marries ROyal Guardsman Otto
* Nalda
* <u>Kamauri</u>
* <u>Licia</u>
* <u>Mirabelle</u>
  » **Newer Secret Cadre** (five years into Damien's reign)
  * **<u>Lady Alanna</u>**
  * Lady Lisa
  * <u>Lord Aaron</u>
  * Lord Devin
  * Master Xavier
  * <u>Lady Emily</u>
  * <u>Miss Tasha</u>
  * <u>Master Derrick</u>
  * <u>Lord Lewis</u>
* **Castle Alsterling Personnel**
  » <u>Maree</u>, knife sharpener for the kitchen, had a huge infatuation with Damien

Provinces of Ilseador

in order of precedence and relevant ruling family members

* *Emeralsee,* duchy – Alsterling family, gold and turquoise (guards wear dark blue and black)
  * <u>Duke Jason (Solway) Alsterling</u>, Crown Prince of the Realm
    * **<u>Duke-Consort Adam (Loveress) Alsterling,</u>** husband of Jason
    * **<u>Damien Alsterling</u>** former duke
    * <u>Genevieve (Stellarine) Alsterling</u>, wife of Damien
    * *Ghost of Queen Marian Alsterling*, great-grandmother of Damien and Genevieve and great-great-grandmother of Jason
  * **Others of note within Emeralsee** (see under 'King Damien Alsterling' at top)

- *Fiefs within Emeralsee*
  - *City of Emeralsee,* <u>Count Antonin</u>
  - *Seasbourne,* county – family Laidly
  - *Brindlewell,* county – Solway family
    - » <u>Countess Alexa Solway</u>, mother of Megan (banished from Court for life)
      - * <u>Lady Megan Solway,</u> only child of Countess Alexa, wife of David, currently a prisoner of Evan Eldridge Alsterling the Pirate-King
        - ◊ <u>Lord David Metreedi Solway</u> (a.k.a. Captain Daffyd Metreedi), husband of Lady Megan
      - * their children (ages given for the 5th year of King Damien's reign)
        - ◊ <u>Elaina Solway</u> – 22yo– lady-in-waiting (Secret Cadre)
        - ◊ *Rudolph Solway* (deceased)(would have been 19yo)
        - ◊ <u>Roger Solway</u> – 13yo
        - ◊ <u>Esmerelda Solway</u> – 11yo
      - * <u>Sir Jason Solway</u>, eldest child of Lady Megan with Grand Duke/Pirate-King Evan Eldridge Alsterling
  - *Cedarwen, barony* – Anvliyar family
    - » Baron Raphael Anvliyar (intended husband of King Damien's sister, Princess Kandra)
      - * *<u>Former Baron Anvliyar,</u>* Raphael's father
      - * *<u>Dowager Baroness Theresa Anvliyar,</u>* mother of Baron Raphael, former Royal Librarian and guardian of King Damien as a child after his parents were slain; died a traitor's death for having conspired to betray Crown Prince Eric, Lady Miria, and Princess Kandra, as well as for Conspiracy Against the Crown due to her role during the Usurpation of Harald Elsevier
  - *Elderwyld,* barony – Eldridge family
    <u>Baron Eugenio Eldridge</u>
      - * **<u>Sir Angelos Eldridge,</u>** one of Baron Eugenio's sons
      - * <u>Julietta Eldridge</u>, an older sister of Angelos, formerly married to Adam's brother, Lorenzo, daughter of Eugenio
      - * <u>Tonia Eldridge</u>, Angelos' oldest sister who has three children, daughter of Eugenio

* *Baroness Dara Eldridge*, mother of Baron Eugenio and Evan; her second husband was Crown Prince Robert Alsterling
* Evan Eldridge Alsterling, a cousin of Lady Miria's, son of Baroness Dara Eldridge and Crown Prince Robert Alsterling, half-brother of Baron Eugenio, sire of Crown Prince Jason Solway Alsterling

- **Ravenscroft**, property, enfeoffed to Elderwyld

  * *David Eldridge*, Lord of Ravenscroft (gifted to Prince Eric and Lady Miria and deeded to her parents), younger son of the former Baron, a failed squire, husband of Alexa, father of seven (Lady Miria was his eldest)
  * *Alexa Eldridge*, David's wife; a blacksmith's daughter, mother of seven
  * *Lady Miria (Eldridge) Alsterling*, Damien's mother, eldest child of David and Alexa Eldridge's seven children

- **Elmirscroft**, property enfeoffed to Elderwyld

  » Lord Enrico Ancellius (underage, father Sir Timothy Ancellius is his regent) son of Timothy and Aryllis Ancellius

- **Lynncrag**, baronetcy – Loveress family
  » Baronetta Linda Loveress
    * Lord George Loveress, husband of Baronetta Linda
    * Their children
    * **Sir Adam** – 34yo, Captain of the Royal Guard
      ◊ Charles (a.k.a. 'Charley') Loveress – 32yo – a forest ranger
      ◊ Lorenzo (a.k.a. 'Lorry') Loveress – 30yo – married and divorced twice
      ◊ Desirée – 28yo
      ◊ Desirée's 2 little boys (8yo and 10yo)
      ◊ Fontaine – 24yo – priestess novitiate (but left before final vows)
      ◊ Martin – 20yo - Healer
      ◊ Marianna – 18yo – lady-in-waiting (Secret Cadre), Spellbreaker

- *Elaarwen,* duchy – Stellarine family, violet and silver
  - <u>Duchess Genevieve (Stellarine) Alsterling</u>
    - <u>**Duke-Consort Damien Alsterling,**</u> husband of Genevieve
    - <u>**Lord Aldred Stellarine,**</u> widowed husband of Duchess-Consort Giendra (Topasirre) Stellarine, father of Duchess Genevieve, only child of Duke Siegfrid Stellarine and Grand Duchess Alicia Alsterling
    - <u>**Ciriis Cellavel,**</u> Lord Aldred's lover and nurse and mother of his child
    - <u>*Duke Siegfrid Stellarine,*</u> father of Duke Aldred, husband of Grand Duchess Alicia Alsterling, son of Duke Emmeren
    - <u>*Grand Duchess Alicia Alsterling,*</u> wife of Duke Siegfrid Stellarine, mother of Duke Aldred
    - <u>*Duke Emmeren Stellarine,*</u> father of Duke Siegfrid
    - <u>*Duchess Shalla (Elemandros) Stelarine,*</u> wife of Duke Emmeren, mother of Duke Siegfrid

    - **Others of note in the duchy:**
      - » <u>Lord Adsel Topasirre,</u> Chatelaine and Regent of Elaarwen, from Genevieve's mother's family
  - *Fiefs within Elaarwen*
    - *Cloudcroft,* property – Stellarine family
      - » <u>**Lord Aldred Stellarine**</u>
        - * <u>**Lady Ciriis Celavell,**</u> Aldred's mistress and the mother of his child
        - * <u>Emmeren Stellarine,</u> infant son of ALdred and Ciriis
        - * <u>Zelda,</u> Cloudcroft's cook

- *Siovale*, duchy – Elsevier family, forest green and silver (guards wear dark green and black)
    - Duke Mark Elsevier - 20yo
        - » *former Duke Tomas Elsevier*
        - » *Duchess-Consort Sildra (Miramar) Elsevier*
        - » Duke Mark's siblings
            - * Arabella Elsevier – 17yo (confined to the care of her aunt and uncle, the Duke and Duchess of Dalziallest for the remainder of her natural life for treason to the Crown)
            - * Lorinda – 14yo (squire in training)
            - * Denis Elsevier – 12yo (squire in training)
            - * Gemma Elsevier – 10yo
            - * Gary Elsevier – 7yo
        - » *former Duke Hector Elsevier,* father of Tomas and Harald, husband of Lydia
        - » *Dowager Duchess-Consort Lydia Elsevier,* mother of Harald and Tomas, died a traitor's death for Conspiracy Against the Crown for her role in the Usurpation by her son Harald
        - » *Harald Elsevier,* cuckoo's *child of Duchess Lydia by King Reginald, died a traitor's death for Usurping the Throne after Damien was crowned... Genevieve Stellarine Alsterling's first husband*

- *Reyensweir*, duchy – family Mirion
    - Duke Quillian Mirion
    - 'second capitol' at Reyenrald is the second-largest city in the Realm.

- *Embervest* duchy – family Eledor
  - **Duchess Tariana Eledor**
  - ***Fiefs within Embervest*** The Lost Provinces of Minglemere (returned) and Everfields (still Lost to Vindalia) are part of Embervest
    - *Minglemere,* barony – family Krakenroost
      - » Lost to Vindalia some seventeen years before King Damien was Crowned
      - » Regained in the 4th year of King Damien's reign
    - *Everfields*
      - » Lost to Vindalia some 40 years before King Damien's reign
      - » Resoted to the Realm in the 6th year of King Damien's reign

- *Alpinsward,* duchy – family Marseill
  - The first of the Lost Provinces to defect (in their case to Mercasia after *Crown Prince Robert Alsterling's* negotiations failed following his murder by 'bandits')
  - The first of the Lost Provinces to return, following King Damien's coronation and negotiations with Queen Genevieve
  - <u>Duchess Laura Marseill, Duchess-Consort Carmencita Merseill</u>

- *Dalzialest,* duchy,
  combined of Dalizell and Zialest when Rosa Teraseel and Zachary Miramar married just after King Damien's coronation – the Miramar family was granted the promotion to a Duchy in recognition of their loyalty to the new king (the counties had been asking for royal permission to merge for several generations)
  - <u>Duchess Rosa (Teraseel) Miramar</u>
  - <u>Duke Zachary Miramar</u>

- ***The Lost Provinces***
  1. Alpinsward, duchy – family Marseill
     - <u>Duchess Laura Marseill</u>, <u>Duchess-Consort Carmencita</u>
     - Lost to Mercasia some 46 years before King Damien's reign
     - Regained in the 3rd year of King Damien's reign
  2. Minglemere, barony – family Krakenroost
     - Baron Densal
     - Returned to Duchy Embervest
     - Lost to Vindalia some 17years before King Damien's reign
     - Regained in the 4th year of King Damien's reign
  3. Elendria, county – formerly part of Duchy Alpinsward
     - Countess Miraly
     - Lost to Deltheran some 25 years before King Damien's reign
     - Negotiations begun to Restore Elendria to Ilseador in the 5th year of King Damien's reign
  4. Farivera – family Marsham
     - **<u>Count Felix Marsham</u>** (father was <u>Count Nathaniel</u>)
     - Lost to Evil Wizard some 30 years before King Damien's reign
     - Resored to the Realm in the 6th year of King Damien's reign
  5. Everfields – formerly part of Duchy Embervest
     - Lost to Vindalia some 40 years before King Damien's reign
     - Restored to the Realm in the 6th year of King Damien's reign

- *Others of Note*
  - <u>Azella the Unpitying</u> (a.k.a. the White Witch of Farivera)
    - Her minions
      - » <u>Jeremy</u> (a.k.a. Mikhail, Jerry, Jemmy, Dandelion)
      - » <u>Denisa</u>
  - <u>Queen Estelle</u> of Deltheren
  - <u>Evan Eldridge Alsterling</u>, Pirate-King, Captain of the Red Sails, Scourge of the Merutian Sea (Ex-lover of Megan Solway, sire of Jason Solway Alsterling, son of Crown Prince Robert Alsterling and Baroness Dara Eldridge of Eldyrwyld)
  - Nobility from Dawil
    - Royal family: Tindilaar
      - » <u>King Eldrig</u>
      - » *<u>Queen Rena of Ilseador</u>,* King Reginald's 4th wife, mother of Prince Eric, grandmother of King Damien; King Eldrig's sister, daughter of King Ezerial and Queen Marlerite
      - » *<u>King Ezerial</u>* of Dawil, Damien's great-grandfather
      - » *<u>Queen Marlerite</u>* of Dawil, Damien's great-grandmother
      - » <u>Princess Livette</u>, King Eldrig's half-sister, mother of Emmerine
      - » <u>Crown Princess Emmerine</u>, King Eldrig's Named Heir and niece
    - noble family of Wave: Elemandros family (descendants of the Turquoise Emperors)
      - » *<u>Lady Giovalla</u>,* former Lady of Wave, Genevieve's great-great-grandmother
      - » *<u>Lady Shalla</u>,* Giovalla's middle daughter, Genevieve's great-grandmother
      - » *<u>Lord Carlos</u>,* former Lord of Wave, Lady Giovalla's grandson and successor, Lord Tedros' father
      - » <u>Lord Tedros</u>, current Lord of Wave. Married in an unacknowledged triad to an Amberdeen princess and a Wavian noblewoman.

MAPS
Ilseador

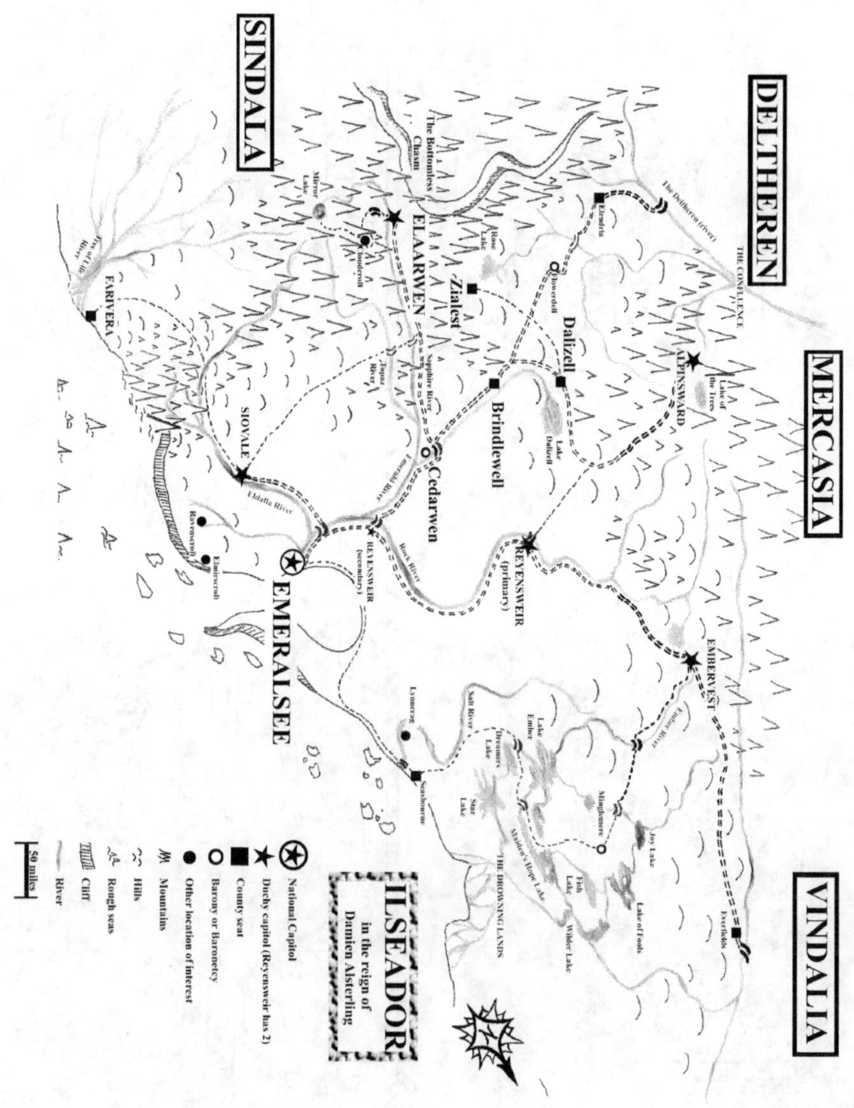

Mangala McNamara

LANDS Around the MERUTIAN SEA

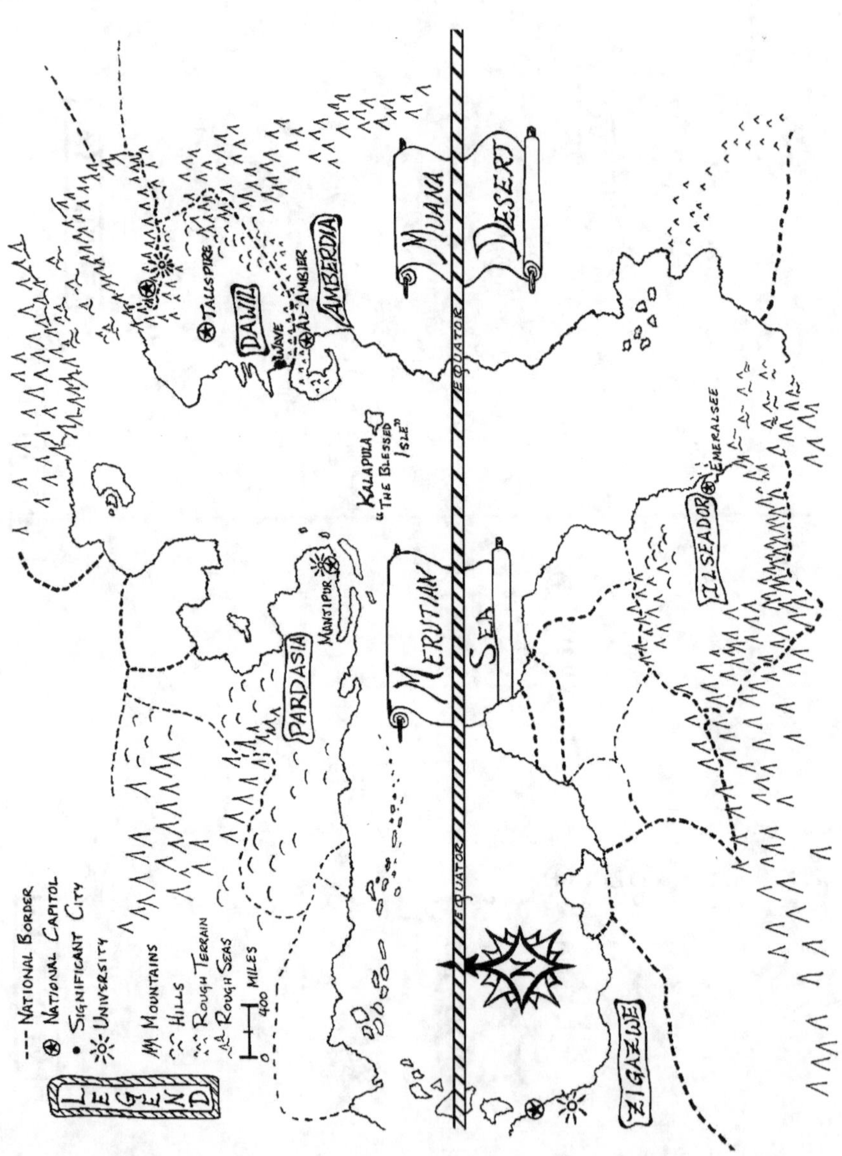

And now, for your delectation...
an excerpt from...

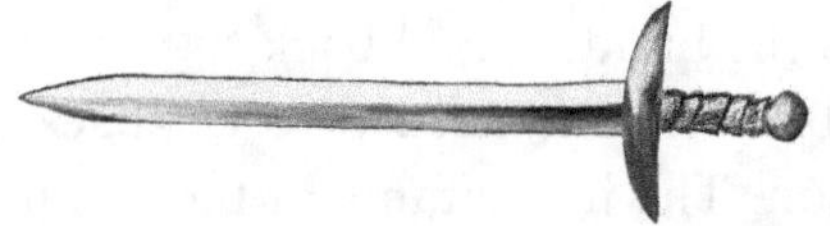

Chapter ONE

Caught!

GENEVIEVE HAD NOT FORGOTTEN THE old king's pet sorcerer. She *had*, however, assumed he would not be a problem. This was clearly not the case.

She ducked into a rubbish-strewn alley and prayed that one of the doors leading off of it would open to somewhere that was not a dead-end. Unlike the alleyway itself. Genevieve really wasn't familiar enough with the layout of the capitol to be doing this sort of thing. As her advisors had repeatedly told her. Her chagrined memory replayed the scene of her tossing her head as she assured them that "the Rebel Duchess" could handle anything.

Not that she had *planned* to have to handle anything at all. She was just going to come in as part of the crowds hoping to get a glimpse of the new young king, on this last day of the coronation festivities. Just another gawker from the countryside. She still had no idea how Lord Prydeen had identified her.

The second door on the right opened at her frantic tug, and Genevieve hurried into darkness, pulling the door tightly shut behind her. She could hear people talking somewhere off to her right and the darkness seemed a little less dark in that direction. Perhaps there was a way through the building and back to the main street she had veered off of so abruptly. She needed to get back to the streets to complete her mission. The inhabitants of the room ahead would be startled, but if she could get past them quickly – before they decided to hold her for a thief – she might make it.

Just as the young woman started towards the sounds, the door behind her crashed open and the sorcerer stepped through.

Lord Prydeen was a master of dramatic effect, some odd corner of her mind noted absently. He stood framed in the doorway, too deeply cowled to see his face, his ankle-length black cloak flapping and curling about him in the sudden cross-currents of air between building and outside. The alley was brighter than the room – so perhaps he merely paused to let his eyes adjust – but in that moment he was more silhouette than shape, more demon than man.

Genevieve could not – *could not* – lead him towards those unsuspecting innocents in the room beyond. Perhaps the completely unexpected would gain her – well, *some*thing.

She took a deep breath, but carefully did not think too hard about what she was doing – though whether it was because Lord Prydeen was rumored to be able to pull one's thoughts from the air itself or because she wouldn't have the nerve if she did–

She spun on her heel and charged directly at the sorcerer, startling him sufficiently that she shoved past him and back out into the dead-end alley. Then to her left and back out to the main street – perhaps she could lose him in the crowd. She had to try.

In her haste, however, Genevieve's own hood was pushed back, exposing her signature red-gold hair – and confirming what had surely only been Lord Prydeen's guess about the identity of his quarry.

Fool that she was for not having dyed it.

Thrice a fool for deciding to skulk about the coronation festivities – like any small child playing "Erawan the Kind Robber" – instead of listening to the reports of her spies as the mature, careful, strategic leader of the rebellion should do. That stupid, romantic title – "Rebel Duchess" – really *had* gone to her head, as Rosa had accused her. She would do the Cause no good by being taken by the king's sorcerer. Even if the new young King Damien lived up to his month-old reputation for fairness, Lord Prydeen would never give her a chance to find out.

No time for this.

Genevieve jerked her hood back up and tried to blend into the crowded market square, trying to outguess Lord Prydeen. Which direction would the sorcerer be unlikely to go? – or which way would he be unlikely to follow? Surely the feared and hated Royal Sorcerer could not make his way through the crowd without causing an uproar that would let her dodge away... though he had before, when she first caught him following her. Could there be *any* safety for her here in the capitol, just six days after Damien's crowning? Surely the old guard was still in place and *no one* (not even the young king?) would dare to gainsay Lord Prydeen.

Abruptly, and entirely on instinct, not daring to look back to measure her pursuit, Genevieve swerved and tore for the royal viewing stand. Damien, if the stories were right – the stories that she had not believed and had come in person to verify – would merely have her executed for a traitor. Lord Prydeen – as she had reason to know – would sell her soul to demons and wring every last memory and secret from her shrieking heart.

The fine bright day taunted her travails, small poofy clouds ambling across a sky as blue as her own eyes. The market square – packed with a crowd of pleasantly frolicking merchants and peasants – impeded her swift progress. The swarms of children playing games of tag nearly tripped her up. The very *joy* of it all nearly derailed her thoughts, for such gaiety could never have been shown in the old king's rule, and part of her could not leave off trying to determine if there was still the undercurrent of desperation that she expected from her previous, and more successfully clandestine, visits to the capitol city.

But the Rebel Duchess knew exactly where the royal platform stood, both due to having marked it well when first she arrived and for the fact that it stood as tall any of the half-timbered two-story buildings surrounding the square. She had hoped to catch a glimpse of the young king from afar when first she arrived, and the royal platform had seemed like the right place to start. She had perhaps stayed still too long, staring too intently at the brilliantly bunting- and flower-clad structure, trying to discern which, if any, of the milling nobles on its three ornately decorated levels was the young king. Then, as now, the top level was empty, save for a matched pair of guards.

Part of her – the part that had insisted on this mad mission against all rational thought and advice – was certain that, if she could but look into his eyes, she would know if Damien was all that the reports claimed... or if he had been corrupted by his grandfather and Lord Prydeen.

Part of her – if she dared admit it – wanted to believe, even if it seemed beyond belief, that he could have been untouched. That the Cause was won, the need for a Rebel Duchess was done. That the Rebellion could quietly fold itself up and her folk could slip back to their homes, to their lives... though perhaps not the Rebel Duchess herself, recognizable as she was as a symbol...

Yet – how could those two old, evil men *not* have insured that the crown prince was a "fit successor" to the king who had controlled a creature such as Lord Prydeen?

Genevieve had met the prince once, when they were both children. He had barely been of an age for his first pony, and she – a few years older – had just graduated to a mild-mannered horse... and her father's half-tamed, firebreathing mare that Duke Aldred had no idea she would even attempt to ride. Her father had brought her to Court to make her curtsy to the old king and see her named his Heir. Damien had been but one of a pack of the old king's grandchildren – a nondescript royal child, good-looking as they all had been, but special in no particular way. They had spent perhaps minutes in each other's presence, on separate ends of the audience hall that had seemed miles-long to her then.

Now those other siblings and cousins, aunts and uncles, were all gone and Damien – unremarked offspring of an unremarkable parent – had been named Crown Prince, and now King. For him to have inherited would seem to signal that he had done something to earn the old king's approval – perhaps by being ruthless enough to have ensured no other contenders were available. Certainly, he had made no mark by protesting his grandfather's policies while the old king lived, no mark of any kind, in fact. Despite all the time Genevieve had spent at Court, she did not recall ever noticing him again.

Yet she could still remember a certain clear-eyed gaze from that long-ago child. A gaze that seemed to recognize and promise to right all the wrongs that existed in the world. A gaze that had haunted her dreams since she had heard he had been crowned, and had kept her skepticism from becoming outright denial when rumors of the new king's beneficence came to her. And so, she had come to see for herself...

She had reached the royal platform at last, and hunted for a spot to clamber up. Not an easy endeavor, as it was so heavily be-ribboned – in every color, not merely royal gold and turquoise – with bright buntings stretched between triple rosettes made of actual rose petals. An elegantly illuminated sign noted that these were the coronation gifts of the Weavers' and Florists' Guilds – but the small barrel that the sign rested upon was of more interest to her, as it gave her a leg up to the first level, which was filled with younger noblemen. These young men were here to satisfy fathers and mothers who wanted them close to the source of power. They eyed her with interest – her cloak had of necessity been pushed aside to climb and she was dressed in hunting leathers fit tight to her athletic frame – and she in turn ignored them, using the spigoted ale kegs at which they were amusing themselves to give her a step up to the recessed second level.

The older noblemen and -women – and their maiden daughters – on this level looked at her quite askance. Genevieve hoped her hood shadowed her face enough to keep any of them from recognizing her, for she knew no few of them, though she did not recognize the barely-grown girls, nor more than a handful of the hardly-older lads below. These nobles had toadied up to the old king while Genevieve – and her father before her – had sought to protect their people. She knew all too well that they would as soon sell her out to Lord Prydeen as look at her. Even now they were trying to toady up to King Damien, bringing their marriageable daughters to parade before him – an array of maidens scarcely past puberty, for their elder ones had been taken to serve the old king and Lord Prydeen in years gone by, many never to be seen again. They, too, must surely be hoping for better from Damien, yet she saw nothing but avarice in the faces of even the children.

A good-looking young man – unusual only for being the only *young* man on this level of the platform, did someone think the new king's taste ran to boys? – with very dark hair and clear grey eyes offered her a hand onto the level. Genevieve was not too proud to accept help, even from a scion of one of *these* families. They exchanged a startled look and nearly let go of each other as an electric spark seemed to jump between their hands. Surely it wasn't dry enough today for such things, and so close to the harbor besides.

Putting such irrelevant details aside, Genevieve brushed off her hands on her breeches as she looked up towards the highest level of the reviewing stand, but saw only the pair of Royal Guards – two blondely handsome men so perfectly matched as almost to be twins – decorating that august space. Knights chosen for their beauty, just as were the horses that pulled the royal carriage. She wondered who they were – might they have enough real skill at arms to have faced her in the Battle of Siovale seven years earlier? She'd caught no more than a glimpse of either of them so far, as they turned, watchfully, eyes raking the crowds. Perhaps they were more than merely decorative.

Hopefully the king himself was sitting down and merely out of view. Genevieve needed for him to be there, before Lord Prydeen caught up with her. It was a wild gambit – praise all the Gods at once that Rosa really could handle the Rebellion, since it looked like she was going to have to. Rosa – would never forgive her for getting herself captured and killed. The Rebel Countess – surely that sounded just as impressive. They had known it couldn't last – this would free Rosa to wed and produce the Heir that she needed. Genevieve's own proper title – Lady Stellarine, Duchess of Elaarwen (she dared not think "Princess of the Realm", though her bloodlines were as good as the king's) – would pass to a collateral line...

No matter. The issue at hand was to get up there to the top level and there was no obvious stair or ladder.

Genevieve dropped her useless disguise of a cloak before it could hinder her further in climbing higher, ignoring the massed gasp from the gathered nobles, and looked for a convenient way to boost herself to the king's level. The balustrade of the king's level – still festooned with those slippery buntings and banners – was more than head-high to her. It was higher than she could hoist herself on arm-strength alone.

That young man was still watching her – looking slightly amused, damn him. Or maybe that was *be*mused. Surely, he had little idea what to make of her and her sudden arrival. But he seemed to come to a decision and wrenched a ring with a large grey pearl on it off his finger, thrusting it towards her. It was the sort of thing a nobleman might offer a noblewoman to indicate interest – a sort of "let's get to know each other" offer, not quite a tryst, but more than an offer of acquaintance. The ring would have a house sigil on it, perhaps even a personal seal – enough information for her to find him again later on. A crazy thing to hand to the highly recognizable Rebel Duchess as she attempted to single-handedly besiege the new king's festival viewing platform. The young man must be completely daft.

And then he bent and cupped his hands as a stablehand might do to help someone into the saddle. The sparkle in his eyes suggested he was prepared to toss her high enough to pull herself up over that balustrade.

Again, the gathered nobles gasped, but this time there were also mutters and a fearful eagerness... and she guessed someone had spotted Lord Prydeen approaching.

There was no time for this. Genevieve stuffed the ring onto her finger – her beltpouch would take too long to open – put her foot in his hands and leapt up in concert with his toss.

And got the – third? fourth? – shock of the day as her reaching hands were grasped from above and an all too familiar voice gruffly said "Young miss, this is the king's place, you can't be climbing... up... her–" The voice cut off as and the hands fumbled and nearly dropped her back down, as their owner peered over the edge and then grabbed her more securely and helped her over the balustrade.

The Royal Guard was looking at her in exasperation and some of the same confusion Genevieve was feeling. It was the strangest and least appropriate timing on anything ever – but the touch of his hands had inflamed her with desire. *Not now, not now!* The Rebel Duchess thought frantically. She'd heard of this, but thought it a fairytale... Rosa, *Rosa* was her love...

"Jason Solway?" she managed to gasp out.

"Genny?" He was as flabbergasted as he was, and if the blush rising in those perfect cheeks was anything to judge, he was suffering from the same reaction. Suffering...

"Here now," said the other Royal Guard, coming forward from his ceremonial position. "Jase, what's this all about?"

She looked almost gratefully at the other man, just as gratefully *not* recognizing him as yet another childhood friend. But his familiar behavior towards Jason – were they lovers? Why did that thought make her heart – or something lower than her heart – do flips? And why, oh, why, *was this all happening at once?*

"Stand back, gentlemen," growled a low, cultured voice.

Lord Prydeen.

Apparently, she wouldn't have to sort any of this out after all.

The two Guards obediently stepped aside, though she rather thought that Jason only reluctantly let go of her hands, and she could see that the sorcerer had come up a set of stairs at the back of the reviewing stand. A brief surge of wind whipped the cowled hood from off Lord Prydeen's spotty, balding head, and tossed his long, drooping mustaches. He had not aged well since the old king's death; his hair had been thinning, but was still full when last she had gotten a good look at him, some months earlier, and the lines around his mouth were graven deeply, where once they had been entirely masked by his whiskers. Genevieve had heard tell that evil sorcerers cast vile spells to keep themselves young – by sacrificing true youths and maidens to demons, some said. She had scoffed, even as she wondered. The old king had lived long past his age, and Lord Prydeen, some said, had not aged at all, even as those noble daughters came to serve them both and were rarely seen again.

"Lady Genevieve." Lord Prydeen greeted her, coldly, but not correctly. He needed nothing besides himself to emphasize his authority, but he had brought a squad of his personal guards up with him. They fanned out behind him, blocking the path, even to headstrong young women who might push past a sorcerer.

She tilted her chin up – her nose was too snub to properly glare down it, but she was tall enough to try... and the arrogance might mask the tremble that the tumult in her stomach had settled into. "The proper title is *'Your Grace'*, messir." She was actually in line for the throne herself, with all of Damien's family gone, and 'Lord' Prydeen was, after all, a sorcerer of no particular breeding.

And if she told herself that a few more times, perhaps she could dare to face him.

A wintry smile passed over Lord Prydeen's lips – gone as quickly as snow in the Summer. "No longer, I fear. My former master stripped you of your titles for your treasonous activities."

Genevieve inclined her head. "So, I have heard. But even a Royal Decree does not make a thing reality. Even His – belated – Majesty never put it to the test in *Elaarwen.*"

Something sparked in the sorcerer's eyes. Anger, perhaps? Could such a one as he even feel something as tender as grief? He gestured to his men. "Bind her and bring her."

Jason bestirred himself to protest, "My lord–!" but the other Guard pulled him back and Genevieve found herself being roughly seized and turned around by hands that made no pretense of not enjoying their task. Even the king's own Royal Guards, it seemed, dared not speak against the sorcerer. Not yet anyways. If only she had waited to see if the young king could consolidate his power; if, indeed, he would continue in the way he had begun!

"My Lord Prydeen! What passes here?" The mild voice interrupted from the direction of the stairs, but was no one Genevieve recognized. She had been turned to face outwards towards the square whilst they bound her, and could not see the speaker.

Lord Prydeen's voice was a curious mix of ingratiating and dismissive. "Nothing you need trouble yourself over, my lord. Some rabble found her way up here, clearly to cause some trouble to you. It is my task and my privilege to safeguard Your Highness. We'll be away momentarily."

Gentle hands cleared away the thongs that had begun to lash her wrists. "Surely you are mistaken, my Lord Prydeen. This is no rabble, but Her Grace, the Duchess Genevieve Stellarine of Elaarwen."

"Yes, my Lord, the so-called 'Rebel Duchess'," Lord Prydeen's voice was growing impatient. "I am taking her to the castle dungeons to have out of her what she knows. You can make an example of her later on – you must not detract from your coronation festivities."

"Nonsense, Lord Prydeen," the mild voice replied. "That isn't how we treat visiting royalty... not to mention that the people would rise in protest and not even you could put them *all* down at once."

He came around to Genevieve's right side, and before she could register that this was the same young man who had cupped his hands for her boot like any stableboy, he gave her that same enigmatic smile, and faced the crowd – who had begun to turn as they saw their king. Damien lifted Genevieve's right hand in his left, holding them high above their heads and called out, "I give you Genevieve Stellarine, the Rebel Duchess!"

It was the sort of moment a Duke's Heir is trained for and – bemused as she was at the turn of events – Genevieve flattened her palm against the king's and stood tall before the crowds, the errant breeze tossing her red-gold curls like a mane. She smiled fiercely, trying to think if this would be taken as some sort of inadvertent admission of surrender.

Even as the people roared their approval – and Lord Prydeen fumed behind them – a sudden, strange crackling noise erupted and ribbons of white fire fountained up between their pressed fingers. It wreathed down to wrap their hands and curl around their arms.

For all that she was the reigning duchess of a province, the leader of a rebellion against an unjust king and an evil sorcerer, and had spent most of her life in that struggle... Genevieve was tempted to faint right then and there. This was absolutely the *last* thing she had expected. If she hadn't seen this happen before, she would have thought it was some new and clever attack by Lord Prydeen.

But she *had* seen this before. And, likely, so had every member of the crowd below.

At least young King Damien looked nearly as befuddled as she felt.

He, however, recovered more quickly than she.

"And your future Queen!" he announced in what sounded like a calm voice.

He pulled her in and kissed her.

And the crowds went absolutely wild.

Read the rest of this exciting story of rebellion and romance!
The Rebel Duchess
now at your favorite online ebookseller in print or ebook!

Also by Mangala McNamara

<u>The Chronicles of Ilseador</u>

The Rebel Duchess: Book One

The Prydeen Prophecy Cycle:
- The King's Champion: Book Two
- The Pirate-King: Book Three
- The Pale Sorceress: Book Four
- The UnCaptive King: Book Five

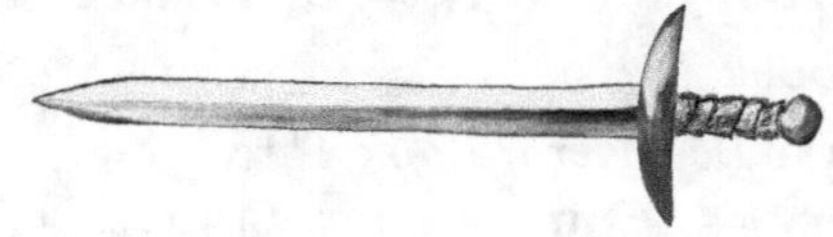

<u>Knightess of the Realm</u>

A Not-So-Sacrificial Maiden

Scaredy Cat:
- A Knightess of the Realm Holiday Prequel Novella

Out of the Woods... Hopefully (a Prequel Novella)

Turns of a Page (A Prequel Story Collection)

The Heir's Journey mini-series (3 books)
- A Not-So-Simple Mission: Book One
- An Entirely-Unexpected Revelation: Book Two
- An All-Too-Surprising Homecoming: Book Three

The Secrets of Dragon Mountain
- An Altogether-Curious Altercations: Book One
- An All-Too-Obvious Choice: Book Two

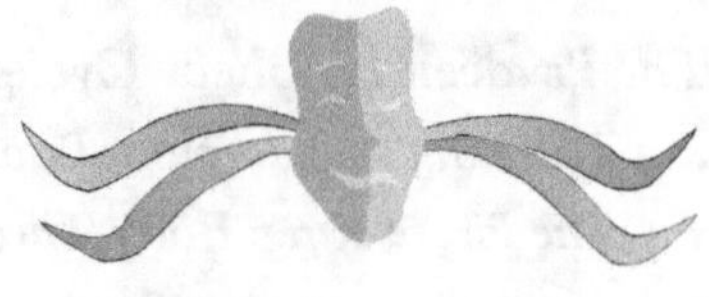

The Prankster Prince

Thony and the Much-Anticipated Adventure

The Raven War Saga (3 books)

Thony Goes Astray! (in the Deep, Dark, and Dangerous Fairy
Wood): Book Two

So You Want to Be a Hero? Book Three

How Thony Stopped a War (and Fixed a Friendship): Book Four

The Pathremiri Problem

Diary of a ~~Runaway Prince~~ Bold Questing Hero: Book Five

And more to come...

Author's Note

Hello dear Reader!

It may come as a surprise to you that *Damien* wasn't who I imagined this series was going to be about.

The beginning of *The Rebel Duchess* – Genevieve and Damien's first meeting – came to me in a recurring dream that *would not stop* until I wrote it. The story ended up being from both of their perspectives (and not neatly in alternating chapters, sigh). It turned out to be a fairly steamy romance. And it turned out to have that *prophecy* at the end that pointed to more books I hadn't planned to write.

At that point, please note, I had an idea of what Ilseador looked like – but I didn't know it was in the same world as Karana's *Knightess of the Realm* stories. (Let alone the rather close connection that some of you may be aware of from the *Knightess* books. Karana and her Companions figured it out in Book 2: *A Not-So-Simple Mission,* but it's a good 40 years in Damien's future… so we're going to let him go on in the hopes that that future can be averted, poor guy.)

At the time, I had thought I was going to be writing YA novels (Karana and her Companions were going to cure me of that – but Genevieve and Damien did it first).

And *at the time* I hadn't written male characters except for Thony in the *Prankster Prince.* (And, honestly, Thony's problem of finding a princess to marry is at least half because he's young enough that he just isn't *interested.* A boy young enough not to be interested in 'romance' is a lot like a girl not interested in 'romance.' Maybe not all of them, but at least the ones I've had the fun of getting to know and/or raise.)

And… I'd never really planned to write anything so DARK.

(*Actually... that's not quite true. By the point* **The Rebel Duchess** *came to me, I'd written Evil Wizards Anonymous – which explores what happens to Azella the Unpitying. She's looking back on her life of perfidy and how she got there while she tries to figure out if there can even be a future for an ex-Evil Wizard. I made the mistake of showing that to an old and dear friend who was... utterly horrified. You need to be in the right frame of mind to read that sort of thing and... she wasn't. I'm still working up to deciding to publish that one... we'll see... If you've read* **The Pale Sorceress** *you may understand why. Oh, yeah, and that one is another at-least-a-trilogy.*)

But that was where I was when that *DREAM* wouldn't let me sleep. For about *TWO WEEKS STRAIGHT.*

And after 'finishing' *The Rebel Duchess* I knew there was at least one more book. We had to see how Lord Prydeen's Prophecy turned out, after all. (I had no idea that Azella was even involved yet... I write these things because *I* want to know what happens!)

I'd sort of picked up on the *L'Morte d'Artur* vibe that was going on by then (hidden prince, sword from the stone... no Morgan Le Fay, since I didn't see Azella coming into the story yet ...) and this seemed like a classing Arthur-Guinevere-Lancelot love triangle. With, well, Adam thrown on for a slightly different twist. I've always been interested in what these stories would look like from the women's perspective – Guinevere/Genevieve seemed like she was going to let me explore the question.

Little did I know...

So, yeah, well, Damien – and Jason and particularly Adam – kind of took over. And Azella – and Evan Eldridge Alsterling, briefly – showed up and...

Well.

That's how we got here.

It got dark, it got *steamy* in ways I couldn't even have imagined four years ago, and it's become a story of *redemption* and *Healing*.

I absolutely adore Damien and his unusual little family.

Those of you who are *noticing* may have realized that I'm writing neurodivergent characters. That's just who they happen to be –

but I grew up in a neurodivergent community (engineers, doctors, scientists) before we used any term like that. We were geeks and nerds and maybe 'quirky' or 'gifted' if people were being extra polite. ADHD and Sensory Issues weren't terms we used commonly until I was an adult – so Damien is *wriggly* and *distracted* and *empathetic*.

These characteristics give him a different perspective that helps him think *outside the box*... and see opportunities and possibilities that others don't. (Neurodivergent people are often the ones that drive innovation, create art that is later categorized as 'great,' and solve problems that seem otherwise intractable.)

Genevieve – and Jason – are much more on the 'neurotypical' side of things. They are intelligent, creative, and highly competent people. But they don't particularly understand Damien (though, it seems that Adam does).

Ironically, Damien was *literally* stuck in a box (the Royal Library... though in the next couple of books you'll see some caveats to that) as a child and as King is sealed into a... much bigger box. But he is also one of the *least* boxed-in people around. He knows the norms – such as sleeping at night and eating at regular times... and having *one* true love – but finds ways to subvert them and is working to bring the rest of the world around to his way of looking at things.

As he himself noted in *The Pale Sorceress,* it's much easier for him to exercise his moralities when his alternative to Evil Wizardry is the luxurious life of a king.

And *this* mini-series is really all about him figuring out how to deal with the boxes that he has put himself into...

...in preparation/acceptance of, among other things, becoming a parent. (If the idea that one has to deal with one's own Issues in order to cope with becoming a parent interests you, you may like my novella *Scaredy Cat* in the *Knightess of the Realm* series. It's about Karana's father dealing with his personal history and beliefs while coping with her as a precocious and 'fearless' toddler.)

Damien's personal journey (which is going to get rocky) in this mini-series, *The Heart of Ilseador,* fits in between the last chapter and the Epilogue of *The UnCaptive King.* After Princess Marli is born, however, we're going to follow him as he takes his Warrior-Queen's place (while she recovers from childbirth) and ends up at the *Battle of Elendria. (Yes, that's the name of the next mini-series.)*

An *empath* on a battlefield? Any surprise that there will be ghosts?

That'll likely be out in 2026 – this year we're finishing the *Heart of Ilseador.* The next book will be *Piled Higher and Deeper* to be released in May 2025.

In the meantime, you can entertain yourself with the next Thony story: *A Court of Mists & Misadventures* in March 2025, and the next Karana book, *An Entirely-Rational(ized) Decision* (the last in the *Secrets of Dragon Mountain* mini-series) in April 2025.

I hope you're finding this as interesting a ride as I am...

Mangala McNamara

P.S.

Those of you who were paying attention to the descriptions of the environmental and social disaster that is Farivera may guess that *Collapse* by Jared Diamond has recently featured in our homeschooling. You would be correct!

The exploding sewers incident references an actual incident in Louisville, KY that was brought to my attention by my 16 year old son (the DungeonMaster) because it featured in a recent D&D campaign he participated in. (Where the sewer explosion was the, er, solution, rather than the problem).

And I'm digging a little deeper into my own background as a microbiologist. What are the real differences between different kinds of life? Damien's empathy for microorganisms rather exceeds my own on a practical level (managing 'resorts' for pathogenic bacteria seems a bit over the top) but his point is a real one. While we naturally prefer our own (and closely related) species as an evolutionary drive for survival... all forms of life are part of the natural world. There is no inherent primacy amongst them.

About the Author

Mangala McNamara writes Epic Romantic Fantasy. Her Knightess of the Realm and Prankster Prince series occur in the same world as the Chronicles of Ilseador stories.

Mangala lives in Flyover Country (the far northern end of the US South) with her husband, The Professor and three of her six children (the remaining children are in college or grad school). You can blame the oldest kid for the excessive amounts of math showing up in Mangala's fantasy novels, the second one for better attention to staging of scenes, the third for all the economics, the fourth for great attention to history – and all six of them for a focus on political science!

Mangala is a former professional bellydance instructor, and used to enjoy knitting, crotchet and embroidering Temari balls, but now is much more boring as she rarely does anything but write… although she also fences (the sport) and plays boardgames with her kids. She owes her love of books and reading to her mother, who was a professional folklorist and could recite – from memory – stories from every nation in the United Nations.

Learn about Mangala's upcoming projects (fiction and nonfiction both) and sign up for email updates at
https://www.RisingDragonBooks.com

More Fantasy coming soon...

A Court of Mists & Misadventures
  Book Six of the Prankster Prince (The Pathremiri Problem)
  (available March 2025)

A n Entirely-Rational(ized) Decision
  Book Three of the Secrets of Dragon Mountain
  (A Knightess of the Realm Novel)
  (available April 2025)

Piled Higher & Deeper
  Book Two of the Heart of Ilseador
  (A Chronicles of Ilseador Novel)
  (available May 2025)

Visit https://www.RisingDragonBooks.com for more
upcoming books, maps, lore, art, and more!